A former teenage tennis champion, Alice Peterson turned to writing with her non-fictional account of her battle with rheumatoid arthritis, with which she was diagnosed at the age of 18. *Look the World in the Eye* is her first fictional novel. She lives and works in West London, and appreciates shopping, 'real coffee' and 'good-looking doctors'.

Visit the author's website at:
www.alicepeterson.co.uk

LOOK THE WORLD IN THE EYE

Katie seems to have it all — she's pretty, successful and has a rich, handsome boyfriend, Sam. But now it's crunch time. Her sister, Bells, is coming to stay and Bells doesn't fit into Katie's perfect world. But that world is about to be turned upside down. Bells strikes up conversations with strangers — including an attractive man at the supermarket — and creates mayhem. Problems escalate when Katie receives disturbing news about her mother. But with help from Bells, Katie finally learns about real love, and that appearances can be deceptive.

ALICE PETERSON

LOOK THE WORLD IN THE EYE

Complete and Unabridged

ULVERSCROFT
Leicester

First published in Great Britain in 2005 by
Black Swan Books
London

First Large Print Edition
published 2006
by arrangement with
Transworld Publishers, a division of
The Random House Group Ltd
London

The moral right of the author has been asserted

British Library CIP Data

Peterson, Alice
   Look the world in the eye.—Large print ed.—
Ulverscroft large print series: general fiction
   1. Sisters—Fiction 2. Disabilities—Fiction
   3. Large type books
   I. Title
   823.9′2 [F]

   ISBN 1–84617–293–4

Published by
F. A. Thorpe (Publishing)
Anstey, Leicestershire

Set by Words & Graphics Ltd.
Anstey, Leicestershire
Printed and bound in Great Britain by
T. J. International Ltd., Padstow, Cornwall

This book is printed on acid-free paper

To my sister, Helen

Acknowledgements

There are many people I would like to thank. Firstly, the idea for the title came to me when I met Alison Rich, who works at *Changing Faces*, a leading charity which supports people with disfigurements. 'Don't hide behind your hair, you look the world in the eye' was something her father used to say to her. Alison gave me a real insight into what it's like learning to live with a facial disfigurement and how it affects relationships with siblings, family and the outside world.

To my superstar agent Clare Alexander for all her patience, hard work and ultimately her belief in getting the script to where it is today.

I have loved working with my editor, Diana Beaumont at Transworld, because she has been so enthusiastic and creative and put all her heart into this book. Also many thanks to Kate Marshall for advising and working on the script; and to Prue Jeffreys, my publicist, for doing such a grand job.

I am grateful to Iris Locke and David Peterson for helping me with different parts of the novel. To Alex Edwards for taking me behind the scenes of the *Cadogan* fashion show; to Gilly for the creation of Sam. Mum and Dad — thank you as always for your love and support.

A huge thank you to my cousin, Emma, without whom the book could not have been written.

And finally, thank you Sophie, for inspiring the story.

1

'Morning, Eddie.' I hand him a white paper bag with a croissant inside.

'The usual, Katie?' He turns to start operating the cappuccino machine. 'You've been away, haven't you?'

'Well, I was in Paris two weeks ago on business. Catwalk shows . . . '

'Paris and models? Sounds like a holiday to me.'

'And racking through three thousand designers' clothes. After a while it's not much fun, I promise! It was like a cattle market.'

'One cappuccino, with organic chocolate on the top.'

'Wonderful.'

'Busy day ahead?'

'Yes, very. Rush, rush, rush. It never stops, does it?'

'You've changed your hair colour again,' he notes.

I smile excitedly. 'I've got my fashion show tonight.' I rummage in my purse, trying to find the right change. 'Got to run, see you tomorrow.'

* * *

'Five minutes to go!' I call out to the models. The dressing room has an overpowering smell of hair spray and styling solutions. I pace the corridor. Where is Sam? I punch in his number on my mobile.

'Katie, I'm on my way, promise,' he says. 'In a cab right now.' He starts to make car noises. 'Yes, left here, mate.'

'Sam! I can hear the phone in the background. You're still in the office, aren't you?'

'Half an hour, tops,' he tells me firmly.

'Sam, I really need you here.'

'Don't pull my hair so tightly,' I overhear Henrietta, one of the models, screeching. 'Are you *sure* you're a professional?'

'Please get here soon.' I hang up, take a deep breath and walk back into the dressing room. Hen sits in the corner, stroking a strand of her blond hair protectively. 'Hen, five minutes,' I say, counting them off on my fingers. 'One, two, three, four, five. No more tantrums, OK? Just let her do your hair.'

I look at the chaos of high-heeled shoes and the racks of black clothes waiting to be modelled. I own a shop in Turnham Green called FIB, which stands for Female In Black, selling day and evening wear and accessories,

2

and tonight is the summer fashion show. The clothes, of course, are mainly black, except for the odd accessory and the occasional burst of colour for contrast. I have started to organize fashion shows twice a year, it's hard work but it pays off. This one is being held at a house in Chiswick, owned by a client of Sam's. The house is so big you could run a marathon in it. It is a perfect location for a show because my local customers will not have to travel far. The owners have also gone for the minimal look: stripped floorboards, white walls, spotlights, large modern paintings covering the walls, gilded mirrors. In fact, it is almost a clone of Sam's house, except his is half the size.

I can hear the audience taking their seats, there is that familiar sound of shuffling and scraping chairs. This is the point when my nerves start to kick in. I pick up a half-full glass of champagne, pink lipstick smudged around the rim. 'Is your glass half-full or half-empty?' was the first thing Sam ever said to me when we met in a bar, followed by, 'Allow me to get you a refill,' and finished off with a wink.

If he had been bald with bad breath I probably would have politely refused. Instead, I was looking at a tall attractive dark-haired man. His skin was so smooth, not a staple of stubble. I had to look around to make sure he was talking to me; that he had picked up my glass of vodka and tonic.

Eve, who works at FIB with me, tells me the photographer wants a quick word before we start, and someone from the press has just arrived. 'Good luck, girls,' I say. 'Look the part, feel the part and you ARE the part.' Was one of the models rolling her eyes at me? I ask myself as I walk out of the room.

Quick look in the mirror. I am wearing one of the outfits we are showing tonight: a black halter-neck dress which floats just below the knee. There is a panel of silver beading around the neckline and bust, and it is cut low at the back and fastened with small sparkling silver buttons. My outfit is finished off with slip-on silver heels. My dark brown hair has been dyed black especially for tonight and is half scooped back with camouflaged clips and pinned together with a white rose.

* * *

The show begins with . . . 'It Started With a Kiss', by Hot Chocolate as the first model strides out in a black satin top and slim-fitting black hipster skirt, offset by a handcrafted black and silver beaded belt which shimmers under the lights. In one hand she clutches a black satin bag with a small silver clasp. In the other she holds a cocktail glass. I wanted to kick start the evening with a heady injection of glamour. She glides up to the fireplace, mushroom-coloured smoke weaving its way across the wooden floorboards at her feet. I think the smoke looks like the clouds you see from an aeroplane. The audience marvels at it and claps as the model leaves the room. I see Emma, my old school friend, taking a seat at the back. You can never miss her entry into a room. She's nearly six foot tall and always played Keeper in school netball classes. She mouths 'hello' to me and looks at her programme. Sam, where are you?

⋆ ⋆ ⋆

Sophie Ellis-Bextor's 'Murder on the Dance-floor', plays as Henrietta walks on, looking miserable but determined, her hair scraped back into a ponytail, high heels echoing on the floorboards. Her mother is in the front row, watching adoringly. 'Henrietta and mother' come together in one package, like bubble and squeak. Hen's mother is lame but loaded, and after you have sat her down in the corner of my shop on the chaise-longue, plied her with a few drinks and generally treated her like royalty, she buys her darling daughter Henrietta almost my entire stock. 'Whatever you want, I don't mind,' she says in a steadily increasing haze. Sam often asks me if the 'old soak in the corner' came by. He knows it's his lucky night if she has.

As the song reaches its climax, Henrietta turns dramatically, looks at her mother, who grunts and stamps her stick on the ground with approval, and sashays out of the room. Going well so far, I think to myself. Everyone is talking, there's a general buzz and people are looking at programmes with interest, writing down notes — always a good sign.

The next girl waltzes out in a zebra-printed evening dress worn with a scarlet wrap. This is one of my favourite outfits. Her hair is dyed jet black with a sharp fringe, very *Chicago*-style. 'Superstition' by Stevie Wonder is on the turntable. I shift in my seat. This song always reminds me of home. Being at school. 'Turn that blasted noise off!' I can hear from Mum's studio when Stevie Wonder's, 'I Just Called To Say I Love You' is played over and over again from my sister's bedroom. I can't help smiling. Another world now.

But I do think about Bells. I can still see her letter slipped into my leather diary, that neat familiar handwriting. I haven't even opened it. I didn't have time this morning. I feel guilty receiving letters from her because I don't write back. I intend to and then one thing happens after another — trips abroad, work, going out, yoga classes, parties, Sam . . . they all get in the way. 'How long does it take to write one letter?' Dad nags me. 'It's a dying art. She really would love to hear from you.' Stevie Wonder fizzles out and fresh clouds of smoke magic their way down the catwalk.

★   ★   ★

The photographer from *Tatler* takes one more picture of all the models standing together. 'Lastly, and most importantly, I would like to thank Mr Todhunter for allowing me to use his fabulous home for the event, especially at such short notice,' I announce. Everyone applauds as I shake his hand. 'Please, everyone, do stay on for a drink, and thank you once again for coming tonight.' The crowd claps one last time and then starts to break up.

I am shaking hands, kissing cheeks, moving through them all in a blur of praise, hearing, '*Loved* the show, Katie,' or 'Stunning,' or, 'Darling! You look a million dollars,' my glass of champagne constantly being refilled and the adrenalin kicking in wildly. Eve tells me the photographer would like to take a final quick photograph for the article. I swing round to greet him and put on my best wide smile, while trying hard not to show too many teeth. 'Thank you,' he says after taking the shot, 'great show,' he adds.

'Thank YOU for coming,' I reply, my balance going for a second. I am already feeling quite drunk; I hope he airbrushes the telltale patches of red from my cheeks.

I feel a warm arm slide around my waist, and turn around. 'Sam.'

'Congratulations, babe, it was sensational.' He kisses me, his baby-soft skin brushing against my cheek.

'You missed half of it.' But I smile, my earlier agitation melting at the sight of him.

'I saw the better half.'

'Sorry for snapping earlier, Sam. I was having my usual panic attack before the show.' I pull a silly frantic face at him.

'It's cool, don't worry about it.' He loosens his tie and then leans towards me and whispers, 'Is the old soak in the corner here?'

Emma makes her way towards me, dressed in sensible black working trousers and a turquoise cardigan which is vivid against her olive skin. She's a doctor and has probably come straight from the hospital. But before we manage to say hello: 'Katie darling, that was the best show yet,' says Antonia, one of my customers who lives around the corner from the shop. 'I need to get rid of my post-birth stomach though before I can even think of purchasing some of those slinky outfits.' She laughs at herself, waiting for one of us to say she looks fabulous considering.

'You've got your figure back so quickly, Antonia,' I reassure her, 'you could get away with wearing any of my clothes.'

'Really?' She blushes, touching her cheek. 'Well, I might pop by tomorrow and have a trying-on session. I have an engagement party to go to. A very smart affair, dinner and all that jazz.'

'Well, I'm sure FIB can sort you out. How's the new baby?' I ask.

'I might take it back to the store,' she chuckles at her own joke, 'and ask for a refund. Just a few nights' sleep would be nice.'

Sam, Emma and I make understanding noises although we do not really have a clue. Emma is the nearest of us to having children as she is engaged to Jonnie. For me, the idea of a baby is terrifying. I would rather live on a compost heap than go through all the traumas that Mum went through. 'Antonia, this is Emma, an old school and family friend, and Sam, my . . . ' Partner? Other half? No. 'My boyfriend,' I finish.

'Well, I strongly advise that you two take precautions.' She nods at Sam and me, laughing again at her own humour. 'It is *exhausting*. If I'm honest, I never wanted to have more than one child, but poor little Billy really wanted a brother or sister. My husband says it's selfish to have only one child. They always say only children are spoilt brats, don't they?'

'I'm an only child,' chips in Sam, running one hand through his hair. I see him wink at Emma.

Antonia reddens again. 'Do you have family, Katie? I'm sure they're so proud of you and what you've achieved. To have your own business and be doing all of this.' She glances around the room. 'Your parents must be here tonight?'

'No, sadly they couldn't make it.' I look at Emma and Sam, hoping they might change the subject. Instead Sam asks me where the loos are and excuses himself.

'That's a shame. Do you have brothers? Sisters?' she asks inquisitively.

I look around. Sam is out of earshot. 'No, it's just me. Little old me.' Emma gives me a long hard look. It's funny how just one small question can have an instantly sobering effect.

'Oh,' Antonia says hollowly. 'Well, never mind. It's OK to be an only child, I mean, like I said, I would have stopped at one,' she continues, digging herself an even deeper hole.

'Emma, don't.' I pull a warning face as we finally move away from Antonia.

'It's up to you,' she says in a spiky tone which makes me feel uneasy.

'It's just easier, then I get no awkward questions or those awful sympathetic smiles.'

'It's fine,' Emma says, but her tone is no more forgiving, 'if you think it's best, you carry on. Don't worry about it.'

I hate it when she gets all self-righteous. The drinks come round again and we each take a glass.

'Right, back to business,' I say, making my way over to Hen's mother with a glass of champagne.

★   ★   ★

Sam turns the key and we walk inside. He and I have been going out for nine months and I moved in with him after only three. Sam works in the City. He used to be a currency trader, that's how he made his

11

money. Now he works in 'mergers and acquisitions', or 'M & A' as Sam calls it. He lives in Notting Hill, a stone's throw from Portobello Market, the famous travel book-shop and the Electric Cinema. It was an impulsive move on my part, but neither of us could see the point of being apart because I was staying with him almost every night. It's easy for me living here as it is only ten minutes away from my shop. I can hop on the number 94 bus which takes me directly to Turnham Green, and my shop is along Turnham Green Terrace. I used to live in Clapham with my old boyfriend, and that was more of a trek. Also, Sam has a wide-screen television in every room, and even a steam room on the top floor. How could I say no when he asked me to move in with him?

Mum was immediately suspicious, firing questions at me. 'Who is this man? Are you sure you're ready, Katie? You jump from one relationship to another like there's no tomorrow.' Her reaction didn't altogether surprise me but it made me want to move in with him even more.

Sam picks up the mail from the floor, which is mostly junk — pizza delivery companies, cab firms touting for business, a card saying the electricity meter man came but no-one was in. 'Nothing that can't wait here,' he says, chucking it onto the small table in the hallway. He wraps his arms around me.

'I'm tired and happy,' I tell him with a hiccup. 'And very drunk. Tonight went really well, didn't it?'

'You are a fashion goddess, my darling.'

I kiss him. 'Thanks so much for helping me organize this evening.' I know Sam went out of his way to ask Mr Todhunter if we could use his house for the show. 'I couldn't have done it without you, you know.'

Sam's face burns with pride. 'It was my pleasure. We're a team, you and me. I was happy to help out.'

'Well, I think we're a top team.'

'Me too. The best.'

I look over his shoulder. The red answer-machine light is flashing.

'Ignore it. How about a liqueur? Cognac?' Sam starts to hum as he skips downstairs to the kitchen.

'Yes, I'd love one.' I look at the machine again. Why do I feel I ought to see who called? I feel certain the message is for me. I take off my high heels, my feet ache from all the standing. I walk away from the machine, tapping my shoes together, and then turn around again and decide that I might as well see who left a message.

'A steam?' Sam suggests before I press the

button. He is holding two glasses and a bottle of Cognac. 'Leave it till tomorrow. It'll only be Maguire. He said he'd call tonight.' He takes my hand and grins. 'I've got a surprise for you, come on.'

'Really?' I laugh and turn away from the answer-machine to follow him upstairs.

2

After a quick early-morning run to blow away the hangover, I arrive at the shop with my usual cappuccino and croissant, and a *pain au chocolat* for Eve who is addicted to chocolate. I find her studying the books to see how last night went. 'We have many orders, especially for the French lace dresses, and many people for the mailing list,' she says, looking even more delighted when I hand her the pastry.

'That's wonderful! Last night went even better than I expected. Eve, I have to tell you,' I continue passionately, 'Sam is taking me skiing this Christmas, to Meribel! It was a surprise, he left the tickets on my pillow.'

'He is a dream,' she sighs. 'Hector and I, we do not get on very well at the moment.' Hector is her boyfriend. 'You two are very serious, *non*?' Eve is French. When I advertized for a new shop assistant six months ago, she was a league ahead of anyone else. She arrived on time, wearing a black ribbed polo neck with a camel suede skirt, and her long honey-blond hair was

15

scooped into an immaculate ponytail. She answered my questions so earnestly, as if her future depended on it. 'I would like to work here with you, Katie. I hope I get this job,' she said, and touched my desk, 'touching wood'.

'I guess we are serious. I'm such a lucky girl.'

'And he is lucky too. Perhaps he is 'the one', Katie?'

'Perhaps.' I smile back at her.

★ ★ ★

It's late in the evening and I am about to lock up for the night. There is a tap on the shop window and I see Sam outside wearing his shades, holding a bottle of wine wrapped in tissue paper and a bunch of lilies.

He kisses me and hands me the flowers. 'Thought I'd pick you up from work today, I finished early for a change.'

'What are these for?' I grin. 'Skiing and now flowers *and* a chauffeur. If you keep this up, I'll never want to leave you, so you'd better watch out.'

'That's the whole idea, Kitty-kins,' he says, as he kisses me again. It's a hot summer's evening, and the restaurants and bars have opened their doors. Already friends are meeting after work, talking and drinking in the last of the sun.

★ ★ ★

'Remember, we're going out tonight,' Sam reminds me as he opens the front door.

'Are we? What are we doing?'

'I wrote it down in our social calendar, Katie. Dinner with Maguire and his new lady.' Sam breaks out into a little tap dance when he says 'lady'. 'He said he was going to get the barbecue going.'

'Great. Sorry, it slipped my mind. It's been hectic today, Eve and I didn't have a moment off, not even for lunch. I'm going to have to employ another person.' I walk over to the answer-machine and press the play button. 'Can you fix us a drink, Sam? A nice glass of wine?' I add.

'Katie, it's your father,' says the familiar voice in a serious tone.

I stand rooted to the spot. This must be the message from last night. I knew something was up. I could feel it. Don't we always expect something to creep up on us and go wrong when things are going too well?

'I need to talk to you. It's . . . ' he coughs ' . . . it's really quite urgent.'

I swallow hard. Oh my God, something has

17

happened to Mum. Or maybe Bells. Has someone in the family died? Aunt Agnes? He must wonder why I haven't called him back.

Sam looks at me curiously. 'Your old man never calls here. He must want something.'

Sam is right. Dad always calls me at the shop. Why didn't he call me there today if it is so urgent? 'I don't know,' I say distractedly, pressing my lips together.

'It's your mother, she's been working herself into the ground,' Dad continues, 'you know what she's like, and we haven't had a proper holiday for years. We went to the doctor's and he strongly recommended a break. I'm taking her away. *So*,' he lingers on the word, 'we need to talk about who is going to look after Bells.'

Bells. Don't say anything more, Dad, please. Ask me to call you back and hang up.

'Who's Bells? Is that your dog?' Sam looks at me.

I nod. 'I'm sure it's nothing serious. Sam, that glass of wine?' I say, praying he will walk away, downstairs to the kitchen.

'Katie, you know I hate pets.'

I wrinkle my forehead at him. 'Drink?'

'Your mother and I are going to France for two weeks,' Dad continues.

Sam is shaking his head now. 'Sitting next to Mum's dog, Doogle, is like sitting next to an old fish. F. Breath Esquire, I call him.'

'Sam! Go! Drink!'

' . . . and Bells will need someone when we go away, we can't leave her on her own,' Dad says.

'I've just bought those new leather sofas too,' Sam protests. 'No dog lifting its leg, please. Oh. Is Bells a girl?'

'Go and run me a bath,' I demand now, feeling myself burning under my skin. Dad is still talking and I put my hand out to press the stop button, but Sam puts his hand firmly over mine. 'What is it, Katie? Jesus, I thought I had a weird relationship with my parents.' Sam has always been cagey about his parents. I remember thinking it strange that he called his father by his first name, Julian. 'Who's Julian?' I had asked. 'My father,' he replied, in an unusually stiff formal voice which invited no further questions.

'I really need to talk to you, to make a plan,' Dad continues. 'I'm out all day tomorrow so can you call me back tonight?' There is a lengthy pause.

I want to say, DAD, HANG UP, PLEASE, OTHERWISE I WILL NEVER FORGIVE YOU, but my mouth has dried and I am unable to utter a word. Besides, I cannot say anything when Sam is next to me. His presence feels like a loaded gun.

19

Dad draws in breath again, a habit I have inherited from him. Sam says I do it when I'm fretting about something. It sounds like sucking a straw. Mum hates it.

Sam laughs. 'He sounds so serious. It's only a goddamn' dog, isn't it, Katie? Anyone would think he was talking about the future of the euro.'

My agitation reaches boiling point. 'Sam, go and run me a bath, PLEASE.'

He pushes past me. 'OK, OK. 'Run me a bath, make me a drink,'' he mimics.

'If I don't hear from you, I'll call you back later,' Dad finishes. 'We must talk.'

I feel as if I can breathe again when I hear the machine indicate the end of the call. Never before have I felt so relieved to hear 'You have no new messages.'

'Sorry, Sam,' I say when he comes back with a drink and I can hear the bath water running strongly. 'I didn't mean to get snappy.' I lift my shoulders and circle my neck. 'It's Dad, he's such a worrier. I'd better call him. You go up, get ready for tonight.'

'Mum's old dog even peed on her wedding dress,' Sam comments, shaking his head as he goes upstairs. 'No dog, Katie. Sorry. You can live here but no dog. End of story. *Capisce*?'

★ ★ ★

It's two o'clock in the morning and I cannot find my cigarettes. The evening was dismal because I could not stop thinking about Bells. Sam would never have known I wasn't enjoying myself. I smiled in all the right places and laughed when Maguire relayed his filthy jokes. But Sam cannot massage this problem away. This is serious. Why did it have to happen now, when things are running so smoothly? And where has Sam hidden those cigarettes? I stare ahead of me at the cupboards. There is nothing in Sam's kitchen. All the surfaces are kept carefully bare; in fact there is nothing much anywhere except for this art sculpture made out of what look like coloured milk bottles. Sam tells me it reflects the mood of the modern world.

I open one of the cupboards and start to run my eyes over the shelves. Sam may have tucked the cigarettes into the pressure cooker, a cunning place as we never use it. No. I stand on tiptoe and run my hand along the top of the cupboard. I could kill him. If I want a cigarette, why shouldn't I smoke one?

I open each drawer impatiently, slamming it shut when no cigarettes are revealed. In my mind I replay my call to Dad earlier this evening.

'Katie, we know it's a lot to ask, but I need you to help,' he'd said.

'This is all so sudden, why didn't you tell me how tired Mum's been?'

'I can't hear you, speak up.'

I had to repeat the question again, keeping half an ear on what Sam was doing. I could hear him upstairs opening our wardrobe, the bath water still running.

'Oh, Katie, you know how proud she is. We'd never go away unless I organized it either. Look, it's for two weeks.'

'How is she?' I asked, biting my lip. 'Dad?'

'She'll be fine, as long as she has a break and we take some time off now.'

'Right,' I acknowledged. 'I know you need a holiday, but I'm not sure I can look after Bells. It's such short notice.'

'It's all booked,' Dad said firmly.

It is so unlike him to go ahead without asking me. How does he know I am free? I might be going on holiday too, or abroad on business. 'Is there anyone else we can ask?'

'Who do you suggest?'

'Aunt Agnes. She'd love to have Bells. Be positively upset if we didn't ask her.'

'Bells wants to stay with you.'

'Why?' My voice was a loud whisper. 'I can't have her to stay here.'

Dad's patience snapped like a wafer. 'Can't or won't?'

'What about my shop? I can't drop

22

everything. I'm sorry. Let's call Aunt Agnes.'

'Now listen here, Katie. Your mother and I have never asked anything of you until now. We need this time together and Bells specifically asked if she could be with you in London. I told her she must write to ask you herself. Didn't you get her letter?'

Dad sounded so stern I daren't say I had not opened it, that it was still in my diary. 'It must have got lost in the post, it's so unreliable these days.'

'Oh, Katie.' He raised his voice in exasperation. 'Why won't you write to her? She's always asking after you. 'How's Katie? Never see Katie.''

I could almost hear Bells saying that and my heart melted for a split second. Dad must have felt it too because his voice softened momentarily. 'It would mean so much to her, and to us.'

Back to reality. 'Dad, two weeks is a long time. It's not even my own home.'

'I understand you would have to ask Sam. We would help towards costs and . . . '

'No, the cost isn't the issue.' Sam came downstairs in his towel at this point and asked why I was taking so long. The bath was ready. A thought came to me. I could persuade him to go on a golfing weekend with Maguire. He would never know. 'I could have her for a weekend?'

'And where is she going to stay for the rest of the time then?'

'Can't she stay in Wales?' was my desperate last attempt.

'Well, she could, but that's miserable, quite frankly,' he said, his voice loaded with frustration.

I understood all of this, but . . . 'I'm sorry, Dad. I really can't. If I had my own apartment . . . '

He cut me short. 'That's not the real reason, is it, Katie?'

'What do you mean?'

'Isn't it high time you shared some responsibility for your sister? Are you going to pretend she doesn't exist for the rest of your life?'

He'd always been able to read my thoughts as easily as looking in a mirror. I inhaled deeply, pulling a strand of my hair tightly. 'What are you talking about?'

'Does Sam know about Bells?'

'Yes,' I said weakly.

'You can't always leave it up to your mother and me. What would you do if something happened to us? Bells would be your responsibility then. Have you ever . . . '

'What do you mean, something happened to you? Like what?'

'If you won't have Bells to stay, you call her and tell her yourself,' he continued. 'I'm not going to be the bearer of bad news.' Dad's voice was trembling with anger now. 'It's for just two weeks of your life then life can carry on as normal, for you,' he added pointedly.

'Dad, what did you mean before?' I pressed him. 'Everything is OK, isn't it?'

'All I meant was, your mother and I aren't always going to be here for Bells. You will have to take over some day, be her guardian. Katie, I'm not trying to scare you, but let's face it, it's something you need to think about.'

But I don't want to. Emma has said this to me too. She wishes I would spend more time with Bells. 'After your parents, you are her next-of-kin,' she always says.

'Katie?'

'All right, I'll have her to stay,' I told him reluctantly.

There was this great sigh of relief. 'That's wonderful, thank you,' Dad said.

⋆   ⋆   ⋆

Frustrated in my search for cigarettes, I put the kettle on to make myself a cup of tea. Is it unfair to expect Sam to have Bells to stay for two weeks? If it were my home, well, that'd be different, I reason to myself. Oh, God, who am I fooling? Yet I am furious that my parents have put me in this position. It cuts both ways, Dad. I have a life to lead. I have a career. I can't drop everything for Bells like you and Mum have. That was always the motto in our household. I thought I'd escaped all that.

I massage my forehead, desperately trying to think of an alternative. Should I phone Aunt Agnes? Bells would have a much nicer time staying with her. I used to love my holidays there.

I can't go back up to bed, I won't be able to sleep. The kettle boils in the background. How am I going to cope with my sister? How will I introduce her to my friends? To Eve? To Sam?

I dig into my handbag to find my diary. In it is Bells's letter. I open it. The address, date and time are neatly underlined in the right-hand corner.

To my sister Katie Fletcher
Mum and Dad to stay in France and it would be very kind you have me to stay in summer holidays.
To stay with Aunt Agnes, Suffolk too far, would be very loveley to stay with Katie in London please.

Its very Longtime, since I saw you and
Wales close to London.
Love, Bells

I fold the letter and tuck it back into my
diary.
How can I say no?

3

1982

I am seven years old. I like staying with Aunt Agnes who lives in Suffolk, near the sea. She makes the best Black Forest gâteau with flakes of real dark chocolate, and she cooks homemade chips with real potatoes in a large deep pan. She is very pretty and wears glasses, attached to small brown beads like a necklace, and a long checked apron when she is cooking. She has these pointed shoes which look like witch's shoes and a train set that I play with in her large garden.

Her husband is funny too. Uncle Roger. Once he sat back in his chair and the whole thing collapsed. 'This house is like an old lady,' Aunt Agnes said. 'It needs a bit of cosmetic surgery.'

I think their house is spooky. Uncle Roger swears to me that he has seen the ghost of his father at the top of the stairs. The stairs creak, even my bed creaks when I turn over. The corridors are dark and smell old and I run as fast as I can up and down those haunted stairs and into my bedroom. 'She is only a little girl but I think she's going to crash right through them,' I overheard Uncle Roger say once.

I am staying with my uncle and aunt while Mum has her baby. Mum finds being pregnant difficult. She has had three miscarriages — Dad explained to me what they were — and during this last pregnancy she has been in bed most of the time. Now it's time for me to go back home. 'Your mother has had a baby girl,' Aunt Agnes tells me. 'You'll need to help your mum a lot. She will be very tired.' She isn't smiling at all and keeps on glancing sideways at Uncle Roger who is shrugging his shoulders.

Aunt Agnes has been so excited all the time I have been staying, constantly showing me baby knitwear patterns and asking me whether she should just 'go for it' and make the booties pink for a girl, or perhaps 'sit tight' in case it is a boy. Every sentence has begun with either, 'Katie, if your mother has a girl . . . ' or, 'I'm sure it's a boy. I can just feel it in my bones.' Even when we went to Sainsbury's she told the girl at the till that I was expecting a baby sister or brother. Aunt Agnes flaps her arms around when she is excited and her eyes flicker like a butterfly. Sometimes she pokes out her tongue when she's in a good mood.

The Sainsbury's girl had black all around

her eyes and didn't seem at all impressed by our happy news. As the dark chocolate Club biscuits and mini packets of cereals slid past her she said, 'Me, I'm never gonna have children or get married. Men, they're only good when you want something done.'

Aunt Agnes roared with laughter as she packed everything into bags. 'What a lot that girl will miss out on,' she told me in the warm car on the way back home. 'When you grow up, Katie, promise me you'll have lots of children? Fill the house with them. Don't be lonely like your old Uncle Roger and me.' Aunt Agnes can't have children, Mum and Dad told me. That's why they like to pack me off to go and see her in the holidays. Supper that night was spent deciding what names to call him/her. Now Aunt Agnes looks as if she doesn't know what to say about the new arrival. It's as if this is bad news.

She hugs me on the platform and tells me to be a brave girl. I cannot understand it. I am seven years old and I always travel on my own to Suffolk. A guard helps me onto the train and then there is Dad to pick me up when we arrive. There is nothing to be brave about. The train trundles back to my parents' home, and I go to the buffet car and pick out a marshmallow biscuit with strawberry filling and a packet of cheese and onion crisps. In between mouthfuls I try to imagine what my baby sister will look like. Will she look like me when I was little? Dad used to say I was blonde and big-eyed with dimpled white skin and chubby legs like baguettes. 'You used to wear your knickers on your head too.' He smiled. 'You pretended they were scarves like the ones Mum wore.'

Dad meets me at the station as usual, wearing his dark-rimmed glasses and looking even thinner and longer than he usually does. My dad is over six foot two inches. Today he is wearing his scruffy jeans which he normally only wears around the house and his knitted chunky grey jumper that matches his hair. He always complains that he turned grey too early in life. He helps me with my little shiny red case as I show the platform conductor my crumpled ticket. I don't have much in my case, just one smart skirt for the evenings, a pair of cords and a jumper, and my toothbrush and flannel. On the way home I want to ask lots of questions about the new baby. Yet I feel as if I have a marble stuck in my throat which makes it impossible to ask. Instead, we drive home in silence. Dad doesn't even put the radio on to hear the news. He loves the news. He turns it on first thing in the morning, at midday, in the afternoon and evening. Mum calls it his 'nervous disease'. Eventually Dad says something. 'Your mother is tired,' he tells me, just as Aunt Agnes did. He tells me I must be a good girl. He is gripping the steering wheel so hard I can see his knuckles turning white. He is also driving faster than usual.

'We're back,' Dad calls loudly. Everything is quiet in the house. Normally, when I return home from school or whatever I have been doing, I hear Mum in her studio with classical music playing loudly in the background. Some mad opera singer will be blasting out of the room, and I always stick my fingers into my ears. Today we walk upstairs, towards my parents' bedroom with their big double bed covered with a quilted bedspread Mum made out of her wedding dress. 'There's no point watching it wilt on a hanger,' she once told me. I cannot think how she managed to make a dress into a bedspread, but Mum can turn anything into something useful. 'She only has to wrinkle her nose and things turn to gold,' Dad says.

Mum is sitting on her bedside chair with her old quilted bed-jacket on. Dad often tries to buy her another bed-jacket, but she won't give it up. 'It's like comfort food,' she says. 'Sticky toffee pudding.' I kiss her on the cheek but she doesn't move, just sits there quietly, like Granny sits in her armchair in the corner of the kitchen when she comes to stay. But there is something wrong about Mum being so quiet. It is unlike her. Shouldn't she be happy if she has just had a baby? Instead she looks small and defeated and her cheeks are cold and dry.

The crib stands in the middle of the room. It looks lonely and no noise comes from it. Mum looks over to Dad, who seems to be making some kind of secret sign at her. Her eyes look red and puffy, as if she has been crying all night.

'Before you see your new sister . . . ' Dad starts slowly. I know then that something is wrong and I am scared. Immediately I walk over to the crib and look down.

4

'Did you really believe Sam would never meet her?' asks Emma. She grinds some pepper onto our houmous. We are eating at a local Greek restaurant. It is our regular Tuesday night out. Emma and I go to a yoga class followed by a drink and supper. Sam plays poker on Tuesdays with Maguire and a few of his other workmates.

Emma tilts her head sideways when she asks questions — she does it when she is watching television too, her forehead furrowed in concentration. Emma and I know almost everything about each other as we have been friends for twenty-five years. She was once my next-door neighbour. We went to school together, ballet classes together, until Emma was told she was too 'big-boned' to have a future in pirouetting. She's tall and willowy now, but when she was little she was 'partridge-shaped' as my Dad used to say. She stole bags of crisps from the cardboard box in their kitchen and ate them at the bottom of the garden. I was the other way round; the teacher constantly asked me if I was eating properly.

We used to have a dressing-up box at home and we would put on my mother's old fur coats and stilettos and strut down to the shops together with Peggy, Mum's dog, held tightly on the lead. Peggy would never walk with me, I had to drag her and she bumped along the pavement. I spent most of my time at Emma's house. When things at home were difficult or if Mum and Dad were at the hospital visiting Bells, I stayed with Emma. I worshipped Emma's sister, Berry, because she was so pretty and everything I wanted to be. Their family house became my second home. Emma is the only person I can talk to about Bells as she grew up with both of us.

Emma still has that incredulous expression on her face, which makes me feel unsettled. Of course, this would be her reaction. Emma is always rational; she knows what is right and wrong.

'I knew Sam would meet her some day, if we were serious,' I finally reply.

'Are you serious?' She dips her pitta into the houmous.

'Yes, I think we are.'

Emma is absent-mindedly coiling her dark brown hair into little horns. Since she was little I can remember her playing with her hair. 'Then in a way this is the perfect opportunity to tell him. It's given you the push you need. Otherwise, when will you?' she asks, almost accusingly.

'It has never been a conscious decision not to tell him about Bells,' I fight my own corner. 'He knows I have a sister, I just haven't told him much about her, that's all. It hasn't come up in conversation.'

'Katie, look.' Emma seems to stare into me, able to see exactly what I am thinking. She has a disarming habit of doing that. 'You're embarrassed, aren't you?'

'Of course I'm not embarrassed.' I blush, feeling defenceless around her, as if she is peeling the protective layers away from me one by one.

Emma chooses not to hear. 'You think the longer you don't mention Bells, the harder it will be suddenly to drop her casually into conversation. You're starting to believe you live in parallel universes, that Bells will never cross your path in this one.'

'Sam's not a curious person,' I defend myself, 'he has never asked me what my sister does, hasn't even met my parents. I've never met his come to that.' Since going out with Sam I have discovered little scraps of information about them. His father worked overseas when he was young, leaving Sam and his mother behind most of the time. 'Mum and I were fine,' he insisted when I asked him once if he'd missed his father. 'We had a great time. Mum had a ball, in fact, when Dad left. Didn't have to get his dry-cleaning done, or put his bloody supper on the table by seven on the dot. She could go out with her friends. Used to take me to all the parties. Think she got sloshed half the time,' he recalled with a short dry laugh. 'Yeah, we had a grand time, Mum and I. Turned out for the best, I'd say.' Sam doesn't like saying anything is wrong or that someone has hurt him. It's a positive thing in that he doesn't ever feel sorry for himself or harbour resentment. 'Life is for living, not for dwelling on, Katie,' he always says.

I know it's not really as simple as Sam makes it sound. Yet I've never felt able to tell him about my family; about how much I hated not seeing more of Mum after Bells arrived. Anyway, it doesn't matter because Sam doesn't ask. That's why I love going out with him. I don't need to explain anything. I can be exactly who I want to be.

'Eat some of this,' Emma demands, pushing the plate of houmous and pitta bread in my direction. 'You haven't touched your food.'

I look at the plate dispassionately. 'I'm not hungry.' Instead I pour myself another glass of wine.

'I think you're overreacting to the whole situation,' she says directly. 'You're not the only one to go through something like this, you know. Dad did exactly the same thing with Mum.'

'Really?' I look up.

'Yes.' Emma nods authoritatively. 'He didn't introduce her to his eccentric brother. You know, Uncle Spencer? Big ears, plays the piano very badly, rides a motorbike and wears dodgy maroon shirts and purple ties?'

'I know Uncle Spencer.' I smile. 'He's the one who can tell you what day of the week you were born from the date of your birthday, can't he? I used to love that game,' I reminisce. 'I was born on a Friday. I always wanted him to be just one day out but he didn't slip up, not once. I remember his wobbly 'Für Elise' too.' I grin. 'Which came out especially at Christmas, along with a few hymns. 'Hark the Herald' was particularly painful.'

'Exactly.' Emma laughs. 'He's wonderful, but he lives on another planet. Dad thought Mum might call off the engagement if she met him. So he was very wily and arranged that Mum's visits never coincided with Uncle Spencer's. They 'courted' for eight months, were engaged, and Mum finally met Uncle Spencer for the first time at the wedding.'

'In one of his dodgy suits?' For a moment I am forgetting my own dilemma and enjoying the world of Uncle Spencer.

'No, even worse, he arrived on his motorbike wearing an extraordinary black shirt with a gold tiger on it.' She wrinkles her nose. 'Totally inappropriate but it didn't surprise anyone.'

'Well, there you go!' I beam triumphantly, topping up my glass of wine. 'Your dad would understand then. *You* should too.' I feel like I have earned back a few points.

'I do understand. But I asked Mum if it would have made any difference had she met Uncle Spencer before they married, and she said no. She was adamant. She would have married Dad anyway. He was a silly old fool who worried too much. She adores Uncle Spencer. We all do. He's entertaining. She finds his sister, Esther, boring and straight.'

'Ems, I do see what you're saying, I just feel Sam has to seriously ... I mean, SERIOUSLY,' I emphasize, widening my eyes, 'fall in love with me before I introduce him to Bells. It's only been nine months and they have been fantastic. I'm happy. I don't want to risk Bells meeting him and whacking him hard in the balls.'

Emma's face dissolves into a smile. 'She doesn't do that any more though, does she?'

When Emma and I were at school we used to meet boys in our lunch hour and clumsily snog them behind school fences and gates. I remember fancying two boys, Toby and Ben, but not being able to choose which one to go out with. So, I decided to put them both to 'The Bells Test'. In the past, boys had met Bells and ten times out of ten left the house vowing never to return. To begin with I had been mortified, but then I started to turn the situation around. There had to be one boy, surely, who could stand up to the test?

I took Toby home first and watched Bells charge at him full tilt and butt him in the balls. You might wonder where the fun was in that, especially for the boys, but the best part lay in studying their reaction. When Bells belted Toby I watched him as he clutched his balls in agony. Then he pretended it hadn't happened at all and asked me what was for tea. Bells started to howl with laughter at that and Toby suddenly said he had forgotten his mum wanted him back for tea after all.

Ben the Bold was much braver. He rugby-tackled Bells and she liked that and kept on asking when he was coming round again. And he did come back! Ben at least had risen to the challenge. Was I scared that Sam wouldn't?

'Come off it, that was when we were

. . . what? Fourteen? Fifteen?' Emma continues. 'And we are talking Toby, the prick who wore tight leather jackets and thought he was in *Grease*. And Ben who drew phallic diagrams all over his pencil cases and files. What a loss!' she laughs. 'Bells did you a favour.'

'I know,' I concede. 'Actually Ben got on quite well with her. But, Emma, it's two whole weeks. It's not a weekend, a few days, it's a whole fortnight. That's three hundred and thirty six hours. That's twenty thousand, one hundred and sixty minutes. That's millions and millions of seconds . . . '

Emma stops me. 'Katie, this is ridiculous. You've got to stop worrying so much. Bells is not your average sister, but so what? She wants you to be a part of her life. Anyone would think you had been asked to solve all the problems of the Middle East, or closer to home even. Just this evening I had to see a young girl with leukaemia, for God's sake. You need to put it in perspective.'

The waiter takes our plates away. 'I know you're right,' I say, hanging my head with shame. 'I'm sorry, Emma, your job must be very difficult sometimes.'

She shrugs her shoulders. 'Bells gets on with it. You need to as well. When did you last see her? I mean, properly?'

41

'Last Christmas. I went home for a night.'

'You need to spend more time with her. You never know, you might actually enjoy her company. Things always come along to test us,' Emma continues. 'Life never stays on a nice even keel, it doesn't work like that.' As she is saying this half of me wants to reply, 'What's ever tested you?' Emma's life is so utterly perfect. She gets on with her family, her brother is an architect, she has a close relationship with her parents, Jonnie adores her, they were *made* for each other, and now she has a large diamond on her finger. It's unfair though I would never say so. But it doesn't stop me thinking it occasionally.

'You don't see enough of your mum either, Katie. You might regret it one day.' She waits for my response. 'What's wrong? There's something else, isn't there?' she probes. 'Is it your mother?'

I tell Emma about my conversation with Dad. 'It seems a bit sudden, that's all. I can't help wondering if he's keeping something from me.'

'Your dad wouldn't lie,' Emma says with conviction. 'Look, I think they just want you to start making more of an effort with Bells.'

'Mum didn't even ring to ask me how my fashion show went,' I tell her.

'OK, but did she know about it? Did you

ask her to be there?' Emma's patience is running out.

'No, not really. Oh,' I wave a hand dismissively, 'I know. I'm nearly thirty, not sixteen. It shouldn't get to me like this.' I sink back into my chair and try to relax. 'I just wish I had told Sam straightaway about Bells, it would have made life a lot easier.'

'Tell him your sister's coming to stay. Describe her so he won't be too surprised, and I bet you he'll be fine about it.'

'But . . . '

'No buts.'

'Yes, but what if . . . '

'NO buts. I know you would be saying the same thing to me if it were the other way around. And I know it's easy, my sitting here giving you advice,' she admits, 'but tell Sam tonight. Don't put it off any longer. He's not a monster, he's your boyfriend. I tell Jonnie everything, he would be hurt if I shut him out. Don't we go out with people to feel supported? Isn't that the whole point?'

'Yes.'

'You tell him,' she says simply. 'What's the worst that can happen?'

5

'Katie,' Dad says sternly, 'don't upset your mother.'

I can't help it. I peer down into the cot again. 'But what's wrong with her?' I turn to look at Mum and Dad. 'Why hasn't my sister got a proper nose? It's all squashed down. And what's that funny hole between her nose and lip?' Mum is crying now, and Dad crouches down beside her, stroking her arm gently.

'Why does she look so funny?' I ask again. I can't look at the baby any more. It's scaring me.

'Katie,' Dad begins, 'this is the way she was born. I am afraid not all children are lucky enough to be born perfect.'

'Why?'

Dad takes off his glasses and wipes his eyes. 'Just because. We're going to have to help her. Your sister will have to see a doctor who will make her face better. It's going to be all right. We're . . . '

'Stop!' Mum sobs. 'Nothing's all right. How are we going to cope?'

'We'll manage. We'll make sure we do,' Dad reassures her. 'Katie will help us, won't you, darling?' He looks at me as if to say, Don't just stand there, come over and give your mother a hug.

Was this what Aunt Agnes meant by being brave? I walk over to Mum and put my arms around her.

★ ★ ★

The doctor is here and I am listening at the kitchen door. I am supposed to be doing my homework in my room.

'There is an excellent local team of specialists in facial-oral problems. They're very experienced in treating children born with a cleft of the lip and palate,' he is saying reassuringly. 'One child in approximately seven hundred and fifty births has this problem. We will also consult a plastic surgeon for advice. He will talk us through the reconstructive surgical procedures. With a series of operations, we can repair your daughter's lip and palate.'

'When can we start?' Dad asks.

'While she is still a baby but a bit bigger and able to cope with the surgery.'

'I don't understand why this happened. I felt fine during the pregnancy, I had plenty of rest. What did I do wrong?' Mum pleads for an explanation.

'It's not your fault,' Dad immediately tells her.

The doctor agrees. 'There is no known cause. Is there any family history, do you know?'

'No, not that I'm aware. I was so sure I had done everything right,' Mum continues oblivious. 'But I should have had a scan. I should have . . . '

'Stop it,' Dad raises his voice. 'Don't continually blame yourself.'

'The specialists will go through everything with you. I know it's hard to take in, but we are very experienced in this field.' The doctor clears his throat. I can feel a terrible silence stretching out before he adds, 'I am afraid there is a further problem. She could be brain-damaged, though to what extent precisely we do not know at the moment.'

'Brain-damaged?' Mum says numbly.

'Yes. We'll carry out more tests but she will need a lot of your time and attention to begin with . . . '

'Her name is Isabel,' Dad cuts in. 'We've always loved that name.'

'Isabel, right. You have another girl too, don't you?' the doctor enquires.

'Yes, Katie. But there's no way I can

46

manage the two of them on my own,' Mum says. 'We need help. I mean, how will I feed Isabel? How will I . . . my baby's really brain-damaged?'

Poor Mum. This is so unfair. I will help. Let me help.

'We'll be fine.' Dad speaks softly to her. 'We'll get through this together.'

I hear the doctor stand up to leave. I rush away from the door and run upstairs to my bedroom.

Mum doesn't come upstairs to say goodnight to me like she usually does. Dad comes instead. It seems dark and cold in my bedroom and I feel very alone as I hear his heavy footsteps walk away from me.

6

I look at the picture of Sam in the silver frame by my bedside. He is wearing the white cotton shirt with the pale blue stripe that I bought him for his birthday, and his dark sunglasses are perched on the top of his head. He is looking directly at the camera with a confident smile. Sam is handsome and he knows it. Virtually every feature is symmetrical except for one of his nostrils which is not as open as the other — he puts that down to his mother smoking when she was pregnant with him. 'The moment Dad was out of the house, she smoked like a chimney. Fag in one hand, vodka in the other.' The only other thing he is conscious of is his receding hairline but I tell him it makes him look distinguished. Noble even. He tells me it makes him look like his father, before he takes a handful of his hair and tries to ruffle it up as much as he can.

I still have not told him about Bells. I have put it off for a week now and she is arriving tomorrow. I am picking her up from Paddington. I don't know why I believe the problem might go away if I don't talk about it. The phone rings, it's Dad. They are leaving tomorrow. 'Who are you staying with in France?' I ask.

'The Walters.'

I don't recognize the name. 'Who are they?'

'Old friends. He used to work with me at Sotheby's.'

'I don't remember them.'

'They moved to France when you were about two.' Dad changes the subject quickly. 'Now, you've got my mobile . . . '

'Actually, could I take down the Wallers' number?' I ask.

'Walters,' he corrects.

'Can I have their number?'

'No, you won't need it.'

'Well, you never know.'

'We'll call you.'

'I think I ought to have it.' Our conversation is like a fast game of ping-pong.

'Just ring us on the mobile.'

'What if there's an emergency?'

'There won't be an emergency.'

'Why can't I have their number? Why are you being so funny about it?'

'Darling,' Dad finally slows the pace of his answers, 'it's simply easier if you ring us on the mobile. That way you can call at any time of day.'

I agree to this, unwillingly. 'Remember to

turn it on then,' I say.

Dad always says he bought the mobile 'for emergency use only', but fails utterly to understand it is useless in an emergency if he doesn't first switch it on.

'Yes, don't worry,' he protests.

'So, what will you be doing with the Walters?'

'Swimming, eating, sleeping, reading books. Darling, I have to go now. Will you thank Sam very much?' he finishes.

I put the phone down feeling uneasy. I am going to have to tell Sam about Bells tonight. I rang him from the shop a little earlier, telling him he mustn't work late this evening, that I am cooking him his favourite meal — steak with homemade chips, just like Aunt Agnes's. I have even made him a pudding: orange icecream cake with dark chocolate sauce. It's his mother's recipe and very easy because even I can do it.

'I'm not sure I'm going to be able to get away early, sweetheart. Busy day,' he told me.

'But I haven't seen you all week. I've got a really special supper laid on.'

He seemed to be considering. 'What have I done to deserve this, Katie?' I could hear his chair swivelling around. 'Are you feeling guilty about shagging someone behind my back?' And then he crowed with incredulity, as if the very idea of someone cheating on him was impossible. Sam has enough arrogance to bottle up and sell internationally. Yet this is what I find most attractive about him. I always thought I would end up falling for an academic or maybe a writer. My last boyfriend was a composer who travelled the world creating soundtracks for television shows and films. I barely saw him, which was why it ended, I knew a relationship like that was heading nowhere. Yet I never thought I would go for someone like Sam. Then again, I fancy Simon Cowell off X-Factor, which just about says it all.

I put the photograph frame back down on the bedside table. I open the sliding doors to our wardrobe and look at my clothes, neatly folded into different compartments, and the dresses, trousers and skirts hanging up. What shall I wear? I go for the dark red lace top with the velvet trim around the neck. I'll wear my black lacy bra underneath. Bottom half will be my Diesel jeans worn with black pointed boots. Sam likes this outfit. I peel off my oyster pink shirt and toss it into the laundry basket, unzip my black cotton skirt and look at myself in the long mirror. My hair, now dyed back to its original dark brown, hangs loose around my face. It's getting long. I pin it up with a clip. I have my father's fine hair. In fact, I have inherited most of my features from Dad; the long Fletcher nose, the high cheekbones, the wide mouth and my dimple.

I open one of the mirrored cupboards in our bathroom to find some cotton wool pads and cleanser. Sam gets infuriated with me if I leave my toothpaste or cotton wool pads lying around in the bathroom, everything has to be packed neatly into the mirrored cupboards. I like it that he is tidy. If he wasn't, his place would look like it had been burgled.

I wipe the day's make-up off my face. From Mum I've inherited a splattering of freckles across my nose and cheeks, and my green eyes. Dad always says he fell for her eyes straight away. They were the colour of olives, and Dad loves olives. When I first met Sam he told me I had 'come to bed eyes'. Wait till he sees Bells's eyes which are far more beautiful. They're a vivid green with no sludgy grey in them at all. I sit on the edge of the bath and start to run the water. I pour in a large capful of neroli oil and finally I step into the sweet-scented water. It has been a long day. I snapped at Eve this morning for eating my Kit-Kat and the dark cooking chocolate that I had bought for Sam's pudding. She ate the entire bar in her lunch hour. The moment I bring chocolate into the shop she can sniff it out like a dog scenting drugs at an airport. Sam doesn't believe me when I tell him that all she eats is chocolate. 'But she's tiny, so petite, so French,' he protests. I once met her in Sainsbury's and she had filled her trolley with bars of chocolate and great big tins of Cadbury's drinking chocolate.

Tonight will be absolutely fine. I will tell Sam, he will be cool with it, everything will be OK, I reassure myself for what must be the hundredth time.

Later I light the dark red candle in its glass candlestick and finish laying the table. I place the new napkins I made out of muslin by each plate. Mum could turn her napkins into the shape of lilies. I used to try and copy her as a child. Now I just fold mine in two. I open the fridge and pour myself a second glass of white wine. Sam should be here any minute now. I hear a key turn in the front door and something jolts sharply inside me. I breathe deeply, I think about Emma's advice to come clean.

'Hi, honey,' I call. I hear him coming downstairs, taking the steps two by two. The room smells of chips frying in golden oil. Dido is playing softly in the background. Sam likes her. He walks up to me and hands me a large bunch of scarlet and orange tulips, my favourite. I thank him with a kiss and he wraps his arms around my waist, pulling me close to him. 'Kitty-kins.' He rubs his nose against mine. 'I'm a lucky boy. I raced home. Not too late, am I?'

'Perfect timing. Good day?'

'Great day in the markets. Fabulous. Wham, bam, thank you, ma'am.' He winks. 'And now I'm all yours.'

'That's brilliant, Sam.' When he's excited about closing a deal I have tried to ask him in the past about it, but he always says, 'Top secret, babe, confidential,' and taps his nose. So I rarely bother now, just make encouraging noises if he has had a good day.

'Smells fab, I am starving.'

'Sit down,' I instruct, leading him to a chair. He sits down and it is me rubbing his shoulders this time. 'Relax and I'll get you a drink first.'

'Are you softening me up for something?' Sam murmurs with pleasure.

'Can't a girl just spoil her boy?' I run a hand over his back. 'Right, what do you want to drink? Beer or wine?'

★ ★ ★

I still have not told him and we have just finished our first course. What is wrong with

54

me? I cannot say a word. Instead, I am listening to Sam tell me that Maguire has bought a Mini Cooper and plans to go racing at the weekend, and would I mind if he goes too?

He leans across the table and strokes my cheek affectionately. 'Enough of me, how's the old soak in the corner? Has she been in lately?'

'No, annoyingly not.' I tell him about Eve instead as I clear the plates. 'She ought to be the size of an elephant, not a mouse,' he chuckles.

I open the fridge. When I put the orange pudding on the table I am going to tell him. The trick lies in saying the first part: 'Sam, my sister is coming to stay tomorrow, is that OK? She's not quite what you'd expect, you might be a bit taken aback . . . ' I am going to scare the living daylights out of him, aren't I?

The pudding sits in front of him. Sam rubs his stomach and smiles. 'I could get used to this star treatment.'

'Sam, I have something to tell you . . . is that *the* watch?' I am staring at his wrist. 'You actually bought it?' I ask in disbelief. I know how much it must have cost. Close to £3,000.

'Yes.' He beams, shaking his wrist at me. Sam has been going on about this watch for months. It's a special 'emergency' model with an electronic device you can press to alert help in moments of crisis. One of his friends works in advertising and his company was involved in its promotion. Sam and I were so excited when we met Pierce Brosnan at the launch. 'You know, I might buy one. Imagine if I were caught in an avalanche,' I overheard Sam saying seriously to Tim, one of his friends at work. 'Yeah, yeah, yeah. Absolutely, mate,' Tim replied. 'Or when your canoe tips up while you're white-water rafting?' I suggested to them both, trying not to laugh. I didn't remind Sam that he wasn't exactly into extreme sports. Falling into a bunker playing a round of golf was about as dangerous as it got for him.

Now he looks at his watch proudly. 'If you pull the emergency cord by mistake you're fined thousands of pounds, Katie, so just be careful, capisce? Anyway, what did you want to tell me?' He slices the orange pudding, cream seeping out around the edges and making patterns in the chocolate sauce.

'I should have asked you before but my sister is coming to London . . . ' I start.

'Really?' He eats a spoonful. 'Yum,' he moans appreciatively. '*Delicioso*. Have you been secretly going to cooking lessons?'

'I was hoping she could stay with us? My

sister Isabel?' I remind him.

'Sure, for how long? I'd like to meet her.'

'Two weeks.'

'Right.' Sam mulls this over, looking surprised that it's for so long. 'No, that's OK, see no reason why not. Isabel's younger than you, isn't she? I could set Maguire up, he needs a bird.'

'But he had a new 'lady' only days ago.'

'Nah, that didn't work out,' Sam says. 'Maguire likes it short and sweet. So Isabel's coming up for two weeks? Perfecto. Done and dusted.'

'Sam, don't talk in clichés. He'll end up a sad lonely old bachelor if he carries on like that.'

'Does she look like you?' he goes on. 'Just a younger, more wrinkle-free version?'

'Sam,' I say with some irritation. 'Is that all you think about? Image?'

'Yep,' he says simply. 'Well, it helps if she's not a complete moose. Come on, girls are just the same. Blokes are more honest, that's all. Would you have fallen for me if I was ugly as sin?'

I pick up my plate and walk over to the sink.

He holds up his hands in a gesture of apology. 'How old is she then?'

'Twenty-two.' I sit back down, stare at the

candle I lit so hopefully. Pudding is over and I still have not told him the whole truth. By the time it burns out he will know everything about Bells, I vow.

'What does she do? I've forgotten.'

'You've never asked.'

'Oh.' He looks blank. 'Well, I'm asking now. Is she a lapdancer?'

'Oh, Sam,' I sigh.

'Don't tell me . . . she works for MI5 or something exciting like that? Seriously, why don't I get Maguire over here one night and introduce them? Do you reckon she'd go for someone like him?'

Bill Maguire. Tall, with very blond hair the colour of an egg yolk, and eyebrows and lashes to match. Always wears a leather jacket, a predator when it comes to women and loves to tell dirty jokes. 'Um, I don't think so. I mean, Bill is great, but . . . '

'Is she single?'

'Yes. Sam, there's something I need to tell you about her, though.' I am staring at the candle, great chunks of wax hardening around the edges. I watch the flame glowing in the dark. I remember as a child running my finger through one and Mum telling me off. 'Don't play with fire, it's dangerous.' Sam comes over to me.

'I'm looking forward to meeting her, babe.

She's coming to stay tomorrow? Great, she can sleep in the white bedroom. What else is there to say?' He starts kissing my neck. 'I love this top,' he tells me. 'Why are you so tense, babe?' He walks in front of me and kneels down, putting his hands on my knees. I know that look. He is about to break out into Chris de Burgh's 'Lady in Red'. Sam knows this always makes me laugh. We tease Emma for liking Chris de Burgh, that's how this started. In fact we have his CD too, but that's our little secret.

Sam pulls me to my feet and we start to dance. We love dancing in the kitchen. It's our time together, just Sam and me. He spins me around, singing softly in my ear, and it tickles. We both laugh together.

Why does my family have to be different? I curse quietly to myself as Sam holds me. Wouldn't it be wonderful to be able to say, 'My sister's a lawyer'? Or an architect, philosopher, psychologist, artist, writer, charity worker. She could even be an accountant, that would be OK. Why can't we be normal, like every other family? Why do I care so much? Surely I should be past this stage? Shouldn't I be mature enough to tell Sam? Like Emma says, if we are in a serious relationship . . .

Finally we stop dancing. 'Thanks for the

lovely evening, Katie. You know how to spoil me.' He takes my hand, gently kissing each finger in turn.

I don't want to tell him, it doesn't feel right to tell him now. *He will meet Bells tomorrow.*

Sam blows the candle out, still holding onto my hand. The smoke evaporates into nothing.

7

1984

As I walk across the school playground I can see my mother standing apart from a cluster of parents waiting by the iron gates. Bells is with her in the pushchair. What is she doing here? A mixture of panic and anger jabs at my chest. Mum never picks me up. What normally happens is I go to Mr Stubbington's corner shop to buy some sherbet dips and marshmallows and then walk home with Emma, my next-door neighbour. I go round to her house for tea because it's nicer there. They light the fire and then we toast our marshmallows.

Mum approaches one of the other mothers and a young girl. She is wearing her grubby apron with paint and oil stains down the front, her bright red shoes which look more like clogs, and her auburn hair is still pulled back tightly in one of her cotton head scarves. All the other mothers wear long navy skirts and frilly blouses with pearls, and their hair is curled and sits like perfect nests on top of their heads. Why does my mum have to look so different? Why did she have to bring Bells?

'Katie, what is it?' Emma asks impatiently. 'I'm hungry. Come on.'

'Mum's here, with Bells.' I pull her back.

'So?' Emma shrugs. 'I want to go home.'

I haven't told anyone in my class about Bells, they wouldn't understand. Emma is the only one who has seen her from the beginning. Bells's face looks so strange. They laugh at anything that looks weird. Mrs Higson, one of the mothers who stands at the gate, is so fat that everyone calls her Mrs Treestump-Legs. Has Mum seen me? I dart behind the boys' outside loo, but cannot stay there for long because it smells. I almost choke. I can hear the parents talking. My mother's voice is louder than any of the others, I think crossly. I am sure she does it on purpose. 'Just GO then,' I tell Emma, waving her away with my hand. 'Tell Mum I had to stay behind in class . . . say anything.'

I can hear people walking off, engines being turned on, prams being pushed, dogs barking. I wait with my fingers clipped firmly to my nose.

'Hello,' I can hear Mum saying, trying to be friendly. 'Don't look so worried, she won't bite you. Her name's Isabel. We call her Bells.'

Who's Mum talking to? I poke my head around the wall. It's Imogen, from the year

62

below, with her mother.

'What's wrong with her?' Imogen asks, unable to take her eyes away from the baby in the pram. 'What's that big hole in her face?'

'Imogen, don't be rude,' the mother interrupts, turning the colour of beetroot. 'It's the inside that counts after all, isn't it?' she says to Mum.

Mum says nothing.

Imogen still stands rooted to the spot like a mannequin in a shop. Piss off, I want to shout. Her mother eventually pulls her away.

I wait until it is quiet and safe to come out. I have to get the timing right. After roughly ten minutes I poke my head around the wall. Mum is bending down talking to Bells. There is no-one else around. I bolt sideways and then stroll forward as if I have come from the main school building. 'I don't care what anyone says, you're my beautiful little girl, and your mother loves you, and we are having a lovely time, aren't we?' Mum is saying.

'Hi, Mum. I had to tidy up the paints . . . and stuff,' I falter.

Mum eyes me suspiciously. 'Emma said you were showing your needlework to the headmistress.'

We start to walk, my head hung low.

'Are your feet suddenly fascinating?' Mum asks.

'Nope.' I shrug.

'I had a call today,' she says, as we walk on briskly, the pushchair rattling against the tarmac pavement. 'From Mr Stubbington.'

My whole body freezes.

'Katie, I am ashamed of you. I leave you to walk home on your own because I think you're old enough. Then I find you have been going into his shop and stealing from the charity bag. What has got into you lately?' Mum stops walking and turns to look at me, her expression demanding an explanation.

Mr Stubbington has banned me from the shop for a week because he caught me trying to steal coins from the charity stocking. Mostly it's full of one- and two-pence pieces but there are always those tantalizing silver and gold coins stuck in the netting of the toe. When Mr Stubbington turned away to put some apples into a brown paper bag one afternoon, I could not resist plunging my hand in to try and get a fifty-pence piece. 'This money goes to help the aged,' he rebuked me, wagging one finger furiously when he saw what I was doing.

I can offer her no explanation. 'Unless you promise to stop stealing, I will collect you every day,' Mum threatens.

I don't look up.

'With Bells,' she adds.

Does she know how I'm feeling? 'I promise I won't do it again, Mum.' Two girls are walking towards us. They stop and gawk when they see Bells. 'What's wrong with it?' one of them asks. I am focusing on a particular crack in the pavement. If I step on this line it will bring me bad luck.

''It' is my daughter, Isabel. She was born with a cleft lip and palate, and your staring doesn't help,' Mum says brusquely, walking past them. I turn to look at them and they are still standing there staring with their mouths wide open. 'What the hell is a cleft lip?' one of them asks the other.

'I'm sorry, Mum,' I say.

'It's all right, but please don't steal again. I have enough to do, just looking after this one,' she says wearily.

After that, Mum and I walk home quietly. 'Hello, Bells,' I say behind the closed door, stroking her hair. 'I'll give her her tea tonight,' I tell Mum because I know she is tired. I like mushing up Bells's food. 'How are you today? Have you had a good day?' I push her into the kitchen. The guilty lump in my stomach is growing.

8

'I'll meet you at the station,' Sam suggests, cramming in a mouthful of toast and marmalade. 'What time does Isabel's train get in?'

'Don't worry, we'll meet you back home.' I don't know why I think delaying the meeting is going to help. At some point the bomb will go off.

'You know, I'm really looking forward to meeting her. I have to be honest, I was slightly dreading it to begin with, but now I'm quite curious to know what another Fletcher sister will be like.'

'Sam, she is very different.' This is the perfect time to tell him. 'I haven't told you everything about her,' I say. 'When she was born . . . '

His mobile starts to ring. 'Hang on a sec,' he says to me as he answers the call. 'Yep, I'm leaving now, Maguire . . . No, I don't agree . . . You've got to look outside the box. Let's talk about this when I get in.' He hangs up.

'Sam, can we talk?' I ask as he puts the phone back in his briefcase.

He pulls a face. 'Can it wait till tonight?

I'm running late already.' He plants a kiss on my lips, opens the front door. 'What's the plan for *ce soir*, by the way? Because I thought you, me, a few of the boys,' he winks at me, 'could take Isabel out for a drink tonight, get her embroiled in London night life, maybe go to a club for a bit of cheeky dancing?'

I can't take this any more, I should have told him straightaway, just as Emma advised. My chest feels so tight that there is no room for further pretence. I have a throbbing headache, a few more grey hairs, and I know that if I do not tell him now I shall explode. Emma did warn me that the longer it took to tell him, the harder it would get. 'Sam, Isabel isn't going to be what you think.'

'What?' He looks puzzled. 'What do you mean?'

'She was born with a cleft lip and palate. It's quite a common thing,' I add when I see his alarmed expression. 'But there was an added complication because she was brain-damaged at birth. She lives in a community in Wales and it's her summer holidays, that's why she's coming to stay.' I feel as if I can breathe again. I wait for a reaction, anything will do.

Sam's face shows little expression. 'Bells? This was what you were talking to your dad about?' He is thinking out loud. 'You let me believe she was your dog.'

'I never actually said that. Bells . . . Isabel.' I shrug my shoulders. 'We call her Bells for short.'

'Right.' He slowly scratches his head. 'Right, I should have clicked. Well, that's OK. No, hang on,' his voice rises, 'why didn't you *tell* me any of this?' He slams his case down.

'I don't know. I'm sorry. I thought you might hate the idea of her staying. And I have no choice, she has nowhere else to go. Mum and Dad are in France. My mother's not well,' I explain, hoping this will make him a little more sympathetic.

'Well, it looks like I have no choice either.' He frowns. 'Next you'll be telling me you have a brother in prison. Katie, I don't know what to say. I'm lost for words. See you later.'

'Don't go, Sam.' I grab his arm. 'We need to talk.'

'We had all week to talk, Kate, we had last night. I'll see you later.' He pulls his arm away and then his mobile rings again. 'Lakemore speaking,' he says tightly. 'No, Maguire, that's *not* what I said. Are we even on the same page?' he shouts crossly.

I close the door after him. I feel terrible. Sick to my stomach. I feel so guilty. I have been lying to myself, to Sam, to Bells. Why am I such a dreadful person? Why am I such a coward? Why didn't I say anything to Sam before?

★ ★ ★

'I hope her train is early, touching wood,' Eve says in her smoky French accent, tapping my desk.

For a moment I think about correcting her English but then I think I prefer it the way she says it. 'Thanks, Eve, if you can lock up . . . '

'Yes, yes, do not worry. I look forward to meeting your sister *demain*, I mean, tomorrow, of course.' She unpins her honey-coloured hair. I have never seen such long hair, I tell her that Botticelli would have loved to paint her. 'My mother says it is like Rapunzel's hair, tumbling down the tower,' she laughs. 'Where are you picking up Isabel?' she asks, tying it back up into a bun and sticking in a long hairpin with a coloured glass kiwi fruit on the end of it.

'Paddington.'

Eve's face lights up. 'It reminds me of my favourite book, *Paddington Bear*. My mother would read it to me as a child.'

A customer comes in looking for a wedding outfit. It's an evening do and she wants to wear a black dress with a coloured shawl which she has already bought. 'Can I leave you to it?' I ask Eve.

'Yes, yes, I see you tomorrow. Please, come this way,' she says to the customer, leading her up the wooden steps to the second floor. 'I think we have just the thing for you.'

★　★　★

As I drive to Paddington in Sam's BMW, I make a mental list of the things I still need to do. I went to Sainsbury's in my lunch hour to buy some fish and chips for tonight. When I agreed to have Bells I called home to get an idea of what I needed to plan for the two weeks. For the first time in years Mum's classical music wasn't on in the background. The house always feels eerily quiet if she isn't in her studio with the radio on.

'In Wales they have a Mexican night on a Monday, she loves chillies and hot spicy food, and they're always given fish and chips on a Friday with mushy peas. I get her the tinned peas, disgusting, I know, but Bells likes them.'

'OK, I'll do that.' If she ate, say, a baked potato on Monday, would that matter terribly? I thought to myself.

'If you don't have time to cook at lunch she enjoys the vegetable samosas that you buy at the deli counter in Sainsbury's. On Wednesdays I think they have their Indian nights. Or is it their organic night? I can't remember.' Mum's voice trailed off.

As I listened, I knew I wouldn't be able to cater for Bells every single night of the week. I rarely cook at Sam's. Most nights we eat out, and if we want to drink Sam pays for a cab home with his company card. 'I don't like cooking, I hate the mess, all the surfaces get gooey and sticky with all kinds of crap,' he says. 'I remember Mum making stock for soup with leftover chicken bones. The smell of it in the morning,' he said with a disgusted frown.

'I think Tuesday is organic night.'

How about Thursday? I wanted to ask, but decided not to provoke her.

'Bells likes her routine, it's very important to her. They eat lunch on the dot of twelve-thirty.'

'I'll do my best, Mum, but she has to fit in with what I'm doing too.'

Mum sniffed. 'She likes her Coke too, but buy her the Diet Coca-Cola or her teeth will rot. And do take her to Sainsbury's and let her cook for herself as well. She loves to cook, always prepares the meals at home.'

'That's fine. Is that all?' My patience was running out rapidly.

'Yes, make sure she always carries her inhaler. Her asthma is much better but we can't afford to take any risks.' I thought she would ask me then if I still smoked but she didn't.

'I'll definitely make sure she carries her inhaler.'

'Thank you, darling.' Mum seemed tired, I could feel it in her voice.

'Mum, nothing's wrong, is it?'

'Wrong? What do you mean? Just because we're taking ourselves off on holiday does something have to be wrong? Don't we deserve . . . '

'Oh, forget it!' I was twisting the phone cable, knotting it around my finger so tightly that it was turning purple. Why was she so defensive? 'I didn't mean that.'

'I'm sorry, Katie. I didn't mean to snap. No, there's nothing wrong.'

I let go of the cable. It had left a deep red indentation in my finger. 'Promise?'

'I promise.'

'It's about time you and Dad had a holiday,' I acknowledged. 'I hope you have a lovely time. I'll see you when you get back.'

'Katie?'

'Yes?'

'How are you?'

'Fine, great.' Why is it that I always want

Mum to ask me how I am, to be more interested in my life, but when she does ask, all I can do is reply in monosyllables?

'Oh, that's good,' she replied disjointedly. 'You really are OK, darling? With looking after Bells too?'

'I'd better go and do all that shopping!'

'I know she'll have a fun time with you. It sets my mind at rest.'

'We'll have a great time. Make sure you come home rested. Love to Dad.'

'Katie?'

'Yes?'

She cleared her throat. 'Do put sun cream on her face, her skin is so delicate.'

'Yep. Don't worry, I'll look after her.'

'Thank you,' she said. 'For helping out. It means a lot to your father and me.'

I sensed she wanted to say something else so I waited for a moment, but she said nothing more. ''Bye, Mum.'

''Bye, my darling.'

★ ★ ★

The train pulls in to the platform. The doors are opened and passengers step out in a heaving mass, each person pushing past me, staring ahead purposefully. The men wear grey flannel suits and carry briefcases. Some of them have taken their jackets off in this heat and loosened their ties. A pregnant woman walks past in a blue cotton shirt and pair of loose-fitting trousers worn with Birkenstock sandals. Another girl totters past me in high heels and a short spotty sundress, pulling a neat little black suitcase on wheels behind her and carrying a plastic cup of coffee.

'I'm just off the train, sweetpea,' a man coos on his mobile. He has blond floppy hair. 'Will be home in time for dinner.' Presumptuous, isn't he? Perhaps the little wifey at home doesn't feel like cooking for him tonight?

The crowds are filtering away, leaving a dull grey lifeless platform. Where is she? She can't have missed the train. I cannot bear it. I start to walk down the platform looking into each carriage but there is no sign of anyone. Then I hear a door open. I see a small figure stepping out of the train. She is wearing a denim jacket with lots of badges on it, a round embroidered hat which looks more like a doily over her head, and a red football scarf. She carries a large purple bag and a couple of plastic Sainsbury's bags.

'Bells!' I say, quickening my pace towards her.

'Hello, Katie. How're you?' I am so relieved

she has arrived that I almost hug her. Instead, I take her purple zip bag. 'Well done, you made it,' I say. We walk away from the platform, past the guard at the entrance. There is a heavy silence after the mobs of people have moved on.

★ ★ ★

We arrive back at Sam's and I show Bells around the house. The kitchen is in the basement; on the ground floor is a large airy room which looks more like a smart waiting room. In here are Sam's new black leather sofas and a fireplace that is controlled by slick silver controls; he has a dark mahogany bookcase filled with glossy hardback books that he hasn't touched. He doesn't read anything apart from the *FT*. On the second floor are the bedrooms, and a cosy room with leather beanbags and a large Stanley Spencer print. The bay window looks out onto the other rainbow-coloured houses along the crescent. If we are in, we pretty much live in this room. Sam plays poker here. On the top floor is the luxury steam room with the big old-fashioned bath. 'This is my favourite room, Bells,' I tell her.

'Sam rich?' she asks.

'Yes, he is. He works very hard.' I take her

back downstairs to her room, a large bedroom with a double bed, wardrobe, a long mirror whose frame I gilded and one small bedside table with an orange and white stained-glass lamp on it. More or less everything in this room is white — the shutters, the walls, the bedspread. The only other piece of colour is the rug with great big orange and red circles on it. Bells sits on the bed, looking around. It is hard to know what she makes of Sam's house.

'What's your room like in Wales?' I ask, sitting down next to her.

'I wish you would go and visit your sister sometimes,' Mum says to me.

'She's a forgotten sister,' Dad adds.

'Not big like this,' says Bells, waving her arm around. 'Have small bed and television and lots of posters. Room looks out on garden and sea. In my plot of land, I grow carrots and potatoes. We grow strawberries this year too. You like strawberries?'

'I do. We don't have a garden here,' I say apologetically. 'I think you have Mum's gardening skills. I'd kill everything! There would only be weeds in my plot of land.' She does not say anything. She is still looking around the room. 'You've got your own television in here, so that's something, isn't it?' I point to the big silver TV with the wide screen in the corner of her room. 'You can watch the tennis. Who do you think is going to win Wimbledon this year then?'

'Agassi.'

'You cannot be serious,' I say, imitating John McEnroe very badly.

She looks at me with no hint of a smile. I'm going to have to try harder than a poor imitation of John McEnroe.

'Shall we unpack?' I open her zip bag and out comes a medley of junk and clothes including a few holey vests. 'Why have you got Mary Veronica's jumper?' I ask, showing Bells the nametag in the jumper, like the ones we used to have to sew on our school socks and PE kit. 'Bells, you don't have many summer clothes in here. Is this all you packed? Odd jumpers, a few T-shirts and a pair of dungarees? Oh, hang on, you have one frilly pink blouse here that says it belongs to Jessica Hall. I think I'm going to have to get you some new clothes,' I say, talking to myself rather than to her. 'You put all this away while I put the fish and chips on. Deal? You like chips on Fridays, don't you?'

'You have crinkle chips, like ones Mum makes?'

'I'm going to make homemade ones, like Aunt Agnes's.'

'Oh,' she acknowledges, and it's hard to tell

whether she is pleased or not. 'How's Aunt Agnes?'

'I think she's fine,' I reply.

'Uncle Roger? He died. Poor Uncle Roger.'

'I know. Poor Aunt Agnes too. I think she gets quite lonely.'

'Poor Aunt Agnes. How's Mum?'

'Well, you know she's on holiday.'

'How's Dad?'

'He's on holiday too. Aren't they lucky? They're in France.'

'In France, that's right. How's Granny Norfolk?'

Our mother's mother, Granny, lives in Norfolk, hence the name. I don't know how she is, I haven't spoken to her in months. 'Fine, I think,' I say. 'Look, you've got your own music system too,' I tell her, trying to stop the tirade of questions about the Fletcher family. 'Come downstairs to the kitchen when you've finished. You'll meet Sam soon.'

I can hear my voice but it's not me. I can't seem to stop talking to her as if she were ten years old.

Sam. I still feel nervous about him coming home. He didn't ring me today at the shop; when I tried to call him his secretary said he was either 'on the other line' or 'in a meeting'. He has her well trained. 'He's really looking forward to meeting you. You'll be good, won't you?' I can't help adding. 'No dramas in front of Sam. We are going to have a really nice two weeks, aren't we?'

'No dramas,' she repeats.

'Good. Come down when you're ready.'

★ ★ ★

I am onto my second vodka. These last few days I have been counting down the minutes until I can have my first drink in the evening. I've been forgetting the cup of tea and going straight to the hard stuff. The chips are frying. First hurdle is over. Bells is here, we are getting on fine, I think. The second major hurdle is Bells meeting Sam. I am sure that once the initial meeting is over, things will revert to normality.

Stevie Wonder starts to blast out of Bells's bedroom. I run upstairs and open her bedroom door. Bells is on the bed, pinning up a poster of David Beckham, his diamond earrings sparkling.

The lovely white room is now covered in football badges and stickers and a Beatles poster is stuck to the door, **SEX, DRUGS AND ROCK 'N' ROLL** written in big black letters at the bottom. It reminds me of Bells's bedroom in our parents' home. She had the master bedroom with the sink that I was envious of, and wallpaper with flowery borders. Bells did not like the wallpaper, though, so she drew pictures of animals and pinned up posters of her favourite pop singers, Stevie Wonder, David Bowie and the Beatles. I remember she had a picture of Bob Marley on the wall too, smoking a joint. Mum did not mind her ruining the wallpaper. She wasn't strict in that sense. She let us get on with it half the time.

Top of the Pops is on the television and the entire floor is covered with clothes, joined by a tattered poetry book, a sketchpad, a small wooden case of oil paints, a collection of CDs and a photograph album. I take a deep breath and bend down to pick the mess off the floor. 'Bells!' I shout. 'Turn it down! It's so loud in here.' I climb onto the bed. 'What are you sticking the posters down with? You're not putting pins in the walls, are you? Sam doesn't like that.' Oh, God, she is. 'Bells, don't put pins in the walls,' I shout at her.

'Why?'

'It leaves a hole.'

She continues to push a pin into the white paint.

'Bells, hey! Don't do that. What did I just say?'

'We do in Wales. Mum lets me too.'

I look down at the bedspread. 'I don't care what you do in Wales, you're staying with Sam and me now.'

'Katie bossy,' she says.

I shrug. 'Bells, can you take your boots off? Sam likes you to take your shoes off when you come into the house.' She is still wearing these peculiar little pixie boots.

'Why?' she asks, and then starts to use the bed as a trampoline because in Wales they have one in the garden and Ted can jump the highest, apparently.

'What is going on? What's all the flipping noise?' I hear from behind. I spin round on the bed and almost lose my balance. 'Bells, keep still! Stop it.'

'Hello,' Bells says, extending her small hand. 'You handsome.'

Sam looks at her strangely. 'What did she just say to me? Katie, what is going ON? What's with the TV and the music?' He looks around. 'This room is a pigsty.'

Bells starts to make piglike noises and I want to disappear under the floorboards.

'Is this your . . . ' He can hardly get the words out.

'This is my sister Isabel. Bells.'

'Hello, you Sam?' she says again, still offering her small pale hand.

He limply shakes it. 'This is Bells?' He

looks around the room again, despair written over his face.

I nod. 'Sam, I'll tidy the room later, don't worry.'

'How has she put the posters up? She hasn't put drawing pins in the wall? Tell me she hasn't, Katie?'

'I'm sorry, I'll deal with it, honey, I promise,' I tell him.

Sam puts his head into his hands. I jump off the bed.

'What's that burning smell?' he shouts above the noise, then marches over to the stereo and turns off the music, followed by the television. 'Jesus Christ, even my grandfather doesn't need the snooker on so loudly.'

'No like Sam,' Bells says.

'Bells! Don't be rude.' Thankfully I don't think he understood what she just said. He's still sniffing the air with a look of disgust. 'Oh, shit, it's the chips,' I yelp, and dart out of the room.

'Fucking hell, can today get *any* worse?' I hear Sam cursing as he runs after me.

★   ★   ★

It has been a long day when finally I make my way upstairs to bed. The chips burned and Sam hated the mushy peas. 'Who eats mushy peas anyway?' he protested.

I looked in Bells's direction and he shrugged. He attempted to ask her a few questions about the train journey but couldn't understand what she was replying. 'I haven't got a clue what she just said,' he kept on repeating when Bells was staring at him for a response. She started to hit the kitchen table with her fork in frustration, repeating her questions in vain.

'If you don't understand Bells, just pretend you do,' I tried to persuade him after supper. 'Just say, 'Yes, very good,' or 'Really?'' I learned this trick from Granny Norfolk. She is getting increasingly deaf so her way of disguising that she can't hear what someone is saying is to reply, 'Really?' or, 'Oh, what a shame.'

I know Sam is still angry with me for not telling him about Bells and I can't say I blame him. What was I thinking? He has gone out for a few drinks with Maguire. No doubt he is telling his friend what a ''mare' he is having and that his house is being taken over by the Fletcher sisters.

I try to read but I can't even focus on one line. I turn off the light and close my eyes.

★   ★   ★

I scream when I see a small figure silhouetted at the end of my bed.

'Bells, what are you doing?' I sit up abruptly. 'Go back to bed.' When I get a glazed response, I jump up and shake her awake.

I can hear Mum coming upstairs and then pacing down our creaky corridor in her floaty nightdress and bed-jacket. 'You shouldn't wake her up,' she scolds me, 'if it happens again just take her back to her bedroom. Bells darling, do you want to go to the loo before you go back to bed?'

'That's right,' she says, lifting up her white cotton nightie and crouching on the floor.

'NO!' Mum and I cry together. Mum starts to laugh, and so do I. And then Bells copies us, doing her mad-lady-locked-up-in-the-attic *Jane Eyre* laugh.

★   ★   ★

I wake myself up with a panicked laugh. I feel disorientated as I turn on the light and look at my watch. It's only midnight. I shiver. I can hear both Mum and Bells now, as if it were yesterday.

The house is deathly quiet. When we were children, Bells used to sleepwalk almost every night. Mum had to put thick white bars over her bedroom window. I step out of bed and walk down the corridor, towards Bells's room. I find myself opening the door, the light glaring out at me. Mum had told me Bells still hates sleeping in the dark and that I must keep a small light on in the corner of her bedroom.

I can hear her deep breathing as she turns over in the large double bed. She is so tiny, just under five foot tall. She looks young for her age because of her height. She could also be mistaken for a boy from behind because of her short auburn hair. Dad says he never wants Bells to grow her hair. 'You must never hide behind your hair,' he told her when she started to be a self-conscious teenager who wanted to look like everyone else. 'You look the world in the eye,' he said.

I kneel down by her bed and watch her as she sleeps, absorbing each line and movement of her face. There is the familiar scar over her upper lip which crosses like two letter Cs. She always wears three small stud earrings in her left ear; one of them is a green stone surrounded by gold.

Her hand pokes out from the duvet, the skin so pale you would not believe there was blood pumping through the veins. I gently touch it and it feels as soft as melting butter. Quickly I withdraw my hand as if I should not have been so bold.

We tidied her room after Sam went out and put the snowy owl that Mum made for her on the bedside table. Bells loves owls. Mum made me a cheetah. His name is Charlie. Bells carefully placed her inhaler on the bedside table, along with her photograph album which she has covered on the outside with David Beckham stickers. Mum told me she takes her album everywhere when she is away from home, it is like her comfort blanket. I pick it up and quietly leaf through the pages. By each photograph, inscribed on a small white sticker, is a precise date, time, location and description of the person photographed. There is a picture of Mum in her studio, her hands caked in clay, smiling right into the camera; there's a terrible picture of Dad with red eyes reading the newspaper; there is a picture of the water meadows where we used to walk as children. My parents live in St Cross, Winchester. They have a pink house that looks like a dolls' house. We used to walk by the lake and feed the ducks and avoid getting too close to the swans. There's a picture of a man wearing a purple tracksuit and football sweatshirt, holding onto a parrot. He has an identity card around his neck. I don't know who he is so I read the sticker. 'Ted, 1990, St David's, in the garden, summertime.'

She opens her eyes and looks straight into me. I panic, thinking I should not be here, but then she shuts them again. I wonder what she dreams about when she goes to bed at night? When she was little she used to have nightmares so we had to keep a light on in her room. It was a little pink light in the shape of a house. Dad said Bells was terrified of the dark as a result of all the surgery she had to go through as a baby and young child. In the end it was Emma's sister, Berry, who came up with a solution called 'The Black Box'. We had to cut off a piece of Bells's hair — it had to be something physical rather than an item of clothing. We put the strand of hair in a box and the alternative practitioner did a kind of absent healing. Mum and Dad thought we were mad but realized there was little to lose. Besides, we were all going insane from lack of sleep. I can still remember Berry asking me to kiss the box. 'Gives it good vibes,' I can hear her whisper. After a few days Bells's howling at night suddenly stopped. It was like magic.

I stand up to leave, the stillness of the room contrasting strongly with the chaos earlier in the evening. I stop when I hear her muffled voice.

'Nothing around me?' she says groggily. I

remember her saying this as a child. 'Nothing around you,' I whisper back, just as Mum used to reply.

'Promise?'

'I promise.'

9

I climb the three steps into Mum's chalky-aired studio. Her classical music is on in the background, just as it always is. Mum's studio is like a play zoo with the parrots, a pair of cockatoos, a zebra, a giraffe, a tiger, a lioness and a few monkeys perched on shelves, some half-finished, some that Mum calls 'rejects' because they slope too far to the right or left. Mum's a sculptor. She makes different kinds of animals out of clay. Her last project was a camel on bended knee. A friend of hers went to the Sahara Desert and fell in love with the camel she rode. She begged Mum to do a sculpture for her from a photograph.

Mum's long table in the middle of the room is covered with jam-jars filled with brushes and open paint tubes. The room has that familiar smell of white spirit, clay and dust. She has an entire pin-board full of postcards and letters from happy customers who have commissioned monkeys or fish or whatever.

'How are you, darling?' she asks, her neck

craned over her work. Her auburn hair is tied back in a navy and white dotted scarf and she is wearing large silver hoop earrings. She looks like a gypsy.

I realize the only time I get to see or talk to Mum is either when she is cooking and the kitchen smells of garlic — Mum likes to put at least ten cloves of garlic into everything — or when she is in the studio.

'Good day at school?' she mutters, continuing with her work and humming along to the background music. I can see her hands are sticky from the clay and she is wearing her denim work apron. Mum, turn around, I think. Instead I walk in front of her. 'Good day?' she repeats distractedly.

I drop my satchel onto the floor. I don't tell her that I got told off yet again for wearing mascara. 'Go and wash that black goo off your face,' my boring maths teacher says again and again. Last weekend I was caught stealing a black eyeliner, mascara and a block of spot cover-up from Boots, and the police came by the house to talk to Mum and Dad. It has been suggested that we need family counselling.

'Stealing is not clever, Katie,' Dad sighed. 'Or if you have to steal, why don't you make sure it's something better than an eyeliner? And don't get caught next time.'

'Not bad. What are you listening to?'

'Classic FM. Puccini, *Madam Butterfly*.' She starts to sing along with the music.

'What are you working on? Who's that for?'

'It's a cheetah.' She sits back and admires it. 'My mother took us to Africa when we were little and we went to a wildlife orphanage. I always remember this cheetah rolling on its back for me like a big tame cat. I was tempted to put my hand through the bars to stroke it. I would have done too if Mum hadn't pulled me away. You see, they could take a bite out of you, and more.'

I flinch. 'What do they like to eat?'

'Beavers, game birds, impala, warthogs.'

'I love its spots.'

'Did you know, the name 'cheetah' comes from a Hindi word meaning 'spotted one'?'

I shake my head. 'What are those dark lines by its eyes? Has your paint run?'

'Run? No! You are funny. Those are tear lines.' Finally she looks at me. 'Do you like him?'

'Him?'

'The cheetah, silly.'

'Oh, I love him. I think he is beautiful. He doesn't look as if he would want to harm anyone.'

'Here, have him, he's all finished.'

'Really?' I smile. 'But who were you making it for?'

'That doesn't matter.' She ruffles my hair and smiles. 'He's yours now. Keep him in a safe place.'

10

I wake up feeling disorientated. My sleep was disturbed. I feel sure I was back at home, in Mum's studio. I can even smell the white spirit. Since the news that Bells was coming to stay I have been thinking a lot about home, particularly about Mum. Yesterday, when I was working in the shop, I found myself thinking about the time when we all went to a New Year's Eve party hosted by Mrs Kissinger. I must have been about twelve. Dad called her Lady Kiss Kiss because she thought she was very grand and did those awful air kisses with sound effects. I remember she had a face like a poached egg, everything squashed and flat. In between bowls of quail's eggs and blinis with smoked salmon being handed around the chandeliered room, Bells lifted her velvet skirt and proceeded to pee on the carpet. You see, unless we reminded her to go to the loo she would forget that it wasn't the done thing to do it on the floor. Lady Kiss Kiss raced over to us saying it was her favourite carpet with hunting scenes on it. It was a red carpet which I had noticed changed colour under the light. Now there was this wet patch over one of the angry warriors on horseback clutching a spear. I remember Mum apologizing and looking around at the other guests who immediately pretended to be engrossed in conversation. I had never before seen so many backs turned towards us. We weren't ever invited back. None of the other guests even acknowledged what had happened.

Sam is still fast asleep. He must have crawled into bed at about four this morning. I never sleep well when he is not with me. I slip my feet into my stripy zebra slippers and put on my silk dressing gown which is hanging on the back of our door. I walk into Bells's bedroom but she is not there. She must be downstairs. I find her at the kitchen table poking the milk-bottle sculpture. She is wearing grey baggy tracksuit bottoms and her red Oxford University T-shirt. Where did she get that?

'Careful, Bells.'

'What's this?'

'Do you like it?'

'No.'

I half smile. 'Don't say that to Sam. It's his favourite piece of art.'

'Don't like Sam.' She withdraws her hand from the sculpture immediately, as if she is touching something dirty. 'He says 'F' word a lot. We not allowed to say that word.'

'You don't know Sam,' I point out firmly. 'You mustn't judge so quickly. You be nice to him, OK?'

'Don't like him,' she states coldly.

'Bells, this is Sam's house. He has been kind enough to have you to stay. You need to get to know him. Do you want some breakfast?'

'In Wales have muesli for breakfast. Make it ourselves.'

'We need to go to Sainsbury's. Do you want to come with me?'

★ ★ ★

As we walk into Sainsbury's I watch us on the CCTV screen. Bells is now wearing her pink frilly blouse underneath a pair of denim dungarees, plus her purple pixie boots and embroidered hat. I am wearing an orange skirt which clings to my hips, with a pale yellow Whistles top and orange beaded sandals. Bells tells me I look like a satsuma.

There is a delicious smell of fresh bread that makes me feel hungry. 'Hello, how're you?' Bells asks an old lady on a light blue scooter which has a black shopping basket at the front. 'How old are you?' She stares at the scooter which has 'Bluebird 2' painted on the back like a number plate.

'Excuse me,' the lady says, reaching across to grab an avocado and avoiding eye contact.

Bells comes back to me with two lemons. 'I wouldn't say hello to everyone,' I tell her quietly as we move on. 'And, funnily enough, people aren't that happy to declare their age.'

Bells is picking out packets of dried prunes, apricots, sultanas, figs and rolled oats for her muesli. 'You have to have Diet Coke,' I tell her when we reach the drinks section.

'Best of luck,' I hear a man saying. I turn sideways to see an old bearded man pushing a trolley filled with oranges. He taps on the shoulder another man who is pretending to be absorbed in deciding what brand of tomato ketchup to buy. 'Best of luck,' he says again, winking. He is wearing a knitted jumper with ducks on it and a pair of black fingerless gloves. His eyes twitch when he talks and for a moment he looks at Bells and me, aware he is being watched. I look down at my feet, hoping the man won't point his fingerless gloves our way.

'A mad man,' Bells says. 'Poor man.'

'Shh, don't stare.' Swiftly I push our trolley on. Bells fills it with everything organic. The only vegetable which isn't organic is the tin of mushy peas. That's the only thing she likes in a tin, she tells me. She puts ingredients I have never even used into the trolley. She wants dried porcini, coconut milk, chillies, coriander, bay leaves, stuffed olives, sesame seed oil, fresh ginger. 'What are we going to do with all these herbs and stuff?' I ask her, slowly panicking that the bill is going to be enormous. 'You cook a lot at home, don't you?' I ask her. 'I bet they love you cooking for them.'

'Yes, they call me Queen of Kitchen.'

I feel relieved when we finally make it to the checkout desk. The queue is long and we stand behind a tall man with light brown tousled hair. Amongst the shopping in his trolley are a packet of crumpets, runny honey, a ready-made lasagne for two, mini Magnums and a bottle of red wine. The kind of food I normally have in mine. Bells taps him hard on the arm. 'Hello.'

I look down at my feet.

He turns around. 'Hi,' I hear him say, and briefly look up. He's wearing glasses, a white T-shirt and dark jeans.

'I'm sorry,' I say, drawing in breath.

'Hello.' Bells whacks him hard on the arm now and then holds out her hand.

'Bells! Don't punch so hard. I'm sorry,' I say, wincing in sympathy. He manages a pained smile as he rubs his arm and stretches out his own hand to Bells.

'You like Beckham?'

I am sure he is wondering if he heard right and I subtly nod. If you can imagine talking without being able to touch the roof of your mouth with your tongue, that's what Bells sounds like. It's easy for me because I have learned her language since I was a little girl. It is like learning a foreign language and even now I have to adapt my ear when I listen to her.

'Yes, I think Beckham's great, and Posh Spice too. I can see you love him,' he intimates, looking at the football badges on her dungarees.

'You have children?' she goes on. Oh, please, stop talking.

I can tell he did not understand from the way he laughs. 'Really?' He smiles.

'You have children?' she asks, urgently now.

He watches her intently, trying to work out what she just said. 'No, I don't have children,' he replies confidently, and I nod, as if to say, Well done, you got it right. 'Well, I hope not.' He pulls a crooked smile.

'How old?'

'Bells!' I say, exasperated. I want to blindfold her and put a scarf around her mouth too.

'It's OK,' the man says, starting to pack his food into bags. 'I'm twenty-nine.'

'My sister, Katie,' she announces, thumping my arm. 'I staying in London.'

He tells her that that sounds like fun. As he speaks I can't help thinking that if he brushed his hair, took off his glasses, fattened up a little . . . he could really be quite attractive.

'You want cash back?' the assistant asks him.

'No, thanks.'

'Nectar card?'

He digs into his pocket which I can hear is full of change and produces a few cards. As he hands the right one to the girl he turns to look at me again. It's strange but I feel like we have met already. And why do I have this strange feeling I am going to meet him again? He signs his receipt, but I can't make out his name.

' 'Bye,' he finally says.

'Yeah, 'bye,' I say, still trying to put a name to his face.

' 'Bye,' Bells adds.

The man turns around once more and looks in our direction. 'By the way, I'm really thirty-four! I find it hard facing up to my age first time round.' I laugh as I watch him walk away.

Bells asks the woman serving us how old she is. I suppose it is better than asking her how much she weighs, I think desperately.

'Excuse me?' she says.

'Bells, stop it!' I demand, before she has time to ask again. I tell her once more not to ask strangers personal questions, especially their age. Sometimes I think she does it deliberately to embarrass me. She likes to do that. It's like being a teenager again. 'Let's just get our food and go. I'm sorry,' I apologize to the checkout girl.

'It's fine,' she says.

I push the trolley brusquely towards the exit door. 'No, don't say anything,' I say sharply each time I think Bells is about to approach someone else.

'No!'

'Don't ask.'

'Quiet.'

'Get in the car.'

I put the keys in the ignition and breathe a sigh of relief that we made it out of Sainsbury's in one piece, that no-one chased us out, threatening to beat us up with a long hard baguette. 'This is only day one, I can cope with this, I can cope,' I mutter to myself.

God help me, I have two weeks of this. I can forget being anonymous for the next fourteen days, can't I?

11

1988

I am thirteen years old. 'How did you meet Dad?' I ask Mum in the car. She is taking Bells and me to watch Dad conduct an auction. It's strange seeing her out of her work overalls. Today she is wearing a green dress and her hair is pinned up in her special tortoiseshell comb. It's one of the first times we have all gone out together. A trip to London! Normally we don't do anything. My best friend Emma occasionally comes round but we stay at home.

'Well, my mother had given me an Impressionist painting so I went to Sotheby's to see if it was worth anything. It was a bit of a mystery as it wasn't signed but it looked like a Pisarro. I was rather desperate to sell it. I'm afraid I was too poor for sentimentality,' says Mum, twitching her nose.

'Was it worth anything?'

'It was worth a free dinner,' she laughs. 'I met your father and he asked me out. I knew he was going to be a part of my life the moment I met him. Sometimes you can't explain it, it's just a feeling.'

'Like love at first sight?' I ask.

'Yes, I suppose it is. He was an assistant back then. He was very naughty, you know. This very lugubrious specialist was explaining that my painting sadly wasn't an original, and as he was talking your father was imitating him behind his back. He was unbelievably attractive, the sort of man who could get away with anything. I remember thinking what a big nose he had. I mean, you can hardly miss it, can you, girls? But it didn't matter, it went with his long thin face. And his eyes were so mischievous and flirtatious . . . ' She was getting carried away now. 'He only had to smile and his eyes were chatting you up. You'll know what I mean when you're older. I remember him giving me his business card. Christopher Fletcher. I liked that name as long as he didn't call himself Chris. Marianne Fletcher, I said to myself.'

'Mum, that's sad,' I sigh heavily. I cannot imagine wanting to marry anyone.

'You'll be doing the same one day. You don't want to marry anyone with a surname like Pratt, or Burk, or Fogsbottom.'

She is right. There is a girl at school whose surname is Smellie and she dreads the school register each morning. Bells is laughing, and this conversation is annoying me now. I turn to look out of the window.

The auction room is dark with lots of people coming in and out. The carpet is red. I am sitting next to a man with such a large moustache he looks like a walrus. Mum was too mean to buy us a catalogue each so I try to lean over and look at Walrus's. I can see lots of stars scribbled on each page next to the prices.

Over breakfast Dad explained how it all worked, his eyes alight as he talked about the auction. 'There is an estimate for each painting and then a reserve price, which means I can't sell below that figure. I'm proud my girls are going to be watching me today,' he added as he ate his last mouthful of toast.

The Walrus peers over at me and I sit straight in my chair. He twirls a pen in his fingers and eyes me curiously. 'You want to have a look?' he says in a heavy accent. He is a French walrus.

This feels exciting. Like when you go to the cinema and everyone is waiting for the main film to start. Everyone is waiting for my dad.

Finally he enters the auction room in his polished shoes, smart suit and tie. I chose his tie this morning. He lets me do that sometimes. He is wearing the black-rimmed glasses which make him look clever. 'That's my dad,' I whisper loudly to my French neighbour. I do think my dad is good-looking.

'Good afternoon, we have a feast of paintings here today so let's get started.' He coughs to clear his throat and I watch him intently. 'Lot number one. Sketch by Matisse of a lady's face. Who's going to start the bidding at twenty-five thousand pounds . . . ?'

The Walrus holds up what looks like a ping-pong bat.

Suddenly the bidding is fast and furious. I turn to the Walrus in amazement as he continues to put up his ping-pong bat. I am enjoying this. As the auction heats up, Mum is growing redder in the face from trying to stop Bells putting up her hand to confuse the bidding. 'Hello, Dad!' she calls out. I can hear people tut-tutting behind us and whispering, 'Why bring a child to a place like this? It's quite ridiculous.' I turn around and give the two old ladies one of my dirtiest looks.

I feel Mum's hand tug at mine. 'We're going,' she mutters. 'Excuse me,' she asks the person next to her. Chairs are shifted, legs are tucked in to allow us to pass. I don't want to go. I was having a good time. I can feel everyone's eyes on us and the two old ladies nudge each other triumphantly. 'Whatever happened to being seen but not heard?' I turn around and stick two fingers up at them. The two ladies gasp and my father looks directly at me, disappointment in his eyes. ''Bye, Dad,' Bells is shouting. People are still staring.

In the car on the way home I scream, 'Why can't you be normal? You're so embarrassing! We can't go anywhere with you.'

Mum brakes suddenly and swerves into the side of the road. 'Mum! Watch out for that man on the bike!'

'Danger, danger,' Bells says in the back seat, laughing.

'Shut up, Bells!' I screech at her.

Mum swerves to avoid the cyclist and goes into the pavement instead, the tyres burning against the curb in protest. The driver behind us beeps his horn furiously as he overtakes us. 'Wanker!' he shouts out of the window. The cyclist turns around briefly and shakes an angry fist at us.

'Now you listen to me, Katie . . . '

'But, Mum . . . '

'No. You shut up,' she says sternly. 'If you ever say that about your sister again, I mean EVER, you forfeit your pocket money for weeks.' She starts to shout, gripping the steering wheel tightly. 'It's *not* Bells's fault . . . '

'You always take her side,' I protest.

'You are very lucky you . . .'

'I am very lucky I don't have a cleft lip,' I finish for her like a robot. If I am difficult, Mum and Dad's invariable answer is to tell me how lucky I am not to have been born with something wrong and that I should count my lucky stars.

'Well, you are,' Mum says.

I don't think I'm lucky. 'You love her more than me,' I tell Mum.

'I do not,' she says wearily. 'That is absolutely not true. All I'm saying is you are the fortunate one and should be more of a role model.'

I shrug.

'All I wanted to do was watch your father today with no dramas but I see that's clearly impossible. No more outings, that is it,' she tells us with finality.

Back to doing nothing.

'On Monday we do nothing, on Tuesday we do nothing,' Bells starts to chant to the theme of *Happy Days*. She does not appear at all upset that she ruined our afternoon.

Mum lights a cigarette with the car lighter and opens the window forcefully. 'Bells, that's enough from you too,' she says, and I start to clap. 'At last, Bells gets told off,' I say angrily.

'It's OK,' Mum starts to mutter, 'it's OK, I can cope. You can cope.'

If Bells hadn't been naughty none of this would have happened. I can feel my chin wobbling but I am determined not to cry. I do not want Mum to see me cry. Instead I shrug as if to say, I don't care, and turn to face the window again. I can feel a few tears trickle down my cheek but no-one can see them. They are my own secret tears. I don't understand it. I wasn't the one causing trouble. Why am I getting the blame? I might as well be the naughty one, because at least that way I get to have some fun.

12

'What am I doing now?' Mr Vickers rubs his large hands together, thinking up his next trick. We are in my shop and Mr Vickers and Bells have been playing this charade game for about five minutes. Already I am finding it tiring having Bells around. She likes to pretend she is a customer and start to unfold Eve's neatly piled clothes; she likes to ask customers how rich they are. 'How much money you have?' she asked a tall willowy girl wearing a lime green sundress. The girl pretended she hadn't heard. And now . . . who is this man with giant hands the colour of a purple cabbage? His circulation is so poor that his feet, squashed into old beige shoes looking more like Cornish pasties, are also a mottled purple.

I sent Bells off to buy a baguette for lunch, and somehow she managed to pick up this man along the way and bring him back here. 'Sorry, who are you?' I asked him as he walked into the shop. 'Who is this?' I looked sharply at Bells. I don't want weirdos in my shop.

'I, er, don't want to intrude,' he started.

'I'm sorry, who are you?' I asked again.

I finally discovered that he is called Mr Vickers and he works at one of the local libraries. He has grey hair and wears mustard-coloured trousers with a smart white-collared shirt. What's even more peculiar about him is that he has a bump about the size of a golf ball in the middle of his forehead.

'Why funny lump on head?' Bells immediately attacked.

'Oh, my goodness,' Eve said, putting a hand over her mouth. 'Bells, it might be personal.'

Our visitor looked at me for a translation. 'She asked you what the, um, lump was on your forehead?' My voice rose at the end. I was oddly curious too; I had never seen one like it before.

'I was, er, born with it,' he replied. 'I'm not quite sure, er, what it is . . . soft tissue or something like that.' He didn't seem embarrassed about being asked such a personal question.

'What am I, er, doing now?' he asks her, and even Eve is joining in. He holds his hand in mid-air, fingers clenched as if he is holding onto something tightly, and starts rocking backwards and forwards, making strange noises.

'You are riding a horse?' Eve guesses seriously, her finger resting on her lip as if she is trying to solve an important crime, and then shakes her head immediately. 'No, that does not explain the hand.' She looks confused, her eyes narrowed.

I glance at the door, praying no-one is going to come in. Don't come in, don't come in, walk on by, I say to myself when I see a couple of women going past.

'Shall I, er, do it again?' he asks enthusiastically, his eyes widening. 'I'll give you, um, another clue,' he adds generously. 'OK. OK.' He positions himself.

Bells starts rocking forwards and backwards like Mr Vickers. It's the first time I have seen her enjoying herself since she arrived. He still makes those odd noises as he rocks back and forth. 'Mind the gap,' he announces sporadically. 'That is,' he pauses, 'er, the clue,' and he smiles at Bells and Eve.

'*Bien sûr!* You are on a train!' Eve claps her hands together.

Bells starts to clap too. 'Choo-choo train!'

'I am on the, er, underground at Waterloo.' He talks slowly, emphasizing every word, in between his stammering. 'I could not get a seat so I am er . . . er . . . '

SPIT IT OUT! I want to shout. Is it only me who thinks this is insane?

110

'I am holding onto the, er, strap.'

He is about to do another role-play and I have to say something now, I am at breaking point. 'I'm sorry, Mr Vickers, we're busy . . . ' Eve, Bells and Mr Vickers look around the empty shop. 'Would you mind . . . ?' I don't have to finish the sentence. He says he has to go anyway. 'I am needed at work. Er, nice to meet you, Isabel, Eve.' He looks at me and nods and then he leaves.

'You come back?' Bells calls after him.

When he has gone, Eve looks at me disapprovingly and I shrug my shoulders. This is my shop, it is not a local community centre.

13

'I'm sorry, honey, I didn't realize it was your
turn to host the poker night,' I apologize
again. Sam watches me as I throw down my
handbag, newspaper and the house keys on
the sofa. Today felt about a week long. No
visit from Mr Vickers but the thing that
makes me seriously draw in breath is when
Bells touches the clothes with her gummy
fingers. Thank God most of them are black,
but even so, no-one wants sticky grains of
sugar on the front of their dresses. Eve took
her up to the box room, a tiny room off the
second floor where I keep a kettle, coffee, a
small make-up bag and my delivery boxes.
She said she would help Bells wash her
hands. 'Hot soapy water,' I could hear my
sister saying.

'You bite your nails? You should eat raw
jelly,' I overheard Eve suggest. 'I will treat you
to a French manicure. You would like?' I
wonder what I would do without Eve. That
manicure gave me enough time to refold all
the clothes.

Now Bells sits down on the sofa and opens
her Magnum ice cream wrapper, oblivious to

my conversation with Sam. She likes the almond Magnums best. I can see Sam now eyeing the sticky chocolate wrapper that is precariously close to his cream-coloured cushion. 'I don't understand why you plonk your crap on the sofa when there's a perfectly good table next to it.' He frowns. 'Isabel, give me that wrapper.'

'You like Stevie Wonder?' Bells asks him seriously.

'What?' Sam squints at her.

'You like Stevie Wonder?' Bells repeats, holding the CD towards him, ice cream wobbling in the other hand.

'Not a fan,' he says dismissively. 'That 'Ebony and Ivory' song he did with Paul McCartney was a pile of pants.'

So charming. Sometimes I wonder what I see in Sam.

'What I really don't like, though, is junk lying around the place. It's my home so if you could respect the rules? Good girl,' he says, avoiding eye contact. 'Wrapper, please.'

She hands it to him and he marches off downstairs to the kitchen. I follow him. I can hear the television being turned on upstairs. Bells is watching Wimbledon.

'I can't go out tonight, Sam, I really need to get my accounts done. Bernard was on the phone today, putting the pressure on.'

'Katie, it's strictly a boys' night,' he tells me bluntly, lifting the bin lid, throwing the wrapper in and slamming it shut.

'OK, what if I told you Kate Moss was coming over this evening?'

A slight smile plays on his lips and then promptly disappears. 'Not allowed access, I'm afraid.'

'What if I'm really quiet . . . as quiet as a mouse?'

'What's Isabel going to do then? I thought Tuesday night was your girls' night with Emma?'

'I had to cancel.' I open the fridge and look inside. Potatoes for baking are in the bottom drawer, as well as a head of organic broccoli and a bag of organic carrots. Cheese, bacon, mushrooms and a pot of olives stuffed with garlic are in the middle.

'I wouldn't hang around if you had a bunch of girls here having a Botox party.'

'I don't do Botox.'

'You know what I mean. Christ, you're pedantic sometimes,' he says, rubbing his nose.

'Sam, Bells and I will stay in our bedroom until the coast is clear,' I tell him. 'We just need to make . . . oh, shit, what does she cook on a Tuesday?'

'What do you mean, on a Tuesday? Get a

takeaway. The boys will be here in an hour.'

'I'll have to microwave a potato.'

'I do not believe this!' He watches me slit the potatoes across the top, waiting for me to change my mind. 'Come off it, this is a boys' night. It's so unfair. This is my house!'

'Stop rubbing your nose so hard. You know what happened last time, it went raw at the end.'

He rubs it gently and then stops. 'I wouldn't come between you and Emma. I don't think she likes me much anyway,' he adds.

I run a hand over my face now and squeeze my eyes shut. I am so tired. 'You sound like a spoilt brat.'

'You're ruining my boys' night.'

'Er, hello, I am saying I won't make any noise. You won't even know Bells and I are here.' He still looks furious. 'Is this really about her? If it were just me, would you mind?' I ask him.

Sam ignores me. 'If you have to bloody well be here, can you go to the upstairs room? I don't want you next-door to us.'

'Sam, as scintillating as it might be listening to you boys, I promise I won't eavesdrop. I've got work to do anyway.'

He makes a disgruntled noise. 'You really promise?' 'Promise.'

Bells sits on the edge of our double bed eating her baked potato. She was cross with Sam because he wouldn't let her cook. 'There's no time,' he shouted at her, and then at me. Bells was opening the fridge and cupboard doors and he was hovering behind her, slamming them shut the moment she moved away. I explained why she couldn't cook her vegetarian risotto with olives and pine nuts. 'Always cook in Wales,' she protested.

I watch her as she eats. She doesn't look impressed by the soggy-skinned potato. 'Try not to get anything on the duvet,' I whisper to her.

'Sam kill me if I make a mess,' she says.

'Shh! Yes, he will. Bells, you can sit more on the bed if you like.'

She slides a bit closer to me but still doesn't look relaxed. 'Do you want to read a magazine? Look, I bought a *Tatler*.' I hold it up towards her. 'My shop is going to be in this next month, I had a fashion show.'

Bells shows no interest.

'Or how about doing the crossword? Or you can watch the tennis but with the volume off? Better that way, you don't hear the players grunting.' Bells is staring absently at

116

the walls. She looks so bored. Mum and Dad told me, before they left, that she did get easily fed up when she was staying with them and often wanted to go back to Wales.

'I know it's boring,' I say, hearing a loud knock on the front door.

Bells puts her food on the floor. 'We've got to be really quiet now,' I tell her.

Any trace of excitement on her face evaporates into boredom again. 'Why?' she asks. 'Bossy Katie. You like traffic warden,' she randomly adds. 'Where's Sam?'

'Sam's here, it's his boys' night.' I'm still smiling at that image of me in uniform with a navy hat on.

'Who's at door?'

Oh, God, I think to myself. Perhaps it was a bad idea staying in.

'Davey mate,' I hear Sam bellow, followed by a few slaps on a manly shoulder.

'Who Davey?' Bells asks loudly.

'Bells, remember, whisper. Davey works in the City with Sam. I told you, they play poker each week.'

'Lakemore,' Davey returns in a ringing tone. 'Am I the first here?'

'Yep, you are *numero uno*,' Sam trills as if he is in a bingo hall. 'No-one else here,' he emphasizes loudly. 'Come on in. Looking sharp, mate,' Sam compliments his friend. I flick my pen between my fingers. I can imagine him winking at Davey now. Sam always follows a compliment with a wink.

'New Paul Smith shoes. They're the business, aren't they?' Davey says proudly.

'Very nice. How about this for style?' Sam challenges him.

He is wearing his new purple silk shirt tonight so I imagine that is what he is pointing to.

'Sharp. I like it, Lakemore. Bet the girls like it too. Your missus pick it out for you?'

'No, saw it down the Fulham Road. Nice, isn't it? Look the part, feel the part . . . '

' . . . and you ARE the part,' they both finish together. 'Sit down, David, pour yourself a whisky.'

'Cheers.'

The door again.

'Crispin, me old diamond geezer.'

'Lakemore.' Another thump on the back. I can hear their shoes clicking across the wooden floor. They go into the poker-playing room. Sam turns the sitting room into the games room, puts out the card table with the polished casino chips. 'Weh-hey, Gravy Daveyeeeeeee!'

'Crisps! How goes it?'

'Who Crisps?' Bells asks me in an even louder voice. Perhaps she is unable to whisper? I never thought of that.

The door knocks again.

'MAGUIRE!' shouts Sam. The door crashes open.

'LAKEMORE!' he shouts back.

'They all deaf?' Bells asks me, rocking forwards and putting her fingers into her ears.

'Good question,' I tell her. 'You'd think so, wouldn't you?'

'Davey mate . . . '

'Maguire, what you up to?'

'Crispin, you diamond!'

I start to laugh quietly to myself. I cannot tell who is talking, they all sound the same.

★ ★ ★

'You OK, Bells?' She is doodling on my newspaper. 'Give us a clue,' I suggest and put my files down. Sam has been playing poker for about an hour now, and I don't know why he worried about me listening to their conversations. Boys together are about as interesting as a night out in Slough.

'I'm gonna raise you twenty quid,' I can hear one of them say.

The chips go into the pot.

'I'll play,' one of them says, more chips going in.

'Fold,' another says.

119

'Are we all on for Ibiza this summer?'

'Absolutely,' one of them says.

'Yeah, yeah, yeah, absolutely,' echoes another.

'Tobes isn't coming this year, his wife has well and truly put the mockers on that.'

'D'you think he played away?'

''Course he did,' one of them guffaws.

'I wonder how she found out? Pub rules. What goes on tour, stays on tour,' someone says authoritatively.

Bells and I look at each other. I pull a silly face at her and she suddenly laughs. I am taken aback by just how pleased I am to hear that. She lifts her right hand, thumb pointing up, near her nose. Sometimes, when I look at Bells, I wonder where she came from. Apart from the colour of her hair and eyes she looks like no-one else in the family, but her laugh is almost identical to Granny Norfolk's.

'Stupid boys,' I mouth at her, hoping to hear her laugh again.

'Very stupid,' she repeats, rocking forward with her thumb up.

I move closer to her. 'Boring, aren't they?' I whisper into her ear.

'Ha-ha!' she grunts, and almost laughs again. 'That's right. Very boring.'

'She was a right moose too,' one of them carries on. 'I said to Tobes, 'Mate, you could have done better than that.' Sam, who was that bird you got friendly with last year?'

I put down my file and go and stand by the door.

'Can we go now?' Bells asks impatiently. 'I'm bored.'

I put a finger over my lips.

'Need loo,' she says, getting up.

'Boys, can you keep the noise down?' I hear Sam asking, firmly but politely.

'What's got into you, Lakemore? You've turned a bit quiet. He must be holding seriously bad cards. Where's your poker face gone?'

'I could be bluffing, Maguire.'

'You're coming to Ibiza, aren't you, Lakemore?'

'Yep,' he says punchily.

'What was that girl's name?'

'Er, I don't know. Cigar, anyone?'

'Scared the missus will find out?' They all laugh.

'I wasn't going out with Katie then,' Sam reminds them. 'I would never cheat on her,' he says loudly, rather overdoing it. 'Music, anyone?'

Come on, answer the question. Who did you meet, Sam? It doesn't matter, we all have a history.

Stevie Wonder starts to play 'I Just Called

To Say I Love You'.

They start to laugh and the music abruptly stops. 'What the . . . ?' Sam is clearly ejecting the CD. 'Must be one of Katie's,' he says, trying to keep his composure.

I put a hand over my mouth to try and stifle a nervous giggle when Chris de Burgh comes on next.

'Blimey, mate. What's happened to your taste in music?' Maguire starts to roar with laughter. 'Next you'll be playing Celine bloody Dion!'

'Katie drives me mad,' Sam mutters.

I can hear Bells now, laughing in the loo, and then there is a flushing sound. Oh my God! I turn around and lean against the door. My stomach feels as if it's on a roller-coaster and we are about to turn upside down, a million feet from the ground. Bells! How could I have lost my concentration and forgotten to remind her not to flush the loo? Sam will kill me. He will kill us both. She comes out of our bathroom.

'Lakemore? What's that sound? Have you got someone here?'

I can feel my heart beating hard. I pull Bells back inside and we lean against the bathroom door.

'Feeling tight, not funny, Katie.'

'We're in serious trouble,' I whisper.

'Serious trouble. Not funny, Katie.'

'No, it's not funny.'

'Lakemore, who are you hiding? Someone just flushed the loo,' one of the boys says incredulously.

I find myself laughing now and Bells copies me. This situation is so ridiculous. Sam has just got to come clean. Tell them we're here.

'No-one is here, boys. Can we just get on with the game?' he insists.

'Come off it!' I can hear a chair scrape back and the click of heels across the floor.

I frown. Yes, come off it! 'Are we *that* embarrassing?' I ask out loud.

'Come off it!' Bells says, stamping her feet.

'Maguire, it must be the neighbours. You can hear everything, and I mean, *everything*. Sit down and finish the game.'

The neighbours? Oh, for God's sake, Sam. Bells is getting restless and wants to leave the room but I hold her arm firmly. I want to see if Sam is eventually going to confess that we are here.

Maguire walks out of the room and looks around. 'Where's the loo?'

'Straight ahead of you.'

I can hear the sitting-room door open.

'Maguire, come and sit down. Come on, who else is going to be here? I've told you, it's the neighbours.'

'All right,' he concedes. Then: 'What the hell was that? There *is* someone here!'

Bells has managed to escape my grasp and is wrestling to open the bathroom door.

'Too tight, not funny, Katie,' she says now at the top of her voice.

'Lakemore, someone *is* in your house.'

Another door is flung open and Bells disappears from the bedroom. I can see her rushing past the sitting room, her arms flailing in the air. This should be interesting . . .

'Who the fuck was that?' one of them bursts out. 'By the way, full house,' he adds loudly.

Bells is running downstairs. 'Who?' Sam asks, but his voice is burdened with defeat.

'That little person?'

'With the funny boots?' another of them says.

'Sam, the game's up. Confess all.'

'I told Katie it was poker night,' he shouts, banging his fist against the table. 'She's here,' he admits crossly.

'But that wasn't Katie,' Maguire exclaims. 'Unless she's shrunk to half her size,' he adds.

I put my shoes on and run past them and down the stairs. 'Hi, sorry, got to go,' I say, unable to turn round and face them.

'Thanks, Katie,' Sam shouts with heavy sarcasm.

'Lakemore,' Maguire now says, clearly wanting an explanation. 'What the fuck is going on?'

14

It is the morning following the disastrous poker evening. I find Bells in the kitchen. She is listening to one of her Beatles CDs, wearing her embroidered hat and dungarees again. They must be glued to her body. I have to take her shopping for Emma's wedding. I don't think I have ever seen my sister wear a skirt.

'How are you, Bells?' I ask, opening the cupboard that houses the mugs and cereal bowls.

'Bored,' she says blankly. 'You know John Lennon lived with Aunt Mimi?'

'No.' I shake my head, flicking the kettle switch on. It's a large silver kettle with a black handle, which matches the toaster.

'They were Nurk Twins before the Beatles.'

'Really?' I nod again. If Bells was in the black chair on *Mastermind* her specialist subject would be the Beatles. 'If you want to go back home, you would say, wouldn't you?' I ask her, feeling ashamed that if she said she wanted to go, I would be relieved. I cannot explain it, but ever since Bells arrived I have had this sinking uneasy feeling hanging over me like an ominous cloud. I can sense something is about to go horribly wrong again, even more so than last night. I wonder if Mum felt like this most of the time when she was bringing Bells and me up? Another reason I feel uncomfortable is that Sam and I have barely spoken since Bells arrived. We are more like ships passing in the night.

'If you want to go home, if you're unsettled . . . ' I try again. However, she has not been here a week yet so perhaps I am being a bit premature. Why am I such a bad sister? Shouldn't I want to spend some time with her? However, more than anything, I want Sam and me to get back on track.

She nods half-heartedly, chopping dried apricots and figs on the table. 'Bells, use a proper chopping board,' I tell her. 'You're marking the table.' I find her a small board. Sam bought a set of five different-sized chopping boards. 'And remember to say sorry to Sam when he comes downstairs.'

'Why?' She bangs the knife into the board angrily.

'Careful, please. You know why,' I tell her again. 'You must say sorry for fiddling around with his music. You don't go around swapping Chris de Burgh for Anastacia. Bells, please. It's really important. Can't you say sorry, for me at least?'

Sam comes into the kitchen and heads straight for the coffee machine. His hair is dark and damp after his shower. 'I'll make you one,' I say. 'Sit down.' I stare at Bells, willing her to apologize, but she says nothing.

'It's all right,' he says tightly. His bad mood hasn't left him and I have run out of things to say. It would help if Bells said sorry.

'Hello, Sam,' she says, looking up at him.

'Hi,' he manages, briefly looking sideways at her.

There is a long awkward silence. 'Wasn't there something you wanted to say, Bells?' I look at her and then at Sam. Still she says nothing. 'You wanted to say something to Sam?' I prompt strongly.

'Sorry, Sam.'

'No problem,' he says. 'Don't do it again, OK?'

That was simple enough, I think with relief.

★   ★   ★

'That was the worst night of my life!' he'd shouted at me last night after the boys had gone. Bells hadn't got far. I'd found her outside our local Italian restaurant with one of the waiters. He was wearing a striped navy and white apron and smoking a cigarette in his break. We sat outside with him drinking a hot chocolate with melting marshmallows on the top. I wanted to give Sam enough time to get rid of the boys before we returned. 'I told you it was a bad idea,' he continued, banging one hand against the other, 'but what do you go and do, huh? You had to wreck it by being there.'

'Sam, it wasn't *that* bad. I'm sorry, but it's quite funny when you think about it.' He threw me another warning look. I was racking my brains trying to think of something that might ease the situation. Isn't it always a good idea to tell someone an even worse story so that they realize they got off lightly? That their ordeal was, in fact, not quite so bad? Great idea, I told myself. 'My parents once gave a dinner party for these clients who had come from America to look at her sculptures,' I started positively. 'It was a really big deal. I mean, Mum even turned the napkins into the shape of lilies, for God's sake.' I chortled but Sam just stared at me. 'So, anyway, it was a really important business dinner.' I stopped again as Sam looked bored. He might as well have had 'So what?' stamped on his forehead. Quickly I got to the main part. 'Anyway, we sat down to find Bells had swapped the lily napkins for her sanitary towels.' I laughed out loud but Sam looked at me with disdain.

'That's revolting, Katie. Disgusting.' He gave a short derisive laugh. 'I'm never going to live last night down. The boys will be dining out on this story for the next year. The whole City will know about it.'

'Don't exaggerate,' I said.

'Katie, all you had to do was keep quiet. You promised you would.' He looked intensely hurt. 'Worst night of my life,' he repeated.

'If that was the worst night of your life, then you've led a pretty charmed existence,' I couldn't help saying.

He turned his face away from me then. 'Poker nights are sacred,' he muttered sulkily. '*And* she swapped my CDs. I mean, Chris *fucking* de Burgh!'

'Sam, don't swear! Bells will hear you.'

'Let me get this straight. *I'm* not allowed to swear in front of her, but *she* is allowed deliberately to swap the CDs to make me look like a fool? Right, Katie, that makes sense. Why do you let her get away with it?'

'She wasn't doing it maliciously, it was only a bit of a game. She was bored, that's all.'

'I think she knows exactly what she's doing. She just pretends to be all innocent.'

Sam is, to an extent, right. But . . . 'Perhaps if you made a little more of an effort with her,' I suggested, my patience beginning to wear thin. 'She thinks you don't like her. That's why she doesn't like you — yet,' I added, seeing his face. He's not used to being told he's unpopular. 'She will like you, it just takes time, that's all.'

★   ★   ★

This morning I watch him making his coffee in the shiny silver machine. Am I imagining it or has Sam hardly touched me since Bells arrived? We have gone from nine months of barely being able to keep our hands off each other almost to taking a vow of chastity.

I watch Bells eating her homemade muesli, and drinking her sage tea. She starts to cough. I think she might be coming down with a cold.

'What are you going to do today?' Sam asks her awkwardly, his head still down.

'Don't know,' she replies.

'You're staying here while I go to my yoga class,' I tell her. I cannot face Bells coming with me. There is one woman who is always at the class who has terrible body odour and Bells would no doubt tell her she smelled. 'And then we're going to my shop.'

'Oh, great,' Sam says, but I know he is not listening. His mind is still firmly focused on his disastrous poker evening. I should think all he wants to know is exactly what date and time Bells's train is leaving and if she wants a lift. 'Well, it's a nice day out there,' he carries on painfully. I look outside and it's drizzling. In fact, the weather forecast has predicted a thunderstorm later this afternoon. Sam is trying but I notice he cannot look at Bells. It is as if he is scared to make eye contact. If he looks at my sister she will see right through him and read his thoughts.

The telephone rings and Sam sees this as the perfect opportunity to go. 'I'll see you this evening.' He takes his car keys off the breakfast counter and is away before I even have time to say goodbye.

15

After my yoga class, Bells and I catch the bus to the shop. The one good thing that came out of Mum rarely taking Bells and me shopping to buy clothes is that I learned to sew.

'Where did you get that material from?' she asked me suspiciously as I had already been caught for shoplifting. It was one morning in the school holidays and I was sitting on the sofa hacking up a red curtain which I'd found at the bottom of a musty old drawer. I had made myself a pattern out of school tracing paper and found Mum's black Singer sewing machine with the foot pedal.

'I'm making a skirt,' I announced proudly.

She peered at it, did her famous disparaging sniff and then turned away, muttering, 'Well, that's very good, darling. Always good to have a hobby. I'll get you some more material.' I think she was in fact delighted that I had found something to do in the school holidays that would keep me quiet and away from the shops, and meant she could carry on working undisturbed in her studio.

Needlework and textiles were the only

subjects for which I received glowing praise in my school reports. None of the other girls in my class were interested and the others would tease our needlework teacher, Mrs Hook, to the point where she would tremble with fear when we entered the classroom. She had a nervous stammer and could never say the word 'bobbin' properly. I was her gold-star pupil. I was the one who was asked to show her work to the headmistress. Mrs Davies sat in her office with a cigarette dangling from her mouth and a necklace that looked like a golden ball on a chain hanging over her black polo neck. She was usually balancing a book in one nicotine-stained hand and stroking her pug, Bertie, with the other. She would duly tell me in her coarse gravelly voice that my kimono-dressing gown or whatever else it might be was indeed a triumph, and as a treat I was allowed to take Bertie for a walk.

I started to make all my own clothes as my interest in fashion grew. I began browsing in all kinds of material and haberdashery shops. I couldn't afford the silks and furs at the upmarket shops but I liked touching all the different fabrics and imagining what I could transform them into. Emma used to come with me, pretending she was interested, but very quickly her eyes would develop that glazed expression while I pored excitedly over exquisite rolls of coloured silks. My pocket money took me to the local markets where I searched for leathers to make jackets and skirts with slits in them. I became good at my bargaining skills, negotiating prices for beads, zips, feathers and fabric off-cuts.

The cheapest and quickest things to make were beaded chokers and belts out of sparkling black and gold beads which I sold to school friends. I created a small factory in my bedroom, the sewing machine kept permanently in the corner by the window, and all the money I made went into an old Nescafe tin which I kept hidden under the bed. All I ever wanted to do was own a clothes shop. I dreamed about leaving home and starting up my own business. I felt imprisoned by my family and longed to be in control of my own life because isn't that what makes you happy, being in control?

I did not want to be financially dependent on my parents any longer than I had to be, so I left home when I was eighteen to live with my electrician boyfriend to whom Mum had taken an immediate dislike because his arms were covered in tattoos. I was longing to be independent and to step out into the wider world. There was going to be no more fearing what people thought of my family, of Bells, of our cut-off existence. I longed to start my own life and make a success of it, with or without my parents.

★ ★ ★

'No touching the clothes,' I tell Bells as I hand her a blueberry muffin wrapped in a white napkin. I'd popped into Eddie's deli to grab us some breakfast. My plan from now on is to stay out of Sam's way. I figure if I can just get through the rest of this holiday with no further hiccups then we have done pretty well. Only one poker night ruined, and Sam will get over it. Eventually.

'No touching clothes.' She coughs again.

'Good.' I sit down behind my large wooden desk which is angled diagonally across one corner of the shop. The desktop has a panel of glass covering black-and-white photographs of our latest fashion show. I have more black-and-white studies screened onto canvas arranged throughout the shop. 'Don't touch the Visa card machine. And no asking customers how rich or how old they are, OK?'

'Yes, Katie, that's right.' Bells nods to me.

I carry on: 'And no coffee near the clothes.'

'No coffee.'

'No commenting on what people are wearing or what they look like. That poor man who had no hair, he was probably very sensitive about it. Or saying hello to customers three times. Fine to say it once,' I allow, 'but once is enough. It's embarrassing for them.'

'Embarrassing for them.' She starts to rock on her feet, something she does when she is nervous or overexcited.

'What did I just say?' I test her, to make sure she was listening rather than merely repeating. Things do not necessarily compute with her, or if they do, she deletes them immediately.

'No saying hello, Katie, answering phone not to. Leave to you.' Bells starts to wave frantically.

'Who are you waving at now?' I ask, my voice loaded with despair, and turn around. Mr Vickers is outside the shop window, peering through the glass. He is carrying a long black umbrella with a duck-shaped handle.

'Hello, Mr Vickers,' Bells calls. He waves tentatively.

I grab her arm in an attempt to stop her from opening the door. 'Bells, I don't want him hanging around the shop.'

She pulls away from me. 'Like Mr Vickers.'

'Bells,' I raise my voice now, 'please don't make me cross.'

She watches him walk away.

'Poor Mr Vickers. Mr Vickers nice man.'

'I know, but I have a shop to run.' I can see through the window Henrietta and her mother approaching and quickly turn to Bells. 'Why don't you go upstairs and start unpacking the delivery boxes? That would be so helpful,' I tell her, pushing her upstairs as if she were a puppet. 'Clean your hands first,' I say, leading her to the sink. 'The boxes are here. These are black T-shirts.' I point to four brown boxes stacked in the corner. 'Scissors are in the drawer. If you could unpack them all before you come back down . . . Thank you.' I don't even wait for an answer.

The simple truth is I don't want Bells saying hello to them at all. I don't want her putting off my customers.

★   ★   ★

Customers come and go. I have made two good sales this morning. Henrietta bought two dresses and three tops while her mother sat on the chaise longue drinking cups of coffee, spiked with a small bottle of Bailey's which she produced from her bag.

Bells has been extraordinarily quiet, I think happily to myself. Perhaps I will treat her to a quick lunch. I find her sitting on the floor, the

T-shirts heaped around her in a muddle.

'Bells, what have you done?' I cry out, kneeling down next to her and picking up one of the black shirts with a small red heart printed on the breast line. I'd thought I could trust her with cotton T-shirts. I mean, how wrong can you go?

'Unpacking shirts,' she says with surprisingly little interest, followed by a cough. Isn't it obvious how angry I am? I open my mouth to speak but nothing comes out. Finally, 'How many have you done?' I whisper in despair, picking up the labels she's cut out that look more like silk raffle tickets strewn haphazardly over the floor. 'People buy these shirts BECAUSE of the labels. They're French designer labels.' I can't look at her otherwise I might hit her. 'What were you thinking of, cutting them all out?'

Bells stands up.

'Don't touch anything else, you hear me? Just leave everything alone.'

'Help Katie. You said unpack everything?'

'No! Leave everything alone. If you touch one more I will be really angry. Why did you cut them out? Did I tell you to cut out the labels? You stupid, STUPID girl!' I scream at her, almost in tears. I cannot cope any more. Please come back, Mum and Dad. I can't do this. You are right, I am a terrible sister.

'Not stupid, Katie. NOT stupid.' Bells rushes out of the room.

I stand looking at the muddle of T-shirts, too paralysed to do anything constructive. All I can do is stare, willing the labels magically to return to where they belong. I hear a door shut downstairs so try to compose myself for the next customer.

'Hello,' I say, walking towards a tall slim man.

'Hi, I'm looking for a present, I wonder if you can help me?'

'Where's Bells?' I say out loud.

'Sorry?' he says, looking puzzled. 'Who's Bells?'

'My sister. Did you see someone running out of the shop?' I can hear the tone of my voice rising in anger and fear.

'No, no-one.' He shakes his head.

'Can you come back later?' I start pushing him towards the door.

'Hey!' he protests, hanging back. 'I came here especially to buy my cousin a birthday present. Her birthday's tomorrow,' he starts to explain then looks straight at me. 'Hang on, haven't we met before? In Sainsbury's?'

'Oh, have we? Right,' I say agitatedly. 'Look, my sister . . . '

'The one who kept on asking me my age? I remember her.'

'Yes, she's run off and I've got to find her.'
I shut the door behind me and then realize I
need the keys to lock up. 'Oh God, oh God,'
I say, going back inside and grabbing my
handbag from behind my desk. I plunge into
it as if it were a lucky dip, hoping to pick out
the right keys. Instead I can feel Bells's
inhaler which I throw onto the shop floor. My
powder compact is chucked after it in
frustration. Why do I always pick out
everything from my bag except my shop keys?
Why can't I have one with practical inside
pockets? My hand is shaking uncontrollably.

'Look, let me help you find her,' the man is
saying. 'Where do you think she might be?'

I let out a frustrated yelp. 'I don't know,
she could be anywhere. If I knew . . . Oh,
where *are* they?'

'Keep calm,' he says.

If my stare were venomous I would kill him
on the spot. Finally I find the right keys.
Where is Eve when I need her? Why did she
have to be sick today of all days? I scribble on
a piece of paper 'Back in half an hour' and
pin it haphazardly to the door.

'OK, here's what we do,' the man says
authoritatively. 'You go across the park, I'll go
on the main road, and we both head for the
tube station and the shops. If you find her,
whistle like this.' He puts his hand to his

mouth and belts out a loud whistle. 'It works in the classroom,' he adds.

I breathe deeply. 'I can't do that, I've always wanted to.'

'Well, use a real whistle then. I'm a teacher,' he quickly explains. 'Always keep one on me for emergencies.' He digs into his black rucksack and pulls out a red plastic whistle attached to a piece of string which he places around my neck. 'She ran off . . . what? . . . five, ten minutes ago? We'll find her, she can't be far away.'

'What's your name?' I ask as I start to run.

'Mark.'

'Thanks, Mark,' I call after him as we turn in different directions.

⋆　⋆　⋆

It's damp and overcast. The park is almost deserted compared to what it normally is on a summer's day. There only has to be a blink of sun and people come out in their bikinis, carrying picnic boxes and rugs. 'Bells,' I shout, and keep on running. 'Bells, where are you?' I walk past a man wearing headphones. He won't know where she is, will he? He might. I'd better ask. I tap him hard on the shoulder. He pulls the plugs out of his ears.

'Excuse me, I've lost my sister. She's short,

about four foot something, really short hair too.' I stare into his vacant expression, urging him to show some sign of recognition. 'And she kind of rocks rather than walks,' I persist. Still no reaction.

'Nope, haven't seen her,' he mumbles finally as he puts his music back on. I see a couple ahead of me. The girl has her hand tucked into the back pocket of her boyfriend's jeans. 'Um, hello . . . hey, you.' I run after them. They turn around in surprise. 'I'm sorry, I've lost my sister. She's short, have you seen her?' I ask with pleading eyes. Please say you have seen her somewhere.

'She's short? That doesn't give us much to go on.' The boy smirks.

'What's she wearing?' the girl asks.

What's she wearing? Good question. 'She's wearing a Chinese embroidered hat and dungarees,' I describe breathlessly. When I get no response, I add, 'And some sort of football shirt with stickers on.'

'You're having me on.' The boy smiles at me. 'Is this some kind of joke? We're on some funny game show, right? *Graham Norton*?' He starts darting his head around looking for the hidden cameras.

I stare at him hard and pin my hopes on the girl. She chews gum thoughtfully and then shrugs her shoulders. 'We've only just got here. Good luck finding her, though.' As I watch them walk on, her hand back in his pocket, I realize this is one of those car breakdown moments. You know, when you see someone break down in their car and feel so lucky that it's not you. You drive on. Now I feel like the girl who's broken down in her battered old car and no-one is offering to help. No rescue team, no phone, no-one's that interested. I fumble in my handbag for my mobile phone then I realize I don't have a clue who to ring. Sam? I stab in the numbers and wait for him to answer.

'I'm in a meeting. I'll call later, I promise. Remember, I'm out tonight,' Sam finishes helpfully.

'She's run away,' I say, my eyes staring ahead. 'What am I going to do?'

'Katie, I'm sorry, but what can I do stuck behind my frigging desk? Do you want me to leave the office and come and help you look for her?' He chuckles as if the idea is absurd.

'No, Sam. That would make you a nice person.' I hang up abruptly. I don't even know why I called him. If Bells comes back I'll tell her that it doesn't matter. What are a few labels? I can sew them back on, no-one will know. Just come back, Bells. Please come back. There is no-one else I can call. It's like living in our own little world again, shut away from what's normal.

''Scuse me . . . she's twenty-two, four foot ten . . . ' I describe her to the next person I meet. I can't see what other people look like any more. I just want to see Bells.

'No, I haven't seen her,' he says.

WHY NOT? I want to scream at him. WHAT'S THE MATTER WITH YOU?

'I'm sure a twenty-two-year-old can look after themselves,' he mutters as he slopes off.

I start keying in my father's mobile number though I know it's crazy. What can he do when he's not even in the country? I listen to the ringing tone but there is no answer. He promised me he would have his mobile switched on in case of an emergency. I put a hand to my mouth and let out a long desperate wailing noise, I don't know what to do, who to ask, where to look . . .

'I've lost my sister. Have you seen my little sister?' I ask a lady sitting on a bench reading a newspaper. The familiar sound of the train rattles in the background. What if Bells is on it?

'What does she look like, darling?' She's American.

I am about to repeat everything I have said before but find myself starting to cry. It's awful but I cannot stop. My chin is wobbling uncontrollably. I put my head in my hands.

What have I done? Bells, I'm so sorry, please forgive me for shouting at you. Bells could be run over and dead by now for all I know, and it's my fault. I look up and the stranger smiles sympathetically as she hands me a tissue from her handbag.

'What does she look like?' she asks softly again. 'Come on, we'll find her. She can't be far.'

I smile gratefully at her. Her auburn hair, the same colour as Mum and Bells's, is piled on top of her head with an assortment of hairgrips and she is wearing dark sunglasses which is strange when it's so overcast. 'If you've seen someone who doesn't blend into the crowd, well,' I sniffle, 'that's her.'

She makes me sit down for a few moments to compose myself. I stare over at the playground where there are a few mothers pushing their children on the swings, and a couple of boys kicking a ball around. Under a tree a pair of boys practise their boxing skills. One stands with a padded shield over his hand while the other practises his punches. I tell her about our argument. I tell her about Bells. It's surprisingly easy telling a stranger about our family. 'I'm sorry for crying,' I add.

'No, don't be. Being sorry for crying is such a British thing. You're going through a traumatic time, you're allowed to be emotional.' I look up at her and smile. 'What is that whistling noise?' The woman looks around.

I can see Mark running towards us, pulling Bells along with him. 'Thank God,' I leap up from the bench and start clapping my hands together.

'Don't thank God,' the American remarks, her dark glasses now perched on the end of her nose. 'I think you should thank that nice young man.'

As they approach I can tell something's seriously wrong. 'She needs her inhaler,' Mark shouts.

I try and find it in my bag, and then remember exactly where it is.

Bells is fighting for breath. 'Her inhaler,' Mark shouts again. 'Where is it?'

'It's in the shop. OK, sit down,' I tell Bells, guiding her to the bench. The American lady stands up to give her room. I can feel the tightness in her chest as she gasps for breath. 'Put your hands on your knees . . . Don't let her lie down, Mark. She has to sit up and try to relax as much as possible. The inhaler is in the shop. I'll be back in a minute.' He sits with her while I run as fast as I can across the park. I unlock the door with trembling hands and rush to pick up the inhaler. I slam the door shut and just about remember to lock it behind me.

Bells takes the inhaler immediately. I stroke her back. We watch and wait.

'How's she doing?' the American lady asks.

'If the inhaler doesn't work we'll have to go to the doctor's or call an ambulance,' I say. Please let me wake up. Please let this be a terrible dream. I draw in my own breath, waiting to see if the inhaler helps Bells.

'I'm all right,' she finally says.

I can feel her breathing becoming more even as I continue to stroke her back. 'You're really all right?' I say nervously. 'Oh, God, Bells, don't ever . . . I mean EVER . . . scare me like that again.'

Mark tells me not to shout, that she's safe, that's all that matters.

'She could have died.' I turn back to Bells who sits, looking tired and crumpled, with her eyes watering. 'Oh, Bells.' I reach out and pull her close to me. 'I'm sorry. I'm so sorry for shouting at you. It'll never happen again.' I feel her arms clutching the small of my back and hold her even more tightly — the way Mum used to hold me when I was younger. So tightly that I thought I would stop breathing. 'Mark's right. You're OK, that's all that counts.'

I pull the duvet over her.

'Tired,' Bells says, turning onto her side.

'Get some rest. Come down for supper later. I'm going to make you your favourite supper. What would you like to eat? Remember, it's me cooking,' I add, smiling.

'Why you hate me?' she asks.

'What?' Should I pretend I didn't hear that? I draw her curtains.

'You hate me,' she states simply.

'Why do you say that? That's not true, I don't hate you.' I turn off the main light and shut the door behind me. Outside I lean against it, taking a deep breath. I feel winded by her question. Bells is no fool, she could hear how hollow that sounded. I can't keep on talking to her as if she's ten years old. Pat her on the head and hope she won't ask me any more difficult questions.

Bells screams then. 'Too dark,' she cries out.

I rush back and turn on the light. Dad once explained to me why Bells hated the darkness so much. After the surgery she developed a phobia about anaesthetics and would scream before each injection. She didn't know what anaesthesia was, but she knew exactly what it meant. Blackness. Dad was good at talking to me and explaining. He was naturally gentle.

I kneel down beside her and make my voice like his. 'I'm sorry, Bells. I forgot. That was stupid of me.'

'That's right, Katie. You don't write me,' she says. 'Mum writes me. Dad writes me. You don't.'

I am about to say something along the lines of no-one writes letters any more, only Mum and Dad's generation, but then I realize how pathetic that would sound. She's right.

'You don't visit me.'

'No, I don't,' I say.

'Why?'

'I don't know,' I reply simply. 'I don't know, Bells.' I try to explain, but I don't even know where to start. 'I don't hate you, but I hated watching you in the park. I was so scared. If anything had happened to you, I would never have forgiven myself. I hated seeing you so vulnerable. I do care. I'm sorry for shouting, and . . . '

'In Wales cut labels,' she mutters.

'Oh, God, I don't care about the labels any more. It doesn't matter. And I will start writing to you, I'd like to.' I realize as I say this that I can't make an empty promise. Bells deserve more than that.

'Mark's nice man. Nice man.'

I smile. 'He is very nice, I am so sorry,

Bells.' Without thinking I kiss her forehead and softly touch her cheek. 'I don't hate you. I could never, ever hate you.' I want to tell her that I love her but I don't feel I deserve to say it. Instead I stand up to draw her shutters and turn off the overhead light. The small stained-glass lamp in the corner of her room is on this time.

'Nothing around me?' she asks.

'Nothing around you,' I say.

'Promise.'

'I promise.'

*   *   *

'Thank you, Mark, thank you so much,' I tell him as I make us both a hot drink in the kitchen. I asked him back to Sam's place as I felt it was the least I could do. Also I wanted to ask him how he had found Bells, and to talk to him without her listening. I'd thought he would say no, that he had to get on with his day, but to my surprise he agreed.

'Is she all right?' he asks, obviously concerned, turning away from the milk-bottle sculpture.

'Yes, I think so. I ran her a bath and now she's lying down.'

Mark tells me he found Bells waiting at a bus shelter. She was clearly in an agitated condition but no-one else at the stop was doing anything.

I feel such a failure as I listen to him recall the drama, realizing Bells is having a miserable time with me. She wanted to see the bright lights of London and the most gripping thing we have done together is go to Sainsbury's. Now I know where I met Mark before. 'That's right, of course,' I tell him. 'You're thirty-four.'

'Yes. But you can forget that bit.' He laughs for the first time today.

I sigh heavily. 'If you hadn't been there anything could have happened.'

'It was nothing, honestly.'

'Thanks, Mark. Thank you so much for everything you did today. You don't know me, know us, you didn't have to help.'

He looks at his shoes sheepishly. 'I did nothing special. Where does Bells live? I mean, I hadn't seen her around before that day in Sainsbury's, and I think I'd remember if I had.'

'She lives in a community in Wales. My parents are on holiday so I'm having her to stay for two weeks. Actually, I need to call them,' I tell him, 'I'll be back in a minute.' I walk out with the mobile and key in Dad's number. Still no answer. I key in their home number. It's their answer-machine. What am

I doing? They are in France. Stop this, Katie.

I walk back into the kitchen. 'Is this your place?' Mark asks, glancing around the bare kitchen. 'I like this . . . um . . . sculpture,' he finishes lamely.

'It's Sam's.'

'Oh, right,' he acknowledges, running a hand through his hair. 'He's your boyfriend?'

'Yes.'

'What happened to Bells? I mean, what . . . '

'What makes her different?' I suggest, sitting down opposite him.

'Yes, exactly.'

I tell him she was born with a cleft lip and palate. 'My parents would visit her in hospital after each operation. Bells had to be strapped to the cot to stop her from scratching out the stitches.'

'That's terrible.'

'She was also brain-damaged at birth. A large part of her brain still works. If you tap into a subject she knows a lot about, then you're OK. But she's never been able to lead a fully independent life like most people can.'

'Is she aware that she's different?'

'Yes and no. I think she is comfortable with herself now, she is her own person, but as a teenager she wanted to be like everyone else. She hated the way she looked. Well, that's what Dad said,' I add. 'You see, I didn't really see that side of Bells because I left home when I was eighteen and she was only eleven.'

'It must have been tough for your parents.'

'Yes, it was,' I say, wondering if I have ever told them how good they were, and still are, with Bells. No, I know I haven't. I've spent too much time feeling left out of the family and resenting all the energy they put into her. 'To be honest, I've never had Bells to stay with me in London before and I'm finding it pathetically hard. I mean, look what happened today.' As I tell him about the problems she's had with Sam, I am surprised by how easy it is to talk to Mark. The words are flowing effortlessly, almost too much so. I suddenly look at him and pray he is not too bored. 'Shall we have a drink?' I say, overwhelmed by the events of the day and in desperate need of relief. 'I could really do with one.'

After a couple of drinks, to lighten the conversation I decide to tell him about the ruined poker night and the switched CDs. He is clearly trying hard not to laugh.

'It's OK, laugh away. It is quite funny.' I tell him how Bells asked a customer's husband why he had no hair, and that triggers another memory. 'When I was about fifteen we had a plumber with a wooden leg and a glass eye — Mr Curly.'

'Mr Curly?' Mark grins. 'Sounds like a Mr Man character.'

I smile. 'Mr Curly was up a ladder in our kitchen one day when a screw in his false leg came loose and then the whole thing fell off. 'Why haven't you got a proper leg?' Bells said immediately, and then started to howl with laughter while Mum and I were desperately trying to find the screw on the floor. I felt so sorry for that man but Bells wasn't being mean, it's just her way. She says what she thinks. If she doesn't like someone she says so. She might tell them they're boring or stuffy.' I decide not to tell Mark that Bells definitely does not like Sam.

'How old is she?'

'Twenty-two. The thing is, you can't put a mental age on Bells. Some things she's very good at, like gardening and cooking, she gets all that from Mum. But if you ask her to visualize something abstract it means nothing to her at all. When my Uncle Roger died, Bells bought some flowers and wrote in the card: 'Dear Uncle Roger, I am sorry to hear you are dead'.'

I notice Mark has a dimple like me. Only special people have dimples, Dad used to say to me when he squeezed my cheeks. I used to hate that. It really hurt, although he never believed me when I said it did.

'It's getting late,' Mark mentions. 'I ought to be . . . '

'No, have another drink. Stay and have some pizza with Bells and me. I'll order some from up the road. You don't live far away, do you?'

'I live near your shop actually, in Chapel Road.'

'No way! That's where Emma lives. She's a really old friend,' I add when I see Mark's blank expression. 'What number?'

'One.'

'She's twenty-nine.'

'My first fake age.' He smiles.

'Exactly. Come on, stay.' The truth is I don't want to be left on my own. 'What do you feel like?' I open the fridge.

'I think I'd better be on my way.' He scrapes his chair back.

'Another beer? How about some wine?' I continue.

'Hey,' Mark says, walking towards me. 'Look, it's been a shitty day, it's not surprising you're feeling like this.' He lays a hand gently on my shoulder.

I'm thinking about Bells and what she said to me earlier this evening. 'Why do you hate me? Why don't you write me?' I start to cry and he holds me.

*   ⋆   ⋆

'I don't think I have ever apologized so much in one day,' I say, as I finally sit down at the table with dry eyes. 'To better days,' I say as I hold my can up towards his.

'To better days,' he agrees.

⋆   ⋆   ⋆

'Bells! Stop!' I scream.

Mum's footsteps hurtle down the corridor. 'STOP HER!' she shouts at me.

Bells is towering over Mum's dog Peggy, clutching a chunky pair of black jagged-edged scissors. Everything turns to slow motion as I watch my sister. She holds the scissors near one of Peggy's ears and smiles as she opens the handles. Peggy looks up at her innocently. I have to stop Bells from hurting her! I try to move. The scissors are open wide, the jagged silver edges gleam. My feet won't move. I cannot move. I am paralysed on the spot. I won't stop her in time. It's too late.

'Stop her!' Mum shouts again.

'MOVE!' I shout. 'MOVE!'

I wake up in a sweat, gasping for breath. Was that me screaming? I take a look around the dark room. It was only a bad dream. Calm down. Deep breaths, Katie. Let it all go. It's all right. I sit up and hug my knees tightly under the duvet. Our bed is empty. Sam is not back yet. Where is he? Why didn't he even call? The room feels black and cold. The least he could have done was call to see if I had found Bells, to see if we were both OK. Why hasn't he? What's the time? Where is he? I lean over to the bedside table, turn on the lamp and hold up my watch. It's just after one o'clock. 'Why didn't he call, Charlie?' I ask my cheetah who sits protectively by the lamp. 'You would have called me, wouldn't you, Charlie, even if you were busy hunting?'

When I go to bed alone I keep my mobile on the bedside table. I pick it up now and ring Sam. It's his voicemail. I want him here with me. I miss him.

I walk down the corridor and quietly open Bells's door. She is curled up in bed, looking peaceful.

I turn off the lamp and lie down again in the darkness. When I was a child I hated the darkness, just as Bells did, but I did not admit it to Mum. I was terrified there was a crocodile under my bed, a witch behind my door or demons lurking under the window seat. *Plop, The Owl Who Was Afraid of the Dark* was one of my favourite books. Dad used to read it to me when he got back from work. He sat on the end of my bed, still in his suit. Now I shut my eyes and try to think of something nice to dream about.

'Nothing around me,' I whisper to myself.

'Nothing around you,' I can hear my mother's voice say.

I hear a creaking noise and quickly open my eyes again. I lie in bed, rigid. Someone is in the house. I am going to be strangled in my sleep! Calm down, Katie, I tell myself. It is so dark that my eyes search in vain for a tiny crack of light or the outline of any familiar object, something to reassure me that I am not going to be in this blackness for ever.

Nothing around me?

Where are you, Sam? I have never felt so alone.

16

I am still awake. I turn my pillow over because it is getting too warm and clammy. I feel so tired I'm incapable of opening my eyes, yet my mind will not switch off. If only it could go quiet at the touch of a button. All I want to do is sleep.

One moment I am worrying about Sam. What if he is so drunk he has passed out and no-one has bothered to bring him home safely? It is nearly three o'clock now. Then I am fretting about what could have happened to Bells if Mark hadn't helped. Bells will tell Mum and Dad about me shouting at her. Mum will be furious.

I decide it is pointless trying to get to sleep. I put my dressing gown on, and walk past Bells's room. She is breathing heavily, still fast asleep. Quietly I shut her door and walk downstairs. I pray Sam has not hidden the cigarettes in too hard a place this time. Thankfully I find a pack in the cutlery drawer.

I sit and think about home again. Bells being here has stirred up so many feelings. Why am I finding it so hard having her around? I knew all along it would be difficult, but hadn't anticipated such a string of dramas in only one week.

After Bells's birth Dad told me that we would get through this together. He told me that life carries on and that things would turn out OK. There are many families who go through exactly what we are going through, he said, trying to make us all feel better.

I felt this overwhelming sense that I had to look after Mum. It wasn't because she was falling apart. Looking back, she was very strong. I simply felt responsible for her. I started to plan what I could do to help. I can remember going shopping with her and how I would slip packets of orange Club biscuits and salt and vinegar crisps into the bags without being caught. I knew we didn't have a lot of money because I'd heard Mum and Dad talking about it. Mum no longer had time to work in her studio and Dad was earning a pretty meagre salary in the auction house. I told Mum she did not have to give me any pocket money and she seemed touched. I said I would raise money at school by selling horse chestnuts in the playground. I wanted to help on the practical side too. I helped Mum feed Bells and dress her. This was something I could do and I enjoyed it, even if Mum pointed out to me that I had missed a buttonhole or was putting her arms where her legs should have gone. Dad was no better. He was once left to look after Bells for the day and Mum came back to find her cardigan put on all askew and her bonnet back to front. It was what Dad meant by muddling through together. It did work for a while.

I was also very protective of Bells. I knew she was vulnerable, not the same as other small children; my sister was different. I probably tried too hard. I remember insisting I should take Bells out for a walk in her pram. I said I'd only take her down our road — up the hill and back again. As I reached the top and was turning the pram around a group of boys came running along behind me, pelting water-filled balloons at one another. One of them barged into the back of me and my hand slipped. The pram started to roll down the hill, gathering speed alarmingly. Mum is going to kill me, was my overriding fear. 'Help!' I screeched to the group of boys. 'Help!' One of them stopped and turned around, the pram crashed into him and toppled over. Bells landed in the gutter. She was cut very badly on the forehead and her right arm.

'How could you have let go!' Mum shouted at me later, pacing up and down the kitchen.

She was throwing her arms up in the air, gesticulating madly.

'It was an accident,' Dad intervened, trying to calm her down.

'An accident? We can't afford any more accidents.'

I started to cry and Dad tried to talk to me. 'Your mother knows it wasn't your fault, she's just frightened,' he said. 'When we are scared, we lash out at the nearest person.'

I started to withdraw from Mum when she spent so much time at the hospital. Bells was about two years old then and I was nine. By this stage she needed a series of operations to start healing her face. It was rather like a puzzle. Piece by piece, the doctors slowly rebuilt the gap between her nose and lip. When the bandages were taken off, it was hard to tell the difference immediately, but slowly Bells started to look more normal.

In the school holidays, when Dad was at work and Mum was at the hospital, I spent most of my time with Emma's family. Berry, her sister, was the one who told us to cut off a piece of Bells's hair and put it in the magic box. She was seventeen then and I can remember thinking how grown-up she was. Berry called me 'Eagle Eyes' because I used to stare at her. Emma still teases me about my crush. Berry was tall and willowy, with long black hair which she dyed with purple streaks. It was so long she could sit on it. She wore Gothic clothes and her eyelashes were coated in thick layers of black mascara. I remember her constantly sucking mint imperials, I realize now to disguize the smell of cigarette smoke.

When Emma's family was away, Miss Grimes, our local babysitter, filled in. I hated my mother for making me put up with her. Miss Grimes wore the same brown tweed skirt the colour of mud every time I saw her, and boring brown lace-up shoes. She wore flesh-toned tights that squashed down the black hairs on her white legs. Her hair looked like one of those Brillo pads we had in the kitchen sink. She wore steel-framed glasses perched on the end of her nose. It was hard to believe she lived only three doors away from us. She looked as if she came from another country. One where all they ate was cabbage.

'She is very nice, poppet,' Mum told me when I wrinkled my nose in disapproval. 'The main thing is I won't have to worry about leaving you.'

Dad loved her because she brought over steamed puddings and lasagnes and 'good wholesome stews' for our freezer. 'She's a one is Miss Grimes,' he chuckled. I will never forget the time she came to look after me for an entire night. Mum and Dad had taken Bells to hospital the day before her next operation.

'You always have your nose in a book,' Miss Grimes scolded me, leaning over to see what I was reading. She was knitting a sludgy green jumper the colour of the damp rotting moss which sat on our garage roof. 'You're far too young for a book like this,' she said in a shocked voice and swiped it away from me. I tried to grab it back, clutching the air. 'Give it back!' I shouted. 'Oh, keep it then, I've already read *Riders* anyway.'

'You'll amount to nothing,' she said to the click of her knitting needles. 'You're just a little piece of fluff. Your sister has a lot more problems than you but she will be a proper little person.'

I shrugged my shoulders and muttered, 'Piss off.'

She lurched forward and hit me hard on the knuckles with her grey knitting needles. 'I beg your PARDON?' She was doing that mad thing with her eyes again. When she was cross or excited they started to roll so all I could see was their whites.

I held in my breath, I did not want her to see that hurt. 'You look like a mad blind lady!' I told her, smiling to cover up the pain.

Before I knew it, I was being dragged upstairs and into the spare room. She pushed me inside and I could hear her turning the key in the lock and saying *that* would teach me. I banged on the door, I screamed and shouted, 'Let me out,' but she ignored me as she watched *Coronation Street.*

Miss Grimes unlocked the door the following morning and told me she was sorry. I told her she was a sad lonely old spinster woman. When Mum and Dad returned I described what had happened. Mum told me to stop lying; she said she knew how much I hated Miss Grimes and that I would do anything to get rid of her. I looked at Dad, who was so often my ally, but he told me not to harass Mum. Couldn't I see how drained and tired she was? Miss Grimes continued to babysit for us, despite my telling Mum I was no longer a child. She carried on locking me in my bedroom; she even locked me in the attic once for being 'insolent'. I never forgave them for not believing me. They closed their ears and eyes to it because they had too much else to think about.

When my father finally became an auctioneer, his salary increased and we could afford to have someone coming in during the day to look after Bells. This was when Mum started to work in her studio again. She started working around the clock, working, working, working, in between looking after Bells. I think it took her mind off the family problems and immersed her in a different world. Her life was divided between trying to meet Bells's needs and working in her studio. It felt like she was not interested in me any more and we started to grow even further apart.

Bells was, 'Mum's girl'. I know both Mum and Dad found her comparatively easy to live with by now, straightforward in comparison to me and my stupid antics. Bells was the 'artistic one'; Mum encouraged her to draw, paint, write, cook — all the things she loved as a child and still loves. Katie was the 'rebellious one'.

'What have you *done* to yourself, Katie!' I can still hear Mum cry in that familiar despairing tone, her heart-shaped face contorting, frown lines appearing, green eyes glaring, mouth opening wider in reproach. 'How could you have been so stupid? So idiotic?' I can see her savagely untying her mucky apron which she then throws dramatically to the floor.

I had dyed my hair blue and pink, like an exotic bird. I was copying Berry who changed her hair colour as often as Madonna.

I can feel Mum's arm pulling mine. 'Which

godforsaken hairdresser did this to you?' she is shouting. 'It looks like you have pink and blue worms crawling in your hair.' By the time we were going home in the car, she was upset rather than cross. 'Why do you deliberately try to upset me all the time? Katie, what's happened to you? You used to be such a sweet girl.'

Wasn't it obvious? Did I have to get my tongue pierced next to get her attention?

I don't think Mum has moved on from describing me as the 'rebellious one'. I think she still believes that I lead this full-on crazy life in London, working round the clock and burning the candle at both ends. I am still the dissident because I never come home.

When I think about it now, it seems almost trivial; people go through much worse things after all. But we don't forget, do we? We do not forget the smallest slight, let alone the feeling that we have been somehow abandoned. Left to play second fiddle to our own sister. It wasn't Bells's fault, I know she never set out to be the golden child in Mum's eyes, and I know how much she has gone through, but there is still a part of me that blames her for needing Mum so much. If Mum wasn't at home she was at the hospital. Bells had speech therapy classes every week, or her eyesight had to be tested, or her hearing aid needed to be fitted. There was always some appointment to go to. I suppose I have never confronted Bells about it because Mum has always instilled in me how lucky I am not to have the same affliction. How dare I be angry or cross when I have my whole life ahead of me? I am a healthy young girl with a promising future. I just need to get on with it. 'You're lucky, so lucky,' I can still hear Mum saying.

In many ways my childhood helped me. It made me become self-sufficient. It made me strive to be independent. Yet I'm still not truly independent, am I? I have this need to be with people; look at the way I move in with every man I meet. I want to feel loved; I want to feel needed. I blame my parents, especially my mother, for not loving me the way she loves Bells. I have this gaping hole inside me which I have tried to ignore for years, yet it will never go away. When I hear Bells talking about Mum so freely all that old anger and jealousy return, as if they have never gone away. Well, they haven't.

There was closeness once, there was tenderness between Mum and me, so how did it all go wrong?

I light another cigarette and blow a smoke ring in the air. I will never forget Mum failing to turn up to watch me perform the leading role in our school production of *Guys and Dolls*. I had reserved two seats in the front row. Something had 'cropped up with Bells' was the tired excuse. I pretended I didn't care. Maybe that is my mistake? I am too proud. But I can still remember how it felt when my father sat down next to an empty seat.

17

'He didn't even call me later in the evening to see if I had found her,' I say quietly down the phone to Emma. I am in the shop the following morning. Eve and Bells have popped out to buy some croissants and cappuccinos.

'NO!' Emma sounds outraged. 'That's dreadful! What did you say to him?'

★ ★ ★

'Sam, a fat lot of use you were.'

'What are you talking about, babe?' He was shaving and I was talking to his reflection in the mirror.

'Yesterday!' I shout in exasperation as I pull on my work jeans. I catch my finger on the zip. 'Fuck, that hurt.' I suck in my breath. 'Bells went missing and you didn't even call.'

'Had she run off then?' he remarks, without a flicker of concern. He might as well have been commenting on the weather. I hurl a trainer at him. It hits him on the back and thuds to the floor.

'Jesus, Katie, what was that for? Damn, I've cut myself now.'

'You could at least try to pretend you're interested. Show a bit of concern.'

'Well, you found her, didn't you?' He turns to me impatiently. 'Katie, I haven't got time for this, I'm seeing my personal trainer in half an hour.'

I throw the other trainer at him. This one hits him bang in the face. Bull's-eye.

★　★　★

'NO! You didn't?' Emma gasps, and then laughs.

'I did.'

'Good for you! I would have done the same too. Then what did he say?'

★　★　★

'What has got into you?' he yells, touching one side of his face. 'Great, I'm going to have a socking big bruise on my cheek. Thanks, Katie.'

'Yesterday was awful,' I say, lowering my voice but making sure it doesn't lose its angry edge. 'If it hadn't been for Mark . . . '

'For who?' There is a slight twitch of interest, at last.

'Mark.'

'Who's Mark?'

'He is a very nice man,' I point out emphatically. 'He found Bells yesterday. He came home for pizza too.' This piece of information has done the trick. At last Sam pays attention.

'For pizza? Why did you have to invite the guy back for pizza?' He waits for my answer.

'To say thank you,' I say simply. 'If he hadn't found her, I don't know what would have happened. She had an asthma attack.'

'Why did Bells run away in the first place?' Sam asks, sitting down on the bed and putting his trainers on.

'Because that is what she does when she gets upset,' I explain to him, as if he really ought to know. 'It used to happen a lot at home.' I tell him about the labels, relieved to find that Sam might in fact care a little. That he is human, after all.

'Well, if you hadn't shouted at her in the first place,' he says smugly, clicking his tongue against the roof of his mouth, 'then none of this would have happened, would it?'

★　★　★

There is an uneasy pause. I want Emma to say, I can't believe he said that. How dare he swing that one back at you? Anything to make me feel less guilty. 'What did you say?' she finally asks.

★   ★   ★

I pick up his cup of coffee which sits on the bedside table. 'Uh-oh, nervous twitch, might spill this all over the white sheepskin rug.'

'KATIE,' he says imploringly, 'put the mug down.'

I do put the mug down as I bought that rug and I love it. Instead, I grab his watch. 'I would say this is an emergency situation, wouldn't you, Sammy? Perhaps if I just pull the emergency cord?' I suggest.

Sam cannot bear to look at me in case I do. He stands up in his jogging trousers, tight T-shirt and trainers. 'Go on, pull it, and you can pay the fucking fine. I'm late for my PT. I haven't got time for this.' He storms out of the room.

I put the watch down. I feel so deflated. A week ago I was happy, things were going fine. My fashion show was a success. I hear Sam coming back and my heart lifts. He is going to say how sorry he is. He will tell me that he has been a complete fool and not at all supportive.

He stands at the door and puts one hand

against the wall. 'You've had your say, now it's my turn.'

'What?' I say, disappointed that he is not going to apologize.

'You never told me about Isabel and now, all of a sudden,' he raises his eyebrows, 'I am supposed to be deeply concerned about her welfare? Katie, I didn't know that she runs off when she's upset. I still don't know a thing about her. I don't feel comfortable around her because *you* haven't made me feel comfortable.'

I sit in silence.

'Did you think I would go off you because of her . . . you know, the way she is?' he finishes. 'It's your own hang-up, Katie. If you hadn't been so ashamed to tell me about her . . . '

Bells is standing behind him now in her cotton pyjamas and football slippers and I desperately try to signal to Sam to shut up. I am frowning madly and buttoning my lips together but he is paying no attention.

'If you hadn't been so ashamed of your own sister,' he stresses, 'things might have got off to a better start. OK, she's different, but so what? I was on the tube the other day and there was this woman sitting opposite me barking like a dog. There are lots of Isabels around, she's not unique.'

Bells looks at me and I put my head in my hands. She walks back to her bedroom and shuts the door loudly. Sam glances round, finally realizing he wasn't talking just to me. 'I couldn't do anything when you called because I was about to go into a meeting. I *am* to blame for not calling you back, and I'm sorry. But don't blame it all on me. Perhaps you should take a good hard look at yourself too, Katie Fletcher,' he says firmly before slamming the door behind him.

I lie down on the bed and stare up into the ceiling. Bells is now playing Stevie Wonder. Stevie Wonder is probably the only constant thing she has in her world at the moment. It is her comfort food.

The closeness we shared yesterday, the affection — well, it has all been undone in one swift blow and I am taken aback by just how much I care. I can't let Bells think she isn't important to me. Lord, oh, Lord, I feel dreadful.

★   ★   ★

Emma is now painfully quiet. Please tell me that Sam is in the wrong, I think. Yet deep down I know that there is a lot of truth in what he said. I should have told him about Bells. What was I thinking? Thankfully she

176

does not say, I told you so.

'Is Bells all right?' she asks. 'Do you want me to take a look at her? Her asthma hasn't flared up again?'

'Thanks, Emma. I think she's OK but she has been a bit quiet,' I admit. 'I know she heard what Sam said but I haven't mentioned it to her yet. I've really mucked up, Emma. When Mum and Dad come home I can hardly say Bells is having a great time. She's miserable. God, what have I done?'

'It's not too late,' she says comfortingly.

'You should be telling me, 'I told you so',' I laugh hopelessly.

'Yeah, yeah. I should but I won't. I'm not doing much today,' she says, as if she is brewing an idea, 'so why don't I fill in for you at the shop and you can take Bells out? Give her a good time, try and make up for it?'

'I would love to,' I say. 'She gets so bored in the shop. Are you sure? You really wouldn't mind?'

'No, Jonnie is being boring and spinning records at home so I'm free. Take her shopping. Spend some proper time together.'

'I could get her something for your wedding?'

'Yes, great idea. I haven't even got my dress yet,' she adds.

'I'll help you. Thanks, Ems, I'd really like to do that.'

★   ★   ★

'How about this?' I suggest to Bells, holding up a pale green skirt and an embroidered silk jacket. I peer at the label on the skirt. Size 12. I will have to take it up a good five inches.

'I like it.' She takes the jacket and skirt from me, without really looking at them. She pulls the curtain of the changing room. 'No come in.'

I can hear her stamping her feet in her big black DM boots. She is giving the purple pixie boots a rest today. I turn to apologize to the shop assistant who says nothing. Instead she looks away. Why did I bother to say sorry? What am I actually saying sorry for? I open the curtain slightly. 'Please let me come in,' I ask. 'Please.'

'All right, Katie,' Bells says.

I sit down on a stool in the corner of the cubicle. 'Do you need a hand?'

'No, can do it on own. Can dress myself.'

'I know, I'm sorry.' I don't seem to be able to do anything right, I think hopelessly. 'What's that funny thing you have in your hand?' I ask, desperately trying to break the ice between us.

178

She shrugs.

'Please show me. What is it?'

She holds out her hand. 'You shake hand,' she says impatiently. I place my hand in hers and something vibrates loudly against my palm; it makes the kind of sound you hear when contestants press their buzzers on a game show. 'What's that?' I shriek, withdrawing my hand and shaking it free. 'Do it again!' I giggle once more. Bells laughs with me for the first time this morning. She said nothing on the bus; she didn't even say hello to the other passengers. I found myself longing for her to ask the man wearing a turban his age. 'I like that,' I say. 'Whose hand would you really like to shake? Apart from Beckham's and Stevie Wonder's,' I add, finally beginning to feel more relaxed.

'Tony Blair's,' she says, rocking forward again. 'Vote Tory.'

'You couldn't say that in front of Mr Blair,' I laugh.

'Vote Labour,' she says.

'I'd like to shake Prince William's,' I tell her, and watch with fascination as Bells starts to take off her clothes. My sister's style is what you'd call the 'bag lady' look. She takes off her denim jacket, covered in yet more football badges and stickers. Under this is her bright red Oxford University T-shirt.

'On the catwalk, Isabel Fletcher now models a grubby football shirt covered in more Manchester United badges and stickers.' I smile as I lean back against the wall. 'Aren't you boiling?' I ask as yet another layer comes off. She is like a Russian doll. I am surprised she can even walk. 'Bells, it's the summer. You're dressed for a day in Siberia.'

'Feel cold,' she mutters, extracting the next top, a holey and faintly smelly tank vest. I must get rid of it. It is followed by another stringy vest with more holes.

I do a bit of fake snoring.

'Ha, ha, very funny, Katie,' she repeats, rocking forward with a smile.

I can see the shop girl's pointed toes. She peers around the curtain and immediately shuts it again when she sees me attempting to get the jacket onto Bells. It is too tight over her bosom. Bells has a heavy chest considering she's only four foot ten. Nature over-compensated. If only we could do a swap. I could give her some of my height — I am five foot nine and a half; and she could give me some of her bosom — I am a mean 34 B. 'I know you're ticklish. Do you remember when Mum used to tickle us under the arms after we'd had a bath? You used to hate her putting talcum powder on you. You would scream and scream.' I stand up and instinctively start to unbutton the jacket. It reminds me of dressing and undressing Bells when she was little. 'Oh, Bells, sorry,' I say, pulling away quickly. 'Sorry.'

'All right, Katie. You help me,' she says, nodding her head. 'You are Fashion Queen,' she adds.

I break into a big smile. 'Well, I think that jacket is too small. Do you want me to see if they have a size 14 for you? And shall we try another colour for fun?'

'No, we don't, I'm afraid,' the shop girl whispers loudly through the curtain. I step out and she is hovering over our changing room like a prison guard, not wanting to let us out.

'Sorry? You don't what?' I ask.

'It only comes in that colour, the colour she's in.' She bites her lip and looks away. If this shop had a box room that is where we would have ended up, and I realize I am no better than this girl. She wants to boot us out of here as soon as possible so we do not put off potential customers. How sad. How truly pathetic I am.

'Really? But I'm sure I saw it in another colour.' I walk over to the rails and, sure enough, the jacket does come in a different colour. In fact it comes in about four different shades and patterns. I take another one off

the hanger and walk past the girl purposefully, back into the changing room. 'Bells, try
it on in a different colour,' I say loudly.

I hear more customers coming in. 'Can I
help you or are you just browsing?' a
sugar-sweet voice asks them.

This jacket buttons up smoothly. I stand
back and tell Bells to come out. 'You look
lovely, come on,' I encourage her. We stand
outside, behind a girl with honey-blond hair.
She poses in front of the mirror in pale blue
jeans, holding up a black dress. Her boyfriend
is sitting in the corner of the shop reading
FHM. Bells shuffles forward, trying to catch
a glimpse of herself. The girl moves out of the
way and I thank her. Bells's skirt trails on the
ground like a train. It's the right colour
though because it brings out the green of her
eyes. Every time I look into them I see Mum.
Bells takes another step and then I hear a rip.
Immediately I push her back into the
changing room and examine the dress closely.
There's a large rip above the hem. 'Bugger,' I
mutter, 'bugger.'

'That black dress is fabulous,' the shop girl
is saying at the far side of the room. 'You
can't go wrong.'

'Bugger,' Bells repeats loudly.

'Shh!' I say, hearing footsteps coming
towards our cubicle. 'Get dressed quickly.' I

look at the pile of clothes. Once Bells is ready we walk out to the shop desk. I am ready to tell the girl what happened and buy the skirt. I can mend it at home.

'Are you going to take that?' she enquires, her voice straining to be polite.

'You married?' Bells asks her. 'You have children?' She steps forward to shake the girl's hand. I can see she has her little electrical device ready. I am about to stop her but when I see the expression on the girl's face I change my mind.

'Oh my God!' she yells and recoils as the device goes off, withdrawing her manicured hand in horror. Bells rocks forward in delight and I smile. The girl glares at us both with nothing but disdain now. 'What happened to her?' she spits, now looking directly at me. 'Is she mad or something?'

''She',' I emphasize, 'is called Bells. If you have a question, why don't you ask her?'

'Born with poorly brain and a cleft lip and palate,' Bells says, just as Mum used to tell her.

'If someone asks, you tell them straight. You have nothing to be ashamed of,' I can hear her saying.

'Will you be taking the skirt?' the assistant demands, clearly not interested and still unable to look at Bells.

'I am afraid it has a rip in it so, no, we will not be taking it,' I say, hardly believing that these words are coming out of my mouth. 'We are not interested in damaged goods,' I carry on, relishing every word now. The shop girl claws the outfit away. 'I'm sure there was nothing wrong with it earlier . . . '

'You could always put it in the sale,' I suggest helpfully.

'You not very nice lady,' Bells says to the girl. I walk out, holding onto my sister's arm. 'Not very nice lady,' she repeats, dramatically shaking her head. 'Katie, not very nice lady.'

'No, not nice at all.'

★ ★ ★

I take Bells out for lunch. 'No more shops, Katie,' she'd said. I order a glass of wine and a Coca-Cola.

We still haven't found her an outfit but I am determined not to give up. The main thing was we bonded over the nasty girl in the shop. It felt surprisingly good, taking on that girl. The look on her face! I watch Bells as she looks at the menu. She still has not mentioned anything to me about that conversation with Sam. I wonder how she feels now? She looked so hurt earlier this morning, so vulnerable, shoulders hunched, head hanging low as she walked back to her bedroom.

Why didn't I tell Sam about her? I suppose the reason is simple. We tell friends about the things we feel comfortable with, proud of. I like to share the good times with Sam, I like the glossy world we have created together. Sam the hotshot guy in the City; Katie who runs her own business. There is little room for imperfection in that scenario. Why would I tell him about Bells when I feel so guilty that I ignore her letters, that I am a useless sister, that I resented her so much as a child for taking all the attention away from me? That I did stupid unoriginal things to turn the attention back on me? Talking about Bells brings back a lot of memories I would rather erase. It feeds the corrosive guilt inside me. But I realize none of this makes it forgivable. Sam was right.

'Bells, about what you heard earlier . . . '

'You ashamed,' she says quickly.

When I hear her say it out loud it makes me feel even lousier about myself. 'I am really sorry. Can we make a fresh start? You have one more week with me in London and I'd like to make it up to you.' I realize I cannot say I am not embarrassed when Bells says hello to everything that moves; when she asks people why they have no hair, or why they have 'only the one leg'. I cannot help it. It's an instinct. 'Bells, it was wrong of me not to tell Sam about you, I don't know why I didn't. It was just one of those things you do and then wish you could rewind time.'

Bells doesn't say anything.

'Where's the thingy that vibrates?' I laugh nervously as I take her hand. 'Friends,' I tell her firmly, but still do not feel I have said sorry properly.

I have that uneasy feeling lingering in the pit of my stomach. I start to think of all the times when people asked me at parties, 'Do you have brothers or sisters?' and I replied I was an only child because I could not face the follow-on questions: Where does she live? What does she do? In the evening, when I am getting ready for bed, I say a quiet prayer to God, asking his forgiveness for denying her. That makes me feel better, that I won't go straight down to hell.

I look at Bells who is drinking her Coke so quickly that she starts to make loud slurping noises through her straw. I am not going to look around to see if anyone is staring. But then she makes one final slurping noise which sounds as if it will blow the door down. Without thinking I do glance around, but in fact no-one is looking at us. They are too interested in their own drinks and food. I order her another Coke. 'Bells, the thing Sam said about being ashamed of you . . . ' I start again.

'It's all right, Katie,' she says, looking at the framed poster on the wall.

'No, it's not all right. I am *not* ashamed of you, I promise you. The only person I am ashamed of is myself.'

'Why?'

'Sometimes I find it hard . . . ' I don't know how to end my sentence so I start again. 'To be honest, I was dreading you coming to stay.' I don't look at her because I am scared I am hurting her. 'You remind me of everything I don't have.'

'Don't understand,' she says.

'I don't feel part of our family, I feel like an outsider. Look at your photo album. Pictures of everyone, Mum, Dad . . . not one of me. It's my fault, I'm the one who distances myself. I'm not blaming you, but you, Mum and Dad are so close, there's such a strong bond between you. When you were young I was palmed off to Aunt Agnes, or stayed with Granny Norfolk, or some horrible babysitter looked after me. You needed their help, Mum and Dad had no choice, I know that, but I didn't cope with it very well. I . . . ' My thoughts are scrambled. 'Do you understand what I'm trying to say?'

'Sort of. Difficult for Katie too.'

'Yes, in a totally different way from what you had to go through. I feel so guilty for feeling like this, I don't want to feel the way I do.'

'That's right. You jealous?'

'Yes,' I reply simply, realizing just how perceptive she is. 'I was really jealous of you for having all the attention. I have to get over it, though, I know it's not your fault.'

'You blame Mum?' Bells asks.

'I guess I do. Mum's always taken on the brunt of it. With Dad it's different somehow, we've always been closer. Shall we make a pact?'

'Yes, pact.'

'That we make a fresh start?'

'Friends.' She holds out her hand, with her short little fingers and bitten nails.

'Yes, friends,' I tell her, clutching that tiny hand.

18

It's nearly six o'clock and I am making fresh price tags with black velvet ribbon. Eve has just left, picked up by Hector who was not at all what I'd expected: short and oily like a sardine.

Eve bought a baby chandelier for the shop today, with shimmering cut-glass drops. She also found some ivory silk cushions trimmed with black lace to decorate the cream chaise longue in the corner of the shop. Very *Moulin Rouge*. We work well together because she has a real flair for design and enjoys making the shop look lavishly aesthetic. We have similar tastes which is lucky.

'Where's Mark?' Bells mentions again.

'Since five minutes ago, I still don't know,' I reply. I can see she is getting restless. She is pacing the shop floor, making fists with her hands. 'Bored,' she says again.

'We'll be going home soon. Draw me something,' I suggest, handing her my notepad. I have a papier-mâché pot on my desk with pens and pencils in it. 'Take one,' I say.

'Mark married?' she asks, stopping the

pacing for a second.

'No, I don't think so. In fact, I'm sure not,' I add.

'Girlfriend?'

'I don't know.'

'Pets? He have a dog?'

'Bells! I don't know. You should have asked him.'

I wonder if Bells misses 'going out' with men, not being able to have a relationship. Does it even occur to her? This is when I feel guilty about envying her. There is so much she cannot have which I take for granted. I wonder what she thinks about Sam and me? She probably isn't envious when all we do is argue. She still says she doesn't like him.

'Mark nice man.'

I can see she is not going to let him slip from her mind. 'Draw me a picture of him,' I say, pleased that she looks interested in that idea. She takes the pad and a pencil and sits down on the wooden stair. I continue looping ribbon through the tags. I like doing this kind of job at the end of a day. 'We going to see Mark again?' she asks as she draws earnestly.

'Maybe.'

She claps her hands together.

Mark scribbled down his telephone number just before he left. The piece of paper is still in my handbag. He told me he was around if I needed him as it was the school summer holiday. I could call him. We could go out. Sam doesn't need to know. Mark is Bells's friend after all.

★ ★ ★

I have thought a lot about Mark and our pizza evening together. It has been a ray of light in the last few days. 'I have a friend who has a brother,' he told me, after the tears and after I had explained how foolish I felt for not confiding in Sam about Bells. 'I had never met the brother until I went to their sister's wedding. I was the very informal photographer,' he added with a modest cough. 'I was in the kitchen with the brother whose name was Ben, and he seemed pretty normal to me, sitting there in his smart jacket and tie, until he asked his father if he could have a Scotch egg.' Mark smiled slightly. 'I thought it was strange,' he furrowed his eyebrows, 'a man of thirty-something asking his father if he could have a Scotch egg, but then I thought nothing more of it until he turned to me, quite randomly, and said that their dog should be put down.'

I laugh out loud, remembering. 'What so funny?' Bells asks as she walks over to my desk clutching the pad.

'Something Mark told me.'

'Mark nice man, isn't he?' She is doing that excited thing with her hands again, as if they are dancing together.

'He *is* a very nice man,' I echo. 'Back to your portrait.' And I am surprised when she sits down obediently and carries on drawing.

'I was amazed my friend had never told me much about him,' Mark continued. 'Baffling, really. I had known him for six years. Been to university with him,' he uttered incredulously.

I smile, thinking about that word 'baffling'.

Then came the awful question which all of us ask though we wish we didn't. 'And what do you do?' I was focusing on the large hole Mark had in the elbow of his navy jumper. It looked like an ancient Marks & Spencer one that needed either replacing or a good darning.

'I'm a teacher, English and drama.'

There is something romantic about being a drama teacher, I think now, tapping my red biro against the desk.

'Really?' I asked. Why do we say, 'Really?' Did I expect Mark to stick his tongue out and say, 'No, only joking'? 'What age?' I continued.

'Teenagers. I like a challenge.' He smiled wryly. 'The holidays are great too.'

With his tousled light brown hair which has

192

no parting whatsoever, the small mole on the right side of his face, even the nerdy round glasses he wears, I reckon a lot of the girls would have a crush on Mark. I had a big crush on my English teacher, Mr Lawrence. He was South African, with a chiselled face and a dark beard with the odd streak of grey in it. I used to imagine him asking me to stay behind after class to go through my essay with me. When all the other pupils trailed out of the classroom I imagined him saying to me, hand on his heart, 'Katie, I can no longer suppress my feelings. I am passionately in love with you.' He would then sweep the contents of his desk to the floor — pencil sharpener, paper, textbooks, register, would all crash to the ground and we would kiss each other urgently.

'Where have you been today then?' I asked Mark, still looking at his holey jumper.

'The library.'

'Really?'

'I took the day off. I'm trying to write a book,' he said. 'I find it difficult working from home, too many distractions like daytime television. 'At nine-ten we can show you how to make yourself look like a Hollywood actor in less time than it takes to boil an egg,'' he said, imitating Lorraine Kelly.

I smile to myself. I often hear Bells

watching *GMTV* in the morning.

'There's Wimbledon too. If Henman's playing I have to leave the house, my nerves can't cope.'

He asked me about my shop. I told him about my time at art college and working for a West End theatre, designing and making costumes, followed by working for a fashion designer for three years. She went bust eventually but taught me a lot about the business. Bells had come downstairs then in her pyjamas, clutching her photograph album. He turned his attention to her as I made a salad to go with our pizzas. They talked about the tennis, Mark said he had the hots for Sue Barker. He asked her about football. I couldn't help noticing the ease between them. Bells was laughing with him and at one point she stroked his arm affectionately, something she has never done with me.

Mark looked at all her pictures slowly. 'Who are they?' he asked.

'Mary Veronica, Ted, in Paris,' Bells said proudly. I went over to have a look. Mary Veronica and Bells were standing outside a café with their thumbs up. Ted was in the middle with his arms crossed. 'We climbed Eiffel Tower,' she told us.

'I would love to do that. Now, who is this?

She is very beautiful.'

'My mum,' Bells said. 'That's my dad. That's Budge, he plays for my football team.'

'Katie, how come there are no pictures of you?' Mark asked, sounding surprised.

★　★　★

I start to clear my desk. It's late and I want to go home. What have we got to eat tonight? Only today I popped out of the shop to post some letters and found myself hoping I might bump into Mark.

Well, he knows where I am. He knows where the shop is too. If he wants to see me, I am sure he will pass by. 'Let's go, Bells. What are we going to do tonight?'

'Sainsbury's? Cook tonight, organic night.'

I pull a face. 'Let's just get a video and takeaway.'

'Mark likes Sainsbury's.'

Good point. 'OK, actually yes, I do need some vodka. What do you want to cook?'

★　★　★

Bells and I are sitting like plum puddings on the sofa, sharing a tub of toffee ice cream with a slice of chocolate biscuit cake and watching the old black-and-white film

Titanic. Earlier Bells cooked us a wild mushroom and aubergine risotto. She showed me how to prepare the aubergines, slicing them and sprinkling them with salt, telling me we had to leave them for half an hour before cooking them.

There was no sign of Mark at Sainsbury's, just the same old man with his trolley of oranges, wishing everyone the 'best of luck'. Bells tells me she has watched this movie at least one hundred times, it is the favourite film in Wales.

'About to hit iceberg.' She claps as she leans forward and laughs outrageously.

'The wallies! Bells, it's coming, it's coming!' I sit forward too.

'Rewind,' she says. I pick up the controls and rewind. I hear the front door shut and Sam coming upstairs. For a second I am actually disappointed he is back.

'SMACK!' Bells cries out. Sam stands at the door, shakes his head disapprovingly and walks out. I follow him downstairs to the kitchen. 'Sam, hello, good evening, nice to see you, did you have a good day? What is this silent treatment?' He is acting like a boy who doesn't get the attention he deserves.

He sits down at the kitchen table which is covered with a baking tray, a greasy butter wrapper, tin of cocoa, digestive biscuits and a bag of sultanas.

'Sorry,' I say, quickly beginning to clear the mess. 'Bells and I made a chocolate biscuit cake for our pudding. I thought we'd have time to clear up before you got home.' I walk past him and put the dirty bowl, licked wooden spoon and tray in the sink.

'Katie, I'm sorry. I'm behaving like an idiot.'

I turn around and lean against the oven. 'Yes, you are. We both are. I'm sorry too. I was scared when Bells ran off. I feel responsible for her, but I shouldn't have taken it out on you. Everything you said, about me not telling you about her,' I scratch my forehead, 'you were right.'

'Take a long hard look at yourself, Katie Fletcher,' he imitates himself.

I sit down next to him and Sam slides his fingers in between mine. 'We are OK, aren't we?' I ask.

'I think so. 'Course we are. Come here.'

'Katie!' I hear Bells shouting.

I pull away from him. 'Where are you going?' he asks.

'To watch the rest of the movie. Coming?'

'No,' he says awkwardly. 'I'm going to make myself something to eat and clear up this mess.'

'Sam, Bells won't bite.'

'I've seen *Titanic*.'

'Doesn't matter, so have I. Bells has seen it a thousand times!' I laugh, wanting him to change his mind. 'Come on, Sam, please come. Bells will clear this up later, she loves washing up.'

'Hot soapy water,' she says as her hands plunge into the foamy basin, a look of extraordinary delight on her face. However much mess Bells creates, she always tidies up after herself. She makes her own bed because that's what they do at home. She cooks her own meals. And even though her room is full of posters and music and looks like a car boot sale, it's an organized chaos. She knows exactly where everything is and gets cross if I move anything. The only thing she's not so hot on is changing her clothes. She doesn't seem to mind wearing the same old thing, day in, day out.

'NO!' Sam shouts at me. 'I will clear it up NOW.'

All the tension between us returns but I don't want another argument. I leave him in the kitchen.

'Katie,' he calls after me.

'About to hit iceberg, Katie,' Bells tells me again. 'Katie, watch.'

I sit down with her. 'The wallies! What do you call them, Bells?'

'Wallies.' She laughs hysterically, in short sharp infectious trills. I watch her face light up as she stares at the screen.

'SMACK!' we both laugh together. 'Rewind.'

19

I had the strangest dream that I was singing 'Purple Rain' in front of Simon Cowell, dressed only in a purple feather boa. He told me that I wasn't quite what he had in mind. I clearly did not have the X-factor. I smile to myself. I often have celebrity dreams. I have been out with Harrison Ford, Tom Cruise picked me over Kate Moss and Gwynneth Paltrow is one of my closest friends. I flick the kettle on. Sam has already escaped from the house. His alarm clock went off so early that I thought it was still the middle of the night.

'Morning, how are you, Bells?' I yawn widely. 'Sleep well?'

'Bored.' She opens a can of Diet Coke.

'You're bored? What do you expect to be doing at seven thirty in the morning?'

She shrugs. She is wearing her grey baggy tracksuit with her red Oxford University T-shirt which now has chocolate stains down the front. 'I need to put some washing on,' I say flatly, still trying to wake up.

I open the blind and squeeze my eyes shut. The sun streams through the window. I stretch my arms out above my head and let out a great big sigh. Bells continues to eat her chopped apricots and figs quietly, occasionally prodding the milk-bottle sculpture. She is listening to Stevie Wonder. Poor old Stevie never has a holiday. I want to turn him off, it is too early. Déjà vu screams at me. We get ourselves so tied up in a routine that we spin round and round like an old pair of cardboard socks in a washing machine cycle. Wake up, go for a run, eat breakfast, go to work, come home, go out, go to bed. I'm not complaining, I like my life, but it is so ordered and planned. I am like a robot.

I am going to skip my run this morning. I am going to make myself a bacon sandwich for breakfast with lots of tomato ketchup. Go on Katie, be wild! I make an even bolder step by deciding I will take two days off in a row. I'll see if Eve doesn't mind being on her own. I think she likes being in charge. 'We are going out today,' I tell Bells, already planning the day in my mind.

'Where? The shop?'

'No, it's a surprise, you'll see,' I say, trying to hide my own excitement. 'Get dressed quickly. Look at the sun, Bells. It's a beautiful day.'

She starts to fidget with her hands, as if she is conducting her muddled thoughts. 'Upstairs!' I tell her again. 'Your dungarees

are in the airing cupboard, I washed them for
you, and it's hot today so wear something
cool. Don't wear five smelly vests!'

'Where we going?'

'It's a surprise.'

'Can Mark come?'

'Yes! Brilliant idea.' I dig into my handbag
and give her the piece of paper, now
crumpled and torn at the edges, with his
number on it. 'Ring him,' I say.

* * *

I feel a tiny twinge of guilt for not being at
work again, but it disappears when I see
Bells. She rocks forward excitedly, tapping
her hands together. After queuing for an hour
and a half we are finally standing in our glass
capsule, propelled one hundred feet into the
air and surrounded by tourists. Mark wasn't
at home. I was ridiculously excited by the
thought of seeing him again but at the same
time relieved there was no answer. It's nice to
spend time with Bells, just the two of us.

'Not moving?' Bells jitters. 'Broken down,
broken down!'

'We are moving, I promise. Apparently
we're moving about one quarter of a metre
per second,' I tell her, putting Sam's
binoculars around her neck. 'Take a look.' I

stand close behind her. She smells of Persil and lime after her shower. 'You can see all of London from here, Bells,' I say, pointing to different landmarks. 'Doesn't that make you feel tiny? Like an ant.' She is breathing deeply. 'There's Big Ben . . . the Houses of Parliament . . . look, you can see Buckingham Palace where the Queen lives. Isn't it incredible?'

'Yes, Katie, yes.'

Bells stops looking through the binoculars and puts her hands behind her head, rocking forward again then turning to face the other way. I sit down on the bench in the middle of our pod and stretch out my legs, the sun beating down on my face. I'm wearing my black and white spotted sundress with flat-heeled white leather sandals, and my hair is scooped up into a loose ponytail. The freckles across my nose have come out in their full glory.

'MIRA! MIRA!' shout the Spanish group sharing our capsule, running over to where Bells is standing. She flaps her hands, getting caught up in their excitement. 'Mira!' They point into the distance. Bells looks in their direction and then looks at me and then turns to them again. They run to the other side in a stampede frenzy and she follows them.

A Japanese couple are taking pictures of

one another at every possible opportunity with their Polaroid camera. 'Ah,' they sigh repeatedly as they look at the pictures. They ask me if I will take a picture of them both and link arms as the flash goes off. Bells rushes over to me and they offer to take a picture of us. Bells is clapping her hands against her thighs now, then she runs to the side of the capsule and calls to me, 'Look, Katie, look! London. Where Sam's house?'

'Turn around for a second,' I say. She swings round and I signal to the Japanese man to take our picture quickly before she runs off again.

$$\star \quad \star \quad \star$$

Bells and I are lying on a pale yellow checked rug in St James's Park, looking up into the clear blue sky. We have just finished eating our picnic: vegetable samosas and a Diet Coke for Bells, a Pimm's and a packet of Marks & Spencer sushi for me, and two large chunks of chocolate biscuit cake.

'There are no clouds, Bells. Just clear blue sky like the sea.'

'No fluffy clouds,' she echoes. 'In Wales we have sea.'

'Do you miss Wales?'

'Yes.' She tilts her head. 'No. A bit.'

'What do you miss?'

'Miss Ted.'

'Who's Ted?'

'My friend.' She laughs mischievously, restlessly kicking her legs and knocking over the cups.

I lean on my elbow and look at her. 'Really? So Ted's the lucky man. You've kept that very quiet. You're a dark horse, Bells.'

'A dark horse,' she laughs back at me. 'Ted just friend, my friend. Ted has parrot like Grandpa.'

'Are you happy there?'

'Yes, Katie, yes. Sometimes sad,' she adds.

'Why sad?'

'Miss home, miss Mum, Dad.'

I notice she does not add me. I bite my lip hard. Why would she? Still, it surprises me how much I want to be added onto the list. 'I'm sure they miss you too,' I tell her. 'Let's give them a call now, tell them we've been up in the sky.'

I take the mobile out of my bag and punch in the numbers. Their phone is switched off. I knew this would happen. They are hopeless. I should have insisted Dad or Mum give me the Walters' number. Why wouldn't they? 'Not there,' I tell Bells. 'How often do they call you in Wales?'

'One time a week.'

Well, they've called twice since she has been staying with me, yet each time have sounded oddly distanced. Why won't this nagging feeling that something is wrong go away? 'Tell me more about Wales. What do you do all day?'

'Go to college Monday.'

'What do you do there?'

'Learn respect.'

'Respect?'

'Towards other people,' she tells me. 'Learn health and safety too.'

'What's all that about?'

'In kitchen. Fire rules and safety.'

'Oh, right. That's important when you're the Queen of the Kitchen, isn't it?'

'That's right. Me the Queen.'

'Do you enjoy college?'

'Yes, love college.'

'What else do you do?'

'I go to football club each week, watch my team play. Watch Budge play. Budge very handsome. I cook. Ted and I make stuff, weave and paint, we watch football videos. Clean room, make beds.'

'Are you on a rota system? You clean and make the beds one week, Ted the next?'

'Yes, that's right, Katie, that's right. Rota.'

'Do you want to clean my room and make my bed?' I ask her with a smile.

'Very funny, Katie!'

I realize how little I know about Bells's life. I know a tiny fragment from her childhood and that's about it. I've never wanted to be involved, but now . . . 'I can see why you get bored with me. You've hardly done anything apart from the last two days.'

'Sometimes bored, that's right, Katie.' She laughs. 'You marry Sam?'

I try to dodge the question. 'How did you learn to cook so well, Bells?'

'You marry Sam?' she asks again, quite insistently.

'I can't see myself marrying anyone, not yet anyway. Bells, you're not burning, are you? We'd better put some cream on, just in case.' I dig into my basket for a tube of sunblock. 'Sit still.' I apply it gently to her forehead and cheeks. She doesn't flinch. Her skin is as pale as a china doll's and soft as cashmere. As I look at her, it is hard to believe she is twenty-two, only seven years younger than me.

'What you looking at?'

'YOU,' I say, as I wipe the chocolate crusts from the corners of her mouth and then dab a large blob of cream on her nose and laugh.

'Not funny, Katie.'

'I think it is *very* funny,' I say to her as I start to pack up our things.

Bells and I sit on the bus and it's rush hour, the traffic is as slow as a slug. After our picnic we went shopping along the King's Road. Bells was like Peggy on the lead, I had to drag her into a few of the shops, apart from a charity one where we found her a pair of red shoes with clover-shaped patterns embroidered onto them. If there was no-one helpful in any of the shops I simply 'threw in the towel', as Sam would say. Why should they see my Visa card? In the end, with the help of a lovely shop assistant, we found a dark red and gold Chinese dress with a jacket for Bells. 'You like it?' she asked the girl.

'I love it.' The girl beamed at her, kneeling down and adjusting the hem. 'I think it's dead stylish, you are going to be the belle of the ball.' I thought my heart might burst as I watched Bells looking proudly at herself in the mirror, her outfit finished off with the shoes she'd bought. I found myself wishing Mum could see her looking so trendy and smart. When Bells was out of earshot I thanked the girl. 'For what?' She looked almost put out. 'It's my job.'

'You know what I mean,' I added.

'I've had more fun today than during my whole time here,' she said. 'And I've been

208

here for over a year.'

I bet you that nice shop assistant goes home tonight and tells her flatmate/boyfriend/whatever that she managed to find a really great outfit for a slightly unusual customer.

'Pull my finger,' Bells says. I turn and look at her dubiously. The moment I pull it she sticks out her tongue and starts to roar with laughter. The grey-haired woman sitting opposite stares at us strangely and then returns to her paperback.

'Pull mine.' I hold out one long tapered finger. I am wearing the three-band silver ring Sam gave to me and have painted my fingernails a pale pink. I have my father's hands with the same long thin fingers. He also has very prominent blue veins. Dad says we have royalty in our blood. Bells leans forward to touch my finger.

'Bad luck, missed,' I exclaim, quickly withdrawing my hand.

She laughs and the woman opposite stares directly at Bells with cold blue eyes. I want to tell her to stop staring. When I was much younger, I hated people staring at Bells in the supermarket or on the street or at the bus stop. I myself am guilty of wanting to hide my sister for fear of being embarrassed by her, yet I am surprised by how much it still angers me when people are rude or stare. Who are they to judge anyone? I shift in my seat. She is still looking at us. It makes me feel uncomfortable but at least Bells doesn't appear to notice, does she? Mum and Dad used to tell strangers what was wrong with her. Dad always explained to me, 'It puts them at their ease. It's normally fear or ignorance that makes people stare. You have to work hard to reassure them. It shouldn't be like that, but that's the way it is.'

'Oh, dear.' I shake my head solemnly at Bells. 'Too slow, miss a go.'

'Not funny, Katie!' she cries excitedly, clapping her hands.

'Pull my finger, come on.' She misses again. 'Sorry, if you snooze, you lose.' That's an expression of Sam's. I doubt he meant it to be used in exactly the same context, however. 'Shit, this is our stop!' I grab our bags and Bells follows. 'Mind the step.'

I wish I had said something, I think to myself, as the sour-faced lady bristles and looks down at her book dismissively.

★   ★   ★

Bells points animatedly to each tray behind the counter — couscous with pine nuts and peppers, carrot cake with a whipped orange and butter icing, warm ciabatta bread with

210

olives or spinach, rice cakes with garlic. We buy some ginger to make a sticky ginger pudding 'like the one Mum makes', she tells me. I buy some pistachio nuts, fresh bread and olives. Emma's coming over tonight especially to see Bells.

'You think Mum eats nice food in France?' Bells asks me.

'I reckon she is eating like a queen and she doesn't even have to do the washing-up.'

Bells rocks forward. 'No hot soapy water?'

'I am not going near those chillies,' I tell her when she asks Eddie for three red ones. She wants to make a chilli sauce to go over her vegetarian sausages. 'The last time I chopped them I forgot to wash my hands, picked my nose, and boy, did it kill!' I laugh. 'Sam almost had to ring for a doctor.'

'Not funny, Katie.' She comes forward and touches me briefly on the shoulder.

'No, it wasn't!' I carry on, still glowing from her touch. It is the first time she has initiated affection and it makes me feel as if someone has wrapped a warm soft towel around me.

'It was supposed to be a romantic evening and I had to spend the entire night with my head dunked in a bowl of cold water.'

'That's disgusting, Katie,' says Eddie. 'Is that all, girls?' I had forgotten he was there.

He is wearing a short blue apron which shows off his hairy legs, finished off with brown sandals and socks.

'You wearing anything under that?' Bells asks him.

'Wouldn't you like to know?' he replies and winks at her. 'How much longer are you here for, Bells?'

'Two day.'

'You make sure you come and say goodbye, won't you?' he says.

★ ★ ★

'No, I'd prefer the table in the corner, please . . . um, say about seven-thirty . . . yep, thanks,' I hear Sam muttering as Bells and I come into the kitchen. He puts the phone down. 'I am going to take you and Isabel out tomorrow evening, for her last night in London,' he announces proudly.

'Are you?' I look at him strangely, wondering what has suddenly brought all of this on.

'I am,' he declares, and looks at Bells for a response.

'Where are you taking us, then? Bells, did you hear that? Sam's taking you and me . . . ' I am tempted to add 'the two bad smells' because he hasn't come near us since Bells arrived, ' . . . out on the town.'

She nods.

Sam looks disappointed. 'We're going to my favourite restaurant. They have the best wine list in town,' he clicks his tongue against the roof of his mouth, 'and serve top-quality steak . . . '

'Bells doesn't drink,' I can't help adding.

'Don't eat meat,' she finishes.

I feel bad for sounding ungrateful. 'Sam, that's a lovely idea, thanks.'

'Thank you,' Bells murmurs, turning Stevie Wonder on.

Sam and I go upstairs. 'I have had one of the nicest days,' I tell him, sitting down on our bed and kicking my shoes off.

'Really? At work?' He lies down next to me.

'No, with Bells. We went on the London Eye, had a picnic, went shopping and Bells bought an outfit for Emma's wedding. I really feel I'm getting to know her.'

'What d'you mean, getting to know her? She's your sister.'

'What I mean is . . . '

'I'm going to the gym tonight, want to come?' he asks.

'No.' I shake my head. 'You go.'

'I need to buy a new pair of trainers,' he's muttering. 'Remember, we're going away for the weekend when Bells leaves.' There is a book on hip hotels on his side of the bed which he now picks up, turning to the marked page. 'I booked the Moroccan Suite, Katie. Look at it, it's beautiful. Next weekend, honey, we need to get away. *Look* at this place.' He points at the picture again. 'Where are my trainers?'

The hotel bedroom looks like a mini-paradise. A four-poster bed with white linen sheets, pale blue shutters, and creamy blue tiles with ornate patterns in the bathroom. Tiny windows looking out onto the gardens. It is very tempting. 'It looks nice . . . '

'Nice? I don't do 'nice', Katie. I do 'amazing'. The place is at its most beautiful now, in the summer when all the roses are out. This hotel ticks *all* the boxes. I mean, even Madonna has stayed there,' Sam boasts. 'I always ask which celebrities have stayed. Remember my theory? If they're soap stars it generally means it's naff. But if Madonna has stayed, I think we can be sure it's going to be a classy joint. I even asked if we could have the same bedroom she stayed in and they said they would see what they could do. Fancy that, me and the missus staying in Madonna's suite.'

I smile. 'You are . . . ' I am about to say 'a sad name-dropper', but then I stop myself when I look at him. Sam's mouth and eyes have not flickered at all. Is he being completely serious? Normally, am I impressed by all of this? Yes, I suppose I am. All I want to say to him now is, Who cares?

'Sam, I had completely forgotten about our weekend away,' I start hesitantly.

'That doesn't matter.' Finally he finds his trainers in his gym bag that he takes to work. 'It's all booked. Done and dusted. All you have to do is enjoy it. There's a spa and beauty room. You can have a seaweed wrap, apparently it gets rid of the build-up of toxins. You girls are funny. Right, I've got to run.'

He stands in front of the mirror to make some last-minute adjustments to his hair. 'I'm looking forward to having this place to ourselves again.'

'Um . . . me too.'

'No offence to your sister, nothing like that, but, well, you know what I mean.'

She touched my arm today and it felt wonderful, I want to shout. You should have seen her expression when I took her on the London Eye. It was one of pure joy, and I was responsible for that. We played silly games on the bus and it was fun fooling around with her. Today made me feel alive. I want to tell all of this to Sam, I am aching to tell someone; but I don't think it will mean anything to him.

I will tell Emma all about it when she comes over this evening. I can't wait to tell her. Only a few weeks ago I was telling her how much I was dreading Bells coming to stay. Now I want to tell her how stupid I've been, how *wrong* I've been. How silly I was to worry about my sister meeting Sam. I want to tell Emma how well we are getting on.

Sam kisses me, bringing me back to reality. 'In a few days it's back to just you and me, babe.' As I kiss him, all I can think is that I should be feeling relieved that the two weeks are nearly up, shouldn't I? And yet, instead, the prospect of waving goodbye to Bells leaves me feeling strangely hollow.

20

'When are you, er, going home, Isabel?' asks Mr Vickers. He was walking past the shop after he had finished his shift at work and Bells rushed out to greet him.

'Tomorrow, catch train from Paddington. Do your funny thing,' Bells demands.

He looks at me nervously. He doesn't do his impersonation of a man on the train, holding onto the bar, which I know he would do if I weren't in the same room.

I clear my throat. 'Mr Vickers, would you like to stay for a cup of tea?'

This question sets him in a spin. 'Er, er . . . ' He looks at Bells.

'Stay, Mr Vickers,' she insists.

'How very, er, kind, er, of you. You are so very kind. Yes, please.'

I leave them downstairs while I go to the box room. Eve nipped out to get some milk, she'll be back in a minute. I make the tea and take it downstairs, only to find Mr Vickers parading about in front of Bells. He appears to transform himself into a confident comedian when he is performing in front of an audience. 'Who is, er, this?' He clears his throat, puckers his lips and places his large purple hands behind his back. 'These plants look very interesting, well worth talking to.'

'Don't know. Who?' Bells punches his arm for an answer.

'Hello, Mr Vickers,' Eve says as she returns with the milk.

I hand him a mug of tea and a custard cream. Bells loves custard creams.

'Thank you so much,' he repeats. 'Do you, er, know who it is?' He looks at each of us in turn.

'I did not see you do it properly,' Eve says. 'Can you do it once more?'

He looks flattered by the attention and prepares himself again, putting on a distinguished voice, his hands clasped behind his back. 'These plants look very interesting, well worth talking to.'

'Oh, my goodness,' Eve says, jumping up and down, 'I know who you are, I know this voice.'

'So do I! Prince Charles,' I leap in before her.

Mr Vickers's face breaks into a smile and I find myself smiling back at him. His eyes are sunken and look grey and weary, as if they have seen too much nastiness in the world, but when he smiles his entire face changes. He has an innate goodness like Uncle Roger, a face that would never tell a lie. 'Er, yes, you are right, er . . . '

'Katie. Call me Katie,' I tell him.

'Another one!' Bells is clapping her hands.

'What is your, er, favourite hobby?' Mr Vickers asks her.

Bells looks at me. 'You like cooking?' I suggest.

'Cooking,' she repeats.

He is thinking. 'I have one.' He picks up his custard cream and takes a bite. 'Delicious,' he drawls. 'It is just the right consistency.' He licks his lips. 'Well, after much ruminating and cogitating I think the . . . '

'I know,' I burst out.

'*Masterchef* man,' cuts in Bells. 'I know!' She is jumping around.

'Lloyd Grossman,' I finish.

'Er, correct.' I notice his stammer returns when he is not performing.

'Another!' Bells demands just as Henrietta and her mother walk into the shop. They gawp at the strange party around my desk drinking tea. 'Do stay, Mr Vickers, and finish your tea.' I smile politely at him. 'My bank manager came round,' I tell Hen and her mother, signalling to Mr Vickers. 'It was so kind of you to come and see me personally,' I add, smiling at him.

That wipes the looks off their faces.

Bells, Sam and I sit in the corner of the restaurant looking at the menus. I take another sip of my vodka and tonic, and start to crunch a large piece of ice.

'Don't do that, Katie. It's bad for your teeth,' Sam says twitchily. A couple enter the restaurant. He casts his eyes in their direction and his shoulders visibly drop with relief when he registers that he does not know them.

'Hello, Katie.' Bells holds my hand and I can see she has the funny toy in her palm. As we touch the vibration goes off loudly. We both laugh.

'What *is* that?' Sam furrows his brow. Bells holds out her hand towards him. 'Um, the waiter's coming over, do it later, yeah?' he mutters.

'I'd like the chicken, please,' I tell the smooth-haired waiter when he stands at our table with his pad poised.

'Chicken?' I feel someone kick me under the table.

'Sam, that hurt.'

'Katie, I'm here to spoil you and Bells. We can eat chicken any old day. Be a bit more adventurous.' He looks at the waiter as if to say, Women, hey! Can't take them anywhere.

'What are the specials?'

'We have salmon, or the smoked haddock risotto is very popular. I would also recommend the medallion of pork.'

Sam closes his menu smoothly. 'Thank you, but I think I'll go for the beef en *croûte*, please.'

'Certainly, sir, a popular choice,' the waiter affirms. 'How would you like it cooked?'

'Rare, please. You can't beat top-class beef.' Sam looks at me again. 'Choose something different, Katie.'

'But I love chicken, Sam.' I don't like the sound of my voice, a whimpering pathetic little sound. The kind children make when they say they don't want to eat their carrots and peas.

He smiles at me as he touches his chin. 'Kitty-kins, you're a funny little mouse sometimes, a creature of habit.' He scans the menu for me. 'How about the scallops instead?'

'Yes, you're right,' I say firmly. 'The scallops would be lovely.'

'How about you, Isabel?' he asks.

Bells has been noticeably quiet. She looks awkward. Perhaps she is quiet because she is leaving tomorrow?

'You have chips?'

Sam's face drops and now I kick him under

the table. 'Yes, I'm sure you have chips, don't you?' I ask the waiter.

'Of course.'

'Why don't you have the homemade beef burger with chips?' Sam says.

'Bells is a vegetarian,' I say yet again. Does he never listen?

He raises his hands in a gesture of apology. 'Sorry I spoke,' he mumbles.

'Bells, why don't you have the vegetarian lasagne, with chips on the side?'

It worries me how quiet she is. I wonder if she is nervous about catching the train tomorrow?

'Can choose my own food,' she shouts, banging her elbow against the table.

'Bells, I'm sorry,' I say. Sometimes I slip into talking to her like a child and I have to stop it. She is twenty-two.

'Would like risotto,' she states boldly.

'You order the wine, Sam.' I push my chair back and it hits the wall. 'There's no space,' I exclaim irritably, 'is this the only table they had?' It feels like we have the children's table in the dark corner.

'I'm afraid so.'

'Really? But there are tables outside. It's warm tonight.'

He starts to rub his nose. 'Let's stay here, shall we?' His mouth starts to twitch too. 'So, what have you two been up to today? Your last night, hey, Isabel. Bet you're dying to get home.'

I know Sam is trying but he just irritates me.

'Mr Vickers said goodbye. I like Mr Vickers, nice man.'

'Mr Vickers? Who is he now? I'll just check I ordered the right wine,' Sam swiftly changes the subject. I look ahead and see a vaguely familiar man joining the group in front of us. Sam is now lifting the menu to shield his face. His mobile rings. Still holding on to the menu with one hand, he picks his phone up with the other. I start to talk to Bells and Sam excuses himself quickly, darting through the doors that lead downstairs to the loos.

After five minutes he still hasn't returned. 'Bells.' She holds out her hand again and the buzzer goes off. I touch her arm. 'Be back in a minute.'

'All right,' she says flatly.

I pull the door and then see a great PUSH sign in front of me.

'Oh, mate, this is a nightmare.' I stand at the top of the stairs, then quietly tiptoe down a couple and lean over the banister just far enough to allow me to see him. Sam is by the cigarette machine, his back to me, one hand leaning against the wall. He starts laughing loudly. I think he is talking to Maguire. 'It's Isabel's last night and I seriously, I mean seriously, mate, need to get back in the good books with Katie. I've avoided them for a fortnight.' Sam is silent; he must be listening to something very profound. 'Too right, Maguire, hopefully more action between the sheets when she's gone. Jesus, it's been like the Gobi Desert!'

I open my mouth and close it again.

'I tell you, mate, when she told me her sister was coming to stay I didn't expect this.' He pauses as he listens. 'Yeah, yeah, yeah . . . absolutely.' He starts pacing the floor. 'Too right, Maguire. This isn't what I signed up for.'

I don't know what to think.

'Yeah, I'll see how it goes. I mean, I do love her. At least, I think I do, and I know she's crazyeeee about me.'

Sharp intake of breath. Who does he think he is? I want to hit him so hard, or better still put him in the stocks and throw rotten eggs at him, in front of Maguire and all his work colleagues.

'Look, mate, better go and butter them up . . . Back to my post, yeah, you know how it is.'

★ ★ ★

The food still hasn't arrived when Sam returns. 'Sorry about that,' he says, 'a client, I had to take the call.'

On the surface I remain calm, but the pit of my stomach is a seething knot of fury. 'Really? Who was it?'

'No-one you'd know, babes. All very boring stuff.'

'What did they want?' I ask casually.

'What's with all the questions? It was a guy from work, that's all. Crikey, Isabel, your sister can be a pain, can't she?' He laughs, hoping Bells will follow.

I watch Sam and can tell he is still preoccupied with the group in front of us. He is drinking quickly.

'Do you know those people, Sam? You keep on looking over?' I ask expectantly.

'No, I don't believe I do. Why don't we eat outside? You're right, it is warm tonight.' He gets up and takes his jacket.

'No, let's stay here.' I smile sweetly at him. 'Look, our food is arriving.'

Sam grimaces as he sits down again.

'Lakemore?' a man calls across to him then. 'It *is* you! Good God,' he bellows.

'Hi,' Sam says, trying to sound surprised, and puts up his hand, his cheeks burning with colour. The stout man with glasses comes over to our table. He is small and round, with curly brown hair and sideburns. I smile at him and wait for Sam to introduce us. After a second-too-long gap I do it myself. 'Hello, I'm Katie.'

'Yes, sorry, this is Katie. Katie, Colin Lucker.'

'Hello, Katie, wonderful to meet you.'

'Hi, Colin.'

'Hello,' Bells says, holding out her hand.

'Hello, er . . . ? Now who might you be?'

'This is my sister, Isabel,' I tell him.

'I'm Bells,' she corrects me.

'Hello, Bells.' Colin shakes her hand. 'Oh, my, what was that?' he laughs nervously.

I am about to tell him when Sam starts to laugh outrageously. 'Isn't it hilarious, Colin? She's a funny one is our Isabel.'

'Better be getting back to my table.' He shuffles back a few steps. 'Nice to see you again, Sammy boy. We must catch up soon.'

'Who was that, Sam?'

'Just my old boss,' he says, cowering behind the menu again and taking another large gulp of wine.

'Really? What a coincidence. We could join them for coffee.' The knot is unravelling in its own way. 'Mr Lucker?' I call out loudly.

I can see Sam shifting uneasily. 'Christ, Katie. Leave it, will you.'

'Er, yes?' Colin Lucker answers tentatively.

Sam now kicks me so hard I don't dare to continue. 'Sorry, Colin, we'll leave you to your dinner, please ignore us,' Sam says to him cheerfully. 'Women! Won't even let you eat in peace!' He rolls his eyes then turns back to face me. 'What is your problem?' he asks in a low whisper.

'You,' I reply. I didn't want to say anything, not on Bells's last night, but I can't help it. I lean closer towards him. 'I heard everything you said on the phone just now. Everything.'

Sam runs a sweaty palm through his hair. There is an awkward silence. 'What?' he finally says.

'This isn't what you signed up for, is it?' I try to look discreetly at Bells.

'Hello, Katie,' she says, holding out her hand.

'Sorry, Bells. Not now,' I say, turning back to Sam.

'Don't know what you're on about,' he mutters. 'I was talking to a client.'

'Don't lie!'

'Don't lie!' Bells repeats.

'You were talking to Maguire!'

'To Maguire.'

'What is your sister going on about?' he says to Bells, trying to keep his composure.

'Sam. I heard.'

'Well, you shouldn't have been fucking eavesdropping.'

'OK,' I say, drawing in breath. 'Let's not go into it now.'

'Sam said F word,' Bells laughs.

'Bells!' both Sam and I say together.

'You having pudding?' she asks me.

'I'm pretty stuffed. Let's get the bill.' Sam turns to get the waiter's attention.

'I want a pudding.'

He allows Bells a quick chocolate brownie. While she is still eating he grabs his jacket from the back of the chair, tells me he is going to pay the bill and that we need to be ready, by the door, in five minutes. Sharp.

★   ★   ★

Sam sweeps round the corner in his BMW.

'Why are you driving so fast?' I ask him as we hurtle round another corner. 'Stop going so fast, Sam.' I press my foot on an imaginary brake.

'It's all right, shut up. These cars are designed to belt along.' He puts his foot down even harder.

'Not funny, Sam, not funny.' Bells is grappling with her seatbelt.

'Bells, don't take the belt off,' I tell her.

I hear a click and now she is unlocking her

door. I twist round quickly. Her door swings open and nearly hits a lamppost.

'Jesus!' Sam shouts. He grabs Bells's floppy jumper and pulls her in, one hand anchored firmly on the leather steering wheel.

'Pull over!' I am shouting, turning from Bells, to the road, to Sam, to Bells again. 'Sam, STOP!'

He pulls over swiftly, the tyres burning against the pavement, and turns off the engine. Thank God no-one was driving behind us.

'Not funny, Sam. Not funny,' Bells berates him.

'Christ Almighty,' he repeats, his head in his hands and almost weeping. 'My new car.'

★ ★ ★

'You nearly fell out of Sam's car, Bells. You have to be careful.' I lift her feet onto the bed.

'Too fast, Katie.'

'I know.'

'Was scared.'

'So was I, but you could really have hurt yourself.'

She is still quiet.

''Night, Bells, sleep well.' I turn off the main light.

'Nothing around me?'
'Nothing around you.'
'Promise.'
'I promise.'

21

I stand on Bells's bed and take down her Stevie Wonder poster. The Beatles poster is pulled off the door. I open her wardrobe and take out her Chinese wedding outfit.

We fold her baggy jumpers, shirts and holey vests together. They go into the zip bag along with the medley of junk, including the buzzing device, her CDs, notepad, photograph album, box of paints and the football badges. 'Do you want to wear these . . . or these?' I hold up her large black boots and the purple pixie pair. Today she is wearing a black T-shirt I gave her from the shop with a little silver star in the middle, which is sadly hidden by her dungarees on top. She decides to go for the pixie boots.

Her large purple zip bag is finally packed, there is only one Stevie Wonder CD we cannot find. 'I'll send it on to you, promise.'

Bells doesn't appear too bothered. She tells me she will take the sheets off the bed, like they do at home.

''Bye, Isabel. It was great to meet you, and come and see us again,' Sam says, standing at her bedroom door in his jeans and leather

231

jacket. It's funny how people are so nice to you when you are leaving. Sam doesn't want Bells to visit again, though I can't really blame him for wanting his home back to himself. He looks relieved as he skirts the room, seeing it clean and clutter-free. Back to his normal routine. Nothing out of place; CDs in their correct boxes; the kitchen surfaces positively sparkling because they are so clean. I am going to miss Bells's meals. What do you do in a kitchen if you don't cook, Sam?

'Thank you, Sam.' She goes forward and shakes his hand.

'It's a pleasure. No problemo.' He looks pleased that she thanked him without any prompting. 'Katie, I'll see you later.' Sam and I didn't say a word to each other last night. By the time I had said good night to Bells he was asleep on the sofa so I left him there. I told him this morning that we needed to talk. Now he walks away and minutes later I hear the door shut.

'Right, ready to rock 'n' roll?' I ask her, and put a hand over my mouth. Without thinking I say things that Sam would churn out and it is starting to worry me. 'Come on, we need to get going.'

Bells says goodbye to her bedroom.

I take her bag and shut the door behind us.

'Passengers going to Haverford West need to change at Swansea,' says the loudspeaker. People are bustling past while Bells and I stand at the information desk waiting for Fiona, one of the staff in Wales, to meet us. She is going to accompany Bells back home. She is late and the train leaves in ten minutes.

'Got your ticket?'

'Yes, Katie.'

'What does Fiona look like?' I am scanning the crowds. Perhaps we are in the wrong place?

'She's fat.'

'Bells!' I laugh at her.

'Like partridge.'

'Eddie and Eve would love to see you again, you'll come back, won't you?' I would love to see you again, that is what I should be telling her.

'Very nice people. Would like to see Mark again.'

'I know, me too.' I still think about Mark and what he did for us. We didn't manage to meet up again, and now that Bells is going, I have no excuse to ring him. Yet I cannot believe that I am never going to see him again. Was he only supposed to come into our lives for that single brief evening? 'If I do see him, what message shall I give him from you?'

Bells starts rocking forwards and backwards. 'Will he write to me.' She starts to laugh as if she has said something very dirty.

'Here's Fiona,' Bells says, her hands in a flutter. I am not sure if she is nervous or excited. Fiona is waddling towards us in a cotton checked skirt and white blouse with a frilly collar.

'Hello, I'm Katie.' I shake her hand.

'Hello,' she says. 'Hi, Bells. How are you?' Her voice warms up. 'How was your holiday? Mary Veronica has really missed you, she got back yesterday.' She takes Bells's bag and I walk behind them. 'We'd better be quick, I'm running late, aren't I? I thought we were meeting at the ticket desk?' She turns briefly to me.

'No, I'm sure we said . . . '

'Never mind, Katie, all is well. Was it fun?' she continues.

'Yes, fun,' Bells says. Fiona marches us onto the correct platform where the train waits. I am not going to have time to say anything now, I panic to myself, my feet pattering along to keep up. I have had all of this morning to tell Bells that I would like to visit her, that I have enjoyed the last few days so much, but I haven't said anything. 'Got your ticket?' is about the sum of it.

'Went on London Eye,' Bells continues. 'Saw all London.'

'How marvellous,' Fiona says. 'It sounds like you've had a smashing time.' She turns to me. 'Thank you, Katie. We'd better get on, the train leaves at nine twenty-one. Two minutes.'

I look at the big clock, the seconds ticking by.

'We want to make sure we're near the buffet car,' Fiona says, stepping up onto the train. Bells follows her. 'Say goodbye to your sister, Bells.'

NO! I want to shout. This is not how I imagined it would be. I want to say goodbye properly. Leave us be.

''Bye, Katie, 'bye.' Bells stops on the step and tries to turn round.

'Stand away from the door,' the conductor instructs as Fiona is stowing Bells's bag in the luggage rack.

'Isabel, be careful. Mind the gap. Get right inside,' Fiona orders.

''Bye, Bells,' I call pathetically to her back. She turns and waves at me. ''Bye, Katie. Thank you for having me.' I watch her and Fiona taking their seats. Bells sits by the window, Fiona next to her. Bells looks out of the window and waves again. She hits her hand against the glass. The conductor blows his whistle.

'NO, hang on, don't go!' I push past the conductor and press the red button to open the automatic doors into their carriage. Fiona is about to say something but I don't let her. 'I just want to say goodbye to my sister, properly,' I say, swallowing hard.

'Hello, Katie,' Bells says.

'Hi, Bells,' I say, my eyes beginning to fill. 'I . . . ' Don't lose it now. The other passengers start to sigh and heavy-breathe around us. 'Excuse me,' the conductor says, 'we need to go. Unless you are travelling to Swansea, can you please get off the train?'

'Get a move on!' a boy jeers, pelting a tennis ball at me. It hits Fiona in the forehead and Bells starts to laugh inappropriately. 'Some of us are in a hurry.'

I wince. 'Fiona, I'm sorry, did that hurt?'

'Well, it did, rather.' She sits in a more upright position.

'Push off!' his friend says. Normally passengers are so buttoned up they don't say a word to one another. Why is it that today everyone is being so vocal?

'Quiet. She wants to say goodbye to her sister,' says the passenger opposite Fiona and Bells. I smile at him gratefully.

'Yeah! Let her stay and say goodbye nice

and proper,' adds another.

Even Fiona smiles at me now. 'Come on, quickly, say goodbye,' she urges.

I lean across and kiss Bells clumsily on the top of her embroidered hat. My handbag bashes into Fiona's large stomach. 'I'll come and see you, and I'll start to write, I promise. Will you come back to London too?'

'Yes, Katie, yes.'

I dare to make one final move before I am hurled off the train. I kiss her on the cheek. ''Bye, Bells. I've loved having you to stay.' I dig into my bag and find the photograph the Japanese couple took of us on the London Eye. I made a copy for myself on Sam's computer. 'Keep it carefully, show your friends in Wales. Put it in your album.'

'Yes, Katie, I will. Loverley photo. Thank you, Katie. Thank you.'

The conductor rolls his eyes at me as he finally blows his whistle. I jog along the platform to keep up with the moving train. Bells waves at me and I wave back, tears running down my cheeks. ''Bye, Bells. 'Bye.' I wave one last time.

I stare ahead, not knowing what to do next. I straighten my dress, flick back my hair and take a deep breath. You walk away and your life carries on, I tell myself. I half laugh. At least I told her. I could have let her go without saying anything, but I didn't. I told her how much I'd enjoyed having her around; I feel we have made a start. I feel one tiny part of my family has come back to me.

I walk away from the quiet of the empty platform and back into the hustle and bustle of the normal world.

22

The house feels so quiet as I walk inside. I go downstairs to the kitchen and expect to see Bells sitting in the corner eating her homemade muesli and prodding the milk-bottle sculpture. I give it a prod for her. I want to see some of her clutter in the room — a cook-book, an empty Diet Coke can or a baking tray lying on the table. Instead the kitchen table is smooth and clean. It is eerily quiet without Stevie Wonder playing in the background. It's almost as bad as Mum's classical music not being played at home. I turn the radio on, anything for some noise. I have to get ready for work, I think to myself, yet am unable to get myself into gear. Finally I walk upstairs and then up the further flight to Sam's bedroom. I can't help looking into Bells's bedroom once more. I want to make sure she really has gone. The room is now a stark white again. It doesn't take long, does it? I am about to pick up the lamp from the corner of the room but then I decide against it. It can stay there. I like it.

★ ★ ★

I take a long shower. I didn't have time this morning. As the hot water blasts against my face I turn my mind to Sam. What am I going to do? Is it time to call it quits? But if we do split up, where am I going to live? Isn't it time I bought my own place? I am twenty-nine, nearly thirty, I have my own business, so what is stopping me?

I have always lived with boyfriends, avoiding the responsibility of a mortgage. But look at Emma and Jonnie. They are getting married, have bought a place together, are taking a risk, stepping into the real world. I have drifted along in my twenties, focusing on my career and going from one unsuitable relationship to another. If I go back to the beginning, I lost my virginity to Scott when I was eighteen. He was the electrician with tattooed arms. I met him while I was studying English, art and French for my 'A' levels. I went out with him for six months and it was wonderful. I practically moved into his bedsit. Mum started to accuse me of using our house as a hotel. 'You only come home to do your washing and have a free meal,' she said. I was permanently hungry going out with Scott because all we could afford to eat in his bedsit were Cornflakes, Cornflakes and more Cornflakes. It was even more exciting when we discovered we could make the best meal

240

out of Frosties and cream, like a *crème brûlée*.

Next there was Alex, a singer and guitarist who toured the country playing gigs. I was at art college in London and quickly moved in with Alex to avoid student accommodation. His flat was more like a hole but that didn't matter. I loved telling Mum that I had landed on my feet. Look at me in London, I wanted to shout. I have a boyfriend, a home, and I have my place on an art course.

Things petered out with Alex eventually. The next boyfriend broke my heart by sleeping with my flatmate, Fran. He was training to be an architect. He was soft, kind, intelligent, the last person I could have imagined cheating on me. I made a promise never to let myself get so hurt again. So I had a series of easy, let's face it, lazy, relation-ships. Look at the last one before Sam. He was always abroad working so in reality I was leading a single life. Emma always says it is better not to be in a relationship than to be in a dead one that is going nowhere. Better to go alone than be badly accompanied, she says. I know Sam isn't exactly one of her favourite people. I wash my hair, the shampoo lathering in my hands. If he and I split up, I lose this place, lose the convenience of living so near to the shop. No need to catch the smelly underground while I live here. I will miss the steam room, too. I mean, who else has a steam room in London?

I start to laugh. Come on, Katie, those aren't real reasons to stay with someone. What about love, commitment, having fun with someone? I did enjoy being with Sam until two weeks ago. Whatever his faults, he has his good points too. He has gone out of his way to book this weekend for us. He is taking me skiing this Christmas. He is confident, successful, he can be charming. I love our secret dances in the kitchen and the way he sings Chris de Burgh songs to me. When we first met he made me feel like the only person in the room he wanted to talk to. He is supportive of my work. Look at the way he organized my fashion show at his client's house. If someone had told me then I would be considering splitting up from him so soon I would have laughed. Has that much changed in two weeks? Will I regret it if I act rashly?

Maybe we just need to talk, I mean *really* talk about *real* things. For instance, I want to know more about his family. I'd like him to tell me about his father. If we stand a chance of staying together we have to be honest with one another and share more. I know I am very much to blame as I started the whole charade off by not telling him about Bells. If we break up I will miss our lifestyle. Sam is handsome, he has money, a stylish house in Notting Hill, a good job. And he has chosen me. What's that terrible phrase: 'You could do a lot worse'? Surely the easiest thing is to do nothing, carry on as normal. Isn't it?

But is that enough for me any more?

* * *

I lock up the shop, but I don't want to go home. The idea of Bells not being there is miserable. Bells gave life to Sam's house, now it is back to being a show home. I find myself going to the bar across the road. It is outside. I order a bottle of wine and buy a pack of cigarettes too since I don't have to put up with Sam telling me not to smoke. A bottle of wine and an hour later my mobile rings and Sam's number appears in the box. I sit staring at it. He tries to call again but I let it ring.

If you could write the script of your life, what would you write? I ask myself. It is another irritating cliché that Sam throws at me from time to time, but at least this one does have some meaning. I would not be sitting here with nothing but failed relationships trailing behind me, I decide. Yet, I can do something about it, I tell myself. I pick up my mobile and am about to ring Emma. Then I put it down. I know what she would tell me, and it is about time I made a decision like this on my own. I need to stop limping along in no-man's-land. Of course I know what I have to do.

⋆ ⋆ ⋆

It's late by the time I make it back to Sam's. He's sitting on the sofa reading the *FT*.

'We need to talk,' I say, walking over to the window.

He puts the paper down. 'If it's about last night, let's just leave it, hey? I'm sorry you overheard me, it was just a load of bravado, Katie. You know what I'm like with the lads, especially Maguire. I didn't mean any of it.'

I think about what he said to Maguire but I'm not even sure how much I care about it now. I don't feel any anger or betrayal. I don't feel a thing. 'I've been thinking about this weekend . . . maybe we should cancel it. I think we've got a few things to sort out.'

'Sorry?'

'The weekend? I don't want to go,' I say once more, slowly and deliberately.

'Katie, you're joking, right?'

I shake my head.

'The room's booked.' He slams his glass onto the table. 'I'm not going to be able to get a refund at such short notice.'

He is unreal. 'Don't you want to know WHY I don't want to go?' I blurt out. 'Sam, this can't go on.' I start pacing the room.

'What can't go on? Stop shouting at me. What has got into you? It is about last night, isn't it?'

'Yes,' I tilt my head, 'and no. Come off it, you probably did mean what you said. This isn't what you signed up for. When we started going out, you knew nothing about my family. Well, now you do. I come with Bells. Also, I know nothing about yours. Why won't you tell me about your father?'

'There's nothing to tell,' he says, exasperated. 'He's a workaholic. I never see the guy, what else do you want to know?'

I frown with frustration. 'Where do you see us going?'

'I don't know what you're talking about.' Sam shakes his head impatiently.

'Where are we heading?' I persist. Why can't he get what I'm saying?

'I thought we were having a great time, having some fun. Clearly,' he huffs, 'I was under the wrong impression.'

'We can go out, get drunk, go to nice hotels and expensive restaurants, go skiing this

Christmas, we can do all of that for another year or so, and then what?' I raise my voice. 'What next?'

'We wait and see. Jesus!' He stands up and faces me properly. 'Why are you so neurotic all of a sudden? What's your problem? What do you want?' His eyes open wide and he laughs sarcastically. 'A ring on your finger?'

'No way.'

'Well, what then? What's brought this on? I thought we were happy the way we were.'

'But what about the future?'

'Bollocks to the future. Seize the day, I say. Worry about tomorrow,' he pauses, thinking, 'tomorrow.'

'If we're not right for each other we're wasting our time. I'm nearly thirty, you're thirty-six.'

Sam ignores me. 'We're going to that hotel, it's all booked,' he says, his tone overbearing. 'We need this time together. Can I have the nice fun Katie back, please? Where's she gone?'

I fidget with the ring on my hand. 'Sam, you meant what you said last night. You couldn't hack Bells, and the two weeks were pretty much a disaster.'

'It wasn't that bad, was it? I'm not used to someone like her, that's all. I thought we got on OK. Anyway, she's gone now, *c'est la vie*, move on.'

'No! Sam, I am not getting through to you at all, am I?' I shout. 'What on earth do you care about?'

'Look, you're not my flipping shrink. What is it with this third degree? I don't know what you're on about.'

I put my hands over my eyes and rub them wearily. This is a lost cause. But I give it one final go. 'What is the point of us?'

'You've changed. Ever since Bells came to stay everything has changed.'

'Yes, it has, and that's no bad thing. I want more than this. I need a lot more than this.' I am about to say that it is not working any more, we are not right for each other and I am leaving him. 'You're a good friend, Sam,' I say, then realize he is not even that. Once we part I cannot imagine just meeting him for coffee. What would we talk about? 'We've had some good times, but . . . '

'No way,' he says, cutting me off. 'Uh-oh, no way, I'm not listening to this.' He gets up. 'I can't give you more. I think you should go,' he states coldly and walks past me. 'You can stay tonight, but I want you out by tomorrow. It's over between us, Katie.' I hear him go downstairs.

'Good!' I shout after him. 'I'm glad! One

more night would be too long.' I hear the front door slam shut.

'Done and dusted,' I say quietly to myself. '*Capisce?*' I sit down on the sofa and stare out of the window. I do not feel a thing. Sam gave nothing to me, and I realize I gave nothing of myself to him, something I have been doing for too long.

I pick up his gin and tonic and drink it in one go. What am I going to do next? I pick up the phone and ring Emma.

C'est la vie, Katie. Move on.

★ ★ ★

I key in the number and Dad answers immediately. They are due to come home in two days.

'Bells left today,' I tell him.

'You had a good time?' he asks, catching his breath.

'Yes, we went on the London Eye, and we bought Bells an outfit for Emma's wedding. Can I have a word with Mum?'

'Katie, we have to go . . . '

'No, don't. How are you both? What have you been doing? You haven't been in touch for ages, I tried to call you the other day . . . '

'Katie, I can't talk right now,' he cuts me off.

I don't want him to go.

'Listen, I'll call you later.' And he hangs up.

I key in the number again but it's switched off now.

I sit staring at the telephone. Something is clearly wrong, why can't he tell me? What is going on, Dad? Why are we such a dysfunctional family?

Why can't we talk?

23

1990

Bells, Mum, Dad and I are sitting in a circle
in a pastel blue-painted room with a plastic
clock ticking in the background. The chairs
were arranged like this when we arrived. I
look around the room. This place reminds me
of hospitals. It has that same clinical feel to it,
the air tangy with disinfectant. Also I don't
want to be here, the same feeling that always
overwhelmed me when I used to visit Bells in
hospital. But this time it is all because of me
that we are here. I feel like a criminal. All I
have done is steal a few eyeliners and records
by Adam Ant and A-ha. I didn't even want
them, the As were the closest to the door,
that's all. Is that really so bad?

Mum looks uptight, legs firmly crossed
along with her arms. Dad is tapping his knees
hard, as if they are a pair of drums. Mum
leans across and slaps his hand. 'Stop that,'
she orders. Neither Mum nor Dad has said
much since we arrived. Mum picked me up
from school. I missed double physics. She
drove Bells and me to our GP's surgery.

'The Fletchers. Would you like to go in,

please,' the receptionist told us and pointed to the door with Family Clinic written on it.

Mum looked frantically around at all the other miserable-looking patients waiting for their appointments before pushing Bells and me through the Family Clinic door with alarming speed. Dad joined us here, out of breath, complaining that he hadn't been able to see his last client at work because of this bloody session we were about to have. Bells is the only one who looks happy to be here. She is flicking through a *Woman's Realm* which she found on a table in the corner of the waiting-room.

The door opens and a small man limps into the room. He is so skinny his grey trousers are held up by a shiny black plastic belt. He carries a file labelled 'Fletcher Case'. He shakes Mum's and Dad's hands and smiles briskly at Bells and me. 'Hello, I'm Simon Shackleton,' he introduces himself. He is wearing a plastic-looking gold watch; black hairs sprout from his wrist to either side of the strap. I wonder what is wrong with his foot as he pulls up a chair to join our circle.

'What's wrong with your leg?' Bells asks immediately. 'You broken it?' I love having her as a sister sometimes. She asks exactly what I want to know and always gets away with it. If I asked like that I would be told off for being nosy.

I watch his mouth twitch as he smoothes his thin brown hair across his forehead. 'We haven't come here to talk about my poor foot, now have we?' He smiles weakly at Mum and Dad and they smile awkwardly back. 'I tend to arrange the chairs like this. It brings everyone close together,' he says, taking control. Bells is rocking her legs up and down as she continues to turn over the pages of the magazine which is so old the pages are tattered at the edges.

I watch Simon Shackleton as he peers at the first page of our file. It looks far too big for a family that doesn't do anything most of the time. His brow is all furrowed, his face looks as if it has been squashed through a flower press. Are our problems really that bad? He closes the brown folder and looks at me. 'Katie, can you tell me a little bit about your family?' he starts, leaning back in his chair. For such a puny little man his voice is surprisingly bold and authoritative.

I look at Mum and Dad who shift in their seats. 'They're all right.' I shrug. 'I don't know what else to say, really.' The plastic clock appears to be ticking even more loudly in the background. The seconds seem like minutes. Mr Shackleton's eyes are focusing hard on me. After a lengthy pause he says, 'Well, perhaps I should make it a bit more specific. Why don't we go around the circle saying the things we like and dislike about each member of the family? It's an excellent way of seeing where the main problems lie. Maybe I should start with you, Mr Fletcher?'

Dad sits up and clears his throat. 'I love my family,' he states firmly. 'I am not going to pick out their bad points.' He shakes his head and sinks back in his chair again. He might as well have 'waste of time' printed on his forehead.

'Ah, so there are bad points?' Mr Shackleton twitches his bony nose.

'No family is perfect. Are you telling me yours is?' Dad's voice rises in indignation as he sits up again. Mum puts one hand on his thigh to calm him down. Already this is not going well. I want to go home. Dad looks over at me and smiles sympathetically. It's a smile that suggests he is sorry for what he is about to say. The ticking of the clock is getting louder. I can hear the pages of Bells's magazine turning over and over. Finally Dad says, 'I suppose I wish Katie hadn't got into trouble because then we wouldn't be here. We were doing fine until this.'

I watch Mr Shackleton shake his head. He clearly does not believe this after looking at whatever is written in our file. 'Please go on, Mr Fletcher.'

'Katie has always been a good child. She has had to cope with a lot, help look after her sister Isabel and so on. I'm sure you are aware of the medical history of our younger daughter?'

Mr Shackleton nods. 'I am.' He taps the file.

Bells looks up from the magazine. 'Drink?' she asks. Mum tells her to be quiet, she has not come to a tea party. She had explained in the car why we were coming here today but Bells has clearly forgotten already.

'We are aware that it hasn't been easy for a young girl like Katie. She has had to grow up very quickly in some ways. Fend for herself more. I think it's a good thing if you ask me, no child should be spoilt and pampered. It doesn't help them in the long run. Katie's a great girl,' Dad continues. 'This is just a phase she is going through, nothing more. I am sure there are other families who need counselling a lot more than us.'

'Mr Fletcher, I am sure that is the case, but every family has their faults . . . '

'Exactly,' pounces Dad. 'We're no different. Do you counsel every family who has the odd hiccup, Mr Shackleton?'

'Mr Fletcher, I don't think you can call this

a hiccup exactly. Stealing should be taken very seriously.'

'No like this man,' Bells cuts in.

Mr Shackleton doesn't appear at all offended by her remark. I look at Dad. He has managed a smile. I am sure he wanted to say exactly what Bells just has. Part of me wants to reach across our circle and hug him.

'And I am sure you would agree with me that it is best to address this problem now, if we can,' Mr Shackleton intones.

Dad turns to Mum, begging her to help him out.

'To go back to what you asked us to do first, Mr Shackleton, dislike is a strong word,' Mum begins. 'There is nothing I dislike about my children. I get irritated and tired because of them sometimes, but that's different. I defy any mother not to feel the same occasionally. Katie is very like I was at that age. Headstrong. She does things to cause a reaction. I think a lot of young girls do. It was very foolish of her to steal but . . . '

'Why are you only going on about me?' I cry out then. 'I'm not the only person in this family. What about Bells? She never gets told off, she's never to blame for anything. Everyone just laughs, don't they? It's all one big joke when she does something naughty. But when I do something bad the police are knocking on the door.'

'Don't like it here,' Bells moans, kicking her legs restlessly. 'Want to go home.'

'It's not quite the same, Katie, and you know that only too well,' Mum points out calmly to me, although I can tell she is desperately trying to keep her voice in check. 'Mr Shackleton, is it really necessary for Isabel to come to these sessions? She doesn't understand why we are here. This is really to do with Katie, isn't it?'

'There you go again,' I screech. 'It's only ever *my* fault.'

I turn to Mr Shackleton, waiting for him to tell Mum and Dad that I am right, it's not fair that I am the one they are constantly criticizing. That he wants us to talk about everyone in the family. Instead he sits back as if to let us take over. I can't stand that smug smile imprinted on his face. What do you dislike about your family? OK, my turn then.

'I hate it when you don't pick me up from school,' I tell Mum. 'I stand there at the gates waiting and all the other parents say to me, 'Does your mother know it's the end of term?' You look different too. They come in long navy skirts and frilly shirts. It's not like I want you to dress in Laura Ashley but you always come to collect me in your painting stuff because you want to be different all the time. I wish I could board there like some of the other girls. And I hate it that you didn't bother to come to my sports day. I had practised every lunch hour and after school, and all the parents were there except you. I won first prize for the high jump.'

'That was nearly three years ago, and I came to it.' Dad hunches forward defensively, now actively taking part. 'Katie, please don't lie. *I* was there so you were hardly ignored. And please don't talk to your mother like that.'

'Darling, it's OK, if this is how she feels.' Mum rests a hand on his. 'We need to listen.'

Dad looks at her with one of his soft smiles. I stare at her again. 'I won the art and needlework pupil of the year award, not that you care!' Each week the school puts up the best drawing, painting or something someone has made, and I had won the most times in the year. Dad's face did go soft with pride when I told them that but Mum didn't say all that much.

'Now, that's out of order, Katie. Of course I care. Stop feeling so sorry for yourself.' She looks pale. 'I'm sorry if I didn't say 'well done' enough or come to your sports day, but you have to understand your father and I only want what is best for you. And I do care,' she repeats. Is that water gleaming in her eyes?

Real tears? 'We work hard so we can send you to one of the best schools. You can't board, we live close by and it's too expensive. And now we need to work doubly hard to make sure we can send Isabel to one of the top schools in the country next year.' Mum and Dad have spoken to me about this. They want to send Bells to a specialist school where she will be with others like herself. She will be taught all the normal things like reading and writing, and do arts and crafts, things like that.

'I'm afraid that sometimes we can't both get to your prize-givings, I wish we could, but at least one of us always comes,' Mum finishes.

'Well, it's usually Dad. You're always working, and I get bored at home. All I do there is read or draw or sew. The same things that Granny Norfolk does. I'll be knitting next. I'm not a hundred, I'm fifteen! I can't bring my boyfriends back to the house because Bells runs at them like a bull and hits them in the balls. They run a mile. When they can,' I add.

Mr Shackleton straightens his hair. He didn't expect any of this, did he?

'You don't have a boyfriend, do you?' Dad asks.

'I don't now! She,' I point to Bells,

'frightens them off.'

'Not funny, Katie,' Bells cries out.

'We hardly ever do normal things like go to the cinema or on holiday,' I continue remorselessly, 'we never do anything. If it wasn't for Emma and Berry I'd run away. I'm going to leave home when I'm sixteen anyway. Then you'll be sorry.'

Mum and Dad look at each other. Dad looks hurt. 'What have I done to deserve this?' is written all over his face. I feel bad that I said that about sports day. He did come, and he entered the fathers' race. He even won the egg and spoon. Mum looks upset too. Good.

Mr Shackleton leans forward. 'I think we should probably call it a day here,' he suggests, looking at all of us except for Bells who is roaming around the room now. 'I think we covered some interesting ground,' he says through thin cracked lips. 'Summing up, I would say, Mr Fletcher, that you and your wife are upper-middle-class intellectuals who have perhaps forgotten that money and the best schools don't necessarily buy a child's happiness.'

I know Mum and Dad won't like that. My words were a slap in the face. Mr Shackleton's have practically knocked them out of their chairs. Dad opens his mouth and then closes it again. Nothing comes out.

'I found it interesting that you focused on the things you dislike and never on the positive things,' Shackleton pronounces. 'All your energy is being channelled into seeing faults in one another, which cannot be healthy. I can see Katie feels neglected, she craves attention like any normal teenager. She wants to be praised. Am I right, Katie?' He turns to me expectantly. I can feel myself turning red now. He didn't have to say any of this. For me to feel it inside is OK, but to hear someone else saying I am craving attention sounds pathetic and sad, like a baby. I am not a baby. Mr Shackleton realizes I'm not going to respond so moves on. 'From this first visit, I feel you all need to spend more time together, set aside a piece of quality time each day just to be with one another. Communication is the key to understanding our own and other people's needs.'

Mum grabs her handbag and we follow her out of the door. Mr Shackleton limps after us, smoothing his thin hair over his forehead again, saying we must book in another appointment for the following week and that we have already made substantial progress by talking about these issues.

We never see him again.

24

I find Sam's car-keys in his jacket pocket. I walk downstairs and out of the house. I find myself unlocking his BMW and turning the engine on. Who does Dad think he is fooling? Something is wrong.

As I drive down the grey motorway, I have this surreal feeling that I am looking down on myself, that it's not really me driving. I tap the steering wheel hard to reassure myself that I am in control. I turn the radio on, and then I flick the switch off, left alone in an oppressive silence with only two thoughts racing through my mind. What am I doing, driving home late at night? Am I going mad?

* * *

I pull into our driveway. Mum and Dad's car isn't there and I instantly feel relieved. They aren't here. I shut the car door and take my house keys out of my bag. They hang on an old rusty silver keyring with the initial K. I bend down to open the bottom lock but the key won't turn. It doesn't need to be unlocked. I consciously try to keep my hand firm as I turn the key in the other lock. The door creaks open. Why hasn't Dad double-locked the door? He never forgets. They are here.

'Hello,' I call out, my voice echoing in the hallway. There is a lot of mail on the floor which I pick up and put down on the hall table. There are no lights on but the house smells lived in. I turn on a light. Coats hang on the pegs, dry, unused. I put my handbag down at the foot of the stairs. The curtains are drawn in the sitting room. The answer-machine is on but it isn't flashing. That's strange. Surely someone has rung them since they've been away? I called once, but didn't leave a message.

My heart is racing as I walk into the kitchen. The blinds are drawn shut but the plug switches are left on, the red bars are there. Everywhere I look tells me they have never gone away, the standby button on the CD player flashes its red warning sign. There are two dirty mugs in the sink. I touch the kettle but it's stone cold. I open the fridge. There's a packet of chicken, sitting in its blue polystyrene tray, curling at the edges. I read the sell-by date and it was only two days ago. There's a box of eggs, butter and mayonnaise on the top shelf. I shut the door.

A saucepan has been left on the stove but it's dry and clean.

I start walking upstairs but my pace quickens and then I'm running up them and down the landing into Mum and Dad's bedroom. The bed hasn't been made, Mum's wedding dress quilt lies haphazardly across the sheets. I walk into their bathroom. There are Mum's and Dad's toothbrushes standing in a china pot in the shape of a fish. Mum's moisturizing cream sits on her dressing table, along with her hairbrush and tortoiseshell hair comb. How dare they lie to me? Where are they? I stand, looking round the room, unable to comprehend what is going on. Then I hear the front door opening and wait to hear voices.

* * *

I can hear footsteps but no-one is talking. The only immediate noise I can hear is my own breathing. 'Katie,' my father says in shock when he sees me at the top of the stairs. Mum stands next to him, her pale face vivid against her auburn hair.

My panic and fear turns to anger. 'You've been lying to me. Why are you here? Why aren't you in France?' Dad looks at Mum but neither of them say anything. I wait for some kind of explanation. 'Can someone tell me exactly what is going on? What's wrong?' Mum walks past Dad, down the corridor and into the kitchen. 'Dad?' I try.

He collapses in a heap on the bottom stair, his face buried in his hands. 'Dad, what is it?' I rush downstairs and kneel down in front of him. 'Dad, please tell me what's wrong.'

'I don't know where to start,' he finally mutters.

'Mum,' I call helplessly, my voice splintered with fear. 'Mum . . . ' I lift my hand off Dad's knee and walk into the kitchen. She's opening the drawer at the end of the kitchen table, where she keeps old letters from her mother and father. She's ripping them into shreds. She holds a letter from Bells and starts to tear that into strips. She hasn't even acknowledged that I am standing in front of her. 'What are you doing? Mum, please.' I start to shake her shoulders. 'Stop it,' I now shout.

She sits down.

'Mum, please, will somebody tell me what's going on?'

'I don't know how to tell you,' she finally says.

'Well, just try. Whatever it is, it can't be worse than what I'm feeling now. I'm terrified. Why is Dad crying?'

'Because I've just been told I have a brain tumour,' she states simply. Then picks up another letter at random and tears it in half.

25

I watch Dad guiding Mum down the hallway. His arm is around her waist, and she moves one of her hands behind her back so that it gently touches his and their fingers interlock perfectly, like a puzzle.

I walk back into the kitchen and sit down. 'This can't be happening, it's not true. Tell me it's not true,' I say over and over again.

'I can't,' Dad finally says as he sits down at the kitchen table.

I have to compose myself. 'How could you not have told me? Why are you going through this all alone?'

'We thought we'd never find ourselves in this position. Our GP told us it was nothing to worry about.'

'*What* was nothing to worry about? A brain tumour?' I utter incredulously.

'Your mother had an epileptic fit six months ago . . . '

'An epileptic fit?' I repeat mechanically. 'Why didn't you . . . '

Dad stops me. 'We didn't tell you because when we went to see the GP he dismissed it as a thing people sometimes get at our age.

'People of your age often get only one attack,' he said. I can remember his words vividly. He told us to go away, not to worry about it.' Dad stands up and goes over to the drinks cabinet. He pours himself a whisky and swallows the lot in one go. 'Then she had another one when she was in the kitchen cooking supper. She was standing right here, in this spot, making my stupid supper. Chopping vegetables.' He slams his glass down on the sideboard.

'And then she had another and another, at monthly intervals, like clockwork. The medication wasn't touching it. I insisted she saw a neurologist. You know what she's like, didn't want to accept anything was wrong. When I called you to ask if you could have Bells to stay, well, we went to see the neurologist two days later. I just couldn't cope with Bells and this at the same time.'

'No, I understand, but why didn't you tell me then?'

'Because we still desperately hoped it was nothing, that the fits could be controlled with medication. She had the EEG and again that showed nothing untoward. She did all those other ridiculous tests, you know, told to count backwards in sevens and to follow the doctor's finger with her eyes. She felt fine, nothing seemed wrong. Then he suggested doing an MRI and we got the results today. We've been at the hospital all day.' Dad collapses back down in a chair. 'There's a tumour growing and the epileptic fits were caused by increased pressure on the brain. The tumour may have been there for years.'

I don't know what to say.

'Believe me, Katie, I wanted to tell you so much, but she wouldn't hear of it. She felt there was no point in worrying you until we knew for sure what we were up against. We were going to tell you eventually, I promise.'

'Can't she have an operation? Have it taken out?'

'Katie, please stop . . . ' Dad is cradling his head in his hands, trying to block out the world.

'Isn't there anything we can do?' I cry out.

'Stop asking questions.' Dad raises his voice. 'Stop it.' He is shaking his head helplessly. He stands up suddenly and pushes the chair away. He crouches down on the floor. I have never seen my father cry. I move forward to hold him, tears streaming down my face now. He clings onto the back of my top, bunching the material in his fingers, twisting and pulling the fabric hard. His face is pressed against my shoulder, and I can feel my top grow damp with his tears.

'I can't live without her, Katie. I can't live without her.'

* * *

I sit on the old dressing-up box which has now been turned into a window seat in my bedroom. I light a cigarette and blow a large smoke-ring out into the dark sky. I can hear voices in the street, they sound happy. Maybe they have just returned home from the pub after another ordinary evening out. Do they realize that their lives could change over-night? That something might happen to them tomorrow which could change everything? Of course they don't. How lucky they are that it probably doesn't even occur to them. They are just like I was a few weeks ago. Blundering on in my own world, thinking that it was a catastrophe when my father asked me to have Bells to stay; thinking it was the end of the world when she cut the labels out of my T-shirts. My mobile rings yet again and finally I take it out of my bag. It tells me I have three new voice messages. I dial 901 to listen to them.

'Where are you, and where's my fucking car?' Sam screams down the phone. 'Can today get any worse? Call me at once.' Slam. 'It's me again,' he bellows. I switch it off. I remember him saying the same thing when I burned the chips that first evening when Bells arrived. *Can today get any worse?* How naïve we are.

The still air and quietness make me feel even more alone. My eyes are so tired they don't seem to belong to me any more. I walk down the dark corridor, past Bells's old bedroom. How are we going to tell her about Mum? We have to tell her. Mum and Dad can't lie to us any more, or try to protect us from the truth. It never helps; it only hurts.

I walk into the bathroom and bend over the sink, feeling sick. I open the mirrored cupboard door and stare at the various bottles and potions. Are there any sleeping pills? I know Mum takes them. There is an assortment of bottles with screw caps and yellowish pills inside. Everything looks ancient. I pick up one bottle, dated 1974, and throw it into the sink. I pick up all the bottles in turn, there are so many — for stomach pains, chest pains, headaches — but none to help me sleep. 'God, help me,' I shout as I hurl them back into the sink.

I stand in front of the mirror, the one where I used to stand and pray to God as a little girl to give me blond hair and blue eyes. 'I know we aren't close, but I want her back.' My voice comes out jerkily. 'Dad needs her.

Bells needs her. I need her. Oh, dear God, make Mum better.'

'Katie.' I hear Dad's voice, calm now. He strokes my back.

'I can't sleep, Dad. I . . .'

'Shh,' he hushes me. He puts an arm around my shoulders and walks me back to my bedroom.

'I can't sleep,' I repeat, walking past the bed and sitting back down on the window seat. I light another cigarette. Dad hates me smoking but he doesn't say anything. He sits down on the other end of the window seat. 'If I was going to start smoking, now would be a good time,' he says, taking off his black-rimmed glasses and rubbing his eyes. His glasses have left a deep red indentation across the bridge of his nose.

I half laugh. 'You don't mind, do you?'

'You smoke; you die. You don't smoke; you die. What sodding difference does it make?'

I inhale deeply. 'How's Mum?'

'She's fast asleep.'

'Good. I still can't believe this is happening.'

'Nor can I.'

'I'm expecting to wake up in a minute.'

'Oh, Katie, what are we going to do?'

'I wish I knew.'

We sit quietly, staring out into the dark sky.

'Make a wish upon a star,' Dad says.

'Dad,' I start cautiously, 'when are we going to tell Bells?'

He turns to look at me, holding his breath. 'Soon. Your mother and I have been talking about it.'

'I think we should call her tomorrow. We need to tell her that Mum is unwell and that she should come home. Bells must be involved. It would hurt her so much if she found out we'd kept it from her for any length of time. She needs to know right from the start. Mum can't go on trying to protect her, or thinking she won't be able to cope, because it only excludes her and makes her feel like she's not normal and . . . '

'Katie,' Dad stops me abruptly, 'you're right, we agree. We want her here with us,' he states firmly. 'She's more precious to us than anything. You both are,' he quickly adds.

I look at Dad. His eyes seem to be a paler blue, a washed-out version of their normal colour. 'Good, because that's right,' I say.

He stares at me quizzically. 'A few weeks ago you wanted nothing to do with Bells. I had to remind you that you even had a sister.'

I bite my lip. 'This is different though, isn't it? We need to stick together.'

'Yes, I realize that, but you've changed. You're fighting for her.'

'I want to make up for being such a lousy sister. Since she came to stay, well, we're good friends. She's worth fighting for.'

Dad leans towards me and kisses my cheek. He reaches out for my hand and grips it tightly. 'I'm so proud of you, Katie,' he says.

26

I wake up from a disturbed sleep. The walls
see-saw around me. Where am I? It takes me
a minute to recollect and when I do my body
feels heavy as I struggle to get up and put one
foot in front of the other.

I find Mum in the kitchen, dressed in her
tattered old bed-jacket and long floating
nightdress with embroidery around the
neckline. She is rifling through the shelf
which holds her cookery books and files.
More letters are on the table, torn to pieces.
She turns to me, a look of total calm on her
face. 'Morning, Katie, did you sleep well?'

Confused more than anything, I tell her,
'Not bad. Mum, why are you tearing up your
precious letters?'

'I don't want you and your father worrying
about any of my business. The more I can get
rid of now, the better.' She goes out of the
kitchen, down the corridor, and climbs the
two steps into her studio. 'What am I going to
do with all these unfinished animals?' she asks
herself. 'Take whatever you want, won't you,
Katie? Otherwise they'll go to waste.'

'Mum . . . ' I pull a chair back and sit at

her worktable. 'Mum,' I start again, slowly, 'one of us *has* to tell Bells. I can't stop thinking about her. She has to know, today.'

She nods. 'OK. Can you arrange for her to come home?'

'I'll call her. If she gets a mid-morning train I can pick her up later.'

'I'd do it, but . . . ' Her voice tails off. 'I can't even drive,' she says shamefaced. 'I feel so useless, your father chauffeuring me around everywhere. One big useless lump,' she laughs mockingly.

I look at her. She is pencil thin, her cheekbones even more accentuated, her eyes even larger and more haunting. Her bed-jacket is practically falling off her shoulders. 'It's all right. I can do it, Mum. Don't be so hard on yourself.'

'How am I going to tell darling Bells?'

'Dad and I will be here. It'll be OK. We just need to be honest and tell her everything. Mum,' I start again, 'what did the neurologist say, exactly?'

'He told me I would be in charge of my pain control,' she replies, her voice once again as calm as still water as she sits down with me.

I can't bear the idea of Mum being in pain. 'Is there anything more we can do?'

'He did say we should see someone else, in

Southampton, a neurosurgeon. He's arranging an appointment, but . . . '

'But what?' A tiny flicker of hope presents itself. 'We will see him.'

'Katie, the neurologist thinks it could well be malignant. I'm not sure I can stand any more tests only to be told exactly the same thing. I feel all right. Funnily enough, I can deal with this. I can't deal with your father spilling coffee all over the cream carpet but . . . '

'Mum,' I try to slow her down, 'I don't care about Dad spilling coffee right now.'

'I can deal with this,' she claims again. 'I need to prepare myself, organize things, that's all. I don't feel ill. In fact, it's hard to believe anything is actually wrong with me. I just want to enjoy the time I have left.'

I shake my head. 'Mum, you need to see the surgeon.'

I don't think she is listening to me as she says, 'I want to go on holiday with your father. We always promised ourselves we'd go on a trip down the Nile, or else go back to Paris again. Or visit our old friends in France whom we haven't seen for fifteen years.'

'The ones you just pretended to be visiting,' I can't help adding.

'I'm sorry. I shouldn't have made your father lie. We were wrong about that. I would

276

love to see them,' she insists. 'None of us will have changed, we'll just have grey hair.'

'You can go, you can do anything you want, but I think we should follow the doctor's advice and see the surgeon.' I lean closer towards her, my elbows pressed hard against her worktable. 'I can't live with the knowledge that we didn't even try.'

'Nor can I,' Dad says as he walks into Mum's studio in his frayed dressing gown and leather slippers. He sits down at the table looking more positive this morning. 'I was going to say exactly the same thing.' He's holding the piece of paper with the surgeon's name and number on it.

★ ★ ★

Dad, Mum, Bells and I are sitting around the kitchen table. Dad has made a pot of tea but no-one has touched their cup yet.

How are we going to tell Bells?

When I picked her up from the station earlier today she shook my hand.

'Nice to see Katie. How's Mum?' she asked. I had told her on the telephone that Mum wasn't well and that she needed to come home.

I took her purple zip bag. 'She's looking forward to seeing you.'

'How's France? They have good holiday?'

How are we going to tell her?

Mum is now wearing slim-fitting linen trousers with a white cotton shirt, her bobbed hair pulled back into her tortoiseshell clip. 'Bells, would you like some of your sage tea?' she asks, handing her a plate of chocolate digestives.

Here we are, trying to be a normal family having tea, when everything is falling apart. Dad and Mum look at one another. It's like a game of 'winking murder', each trying to signal the other to start.

So I begin because I cannot bear the heavy silence. 'Bells, Mum and Dad wanted you to come home because . . . '

Mum stops me. 'Katie, can I?'

I nod. 'I'm sorry.'

She has too much pride to let me be the one to explain. 'Darling,' Mum starts, looking directly at Bells, 'I wanted you to be here because I have something to tell you. I'm so sorry,' she says, reaching out to hold Bells's hand. But Bells won't let her take it.

'Why?' she asks.

'I have a brain tumour,' Mum states in one bold sentence. The words are out so quickly that I have to catch my breath.

We all wait for Bells to say something. Anything. She has clenched one of her hands

278

into a fist and uses it to hit the other. 'You going to die like Uncle Roger?' she finally asks, rocking backwards and forwards in her chair. The room is utterly silent except for Bells's heavy breathing.

'Yes, I'll be joining Uncle Roger. I'm sure we'll have lots of fun up there together,' Mum says, her eyes looking upward as if to heaven. 'We'll have whisky and cherry cake parties.'

Bells stands up and leaves the kitchen. 'Going to watch *Titanic*,' she says.

Mum sits back with a look of relief, as if she has done the hard part. 'I'll talk to her again when she's ready. We'll let her watch *Titanic*.'

Dad nods and finally takes a gulp of tea. Mum takes a digestive biscuit. 'Well done, darling, you bought the dark chocolate ones.'

'No!' I shout, slamming my cup onto the table, tea spilling everywhere. 'You talk to her now. You tell her that we're going to see the surgeon, that we're waiting for the scans to be sent to him and that when they are,' I have to take a deep breath because I feel I am suffocating, 'we are seeing him.'

Mum and Dad stare at me.

'Bells doesn't want jokes about Uncle Roger, for Christ's sake. She needs to understand. I am fed up with none of us talking, bottling everything up and pretending it's all normal and everything is OK, when it *isn't*.'

'Katie? Are you quite finished?' Mum asks.

We can hear the theme music to *Titanic* playing in the background.

'No, not quite,' I reply simply. 'I don't care if the boat's about to hit the iceberg. You go in there and turn *Titanic* off. You tell her now.'

★ ★ ★

I am eavesdropping outside the sitting room door. 'You scared?' Bells asks Mum.

'Yes, but I've got all my family around me.'

There's another long silence. I think Mum is comforting her. Suddenly the door opens and I quickly move away, but it's obvious I've been listening. 'I'm sorry . . . for shouting earlier,' I say to Mum.

'You were right. Now, if you don't mind, I need to be on my own. I'm tired.' She touches my shoulder gently before walking upstairs. I hear her bedroom door shut before I go into the sitting room to join my sister.

27

It is the morning of Mum's operation.

'I think we can do something about this,' the surgeon had said, holding the MRI scan. 'I think the tumour could be benign, I can't be absolutely sure until we operate, but I would strongly advise you to have an operation.'

'What makes you think it might be benign?' Dad asked, trying to contain his hope.

'From how it looks on the scan and it may have a clear margin to cut around.'

'So you're saying it isn't malignant?' I asked. Was I dreaming? This conversation couldn't be happening. We had been expecting confirmation, not a different assessment altogether.

'I can't be absolutely sure, but if we do nothing, we shall never know.'

I wanted to hug him, get down on bended knee and pray to God but I tried to control myself. Dad held Mum's hand so tightly that I thought her bones might crack from the pressure.

'Thank you very much,' she said, as if he had just told her she could have pickle with her cheese. 'When can you slot me in?'

Now Dad sits awkwardly in the light blue armchair next to Mum's bed. I know he hates hospitals despite being so used to them. 'It never gets any easier,' he'd confided in me. Bells is sitting next to him. She hasn't said a word this morning. The only thing I can hear is her rattling chest.

'How are you feeling?' I ask Mum.

'I'm OK.' She clutches my hand. Besides her hospital gown, she is only wearing her gold wedding band and the plastic hospital wristband with her name and date of birth on it. Normally Mum wears her aquamarine engagement ring, her gold watch and her two gold bracelets that jangle together like a wind chime. Everything about her looks bare; stripped down.

'I'm ready to face it.' She breathes deeply. 'I'm so glad you're all here with me.'

Bells starts banging her forehead with her fist. She stands up, sits down, stands up again and then starts circling the bed like a trapped monkey in a cage. 'Sweetheart, will you sit down?' Mum pleads, clearly upset. Were we wrong to bring Bells here? No. We couldn't have left her at home. Besides, Mum wanted her here.

Bells grabs her inhaler from her pocket.

'I'm really thirsty. Can you get me a drink?' I ask in desperation. Dad immediately takes Bells off 'on a coffee run'.

I look at Mum. It is the first time we have been on our own today. Her green eyes are large and staring. 'Tell me about Sam,' she starts. Anything to fill the silence. 'Why did you break up? Was it because of Bells?'

'In a way. I think I would still be going out with him had it not been for her staying with us,' I admit.

Mum raises her eyebrows inquisitively. 'What do you mean? Did she hit him in the balls?' A small smile lights up her face, making her eyes look less penetrating.

'No, Bells has replaced whacking men hard in the balls with swapping their CDs around.'

'Your father hates me not putting the CDs back into their boxes.' Mum smiles. 'It's his biggest fetish.'

I smile back because I know he hates it too. 'Sam wasn't nasty to her,' I continue, 'he did take us out for a meal once, but he was so embarrassed because we met his old boss at the next table. Some of it's my fault. I never told him about her properly, he didn't know what to expect . . .'

'Oh, rubbish, Katie.' Mum does that familiar crow of incredulity that I have always found off-putting and heavily critical. Funnily enough, now I am pleased to hear it.

'I don't know Sam, but all I will say is that when we had Bells it sifted the good friends from the bad instantly. Some of them disappeared overnight; they couldn't handle it at all. Will-o'-the-wisps,' she finishes neatly.

I can't help but smile. 'Will-o'-the-wisp? Wasn't there a TV programme called that? He was a kind of smoky cartoon character, like a ghost?'

'I don't know, darling, probably. Off they go at the first sign of trouble, and then — puff!' She claps her hands together. 'As if by magic they come back when it suits them. Gerald and Sue are like that,' she says.

'You're right. Sam is a will-o'-the-wisp.' I have this image of him disappearing from my life like a plume of smoke evaporating into nothing. He came to collect his car, told me how sorry he was to hear about Mum, handed me my mail, and then he was gone. He told me he would keep in touch but I have a strong feeling I shall never hear from him again.

'Sometimes you find out about people the hard way,' Mum says. 'It's often the least likely ones who become wonderful friends or even lovers.'

I don't like the word 'lover' but so what? Everything else seems so unimportant to mention now. Let words, thoughts, slip away into oblivion.

'There are people who are outstandingly nice, others who are mediocre, and some who are just bloody awful,' she concludes, as if visualizing ticking the appropriate box. 'It sounds to me like Sam was pretty mediocre. Not good enough for you, Katie.'

'We just weren't right for each other.'

'No, he wasn't good enough for my Katie.' Her voice is starting to crack. She looks tired, deep circles of grey under her eyes. I can see her trying to compose herself, not allow herself to cry. 'Tell me more about Bells's visit,' Mum continues.

I decide to tell her about Bells running away that wet afternoon. I tell her about my saviours, Mark and the American lady in the park. 'I was terrified. I would never have forgiven myself if something had happened to her. I shouldn't have got so angry.'

'It's easy to lose your rag.' Mum looks directly at me now.

'I didn't realize what a full-time job it is,' I run on. 'I had to watch Bells all the time and my patience did wear out. We had to stop and talk to almost every passerby in the street too.'

Mum laughs knowingly. 'It takes me a good two hours to get round Sainsbury's.'

'How old you are?' I imitate.

'What wrong with you?' Mum follows.

I tell her about the poker night and Mum laughs so loudly while thumping her hand against her thigh that the other people in the ward cannot help but look our way. 'It sounds like you had a very funny time. You see, it's much more fun for Bells to visit you than her old parents all the time. She gets bored with us.'

'We went on the London Eye. Mum, it was wonderful. Bells and I did bond, we got to know one another again. I want you to know that.' I reach into my bag and take out a letter she wrote to me. I want to read it to Mum.

' 'Dear Katie Fletcher',' I start. 'I love the way she writes my surname,' I add, smiling. ' 'Very kind you to have me to stay in London. Very nice bedroom, lots of white. Nice house. You do that remember going to London Eye. I . . . ' '

She has Tippexed a word out here.

' 'I loved to go, saw all London and very loverley time with you on London Eye. Mark a very loverley man. You seen Mark? Mr Vickers too a very nice man. I am sorry I had to go, very kind you to invite me to come to London. Wonderful you. Hope not very Longtime to see you again. Nice you, very kind you, please send you my love. Thank you.''

She has signed it in pen: ''Love, Bells. Ps Please RSVP me soon.''

Mum rests her head back against the pillow. 'Your father knew it would be good for you to spend time together. He's a wise old thing.'

'When you're better, we'll go on the Eye. You are going to come up to London and we'll go out for lunch and do fun things. Pact?'

I wait for her to answer.

'Katie, if I die . . . '

'You won't, you're going to be fine.'

'If I die,' she continues calmly, 'you'll take care of Bells and your father, won't you?'

'Mum, don't . . . '

'You were the one who made me realize we must be honest now and say what we feel.'

'Yeah, OK,' I acknowledge.

'I need to say it while they're not here. They'll be back in a minute.' She adjusts her position in the bed. 'Your father and I were going to redecorate the house and . . . well, he wouldn't have a clue,' she whispers, leaning closer towards me. 'You'll help him?'

'OK,' I say, feeling my bottom lip quiver, just like Dad's does when he is about to cry.

'And you'll be there for Bells? You'll go to

her open days and visit her at weekends?'

'Yes, I promise I will,' I say.

'I'm so glad we can talk like this, that we didn't need Mr Simon Shitty Shackleton!' Mum starts to laugh and cry in between with relief. 'Do you remember his plastic belt and weasel face? Your father still won't talk about it.'

'I do remember him. Funnily enough I was thinking about him only the other day. I remember he called you and Dad upper-middle-class intellectuals.'

'Ha!' she sniffs. 'What rubbish! I'm sure intellectuals don't watch *Who Wants To Be A Millionaire?* and I bet they're able to finish the *T2* crossword.' Mum looks like she is gearing herself up to say more. 'But who will look out for Katie?' she says, taking my hand again.

At that moment Dad and Bells return. Dad is holding a plastic tray with two cups of coffee on it. He sits down at the end of the bed. 'How're you, Mum?' Bells asks, rocking forward.

A nurse comes to the bedside. 'They're ready for you now,' she says.

Then they will shave Mum's hair, I can't help thinking.

Bells walks away. 'Don't like it here . . . not nice here.'

'Bells!' Mum cries out. 'Please come back. Will you go and get her?' she urges Dad. 'Let's get this over with as quickly as possible. I can't stand it any longer.'

Dad brings her back, trying to reassure her that nothing bad is going to happen.

'Say goodbye to your mother,' the nurse says impatiently to Bells.

I give her a hard, accusing look. How dare she make it sound so final?

Bells is rubbing her head and breathing heavily. ''Bye, Mum,' she finally says, throwing an arm over Mum's stomach and resting her head against the theatre gown. ''Bye, Mum.'

Mum strokes her hair. 'I love you. I'll see you later,' she says.

★ ★ ★

Dad is furiously writing lists at the kitchen table. I'm not sure what he's writing but it seems to help him take his mind off the operation.

Bells is watching *Titanic* but she doesn't make any sound when it's about to hit the iceberg.

I don't know what to do with myself. All I can do is look at the clock and watch the seconds tick by. Slowly.

Eventually the telephone rings and Dad and I move to it like lightning. 'You take it,' I quickly say. I can hear Bells switching off the television.

Dad picks up the receiver. 'She's conscious,' he is saying, clearly repeating what the surgeon is telling him. 'It certainly looked benign.'

'Bells!' I scream, jumping up and down like a mad monkey. 'Bells! Mum's OK!'

'Mum going to be all right,' Bells says, joining us.

'But what?' Dad now asks slowly.

I stop abruptly. Bells stands next to me. 'Mum all right,' she repeats.

'Oh, I see,' Dad says gravely.

'What? What?' I demand.

'What?' Bells follows.

Dad flaps his hand furiously to shut us up.

'Can we visit her now?' he continues. 'OK, we'll be there right away.'

28

'Go home,' Mum insists again, after I have given her some more water. 'You look even worse than me.'

I look at her. Her skin is so pale that she is almost camouflaged by the white pillow and sheets. Nothing covers her head except for a fine stubble of hair and a scar on the left-hand side of her face, curved like a question mark. It is two weeks after the operation. It was a success in that the tumour was benign and was taken out; but the surgery left her very weak and with virtually no movement on her right-hand side. She couldn't even turn herself over in bed. Everything had to be done for her and she slept a lot of the time. None of us had had any idea that she might not be able to walk after the operation. 'What's a Zimmer frame doing at the end of the bed?' was the first groggy question she asked us. Her next concern was not being able to sign her own name. 'Mum, why are you trying so hard to write your signature?' I had asked her, watching her wrestle with the pen and paper.

'I've told you. If I am going to be like this

for ever I want at least to be able to get at my money,' she said breathlessly. Any small effort makes her tired.

Thankfully the physiotherapy is already helping her to regain strength and mobility. She has just started to get up and walk very slowly, up and down the ward. To say we are relieved is a gross understatement. It is a miracle. When I watched Mum walk for the first time, I was clapping so vigorously that the palms of my hands were burning red.

'Please, Katie, go home, darling. Take the awkward squad home too.' She is referring to Dad who is talking to one of the doctors. She thinks he fusses too much over her. She shuts her eyes. 'I need to get some sleep. And you do too,' she adds.

Mum's right. I do need some sleep. I haven't slept properly for days. Dad drives us home. We don't say much. 'Is there anything on television tonight?' is the only question he asks me mundanely.

When I walk into the house it's very quiet. No Stevie Wonder. No Beatles. Bells doesn't seem to want to play any music. I find her in the kitchen again, wearing Mum's denim apron, now quite grubby with a blob of spinach down the front, her small hands encased in red spotted oven gloves. Yesterday Dad and I returned home and she had made us a cauliflower cheese, using all the leftovers in the fridge. It was the most delicious cauliflower cheese I had ever tasted too. The day before that she cooked a courgette and asparagus quiche. She chose not to come to the hospital today. In fact she hasn't been since the morning of Mum's operation. Each day we ask her if she wants to come but all she says is, 'Tell Mum get better.' Dad and I make a point of not leaving her for long periods of time on her own. We come and go in shifts.

'Hello, how's Mum?' she asks immediately, putting a large white dish into the oven and then turning to face me. 'Mum all right?'

'She's OK, a bit grumpy and tired. She sends lots of love. Bells, wow, what are you cooking?'

'Stuffed pancakes with ricotta and spinach.' Suddenly the smell makes me ravenous. 'Made strawberry fool too. You like straw-berries? Mum loves strawberries.'

'I love them. You are a star,' I tell her, collapsing into a chair. The table is littered with a cooking bowl, broken eggshells, flour for the batter, a greasy block of butter and a few bruised strawberries which haven't made it into the fool. It's a comforting mess.

'How's Mum?' she asks again, yet I know she is not expecting another answer. 'Make you drink,' she says, opening the cupboard. The bottle of vodka is laid out for me; Dad's whisky is ready for him.

She hands me my vodka which I take gratefully. 'Bells, you really are amazing.'

Dad walks into the kitchen. 'Bells has made pancakes for supper and fixed us a drink,' I tell him and he smiles.

'How delicious,' he says. 'Thank you, Bells.'

'I might take my drink up with me, have a bath,' I say, prising my heavy body from my seat.

'Sit down, Dad,' Bells insists, guiding him to a chair. 'Sit.'

I walk upstairs and into my bedroom. Bells has made my bed — just as she has done each day since the operation. She has even left a small bowl of lavender on my bedside table.

I find myself walking into Mum and Dad's bedroom. She has stripped that too and there are clean sheets waiting to be put on; all of Dad's dirty laundry is in the wicker basket by the door. I notice she has placed the photograph of Mum and Dad's wedding by his bedside light, along with another small bowl of lavender. Bells is like a fairy godmother. I sit down on the bed and pick up the photograph. It's funny to think she and I weren't born when that picture was taken; it was just the two of them together, starting out. Mum was twenty-six when she married. At the age I now am she would have had me.

I don't even hear Bells sitting down next to me. 'Mum all right?' she presses again.

'She's fine. She wants to come home though. She hates hospitals.' As I say it I quickly turn to Bells. That wasn't the most sensitive thing to say in front of her. 'Sorry, you more than anyone know what I mean.' I put my head into my hands.

'What wrong?'

'I'm tired.'

'How's Sam?'

'We're not going out any more,' I tell her. I've told her before, she must have forgotten.

'Not nice, Sam.'

'He was all right.' I hold the wedding picture in front of both of us.

'Beautiful Mum,' Bells says.

'Very.' I put the photograph back on the table. 'Thank you for my lovely lavender.'

'Lavender smells nice.'

'Thank you. You've done so much these last few weeks. Dad and I, well, we're really grateful.'

Bells rocks forward, scratching her forehead. She doesn't blush but I don't think she knows what to say or do when someone compliments her. 'In Wales, have cleaning rota,' she tells me. 'Clean Ted's room. Ted my friend.'

I smile at her. 'Ted's lucky. I just want someone to make things better, Bells. For you, Dad, for me, and for Mum, particularly Mum. I want us all to be happy.'

Right now I feel my entire life is slipping away from me.

'Mum didn't die like Uncle Roger,' she says.

She's right. I know I should be feeling fortunate. Mum is going to be all right. Yet, now that we know she's going to get better, I can't help thinking about everything else. My job doesn't feel that important any more, I have no Sam — not that he's a great loss, but I do miss that feeling of security. I have no home. I'm worried for Dad. I'm worried about Mum and how we are going to cope when she comes home. I'm worried about everything; it's no wonder I can't sleep. Bells is the one ray of light. Dad and I would have been lost without her, eating takeaways and sleeping on grubby sheets, with no lavender by our bedside.

'Do you get lonely, Bells?'

'At times.'

'When?'

'Night-time.'

'Me too. Why at night?'

'Dark. Don't like dark.'

'I just want everything to go back to normal. I want . . . hey, where are you going?' Bells has just walked off without listening to me. She's bored of me. I stare up into the ceiling. Two minutes later I am still staring at the same spot, unable to move or think about anything.

Bells now stands in front of me with the telephone.

'Who is it? I didn't hear it ring,' I say.

'Someone on phone for you.'

'Who?' I repeat, not wanting to take it until I know who it is. 'Is it Emma?' She rings every evening, around this time. It must be her.

'Mark,' she says simply.

'MARK?' I utter incredulously. 'Mark called?'

'No.'

'What?' I whisper. 'It's not Mark, is it?' Bells has a strange sense of humour. I take the phone from her. 'It's Aunt Agnes, isn't it?'

'Katie?' I can hear in the distance. 'Hello. Katie?'

It's definitely not Aunt Agnes because it's a man's voice. 'Who is this?'

'It's Mark.'

'Mark nice man. Mark nice. Mark helps.'

'Bells!' I say, holding my hand across the mouthpiece. 'Why did you call him? How did you get his number?'

'Mark nice man. Asked him to see us.'

'I know he's nice but . . . Oh, bugger . . . ' I take my hand away from the mouthpiece. 'Hi, Mark,' I try to say casually.

'Katie, I'm so sorry to hear about your mum.'

Just hearing his voice makes me want to cry. 'It's OK, it's fine. We're fine,' I stutter.

'Bells asked me if I'd visit. I know this is weird, I hardly know you, but I'd like to. I mean, if there is anything I can do to help, or . . . '

'Bells would love to see you.' I can't believe he is on the phone. I tell him Mum is still in hospital and that they think she will be there for one more week, until she can walk independently. 'Maybe you could come when she's home?' I suggest.

'Fine. Just call me.'

'That would be great,' I say, realizing how much I would like to see him too. 'Really great. I'll be in touch.'

After our conversation Bells claps her hands. 'Mark coming!'

'How did you get his number?' I asked again.

'Took it from bag. Had it in London. Kept it.'

I can't stop smiling. Mark is coming to see us! This is so random, so unexpected. Yet, at the same time, nothing feels more normal.

29

Bells and I are standing on the station platform, waiting for Mark to arrive. Things are looking up, at last. Mum climbed ten stairs at the hospital and was finally discharged. She has been at home for two days. It is fantastic having her back. The only worrying thing is that already she is trying to cook and do too much. Determined to get back to some semblance of normality, she was trying to make some homemade elderflower cordial, bent down to get a large bowl and then bashed her head against the cupboard. Her eye-sight has been affected by the surgery and she often knocks or bumps into things. Dad immediately rushed her back to hospital as he was terrified she had dislodged the stitches. 'The awkward squad is back,' Mum said when the doctor told her she couldn't keep away. Thankfully it was fine, nothing more than a nasty bruise.

'Three minutes,' Bells says, looking at the flashing sign hanging above the platform.

'Two minutes . . . One minute . . . Mark!' Bells waves.

He walks towards us. His hair looks

unbrushed and he is wearing the round glasses that make him look like a professor. I can imagine him wearing a white coat and working in a laboratory. Instead, he's wearing dark jeans, a pale blue striped shirt, and his face looks tanned. My face is a sickly drained colour from spending too much time in hospital. Bells hits his arm. 'Hello, Mark.'

'Hi, Bells.' He shakes her hand affectionately. She hits him again, and he gently hits her back. Then he turns to me. It's that awkward moment when we don't know how to greet one another. Hug? Kiss? Hold hands? I lean towards him, ready to kiss formally on the cheek, but he puts his arms around me. 'I couldn't believe it when I heard the news. I'm so sorry.'

'Thank you for coming,' I say, not wanting to let him go.

⋆ ⋆ ⋆

When I open the front door Mum calls, 'Darling, we're in the kitchen.' She is longing to meet Mark. 'Is this the nice chap who helped you find Bells?' she'd asked me. 'Is he a boyfriend?'

'No,' I insisted. 'I've only met him a couple of times, Mum. He's Bells's friend as much as mine.'

'So, as Cilla says, there's no need to buy a hat yet,' she laughed.

'Oh, Mum.' I cringed, feeling myself turn bright red. 'Stop it!'

Now Mark, Bells and I walk into the kitchen and are confronted by the sight of Mum, Dad and a very plump man standing behind a trolley stacked high with wigs.

'Hello, Mark,' gushes Mum, holding out a hand. Mum loves men. I always suspect she wanted to have a son. 'Katie, Bells, Mark,' she says, examining him closely again to see if he could be potential husband material, 'this is Mr Marshall, the wig man.'

He extends one thick hairy arm and shakes our hands. 'Isn't your mother doing well?' he beams. 'All we need to do now is fit her up with a nice wig and then she'll be the talk of the town!'

Mum pats her head nervously. Her hair hasn't grown back apart from a few wisps. Dad tells her she looks like a fluffy chick.

Mr Marshall opens the first page of his portfolio. 'This is Mrs Henderson, she had a terrible time of it, lost all her hair she did. You know that rare disease where it all falls out? For the life of me, I can't remember what that disease is called. Anyway, she was lying in the bath, she was, and when she got out, all her hair was floating around in the water. It was a terrible shock. She was beside herself.'

He shows us the picture of Mrs Henderson before and after. In the after shot she wears a brown wig that looks more like a wooden salad bowl tipped onto her head.

Mr Marshall takes us through the entire portfolio and by now I am dreading what he is going to suggest for Mum.

He closes his portfolio and we all wait with bated breath. 'Now, how about this for starters?' Mr Marshall bends down and takes a wig from his trolley. He holds up something ginger and cabbage-shaped, and I am dangerously close to laughing out loud. I know Mark is too, I can feel the vibes coming from him. Mum looks horrified. Dad is speechless. Bells roars with laughter. 'Very funny,' she says. 'Ha-ha, very funny!'

Mr Marshall looks puzzled but gamely carries on. 'This is a close match to your original colour. Shall we give it a go?'

He places it carefully on Mum's head, smoothing it over and making sure there is not a single hair out of place. He proceeds to stand back in admiration. Mum looks at Dad, waiting for a reaction. Dad looks at me. I look at Mark. Mark turns to Bells.

'You need a mirror,' Mr Marshall says when none of us utters a word. He holds up a square mirror in front of Mum. 'It looks super on you if I say so myself.'

Mum shrieks with dismay. 'But I had auburn hair, like my daughter, Isabel.' She glances at herself again and then quickly averts her eyes. 'I don't want to wear this. It looks like I have a satsuma on my head. I'd rather be bald.'

'Mum, we can buy you some really pretty silk scarves,' I suggest. 'You don't have to wear a wig.'

We all agree, except for Mr Marshall who looks crestfallen as Dad and I show him out with his trolley of untouched wigs.

'Thank you for coming anyway,' Dad says quietly. 'I'm sorry if we sounded rude or ungrateful, but I don't think a wig's the answer.'

'No problem,' Mr Marshall says, 'but don't hesitate to ring me if you change your mind. The wig door hasn't been totally shut, I shall leave it, let's say, slightly ajar.'

Dad and I try not to laugh again. The wig door?

''Bye for now.' He bustles his trolley out of the door.

When we walk back into the kitchen Mum pats her head self-consciously. 'It really is very nice of you to come and see us,' she says to Mark, but I can tell her mind is still on that wig.

'I think you made the right choice,' he assures her. 'A silk scarf would suit you much better.'

I smile gratefully at him. I am so glad he is here. Dad tries to break the ice by asking us if we want a drink before lunch.

'Bet you didn't think I'd end up like this, did you, darling?' Mum can't help saying, still touching her very short hair. 'I hardly look the part, do I?'

Look the part, feel the part and you ARE the part, I can hear Sam chanting in front of the mirror as he shaves.

Dad steps forward and kisses the top of her head. 'I love you, no matter what. You don't ever need to hide behind your hair. What did we always say to you, Bells?'

'You look world in the eye,' she says.

'Dad used to say it all the time when we were children,' I explain to Mark.

'That's right,' Dad confirms. 'You look the world in the eye.'

30

Mum and I are watching an old black-and-white film on television, *Roman Holiday* with Audrey Hepburn. Mum is making a new tapestry cushion. She can never sit still and do nothing. Her colour is returning and her mobility improving each day with physiotherapy.

She looks pretty in her rose-patterned scarf and the large dangling earrings that I bought for her. When Mark came down for the day, Bells and I took him shopping. 'They look like chandeliers hanging off your ears,' he said, when I held the earrings up to my face. It was lovely seeing Mark, even though we had no time on our own. Mum and Bells monopolized him. I did tell him though how much his visit had meant to us.

'Katie, you need to think about going back to London,' Mum says to me out of the blue.

'What?'

'You need to go home.'

'No way. I can't, not yet. Do you want another drink? Hot water with lemon?'

'I'll be all right,' she reassures me.

I don't want to go. The idea fills me with horror.

'I feel guilty, keeping you from your friends and your life.'

'That doesn't matter. God, nothing matters except you getting better.'

Mum puts her needle down and turns to me. 'You've been wonderful but you can't stay here for ever.'

'But who's going to make you breakfast in bed and cook? Dad can't cook. No, we can't leave you, not yet.'

'I'm getting better all the time and your father is a good nurse. It's time you and Bells went home.'

'I'm not sure,' I say nervously.

'I'm sure. You need to start thinking about where you are going to live,' she says with concern.

'I don't know . . . '

'Katie,' Mum puts her sewing on the table, 'I can't thank you enough for everything you've done.'

'I haven't done much.'

'You have. Katie,' Mum says again, 'I've been a dreadful mother.'

I feel a rush of blood coming to the surface.

Yes, you have. You were too wrapped up in your work, you distanced yourself from me and put all your time into Bells, saving only a crumb for me. I felt invisible most of the time. I've always felt second best with you. I never seemed to be good enough; it felt like you didn't want to be involved in my life. That's what I would have said to her six weeks ago. Yet none of it really matters now.

'Mum, don't . . .'

'No!' She stops me abruptly. 'I want to. Let me. I've never been any good at saying how I feel. No better than you in fact.' She laughs painfully. 'I close up like an oyster.' Mum's voice is cracking around the edge like a broken shell. 'If I can't say it now, I'll never be able to.'

'OK, tell me.'

'I've never let myself accept that I didn't give you enough time, that you needed me as much as Bells, just in a different way. I should never have said how lucky you were not to have her problems, it was the easy way out. I didn't applaud you in your own right. But look at you now. A beautiful successful woman . . .'

'I'm not.'

'You are. I've missed out on such a large chunk of your life, and I want to make up for it. I'm so sorry.'

'You just had a difficult, demanding child. I should have realized how hard it was for you and Dad instead of thinking about myself all the time! I admire you both so much for bringing us up, with no help. I admire you more than I can say.'

'It wasn't good enough, though. I'm your mother,' she says, full of self-reproach. 'If I can't look after you, who can? I know I retreated into my own world. My work became everything because it took me away from the everyday grind. Then you left home and suddenly you didn't need us any more. I've carried this guilt for neglecting you all my life. I buried it in my conscience.' Mum stands up and walks slowly out of the room. 'I've got something for you,' she says. 'Stay there.'

She returns, holding a small gift wrapped in white tissue paper.

'Mum, you didn't have to.'

'Just open it.' She sits next to me as I unwrap the present. It is an oval silver box with an inlay of tortoiseshell and inside is her precious tortoiseshell comb. 'My mother gave both of them to me as a wedding present.'

'I love this box, it's beautiful. And your comb . . . you always wear it.'

'Well, it seemed perfect timing,' she says, adjusting her scarf. 'Besides, I want you to have them. It's a thank-you for all you've done.'

I put the box down and hug Mum.

'Why did it take us so long to talk? Why did it have to take this to bring us together?' she asks, holding me close.

31

Back to normality. Back to stocktaking, ordering from suppliers, organizing the next fashion show. Back to yoga and swimming, going out again and socializing. Back to the daily grind of London; noise, traffic, rude people pushing and barging. It is terrifying.

I have moved in with Emma and Jonnie. They have a small house with a garden near Turnham Green Terrace, and Emma insisted I stay in their spare room until the New Year, just before they get married. Being with her has made the move far less daunting and it's ideal when they live so close to my shop and so near to Mark. I need to call him soon to let him know we are temporary neighbours.

★　★　★

This evening I am going to Jonnie's parents' home near Lisson Grove for supper. Since being back in London I haven't seen that many people. Last week, I went over to Sam's to pick up my sewing machine. It was the last thing I had to collect. I still have keys so I went in my lunch hour when he was at work.

His house looked just the same, not that I had expected it to change. Everything spotless and in the appropriate place. It didn't look like I had ever been there. I put the keys through the door. ''Bye, Sam,' I said. As I predicted, he hasn't been in touch since he heard the news about Mum.

As I wait in the sitting room for the taxi, I look at Emma and Jonnie's engagement photos taken in Battersea Park. They are in black and gilt cardboard folding frames. I pick one up off the mantelpiece. They remind me of those cards I used to be given with the end-of-year school photographs. ''The entire photograph was ruined because Katie decided to pull up her skirt and show us her knickers,'' Mum would read out. 'What have you got to say about THAT, madam?' She always waited for an explanation, but I was sure I could see a small smile trying not to surface. Just thinking about home makes me miss it. It's ironic. All I wanted to do was leave home when I was a teenager. Now, it's the only place I want to be. I felt safe there, harboured in a cocoon. I felt needed.

The day I left, Dad and I stood quietly on the platform waiting for my train to arrive, both locked in our own thoughts. I was thinking about being a child again, climbing onto the train with my shiny red suitcase to see Aunt Agnes, and Dad waving goodbye as the train started to move.

'I don't want to, I'm not going,' I said as the train approached.

Dad smiled as he brushed a strand of hair away from my eyes and tucked it behind my ear, like he used to do when I was young. 'You have to go.' He opened the door and helped me in with my luggage. 'Mum and I will be fine on our own.'

Bells had left the day before. 'One down, one to go,' Dad had said. She was happy to go back. She missed college, her friends, her football and her normal routine. I hadn't missed anything and that scared me. 'Who's going to cook for you, Dad?' I called out as the train slowly started pulling away.

He waved his hand at me. 'I'll manage without Bells, don't worry.'

I laughed. 'No more secrets, EVER!' I shouted out of the window. 'We tell each other everything, good and bad. Great or bloody awful!' Strange the way our family does this. Dad and I had what seemed like an eternity of time waiting on the platform together and now that I was actually going, the words were tumbling out and fizzing at the surface like champagne bubbles. I had a few more seconds before he would be out of sight.

'Everything,' he agreed.

'Promise?'

'I promise.'

We blew kisses to each other. It was like a contest to see who stopped first. Dad's figure quickly faded into the distance. He was the only person left standing on the platform.

I open one of the photographs again. Emma is sitting down, Jonnie behind her with his arms wrapped around her shoulders. She's wearing a red dress which contrasts with her cropped dark brown hair and brown eyes. He's wearing a pale blue shirt to go with his blue eyes. It's all very colour-coordinated and very grown up. The doorbell finally rings and I put the photograph back in its place.

$\star$ $\quad$ $\star$ $\quad$ $\star$

Emma hands me a large glass of wine. It's a solid wide-brimmed glass that can hold almost a quarter of a bottle. Perfect. Jonnie leads me into the sitting room. 'You must meet my parents,' he says. They are standing expectantly by the fireplace. 'Mum, Dad, meet Katie.'

'Call me Will.' He is a big beefy man so it's forgiven that I nearly laugh out loud when I hear his soprano voice.

'Call me Hermione.' Jonnie's mother steps

forward to shake my hand. She must come up to about my waist. She looks like a little mouse and is wearing these peculiar multi-coloured pointed shoes which curl up at the toes like the end of a gondola. She looks the way Will sounds.

'What do you do, Katie?' he enquires, wide-eyed and smiling. I am still trying to keep a straight face. Why didn't Emma warn me about that voice? She must have known how I'd react.

'I own a clothes shop,' I tell him.

'Oh, how interesting,' he squeaks, touching his navy V-neck jumper with both hands. It reminds me of the jumpers golfers wear. He just needs the checked trousers and the visor to go with it.

Think of a sad story, SAD story, I'm telling myself as I look at them both goggle-eyed. Starving children of the world . . .

'What's it called?' Hermione chirps enthusiastically. 'I know someone who works in fashion. She gets to travel abroad to Paris. I think she works for Gucci or Givenchy, something like that.'

'Well,' I cough, 'it's called FIB.'

'Fib?'

'It stands for Female In Black,' I tell her.

'Oh,' she says, her voice heavy with disappointment. 'I think black is so dreary, all you young things wear it,' she comments, scanning my outfit. I am wearing a soft black rounded-neck jumper with sequins edging the cuffs. I get distracted as Jonnie hands me a plate of mixed nuts, and winks at me.

'So, you're living with Jonnie and Emma, I gather?' Hermione has lost all interest in my career, then.

'Yes, that's right,' I say, and then add, 'for the moment, that is,' when I can see from her face that she is faintly dismayed. 'It's strictly temporary until I find my own place.'

'You're not married then, Katie?' Both Will and Hermione look at me expectantly, like Little and Large. I gulp down some more wine. 'No,' I say, and feel compelled to add, 'not yet.'

'Oh, what a shame,' peeps Will, his big moon face looking downcast.

Hermione's mouth shrivels like a prune. 'You young people wait for so long. I married Will when I was just twenty. I had three children by the time I was your age. You're all the same. I mean, look at Jonnie, he took his time,' she grumbles.

I am tempted to say she probably had to marry her husband quickly before he changed his mind and did a runner.

'What do your parents do?' she continues. She really does look like a hamster. I want to ram some of the nuts into her mouth. 'Well, my father works at Sotheby's,' I tell them.

Hermione graciously acknowledges this, saying it must be a very interesting job. I can almost see her conferring a tick of approval. 'How about your mother?'

I clear my throat. 'My mother's recently had a terrible time, she had a brain tumour.'

'I am sorry. How awful for you all.'

'It was awful, terrible . . . ' My heartbeat quickens. I only have to think about it for a second and I feel so lucky, everything else fading away into the background. 'No, well, it was awful, but she's OK now. She got through it, she's doing well,' I tell Hermione proudly. 'The tumour was benign, but had it been left . . . well . . . ' I trail off, unable to think about it. 'It will take a good six months to a year before she gets back to normal totally, but she is great, really great.'

As I say it, I can hardly believe it's true. Mum pulled through. We pulled through it together. I can see her now, sitting at the kitchen table, her bright red and gold silk-patterned scarf coiled around her head, reading out to Dad how to cook a fish pie for their supper.

'Isn't she brave,' Hermione comments.

I have to stop myself from frowning. This kind of reaction drives me mad. 'Yes, she is.

She took a massive risk having the operation, but to be honest, she had no choice.'

'Flake the fish, darling,' I can hear her repeat because Dad is chopping it instead. He can only really cook scrambled eggs.

'Well done her,' Will chirps.

'I'm very proud of her. I feel so lucky she's still with us, and . . . '

'Do you have any brothers or sisters?' the hamster enquires hopefully.

I take one more glug of wine to brace myself for the question which I know is coming next. One tragedy surely cannot lead to another? There must be some light at the end of the tunnel? I bet you that's what hamster is thinking.

'I have a sister.'

'Is she married?'

'No.'

'Mum! Stop being so nosy,' Jonnie calls from the kitchen. 'Mum thinks everyone over twenty-one should be married,' he warns me.

'Oh. What does she do?'

Of course she was going to ask that. Asking people what they do is a kind of nervous tic with the middle classes. I cough even though I don't need to and draw in a deep breath. 'Well, Bells is a slightly unusual case. Er . . . she . . . '

'Bells? Is that what she's called?'

'Sorry. Bells — Isabel. We've always called her Bells for short.'

'Oh I see. Why is she unusual?'

'She lives in a kind of community, it sounds like a farm but it's not,' I add.

'She works on a farm?' Hermione creases her forehead in confusion. 'Is she a volunteer?'

'No, she's not a volunteer,' I say, twisting the silver ring on my finger. 'She lives there, it's her home.'

'Oh,' says Jonnie's mother, looking even more puzzled.

'It's a special home for . . . ' I pause, thinking of the correct way to word it, 'people with disabilities.'

If Hermione was in one of those hamster wheels which roll around the floor, she'd be spinning out of control by now. 'You mean, she's mentally handicapped?'

'Yes, I suppose if you put it that way,' I say stiffly, 'she is.'

'Oh dear, oh dear. What a shame,' Will pipes up.

'Poor, poor thing,' the hamster adds, her mouth drooping mournfully.

'She is not a poor thing,' I voice defiantly. 'She's wonderful. She's a very good cook, loves her music and football. There's nothing she doesn't know about the Beatles or Stevie Wonder. She has this magical sense of humour, too. Bells is her own person, and if you told her she was a poor thing she would hit you hard in the balls.' I want to take back the last bit but it's too late. Jonnie roars with laughter; I hear Emma choke and then let out a snort. I look at Will and Hermione but their expressions are still pitying. They aren't even listening.

AND I HAVE CANCER OF THE BOWEL, I want to shout, pointing to my cigarettes regretfully, but bite down on my lip hard. When I start to envisage Bells hitting Will hard in the balls, I have to try hard not to laugh. Imagine the high-pitched squeak that would come out of him! I let out a desperate, 'Do you need a hand?' to Emma and Jonnie in the kitchen.

'No, we're fine,' Emma calls back and I can hear the smile in her voice. Jonnie sympathetically tops up my glass.

I change the subject by talking about the photographer Emma found for the wedding. Has Hermione seen the picture of the chocolate cake she has chosen which will be garnished with white flowers? What is the mother-of-the-groom going to wear? I am going to design and make Emma's veil. Hermione tells me she loves winter weddings because that's when she got married. All fun, pretty things to talk about.

★ ★ ★

'What's a pretty girl like you doing on her own tonight?' my taxi driver asks as he turns on the engine. Emma bundled me into the cab because she is staying with Jonnie and his parents tonight. 'Do you have a boyfriend?'

This cab driver is very forward, isn't he? 'I have one, thanks,' I hiccup, deciding it's much more fun to lie. 'I'm afraid I can't talk too much about it, though,' I say, crouching forward into the space between his seat and the front passenger one. 'A bit complicated. Wouldn't want it making headline news. We have to leave separately, too risky otherwise with the paparazzi.' I sink back into the padded leather seat and hiccup once more. 'Oops, sorry 'bout that.'

'I don't believe you, man,' he laughs. 'Should I be getting your autograph?'

'OK,' I concede. 'I'm on my own. I've just split up.'

'I knew it,' he exclaims. 'I can sense things. Oh, that's sad. Too bad. I missed my wife when we split, you know what I mean?'

'I'm a bad picker of men. What's your name?'

'Fourque.'

'For what?'

'Fourque,' he says and proceeds to spell it out. 'F for Freddie, O for orange, U for umbrella . . . '

'Well, Fourque, I pick men who are no good in the end. My second to last boyfriend was a commitment freak, and my last one was shallow and said silly things.'

'You pick the vermin?'

'What?'

'Vermin. That's what I call all those people who aren't any good. There are a lot of them out there, you know what I mean? You have to be careful.'

'Vermin! I like that. I have this picture of rat-like people scurrying around with red flashing lights to show they are hazardous.'

'Yeah, rodents, man,' he laughs with me.

'Rodents,' I shout out of the window, feeling the fresh cold air blast my face.

'Thing is, I wish they did have red flashing lights. You see these well-dressed nice-looking people around but half of them are probably vermin too, rodents, man. I just wish you could tell them apart.'

'What about you now?' I ask, sitting forward again.

'What about me? Well, I want to make it in the music world. I don't want to do this for the rest of my life,' he says, pointing to the steering wheel. 'I have an interview next week. It's like my chance to do something I've always wanted to do. You have to take it, don't you? You know what I mean?'

'I know *exactly* what you mean,' I say with certainty. 'Life is way too short to waste it. Whoah, slow down, stop here.' I want to buy another bottle of wine from the off-licence.

I clamber out and pay him through the front passenger window. He smiles at me and his eyes light up like fairy lights. 'Will you pray for me to get the job?' he asks. 'And I'll pray for you to find the right man.' I find myself nodding because I like him. 'And stay away from the vermin,' he adds.

★ ★ ★

I head into the off-licence and stare at the various bottles of wine in front of me. In the end I take any old one and totter to the till. 'Thank you,' I say, clutching the carrier bag. 'Have a good day.'

'Katie?' I hear.

I stop and turn round. I know that voice. I tilt my head at him. He's wearing a cord jacket and holding a bottle of water and a large packet of barbecue-flavour crisps.

'Mark.' I smile, unable to conceal my delight at seeing him. I realize my mouth is wide open and quickly attempt to look less like a goldfish.

'What are you doing here?'

'I live here.' I explain I am staying with Emma temporarily.

'That's great. How are you? And how's your mother?'

'She's not here.' Why did I just say that?

Mark looks at me strangely. 'I have to pay for this, hang on a sec. Don't go anywhere.' He delves into his pocket to find some notes and loose change.

I tell him I'll wait outside and do a quick drunken skip on the pavement. This is turning out to be a much better evening than I thought. Hallelujah! I love Mark!

We start to walk home, me cursing that we will be there in thirty seconds. Why can't we live at least a mile away? 'I've been waiting for you to call. When did you get back?' he asks.

'Five days ago. I would have called but I've had so much to do in the shop, a lot of catching up, you know what it's like. I'm sorry, I should have . . . '

'Don't worry, I understand. Well, this is me,' he says, standing outside a black door with two steps leading up to it. 'But I'll walk you back to Emma's.'

I don't budge an inch. I can't let him go. I like him. I wanted to call him but I lost my nerve without Bells as an excuse. I need to pluck up the courage now. What have I got to lose any more? 'Can I come in? Let's crack open this bottle of wine.' I start walking up the steps.

He takes an arm to steady me. 'Don't you think you've had enough?' he asks, amusement in his tone.

I frown at him disapprovingly.

He gives in.

Mark's flat is small. His bike leans against the corridor wall. We go into the sitting room and I collapse into a soft sofa.

'I'm going to put the kettle on,' he tells me as he walks out of the room. 'Do you want a coffee?'

'What do you do?' I start talking to myself. 'What do you dooooo?' I can hear Mark laughing in the kitchen. Five minutes later he comes back with two mugs. I peer into my coffee as if I don't know what it is. 'It's Saturday night. I've been terrorized all evening by Jonnie's parents. Believe me, I need a proper drink.' I kick a wine glass on the floor at my feet. 'Oops! What are all these wine glasses doing?'

'Doing?' Mark grins. 'They're having a party.' He takes his jacket off.

There's an open bottle of white wine on the coffee table in front of me. I pour some into the nearest glass, spilling a little over the edge. Mark picks up the other glass that is precariously close to being kicked over. I can smell his aftershave. He's wearing a soft white shirt. I suddenly want to nuzzle into his shoulder and have a proper man hug. 'This place is a real tip, isn't it? Did you have a party tonight?'

'I had a few friends over.'

'You had a few friends over,' I repeat seriously, followed by a large gulp of wine. 'You know, Mark, it really is dandy to see you.'

'Dandy?' he laughs. 'I like that word.'

'You English teacher, you. D'you think it's fate, Mark, the way we bump into one another? There I am, at the off-licence, and — poof! We bump into one another, just like that. Or you living so close to Emma and me moving here, right next door to you. It's meant to be. Has to be.' Mark raises one eyebrow.

'I've always wanted to do that!' I peer closely at him, my mouth hanging open. 'How'd you do that? Can you roll your Rs . . . ' I flop back against the sofa like a rag-doll.

He rolls his Rs and then abruptly stops. 'This is a pretty strange evening.'

'D'you know, I think it might be destiny,

Mark. D'you believe in destiny?' He looks unsure. I lift myself up off the sofa to walk over to his music machine and look through his CDs. '*My Fair Lady*? Oh my God, you're gay. Haah!' I sigh deeply. 'It makes sense.'

Mark looks bewildered now. 'I am not gay, it's a school CD. We're putting on a production this year.'

'What's all this paper?'

Mark stands up abruptly and takes it from me, shuffling it back into order. 'It's my book.'

'Oh. Shall we dance?' I twist around and Mark catches me, releases the glass of wine from my hand and holds me still. He could let go of me now, I think. Eventually he does and I collapse back onto his sofa.

'Look, I think you need your bed. Do you want me to take you home?'

'Do you want me to go home?' I ask coyly, trying to be seductive. 'You know, you're very attractive, Mark. There's something about you.' I linger on the word 'you'. 'Come a bit closer.' He edges nearer to me. 'Don't look so worried, Mark.' I close my eyes for a second, in anticipation of a kiss.

'Katie.' I feel a hand shaking my arm. 'Oh, shit, Katie. Wake up, Katie, please. Wake up.'

The words are echoing around me but I ignore them as I fall into a deep blackness.

32

I wake up the following morning on a soft sofa with a rug over me. I attempt to move. My head! I start to groan. I hold it heavily in my hands. I swallow. My mouth feels like a sewer. I summon all my strength to sit up, pulling the rug with me. Where am I? There is a glass of wine on the table in front of me and the smell of it makes me feel sick. I'm still wearing my clothes from last night. My neck creaks when it moves. It's too painful sitting upright. This is a bad dream. My head hits the pillow again. The last thing I remember vaguely was drinking stewed coffee. I shut my eyes and go back to sleep.

★ ★ ★

I am woken up abruptly by cramp in my arm. Quickly, I fling off the hairy tartan rug and stand up and start to shake my arm about. The wine glasses have gone. I look around me once more, trying to piece together the events of last night. Papers and books overflow from a desk and a tall silver lamp with long spidery legs stands to one side of a computer. There's a white-painted shelf holding even more books and a small television in the corner of the room. Sam would have a breakdown if his place looked like this. I pick up a glass of water from the floor and drink it steadily in one go. I am so thirsty. Next to the glass is a packet of white pills. There's a scrap of paper on the floor with a torn-off ring binder edge.

'I've gone for a run, will be back soon, Mark. PS. These are for the sore head.'

Mark. I saw Mark last night! Of course I did. Where did I think I was? I start pacing the floor, knocking over a white plastic bowl — the kind Mum uses for sifting flour and sugar to make cakes. This is embarrassing. Did he think I was so drunk I was going to be sick in this during the night? Obviously he did.

He'll be back soon. How come I stayed here? I remember meeting him, but staying the night? Why can't I remember that? I sit and think hard about what we talked about last night. Mark must have gone for a long run. I bet you he's hoping I will be gone by the time he gets back. He's probably having brunch with his friends, telling them that I crashed out on his sofa last night. I rub my eyes. Try to remember, Katie. My head feels cobwebby. What I could do is run back to Emma's and Jonnie's, have a shower, get myself looking decent and return to say thank you for . . . what? I'll figure that out later. That's a good plan, Katie. Desperately I try to kick myself into action but nothing is happening. I am standing, transfixed, like a limp piece of lettuce. I hear the distant bang of a door followed by a key turning nearby. My heart jumps again at the thought of seeing him. I sit back down and attempt to look relaxed.

Mark comes into the room clutching a bottle of water and a newspaper. His face looks fresh and squeaky clean. 'Good morning.' He smiles as if he has won a premium bond. Why does he look so happy? 'How are you feeling?'

'Fine!' I lie. I wait for any clue as to why I found myself on his sofa.

'Really? You look terrible,' he says.

I laugh and admit, 'I feel dreadful. I feel worse than I look and that is saying something.'

'I bought us some breakfast. Well, lunch really. I've already had a bit of cereal. Stay for brunch, shall we say? I'm not going to take no for an answer so come into the kitchen when you're ready.'

I pat my greasy hair self-consciously. Look the part, feel the part . . . Oh, shut up, Sam.

'Have a shower, if you like.'

My God, he is offering me a shower. Next he will be offering me his toothbrush. How has this happened? I rub my head. I remember Will and Hermione clearly from last night. Then I bumped into Mark and we drank some more wine and coffee. I am sure nothing else happened. Convinced, in fact. He wouldn't have left me on the sofa, surely? I would have woken in his bed. 'Mark,' I call, making my way to the kitchen.

I find him at the stove frying bacon. I love the smell of bacon and toast. I sit down, suddenly starving. 'Mark, what were we talking about last night?' I ask tentatively.

'Nothing much.' He is wearing those black-rimmed glasses which remind me of my father's.

'I wasn't talking crud?'

'Crud? I love your turn of phrase. I particularly like 'dandy'.'

'Dandy? What was I saying last night?'

'I can't really remember,' he says, the corners of his mouth turning slightly upwards as he pretends to be absorbed in cooking. The oil spits and hits him near the eye. 'Ouch! I hate it when it does that.'

'Come on,' I gently encourage. 'You can remember, I can tell.'

'All right then. You said it was dandy seeing me, and then you conked out.'

I put a hand over my mouth. 'I'm sorry. How lame am I?' I lean my elbows against the table. 'I feel so ill,' I groan. 'Was I really so drunk I couldn't make it five steps back home?'

'Yes, pig drunk.'

'Pig drunk?'

'I tried to lift you . . . '

'I am definitely going to start swimming,' I promise virtuously.

'Katie, I didn't mean that. It's just that a dead weight is heavy.'

I think I would rather be called overweight than a dead weight.

'Look at you, you're stick thin.'

'I eat like a horse but I run on my nerves. I've got my mum's genes.' Mum. I must ring today and see how she is. 'She's thin too but we both have round curvy bottoms,' I add proudly.

Mark raises an eyebrow as he scoops the bacon from the pan and puts them on the kitchen roll. The grease settles onto the white paper with hens lining the edge. He turns to me with the spatula in his hand. His pale blue shirt collar is sticking up rigidly and he is wearing that navy jumper with holes in the elbow again.

As we eat our bacon sandwiches and drink coffee and orange juice, Mark asks me about

Sam and why I am not living with him any more. 'Katie, you've got a bit of orange stuck on your tooth,' he points out as I start to answer. I censor the story. I don't tell him exactly why; I don't mention what Sam said in the restaurant; all I say is that the relationship had run its course. Mark nods thoughtfully. He knows I am cutting the story down to make it simple. 'I'm sorry. Is there a chance you can get back together?'

I shake my head adamantly. 'There is nothing left to say. I pick rodents.' I start to smile, slowly remembering the cab drive home.

'What?' Mark has that baffled look again.

'Never mind. What are you doing today?'

'I've got to finish my book. Deadline is tomorrow.' Mark looks at his watch. 'In fact, I must go soon.'

I feel a sharp twinge of disappointment. I have enjoyed eating breakfast with him. It seems like an extension of my night out and I don't want to go yet. 'Your book? Don't you write from home?'

'Sometimes. I've just rented out this tiny office space because I find it easier writing away from here.'

'That sounds like a good idea. And then it's going to be sent to publishers, is it?' *Do you believe in destiny?* I gulp hard, feeling a flush of red creep up my neck. Did I really say that to him?

'Yeah, it's frightening letting it go out into the lion's den.'

'I can imagine. I like reading. My headmistress inspired me to love it. By the time I was fifteen I had read all of Tolstoy, Emily Brontë and Jane Austen. I wish I could write. What's the book about?' I now feel I have to keep the conversation steered away from last night. Flashbacks are suddenly appearing in front of me like warning hazard lights. *Do you think it's fate, Mark, the way we bump into each other?* I sink further into my seat.

The doorbell rings.

Mark picks up the entryphone. 'What a surprise,' he exclaims. 'I thought you weren't coming down until tonight?'

Oh my God, you're gay. I don't know when to stop, do I? Oh, well, what does it *really* matter? I try to convince myself. He's probably flattered by the attention.

'Are you going to let me in?' I hear from outside the flat.

'Sorry.' He presses the entry button.

'Who is it?' I ask casually.

'My girlfriend. She lives in Edinburgh.'

'Oh, right, that's nice.' A deep thud of disappointment hits the bottom of my stomach. 'Right, I should go,' I say, trying to sound like I have a busy day ahead.

A tall girl with light brown hair held loosely in a ponytail walks into the kitchen. She's wearing jeans and a fitted white shirt with small black dots on it. She steps forward to give Mark a kiss. 'Hello, you,' she says and they briefly hug. 'Surprise! I decided to catch an earlier train. My work can wait.'

Mark coughs. 'Jess, I'd like you to meet Katie.'

'Oh, hello.' She swings round in surprise. She smiles uncertainly at me and I can tell she is trying to work out why I am in Mark's kitchen, dressed in a black evening top, with heavy smudged black-ringed eyes.

'Right, I'd better be off,' I say.

'Mark, sorry, but who . . . I mean, what's going on?'

'Nothing is going on,' he states firmly. 'I've told you about Katie,' he assures her. Then he looks at me. 'Sorry, but I told Jess about your mother, I hope you don't mind?'

'Oh, you're Katie,' she exclaims with some relief. Then bites her lip and looks at me closely again. 'How is your mother?' she asks slowly, her eyes narrowed. She is still trying to work out why I am in Mark's kitchen.

'She's much better, thanks.' But Jess isn't listening. I could have said any old thing.

'What exactly is going on?' She stares at Mark hard. 'Is there something you're not telling me?'

'I should go,' I say nervously.

'Did you stay the night?' she asks me coolly.

'God, no,' I blurt out.

'Well, could you just explain to me what you are doing here?' Her voice is calm but there is an uncomfortable edge to it.

'Well, I did stay here, but obviously not in the way you think I did.'

'Jess, this is ridiculous,' Mark says.

'Ridiculous? Is it?' she queries, still remaining remarkably cool and not taking her eyes away from mine. I want to go home.

Mark makes Jess sit down at the table next to me, and pulls up a chair for himself. 'Katie and I bumped into one another last night at the off-licence. I was buying barbecue crisps and a bottle of water . . . did I buy anything else?' he asks himself. 'Well, that doesn't matter,' he continues, waving his hand dismissively. 'Anyway, I walked her home, I wanted to find out how her mother was. She came in for a drink — and you were so tired, weren't you?' He gestures towards me. 'Then she fell straight to sleep on the sofa,' he finishes earnestly. 'And there is nothing more to say.'

'I'm sorry, Jess, Mark was just being a good friend. I was really tired.'

'So nothing happened,' she says, more of a statement now than a question.

'Nothing,' Mark and I say together.

'Look, Katie slept next door.' He leads her into the sitting room.

'Mark, if you're lying to me, I couldn't bear it,' I can hear Jess saying quietly to him as she knows I am only a room away. 'I'd rather you told me now.'

'You know I wouldn't lie to you,' he reassures her. This is the perfect time to make my escape. It's clear they need to talk about this and I don't think I'm helping by hanging around.

I edge my chair back, trying not to disturb them. I open the front door. 'I know it might look suspicious but I swear nothing happened. Come on, Jess,' Mark is saying.

Gently I shut the door behind me.

★   ★   ★

I start walking home, taking each step very slowly.

I see the empty stretch of road ahead of me. Thank God I am outside that flat; I am too hungover to deal with this.

The shock of Jess's arrival is now replaced

with a nagging sense of disappointment that Mark has a girl-friend. *You know, you're very attractive, Mark. Come a bit closer. Don't look so worried . . .*

I have made a complete fool of myself! Oh well, I think, kicking a stone across the pavement. What did I think would happen? Break up with Sam and then fall predictably into the arms of a tall attractive elusive stranger who is, of course, the complete opposite to Sam, single *and* the answer to my dreams? For God's sake, Katie, this isn't a movie.

'Hey, why did you go without saying goodbye?' I hear. I turn round and see Mark racing towards me on his bike, his typescript balanced between the handlebars. He comes to an abrupt halt and the script flies onto the road and scatters into a hundred sheets.

'I'm sorry, I shouldn't have stayed last night.' I bend down to try and retrieve the paper. I reach out for one of the sheets and the wind blows it in the opposite direction so I end up clutching air.

'Shit . . . bugger . . . shit!' Mark curses on his hands and knees. 'I knew I should have put it in a bag.' He is desperately grabbing sheets of paper. One floats off into the middle of the road.

We start to laugh helplessly. I don't feel it is

the right time to ask what the book is about as I pick up the pieces of paper and dust them over. 'They're not too grubby,' I say. 'At least it's not raining.'

'You weren't going to say goodbye?' he mutters, scooping the remaining pages off the road.

'I need to go home, get out of these smoky clothes and have a bath.' I smile at him. 'Is Jess OK?'

'She's all right.'

'Shouldn't you be with her?'

'I have to get this work done, it won't take long,' he says. 'It's fine,' he reassures me.

'I don't blame her for being suspicious, I would be.'

'We know nothing happened so we have nothing to feel guilty about.'

'Exactly.' He stands up and I stand up with him. I start walking. He grabs his bike and follows me. 'Well, this is me.' I stand outside a red door with bits of paint flaking off it. 'Thanks, Mark, I'll see you soon.'

'Dandy.'

'Dandy,' I repeat. Mark doesn't say anything now. ''Bye then.' I start to turn the key in the door, aware that he still hasn't gone.

'Katie?'

'Yes?'

'I feel I should have told you — about Jess, I mean.'

'It doesn't matter,' I say, an octave too high.

This time he makes no reference to Bells. 'I'd like to see you again. There's no harm in us meeting for a . . .'

'Coffee?'

'And a sticky bun?' He pulls that funny crooked face.

'You know where I am.'

'Great. Friends?'

Ouch! That's painful. Did he think he had to say it so I wouldn't make a pass at him again? 'Friends,' I say.

'Good luck with the book,' I call after him, wrapping my shivering arms around myself for warmth. I watch him as he pushes off on his bike, the script back in position in-between the handlebars. He uses one hand to wave at me from behind. It looks dangerous to me. 'I hope those publishers are going to love it!' I call out. I want to shout, 'Be careful,' but I don't want to sound like his mother.

33

The house is modern, down a very steep drive. Mum warned me how steep it was and that I must leave the car in gear. I have bought my own second-hand car and I love it. It's small, silver, shiny and fast. The next thing I need to do is buy a flat. I have saved enough now to put down a decent deposit. What am I waiting for?

My legs are stiff and aching from the long journey. I should have arrived at least half an hour ago had it not been for getting lost along the endless winding narrow roads which all looked the same and seemed to lead nowhere. There are no signs outside Bells's house, it really was a stroke of luck I suddenly came upon it. I spotted a tall man wearing a tracksuit, with a bright blue jumper and an identity card around his neck, motioning me into the drive. I recognized him immediately from Bells's photograph album.

'Hello, I'm Ted,' he says, holding out a large hand which I shake. He has curly brown hair, the colour of a conker, and bright blue eyes which almost seem to pop out of his head with enthusiasm.

'Hi, Ted. I'm Katie, Bells's sister.'

'Hello, Bells's sister. Welcome to Wales.'

A tall man with dark hair walks out and says hello too, asking me how my journey was. His name's Robert. He is one of Bells' 'key workers'. He leads me inside, down a long corridor, past a pin-board which gives details of the events of the month, and into the kitchen. 'Isn't the weather remarkable today?' Ted says, following closely behind. 'They said there would be lots of rain, but we haven't had a single drop.'

'Ted is fascinated by the weather,' Robert mentions with a dry laugh. 'There's nothing he doesn't know about weather fronts across the country.'

The kitchen's a soft yellow, the colour of primroses, and kept immaculately clean, not a spot of dirt or clutter anywhere. I like the feel of the place immediately. There are glass doors behind the long wooden kitchen table which open out onto the terrace and garden. 'What a lovely house,' I acknowledge, looking around the room.

'We like it,' Ted says proudly.

'Bells will be down in a minute, she heard your car arrive. Would you like a tea? Coffee?' Robert stands ready at the kettle.

'I'd love a tea, please.'

'You haven't been here before, have you?'

he asks as he switches on the silver kettle.

'No.' There's no accusation in his tone at all, but I can't help but feel a heavy sense of guilt that up until now I have shown no apparent interest in where my sister lives. 'I want Bells to show me round.' Above the larder fridge is a black-and-white photograph of her wearing her dungarees, standing over a wheelbarrow filled with cooking apples. She's smiling with her thumbs up. Robert can tell I'm looking at it.

'She's a great girl, Bells,' he comments. 'She's always doing something. She can't sit still, can she, Ted?'

'Never,' he says with authority. 'Bells and I go to college together. Every Thursday we go. We learn all kinds of stuff, like art and writing, and I'm learning to dance too.'

'Really? What kind of dancing?'

'Ballroom dancing.'

There's another photograph, on the other side of the room, to which Ted leads me. He is large with broad shoulders. 'Guess where I am?' he says. I peer closely at the photograph. I can see Bells dressed in an Elvis outfit, strumming a tennis racquet as a guitar. Ted is just behind her, wearing what looks like a shiny all-in-one outfit, with enormous fake sideburns. He's playing the drums. 'There you are!' I say, pointing.

'Groovy, huh?' He starts to laugh. 'It was my birthday party. Everyone had to dress up as Elvis Presley. Bells and I formed a band together, we called ourselves the Gold Fishfingers.'

'Really groovy.' I smile back. 'Why the Gold Fishfingers, though?'

'Well, I love fishfingers,' he replies simply, as if I really should have known, and walks out of the kitchen.

'How is your mother?' Robert asks me.

'She's OK. Gets frustrated because she still can't drive, but Dad is so patient with her. He sets her tasks, like putting photographs into albums and other things you never normally get round to doing.'

Robert sighs with relief. 'We were so worried, you know.'

'Has Bells talked to you about Mum?' I ask.

'No, no,' he says shaking his head. 'She wouldn't do that.'

I'm dying to see her so I ask if I can go upstairs, but then she walks into the kitchen. She's wearing her red football slippers, a pair of tracksuit bottoms which I haven't seen before and the black T-shirt I gave her with the silver star on it. 'She's wearing it in your honour,' Robert says, winking at Bells.

'Hi, Bells.' She walks towards me. I'd like

to hug her but Bells doesn't really do hugs. Instead we shake hands and then she hits me affectionately on the arm and I hit her back. 'That's right,' she says.

I pick up my bag. 'I brought you some olives and some cheese biscuits, and Eddie asked me to give you this ginger cake.'

'Eddie at deli.' She rocks forward and takes the bag of food. 'Thanks, Katie.'

⋆ ⋆ ⋆

Bells leads me upstairs. There is a large DO NOT DISTURB sign stuck to her door, along with lots of peeling off football stickers. Her room is small, with a single bed in the corner, and unlike the kitchen there is no space in here which hasn't been filled with paintings, stickers, posters, CDs and newspaper cuttings. I have to tiptoe in between a painting on the floor of the Union Jack flag and a poster which reads in red pen, Come on ENGLAND.

There's the familiar poster of Bob Marley smoking a joint, and the one of the Beatles, both of which she pinned to the walls of her bedroom in London. I sit on the edge of her bed. Her inhaler sits on the bedside table together with her photograph album and a mug of tea.

'How's Mum?' she asks, sitting down next to me. Her chest is wheezing. She picks up her inhaler.

'She's much better.'

I stand up and walk over to her window. I catch a glimpse of the sea. 'Bells, wow!' I sigh. 'What a view you have. It's beautiful.'

She stands just behind me, breathing heavily. 'You like sea?' she asks, clearly pleased that I am impressed.

'I love the sea. It makes me want to move out of London,' I say, turning to her. 'Come on, let's go for a walk.'

★   ★   ★

It's warm, but as Ted summarized, there are some dark threatening clouds hanging over us. We walk across the pale sand. I bend down and pick up a handful, letting it sift through my fingers like grains of sugar. Bells walks ahead of me. 'Do you swim in the summer?' I ask, catching up with her.

'No, too cold.'

I ask her if we can sit down for a minute. We have walked a long stretch of the beach. It's so peaceful here, looking out to sea. There is not another soul in sight and the only sounds we can hear are from the seagulls.

'How's Dad?'

'He's all right. A bit tired from Mum bossing him around.' I gently nudge Bells.

'That's right.' She nods thoughtfully. 'Poor Dad. How're you?'

'I'm back in London, staying with Emma.'

'How's Emma?'

'She's fine. Getting ready for her wedding.'

'How's Sam?'

'I don't know. I haven't seen him. Did you get my last letter?'

'Yes. How's Aunt Agnes?'

After Bells and I have discussed every friend and member of our family, we start walking back. She continues to show me around her home and I can tell how proud she is by the way she points out everything. This is her territory; her world that I am entering. The sitting room has a piano. 'Ted plays piano,' she tells me. 'Poor Ted,' she adds, striking a key.

'Why poor Ted?'

'Very lonely, has no family.'

Bells would hate to be called a 'poor thing', but I have noticed how often she refers to other people in that way. It must give her a sense of security, feeling better off than the person next to her.

'No-one visits Ted,' Robert says. He stands resting one hand on the door handle. He must have overheard us. 'I've worked here for twelve years and Ted hasn't had one visitor in that time,' he reflects incredulously. 'You wouldn't think it could be true but some families just leave their children here. Dump them.'

'That's terrible. Why have them at all if that's what you're going to do?' I say angrily. It makes me realize how together my parents are, how strong they have always been. They would never have rejected Bells, it wouldn't even have occurred to them. It also makes me realize just how much I do not want to be lumped in the same category as Ted's family — the sister who never bothered.

'I know. It's the pits,' he agrees, tapping one foot against the floor. 'Everyone loves Ted, they don't know what they're missing out on. He looks after us all.'

'Ted champion on trampoline,' Bells adds. She is looking at the collection of videos next to the television.

I turn to Robert. 'So you've worked here for twelve years? That's pretty good going.'

'Yep, and I haven't had one solitary day off,' he claims.

'No way!'

'Well, maybe one or two, but I love it. My father worked here, so it runs in the family. I don't know what else I'd do.'

'You could do with a holiday though, couldn't you?'

He smiles. 'Yeah, I suppose,' he says, 'I'm just not sure where I'd go.'

'You seen *Trading Places*?' Bells asks me.

'I love that film,' I exclaim. Robert and I walk over to join Bells, and I look over her shoulder at the videos. 'Oh, wow, *Tootsie*, that's my favourite!'

'Very funny, *Tootsie*,' Bells agrees.

★ ★ ★

It's now three o'clock in the afternoon. Bells and I have tea and some chocolate digestive biscuits, and then I drive us to the local football club. She is now wearing a football shirt and her red Manchester United scarf wrapped snugly around her neck. Her team are playing a match late this afternoon, she tells me excitedly. We enter the clubhouse. There are a couple of men sitting at the bar.

'Hello, Budge,' she calls out. 'He's captain,' she quickly tells me, her breathing intensifying. 'Hello, Paul. Hello, Budge.' She punches each one in turn. They turn round and hold up their hands to give her a high five. Bells's hand barely covers the palms of theirs.

'My sister Katie,' she tells them. They briefly look at me and say hello.

Budge is very good-looking. He has dark brown hair and dark eyes that turn very slightly upwards. 'Hi,' I say back, but I can see I have lost his attention already.

'Bells, you're going to watch the match today, aren't you?' Budge asks, pulling at her scarf. He starts to uncoil it. She laughs furiously, saying it's tickling her. I can see her blushing.

''Course she is,' says the other one. Another army of men walk into the clubhouse. They take it in turns clapping Bells on the back.

'How you doing, Bells?'

'How's our favourite mascot?'

'Bells, good to see you.'

'We've missed you,' Budge adds.

'I tell you,' one of them says to me, 'we need Bells back on the pitch. She's our good luck charm.'

I'm about to say something when a beefy man, who looks like he works out in the gym seven days a week, sweeps in from behind and gathers her up in his arms. They all cheer and I start to join in. He puts her onto his shoulders. Bells is laughing and clapping her hands. 'Come on, St David's,' they are starting to chant like a tribe. I have never seen her look so happy, nor so at home anywhere. She fits in here like the missing piece of a jigsaw that has been lost for a long time. No-one else will do but Bells. I stand back, letting them pass me. They're filing out now and onto the playing field. 'Katie,' I can hear her call, looking over her shoulder to try and find me. 'You coming?'

★ ★ ★

I drive back to London early the following morning feeling happy. Bells's team won, 2–0. I watched the match, spending most of my time asking her, 'Are they allowed to do that?' I need to get up to date on the rules of football, clearly. After the match, I drove Bells home and found a crowd of people in the kitchen. I met Mary Veronica, a girl called Jane, another man called Alex, and Ted was still in the kitchen, looking after everybody. He said Bells was going to cook for us all. She made one of her famous vegetable roulades and, to follow, we had chocolate mousse. Bells opened her tub of olives and passed them around. Mary Veronica hated the taste and spat hers out. They turned some music on, Stevie Wonder of course.

I can now put faces to names; I can imagine what she does on a Saturday afternoon. I can see her being picked up like a trophy and carried onto the football pitch. I

351

can hear her laughing and clapping.

I can see her cooking in the kitchen.

The different nametags in her clothes make sense now.

I can see her when she picks up the phone in the corridor, in front of the pin-board.

It didn't feel sad leaving because I know Bells is in the right place. It's not perfect, nothing is, but it's almost perfect, and it's her home. We've made a pact that I'll see her once a month and phone her every Monday and Friday night. I know how important it is for Bells to have her routine. 'Promise?' she said as I left.

'I promise.'

34

I am sitting at the kitchen table flicking through one of Emma's many *Brides* magazines. Brides with flashing white smiles and pearls the size of quail's eggs stare out of the pages at me. Emma will look nothing like them, I hope. I can overhear Jonnie and her next door talking about the wedding. They are getting married in London, at St John's Church, Hyde Park. Double-decker buses will take the guests from the church to the reception at the National Liberal Club.

In fact, Emma can't stop talking about the wedding.

Should she choose Selfridges, Harrods or Peter Jones for their wedding list?

Should their invitations be modern or traditional?

Should they invite friends' girlfriends and boyfriends?'

'If I invite Josh, I have to invite Rebecca too, although I hardly know her,' she is saying. 'And what about children?' she cries out. 'I really don't want children.'

I realize how much I want to buy my own flat. I need my own place.

I put my head into my hands. Why do I feel so flat? It's been two weeks now since I saw Mark. For some reason I'd imagined he might pass by my door . . . well, Emma and Jonnie's door . . . but nothing.

I picture him on his bike again. I wonder what his book is about? Crime? Thriller? Love story? Science fiction? An autobiography? Perhaps he has had a fascinating past. On the cover will there be a photograph of Mark set in a square border, and will it be called *Mark's Journey*? I laugh at this idea. I feel a lot more interested in everyone else's life at the moment. *If you could write the script of your life, what would you write?* I hear again, but this time it's not in Sam's voice. It's my own.

I march into my bedroom and pick up my sketch-book which sits on the bookshelf. I'm not sure what I would write but I know I want to start sewing again. Since splitting up with Sam I have had more free time and I want to make the most of it. Maybe I want to take life less seriously too. No more writing lists of what I want to achieve by the end of each decade. Sam did those — he wanted to retire by the time he was forty. I just want 'to be'.

With renewed enthusiasm, I decide to go for a Sunday walk with my sketchpad. I could buy a coffee and people watch. I need to get ideas about what people want to wear. It's cold outside, but the autumn sun is warm. I put on my blue and red poncho over my dark jeans.

Jonnie looks relieved when I walk into the room. 'What are you wearing?'

'It's the latest fashion.' I twirl around for him.

'Where are you off to, cowgirl?'

'A walk.'

'Who are you hoping to bump into?' he asks with a naughty smile. Jonnie is not good-looking. If you analyse his features they are in fact quite ugly. Two crooked front teeth, a long chin, and he's too thin because he works too hard. Yet when you put it together with his blue eyes, dark hair and his sense of fun, he is one of the most attractive people I know.

'Jonnie, we have to carry on with the wedding list,' Emma insists, her face crumpled with despair.

Jonnie pulls a desperate face. 'See you later.'

★ ★ ★

I sit down by the café window with my cappuccino and gaze ahead. It's mid-morning and a few people are out. A girl walks past in a long dark brown skirt with ruffles around the bottom. She wears brown boots and a cream-coloured wrap-around cardigan. She must be cold without a coat. I quickly sketch the overall effect. Tassels and fringes are back in, I notice, when I see yet another young girl walk past in a hippy layered skirt and a belt with a large golden buckle. I am sure that's a Jigsaw belt. I saw them in there the other day. The latest fashion reminds me of what Emma's sister Berry used to wear. Another girl passes in jeans, a green and white stripy woollen hat that covers her ears and a long black coat. I notice how many people are jogging too.

I start sketching but my mind keeps wandering. I think I would rather write to Bells instead. Ten minutes later I have written nearly two pages.

I loved visiting you last weekend and seeing your home. It meant a lot to me, Bells. I'm only sorry I haven't visited before. I still think about the view from your bedroom window. You are so lucky to be able to look out onto the sea every morning. That would put me in a good mood.

I thought Ted was lovely, tell him I look

forward to seeing him dance at your open day. I also loved the football — are your team playing this weekend? If they are, I hope they win. Mr Vickers pops in for tea almost every day now. Eve and I miss him if he doesn't drop by. He helps himself to a custard cream and makes his own pot of tea.

I forgot to tell you, but Mark asked after you. I saw him the other night. In fact, I made a real fool of myself and drank too much, and then told him how much I liked him. I feel a real idiot now because he has a girlfriend. Anyway, it doesn't matter because we are still friends. Next time you come to London I am sure we can all meet up for . . .

I stop writing for a second, and think about what Mark said to me. I can still see him standing at Emma's front door.

I pick up my mobile and call him. 'Just wondered if you wanted to meet up for that coffee and sticky bun?'

★ ★ ★

My pen flies across the page as someone taps me from behind. A large smudgy ink mark splatters against the last sentence. 'Damn.

Don't ever creep up on me like that again! You frightened me.'

'Sorry, Katie.' Mark smiles, leaning over me. Is he trying to read my letter?

'I was waving at you from outside but you looked so serious. You're not writing your will, are you?'

'Mark!' I cover the page, the way I used to if I thought someone at school was trying to cheat and steal my answers.

'Who are you writing to?'

'Bells.'

'Can I add something?' He sits down next to me and peers over at the letter.

'No!' I shut my sketchpad firmly now. 'You can write your own letter.' Bells is right. I am bossy. I *am* a traffic warden.

'Sorry,' he says again. 'I'm glad you called.'

Mark has this disarming way of being polite and formal with a naughty streak too, all at the same time. I begin to relax now that the letter is well and truly out of sight.

'Give us a cigarette,' we hear an old man in a raincoat asking in the doorway.

'You scrounger,' says a younger man who is about to walk inside. He digs into his pocket and finds a cigarette for the old man. 'There you go.'

'You have a lighter?'

'Bloody hell! What has this world come to?'

Now he lights the old man's cigarette. 'Anything more I can do for you?' he calls after the old man who is now limping off into the distance, sucking his stick of nicotine. 'Polish your shoes, buy you a drink,' he mutters to himself as he walks over to the counter.

'I love people watching,' Mark remarks. 'It's even better if I'm sitting in a hot country, by the sea, drinking beer.'

'If only. Any news on the book yet?' He's wearing that navy jumper with holes in the arm.

He lets out a long frustrated sigh. 'No. My agent says it needs more work. If you want instant gratification, don't be a writer.'

'You never told me what you are writing?'

'Just a fantasy adventure story,' he says modestly. 'It's for children and adults. I'm trying to be the next J. K. Rowling, only better,' he confesses. 'My grandmother used to read me *The Adventures of Uncle Lubin*. It's a book I've never forgotten. I'd love to be able to write something as good.'

'I don't know it. What's it about?'

'You don't know it?' he exclaims in disbelief. 'You must read it. Uncle Lubin looks after his young nephew Peter, but one day a great Bagbird swoops down,' Mark does the actions, 'and whisks the child away. Uncle

Lubin has to find him. He travels around the world and up to the moon in his floppy hat and striped stockings. Uncle Lubin has a dream that he sees Peter under the sea, flanked by mermaids, and he's safe. When he wakes up he is distraught to find himself alone. Uncle Lubin never gives up, though, and in the end . . . '

'Don't tell me!' I bang my hand against the table. 'He rescues Peter?'

'Yes, sure.' Mark looks disappointed by my reaction. 'But it's more than that. It's about the human spirit and enduring love. It's about never giving up hope. I wish I still had that book, I don't know how Mum could have lost it.'

'Have you read *The Old Woman in the Vinegar Bottle*?'

Mark shakes his head.

'It's about this woman who lives in a vinegar bottle. She has a little ladder to go in and out by,' I wiggle my fingers as if climbing an imaginary ladder, 'but she grows discontented.'

Mark grins. 'I'm not surprised. Living in a vinegar bottle doesn't exactly sound enthralling.'

I smile. '''Tis a shame, 'tis a shame,' she grumbles, and pictures herself in a little white house with roses and honeysuckle growing over it, pink curtains, a pig in the sty. A fairy passing by feels sorry for her. 'Well, never you mind,' she says. She tells the old woman to go up to bed and turn around three times in her bottle. 'When you wake up in the morning, you'll see what you will see!' When the old woman wakes she's in a room with pink curtains and she can hear a pig grunting outside.' I do the sound effects. 'What's wrong?' I am put off from telling the rest of the story because Mark is looking at me in a strange way.

'Come on, tell me what happens next,' he insists.

'Well, the old woman is delighted but it never crosses her mind to *thank* the fairy. The fairy goes east and west, north and south, and then comes back to the old woman, knowing how pleased she will be in her little white house. 'Oh! 'tis a shame, so it is, 'tis a shame. Why should I live in a pokey little cottage? I want to live in a red townhouse and have a little maid to wait on me.' 'Well, never you mind,' the fairy says.'

''When you wake up in the morning, you'll see what you will see,'' Mark finishes for me.

'Next she wants to live in a house with white steps and men and maids waiting on her. Then she wants to live in a palace. 'Look at the Queen. Why shouldn't *I* sit on a gold throne with a gold crown on my head?' The fairy grants her wish, but when she returns to hear the old woman complaining that the crown is too heavy for her head, she gives up. 'Why can't I have a home to suit me?' the old woman moans. 'Oh, very well, if all you want is just a home to suit you . . . ' the fairy says wearily. The old woman wakes up and finds herself back in the vinegar bottle, where she stays FOR THE REST OF HER LIFE.'

'Serves the old woman right.'

'I remember that story so well, Mum read it to Bells and me. What about your family?' I ask. 'I've been so wrapped up in my own dramas that I know nothing about you. Are you close to your parents?'

'We've had our moments. I felt I'd let my father down when I told him I didn't want to be a lawyer. My brother emigrated to New Zealand and became a sheep farmer, Dad couldn't understand where his genes came from. I was his last chance. Law is in his blood, his father was a lawyer. Jess is a lawyer too so that helps.' He laughs drily.

For a moment I feel that terrible atmosphere in the kitchen again. 'That must give her brownie points?'

'Yes, they really like her. Jess is like family. My Scottish lass, they call her.'

So not only is she good-looking and bright,

she is also like family. Bugger. 'How did you two meet?' I ask casually.

'At school, funnily enough. In Edinburgh.'

'Why were you in Edinburgh?'

'One of my father's first jobs was there and my parents loved the place so much they decided to move permanently. I think I am about one-eighth Scottish by now.' He smiles.

'So you've been going out with her for how long?'

'Only six months, but it feels like longer,' he adds, and I can't tell whether that's a good or a bad thing.

'How come it took you that long to start going out?'

'I don't know,' he says, his voice clipped and considered. 'We kind of fell into it. We went on holiday with a group of friends and that was it. We were worried it might affect our friendship but it's fine.'

Fine? Fell into it? That was it? Mark's vocabulary lacks a certain passion. Where's the romance? Where are the fireworks?

'I guess it's true,' he says with a sense of defeat . . . or am I reading too much into his voice?

'What?'

'Somewhere along the line, girls and boys can't just be friends. At some point . . . '

'You don't believe that rubbish, do you?

363

Come on. We're friends, aren't we?'

'Yes. You're right.'

'Are you happy?'

'Am I happy? Well, that's a difficult question.'

'With Jess, not in general,' I say, hoping that I am not being too nosy.

'She's one of my closest friends. She's always been there for me. It's funny, though,' he shuffles his chair in closer, 'she's intelligent, but if you ask her where Guatemala is, she doesn't have a clue.'

I sit, frozen, trying to picture where exactly it is. 'Africa?' From his expression I see I'm wrong. 'America,' I burst out. 'Of course, it's America.'

'North or South?'

'Er, South? No, North.'

'It's south of Mexico, next to Honduras, and not so far from Panama.'

'Shut up, clever clogs, we can't all be geography wizards.'

'Which direction is north?'

'Shut up!'

'How did we get onto Jess?'

'We were talking about your parents. They wanted you to be a lawyer.'

'Oh, yes. It's all about approval, isn't it? You want them to be proud, whatever you do.'

'I admire anyone who teaches, I couldn't

do it. Is your father proud of you?'

'I don't know,' he shrugs. 'I think so.'

'He should be.' I smile. 'You see, if you were to die tomorrow — God forbid,' I add, touching his arm briefly.

'Thank you,' he nods.

'I'm sure your father would be saying, 'I wish I had told Mark we were proud of him.' I would never have forgiven myself if Mum had died and I had left so many things unsaid. I felt so hard done by when I was little because she was always in hospital with Bells, but look at people who have no proper homes or divorced parents who screw them up. Emma says she sees people . . . '

'Don't start saying how much worse off they are than you,' Mark says, disgruntled.

'Well, they are, aren't they?'

'Look, we never really go around thinking like that. There's always someone a lot worse off than you, sure, but if someone said to you, 'Think of the starving children in Africa,' every time you came to them with a problem, you'd want to pelt them with frozen peas.'

I laugh. 'Why frozen peas?'

He shrugs. 'I couldn't think of anything else. What I'm trying to say is, each problem, each situation, it's all relative. OK, you had a damaged relationship with your mother, but if someone tells you they don't get on with any of their family, mother, father and all six sisters and brothers, and that you should count yourself lucky, does that really make it better?'

'You should become a counsellor, you know. I've never thought about it like that.'

'That'll be fifty pounds, please. See you next week?'

'Yes, please.' The scary thing is I really mean it too.

We sit quietly for a few minutes watching people go by. It doesn't feel awkward saying nothing. It feels peaceful.

Eventually I break the silence. 'Do you have any unusual characters in your family?'

'How about the grandmother who kept a lion under her bed for starters?'

I laugh. 'Well, I'm glad it's not just our family then.'

From the corner of my eye I can see a girl walking by outside, wearing a baseball cap on back to front, a black bra, black vest, a black mini skirt, a small backpack and black knee-length platform boots. A group of young friends walk past and I hear them laugh at her mockingly, but the girl boldly marches on.

'You see that girl?' Mark says.

'You can hardly miss her, can you?'

'She looks a bit weird . . . '

'She's wearing a shocking outfit,' I interrupt.

'Fine, all that's true, but she's far more interesting than the other girls who look like clones of each other.'

I look at the backs of the three girls, each with dyed blond hair, all roughly the same height, and all wearing baggy trousers, skin-tight tops and trainers.

'She'd be the one the author wrote about. Eccentric, unusual, out-of-the-ordinary characters make the world go round,' Mark says. 'God, life would be boring without them.'

★　★　★

When Mark leaves, I finish my letter to Bells and then go to the newsagent's to buy copies of *Vogue*, *Tatler*, *Harpers & Queen* and *Glamour*.

Two weeks later I have made myself a suede coat with panels on the front and a soft lining. I have also been working on my designs and compiled a small portfolio. I would like to have my own label in the future; it's something to work towards. 'I've bought a Katie Fletcher top,' I can hear someone saying excitedly. I've been people watching constantly, looking around various shops in my lunch hour and seeing what's out there. I have been working late in the evenings after I close the shop too. It was time to change my image as well so I went to Ariel's, my Spanish hairdresser's, and he made me 'feel like a different woman', as he put it. He cut and layered my hair in the front. I like pulling it back into a short neat blunt ponytail. It feels symbolic of a new start on so many fronts, most importantly with Mum.

And, even more impressive, I have bought a pair of luminous purple goggles and a black costume and have been swimming each morning before work.

I have even stopped smoking.

I like the new Katie Fletcher.

35

'Jonnie, who was on the phone?' I call. It's the evening and I'm about to go to bed.

'I don't know, he hung up again.' I walk into the sitting room. Emma is sitting next to him doing the crossword.

'He?'

'Well, the only person I can think of is Sam,' Jonnie suggests. 'D'you think he might want to get back in touch?'

'Possibly,' I say. Sam has called me a few times. He keeps on saying he wants to meet up, we need to talk, but I cannot see the point. What is there left to say? I told him we should accept it's over and no hard feelings. 'You sound different. Are you seeing someone else?' he immediately pounced. I assured him that I wasn't. 'Sam, I've been at home looking after Mum, the last thing on my mind has been finding a boyfriend,' I said wearily. Maybe I should just meet him and be done with it.

Jonnie studies my expression. 'There's nothing going on between you two still, is there?'

'No! No,' I say more calmly.

'Is it safe to talk about Sam now?' he asks.

'Quite safe.'

'Well, I always thought he was a bit of a tosser,' Jonnie comments.

'Jonnie!' Emma puts the crossword down.

'It's fine, honestly.' I shrug. 'If you look the part, you feel the part . . .'

'And you ARE the part,' we all finish, and start to laugh.

'How about, 'You have to think outside the box'?'

'I liked 'done and dusted',' Emma says now, growing animated, clapping her hands together. 'He actually said that to me when one of my patients died. Admittedly he was ninety-nine and had had a good innings but . . . ' the corners of her mouth curl upwards . . . 'he was being cremated, so it didn't seem quite the right thing to say. 'Emma,'' she puts on Sam's voice, ''it's the nature of the job.''

I sink down on a corner of the sofa. 'He didn't?' I exclaim. 'He *is* a tosser.'

'I always thought you could do a lot better,' she finally admits, and then pauses as if she is not sure whether to say whatever is on her mind next. 'Like this Mark person?' she finishes, trying desperately to sound casual. 'I mean, you've been spending quite a lot of time with him.'

'Uh-oh, no, I want to be on my own. No men, thank you. Anyway, he has a girlfriend.' I change the subject quickly. 'If the phone rings again in the next few minutes, let me get it, OK? I'm going to put the rubbish out, it's bin day tomorrow, isn't it?'

'It is,' Jonnie confirms 'Bin day. What an exciting fast-paced world we live in.'

I haven't smoked for a month now, no ash and stubs in the bin this time. I have not cut out the drink though. Come on, life is too short. I wobble out of the front door with two large black bags in my hands. I am tempted to go for an evening walk, I might bump into Mark. Since that Sunday morning, nearly a month ago, he and I have been out many times. I often go round to his place after work and we have a drink together. We made spaghetti Bolognese the other night and watched one of Bells's favourite Dustin Hoffman movies, *Tootsie*. Last week Mark shoved a note through the door: 'Sticky bun and a coffee tomorrow?'

It's a Monday night, he should be in. It's only ten o'clock. I feel like some company, that's all. Just as I knock on the door to his flat I hear his bike outside and now he is coming through the front entrance. His face looks pink from the cold night air and he's wearing a bright yellow strap across his coat

371

which he pulls off when he sees me. 'Hi.' He rubs his hands together. 'How are you?'

'I'm fine. I was just putting the rubbish out then I thought about you.'

'Charming! Do you want to come in for a drink?'

'Would love to. Where have you been?'

'School. God, I'm tired,' he says as he walks into the kitchen. I follow him. 'We're rehearsing for *My Fair Lady* and there's so much work to do. Lines to be learned. Singing classes. Dancing. Professor Higgins has ducked out now so I've had to replace him with Matthew, and I don't know if he's up to the task.'

'Sit down,' I order. 'Tell me where everything is and I will make you something to eat and drink. My turn to fuss over you.'

'Wonderful,' he sighs, taking off his boots and the bicycle clips from his trousers. 'What luck I ran into you. The mugs are in the cupboard above the sink.'

I open a cupboard and find plates and soup bowls. 'To the right,' Mark instructs. 'The coffee's in the fridge.'

'You keep it in the fridge?'

'Keeps it fresh.'

'Why do you keep mustard in the fridge?' Mark looks at me wearily. 'Sorry,' I apologize. 'Everyone's kitchen's a novelty. You like these!' I turn to him in amazement. On top of his fridge sits a packet of marshmallows covered in chocolate with strawberry jam filling. 'Emma teases me for still liking these. She told me they are the sort of things mothers put in packed lunches and that I should have grown out of them by now.'

'Well, she's missing out then, isn't she? I love them, could eat a whole packet at once.'

I am delighted to hear this. I make two cups of coffee and Mark eats some toast with Marmite.

'Katie, I have a big favour to ask. I was going to come and see you about it tomorrow.'

'This sounds serious.'

'Jess can't come to *My Fair Lady*. Obviously Edinburgh's a bit too far to come just for a school play. Also, she fell into her mother's flowerbed and sprained her ankle.'

I burst out laughing and Mark looks at me strangely. 'Oh, Mark, sorry, it's just the way you put it.'

'She was trying to find the house key under the flowerpot, you know the way parents think that's such a clever place to leave keys? Well, she picked up the pot, lost her balance, and fell backwards into the rose bush.'

'Stop it!' I say, bending over double, unable

to control my laughter. 'Is she going to sue the rose bush?'

'I can't think why you find it so funny,' he says, but I know he is smiling without even looking at him. 'Anyway, I was wondering if you would come with me instead?'

'Really?'

'Yes. What do you think?'

'Have you asked Jess?'

'I will, but I'm sure she won't mind. She knows now that we're just friends.'

'All right, I'd love to come then. I've never been to a school play. The only time I remember Mum coming to watch me at school was when I was nine. The entire class played recorders. She tells me we were *terrible*. Granny Norfolk came too, and apparently nudged her in the middle of our rendition of 'Greensleeves', saying, 'The *crème* of Southampton is here tonight,' followed by a squawking laugh.'

'What, a laugh like yours, you mean?'

'Do I squawk?' I panic.

'You do,' he admits. 'It's quite infectious, though.'

'When is it?'

'Friday night.'

For a moment I long to have something else on to make him think I have a hectic and exciting social life. 'Right, fine, see you

Friday. I'm going. I've had enough of you for one night.'

* * *

A school play. Do I dress smart? Casual? Trendy? Finally I go for smart and trendy. I have decided to wear my black dress and the gold necklace with the medallion-like pendant. I look at myself in front of the long mirror. Since I stopped smoking I have put on a few pounds around my hips and my face looks less drawn. I put some shimmering grey round my eyes to bring out the green in them and dust my face with some tinted powder. I scoop one strand of hair back into a clip and the sharp layers kick forward.

* * *

I am singing loudly in the street, pretending to be Eliza Doolittle.

'Shh!' Mark laughs, holding me back from swinging around the next lamppost. 'We're getting some really strange stares.'

'Who cares, Mark? You shouldn't mind what people think.'

'I don't,' he agrees.

'I've spent far too much time caring about

what others think,' I tell him. 'It's a waste of time.' I turn to him. 'I really enjoyed tonight. I think your class are wonderful.'

'They sang their hearts out, didn't they?' he says proudly. 'Helen really belted it out.'

Helen played Audrey Hepburn's part, Eliza. I don't want to tell Mark she nearly deafened the audience and that I wished I had taken my earplugs. Mark stayed so intent on the performance that I didn't dare breathe in case he missed a note or a word. The real low point was when Professor Higgins tripped and fell off the stage. He was dancing with Eliza in triumph because she was finally speaking 'proper' and he stepped too far. Everyone gasped and Mark rushed to the stage as if he was acting in *Casualty*. I couldn't help watching him more than the play. What was so fascinating was the passionate interest he felt in these children who couldn't really sing. Mark was with them every step of the way. His changing expressions told the whole story.

He would screw up his face when the piano teacher hit a wrong note. There was one part where they had to start the 'Rain in Spain' song again because she hit a series of wrong notes and I thought Mark was going to have a heart attack. 'We rehearsed this one time and time again.' He grimaced. 'That hairy baboon never gets it right first time, look at her ridiculous tinsel tiara,' he went on, and then looked at me remorsefully. 'I mean, she's really very nice, but . . . '

'Shh, they're doing really well,' I whispered back, reaching out to hold his hand in support. He clutched his fingers over mine. His palm was sweaty. The best part, however, was the end. Everyone stood and applauded for what seemed like five minutes. The headmaster called Mark up onto the stage and he bowed together with the cast. Bells would have enjoyed this too, I thought. She should be here. The cast bunched around him, one actor hit his arm affectionately, another one did a high five. Mark was congratulating them all. Eliza gave him some flowers and then looked shyly at her feet. 'Who's that babe with you?' one of the boys asked loudly, pointing at me. I almost burst with pride at this point. Nearly thirty and called a babe! 'Is that your girlfriend?' he continued.

I know I blushed furiously at this point and had to pretend I needed something in my handbag. When I looked back Mark was smiling at me.

★　★　★

'Taxi!' Mark shouts as we see a black cab with its yellow light lit up.

He and I sink back into the seat. I break out into another *My Fair Lady* song and Mark joins in. The cab driver is shaking his head at us.

'What's your favourite thing in the world?' I ask. 'Apart from porn.'

Mark scratches his chin playfully. 'If it can't be porn, it has to be . . . um . . . marshmallow biscuits.'

'Don't overexcite yourself.'

'Come on, you then?'

'The smell of fresh coffee and bread.'

'Skiing on a beautiful day with fresh-powder snow.'

'Going to bed.'

Mark raises an eyebrow. 'With anyone in particular or on your own?'

'On my own and having the duvet all to myself.'

'Wow, aren't we a wild pair? OK, what do you hate most in the world?' he quickly moves on.

'Rude and narrow-minded people.'

'People who look over your shoulder when you're at a drinks party.'

'I hate that!'

'The trick is to start telling them you drank a bottle of gin with twenty Anadin and see if they say, 'Oh, how interesting',' Mark says drily.

'Traffic wardens,' the cab driver shouts through. Oh, no, I think to myself. 'And people who tell me which route I should take — that gets me, that does. Think they know better when I've been driving around London for years,' he rambles on.

'Ooh, I've got one! Christmas starting in August.'

'I like this game. People who trump you,' Mark goes on. 'I tell someone I went to Vienna and they tell me the place I really ought to go to is Budapest.'

'Oh, yes,' I agree. 'Nothing more annoying. People who trump are the same people who look over their shoulder. Vermin, that's the new name for people we don't like. Rodents, man.' We laugh.

'If you could change anything about yourself, what would it be?' I start again.

Mark wrinkles his nose as he is thinking this one through.

'I'll start,' I suggest. 'I wish I wasn't so stubborn.'

'I'm too soft.'

'You're not soft. I saw how you pulled those children into line. They respect you. You're kind but that's different. I can be too proud.'

'I love the way you say what you think.'

'I don't, Mark, not always. Look how long it took Mum and me to start talking properly. I bottle things up, let myself stew over problems.'

'Well, I wear my heart on my sleeve. I'm too emotional. I even cried reading *Bridges of Madison County*.'

'You're a wimp. But I cried too,' I add.

'So did I.' The cab driver is still eavesdropping. 'Now, is it left here?'

Our legs gently brush. 'Mark.' I lean closer towards him. 'I've never noticed your eyes before.' One is tinged with brown, the other is blue. We look at each other for a second too long. I turn away first.

'Oh,' he says, 'a freak accident. I was about to score for a cricket match. I was spinning a pencil in between the guy ropes that hold up the nets for practising when it spiralled out of my hand. The likelihood of that pencil hitting me was a million to one, but . . . ' he gestures to his eyes ' . . . I had to have three stitches. That's why I need the glasses. It's my excuse whenever I lose a tennis match,' he smiles.

'You can barely tell. I mean, it's really subtle.'

'You're shivering. Here, have my jacket.'

He places it around my shoulders and I feel acutely aware of the warmth of his touch.

'You're such a gentleman,' I say.

'What is it with you two lovebirds? Is this some kind of mutual admiration society?' says the cab driver.

His intervention breaks the tension. We both smile. 'Lovebirds?' I start to laugh ironically. 'Have you ever had your palm read, Mark?'

'No way, I don't believe in any of that.'

I take his hand and turn it over. 'You have a very long life line,' I tell him.

'Oh, no, don't say that. I think there should be a finite age. Say, eighty? We just fall off our perch at eighty before old age really sets in.'

'Oh, dear me. Your love line is very poor. You haven't got much going on in *that* department. You have a very small . . . '

He pulls his hand away abruptly and takes mine. 'OK, Katie Fletcher, let's see what's in store for you.'

He circles my palm gently. 'Oh, no,' he starts saying. 'Oh dear. Oh dear.'

'Mark!' I nudge him in the stomach.

'You are going to come back as a . . . ' he's thinking ' . . . centipede in the next lifetime.'

'Mark, you are mad. If I come back, I am going to be a pop idol and frolic in front of Simon Cowell, thank you very much.'

'I don't understand the attraction. Jess likes him too. It's right here, thanks. Do you want to go somewhere for a drink? Do we really want to go home yet?' he says with unusual urgency in his voice. 'Shall we tell him to go around the block while we decide?'

'Emma and Jonnie aren't in tonight. Why don't you come over to my place?'

'Yes, sounds good. Stop here, could you?'

Mark takes my hand as I step out of the cab. 'M'lady,' he says. 'By the way, I never said it but you looked beautiful tonight.'

'Why, thank you, sir.' We stand holding hands, neither of us moving. 'My place, then?' I say, finally letting go.

'Whose place?' Sam is waiting outside Emma and Jonnie's front door, wearing his old leather jacket. He starts walking towards us.

I can see his hands are trembling and feel almost sorry for him, standing out in the cold on his own. He doesn't look like the confident Sam who used to stride along to the click of his shoes. He hasn't shaved properly either. 'What are you doing here?' I ask him.

'More to the point, what are you two doing together? This looks cosyeee.'

'Sam, it's none of your business.'

His eyes narrow as he looks at Mark. 'Who are you?' he demands aggressively.

'Mark.'

'Well, hello, Mark. Where have you just taken Katie?'

'Look, it's got nothing to do . . . '

Mark stops me. 'Well, if you really want to know, I took her to see *My Fair Lady*.'

'But Katie hates musicals.'

'I do not,' I cut in. 'I loved *Mama Mia*.'

'Well, even nicer of her to come along with me then,' says Mark calmly.

'Are you two on or something?' Sam says, as if he is imagining the two of us together and it's not a pretty sight. 'Having said that, I can't imagine it. Katie's more like a nun these days. Acts like she's wearing a habit and a chastity belt.'

I don't feel so sorry for him any more. 'Sam, you're drunk and being stupid.'

'Mark who loves gay musicals, my ex-girlfriend's turned into a nun. So are you two together? Probably not, I'd guess.'

'Well, as her modesty's ensured, I'm surprised you had to come and check on such an unthreatening situation,' Mark says, taking my hand.

Sam pulls our hands apart.

'Sam, it's late, I think you should go home,' I tell him.

'It's not even midnight, Sister Fletcher.'

Mark and I continue to walk on without him. 'Do you want me to call a cab for him?'

Mark asks quietly.

'I miss you,' Sam cries out. Mark and I stop and look back. 'I miss you. Katie, you can't go out with someone, live with them, and then never want to see them again,' Sam protests. 'Why haven't you been returning my calls? I'm not going to leave until you talk to me.'

I tell Mark to go on without me, that I'll call him when Sam has gone. 'If you're sure?' He looks at me intently. 'Katie, I'll stay with you if you want?' Sam throws him a hostile look.

'I can't leave him out here. Honestly, go on.'

'All right,' he says. 'Come over later.'

★ ★ ★

'Make this quick, Sam,' I say as we step inside.

He sits down on the sofa. 'I've been an idiot, you were right. We need to start talking about you and me,' he says, moving his arm towards me and then letting it drop. 'Everything you said that night, I've been thinking about it.' He pats the space on the sofa. 'And you've been through so much since then. Come and sit next to me, sweetheart, come on.'

I pull up Jonnie's leather chair and sit opposite him. He looks at me with that familiar puppy dog look, as if butter would not melt. 'You're lucky I even let you in,' I remind him. 'You were behaving like an idiot outside.'

'I know.' He smiles. 'I can't help it. I'm going crazy here.' He pulls a mad face, attempting to make me laugh. He beckons me towards him again, tapping the sofa as if I am a dog that is about to jump up and join him. 'Come on, Kitty-kins.'

'I'm comfortable over here, thanks.'

'Kitty-kins,' he tries again, putting on a silly baby voice.

'Sam, what do you want?'

He looks at me with surprise. 'OK, well, here goes. Nothing makes sense to me if you're not around. I rattle around in that house of mine. I want you to come back, I'm sure we can make a go of things. We used to have fun together. Come on, what d'you say?'

'Sam, too much has happened, I don't think it would work.'

'Well, we can only find out for sure if we give it another go, can't we?'

'Why do you miss me?'

'I just do. End of story.'

'You don't need me. It's because you're scared of being on your own.'

He laughs but I can tell he is trying not to lose his cool. 'That's not true,' he splutters, 'I'm not scared of anything. I valued our relationship . . . clearly a lot more than you did.'

'That's unfair,' I say, then realize he is right. It was easy letting Sam go. I haven't missed him at all.

'I think you and me are worth fighting for.'

'Why, Sam? You didn't call me once when Mum was so ill.' I can't keep the hurt out of my voice.

'I know,' he says quickly. 'I'm sorry.'

'She could have died, Sam. You didn't even call me as a friend. That's what it's all about, getting through the hard times as well as having fun together. We're great when everything's going well, but we fall at the first hurdle when life throws us a challenge. What does that say about us?' As I am saying this I am thinking of Mum and Dad who have stayed together through the good and bad times because they are a team. Having Bells and me, and all the problems that came with us, just brought them closer together.

'Haven't I said I'm sorry a thousand times? I'm no good at dealing with stuff like that . . . illness, you know, I don't know what to say. Your mum's all right now, isn't she? What do you want? More sympathy? What more can I do?'

'You don't need to do anything. It's over,' I say.

Sam starts telling me that if I don't go back to him his life will fall apart, he cannot live without me. He wanted to call me when Mum was in hospital but he didn't know what to say. 'My family, we never talk about things like that. My father doesn't allow room for anything personal or . . . ' He stops. He tells me he knew I would call him if there were any news.

'I'll even marry you, I'll do whatever it takes,' he says, gambling that this last pledge of commitment will work. 'Katie, I'll do anything.'

'Sam, please stop,' I cry out.

'What's wrong?'

I try to compose myself. 'I don't know how to say this,' I start. 'I wish I didn't have to. I don't love you.'

'I know I was angry, I shouldn't have made you leave like that. I should have called you, been more supportive,' he says, choosing not to hear what I have just said.

'Look, it's OK,' I reassure him. 'Let's just move on.'

'It's not because of Mark, is it? Katie, you can do better than that. I mean, who is he?

What's he doing taking you to a bloody musical? You can't be serious, picking him over me?'

I should have known he'd say that. I start to feel sorry for Sam and then he goes and says something like that. 'For your information, I like Mark. He's a friend. He's the same Mark who helped me when Bells went missing. Remember?'

'He ticks all the right boxes, does he?' says Sam with heavy sarcasm.

'Why are we even arguing about it? This is boring. Let's just admit it's over. Couples split up. One in two marriages breaks up.'

'Did we split up because of Bells? We were happy before she came along. I know I didn't hit it off with her, but we can work on that.'

Has he listened to a word I have said? 'No, we can't. You can't change who you are. I've changed, things change, that's all. I'm tired, Sam. It's late. I'm going to call you a cab.' I walk over to the small table by the sofa and pick up the phone. I start to punch in the number of the local cab firm.

Sam snatches the phone from me and hangs up. 'I'm not going.'

I pick up the phone again. 'Well, you're not staying here.'

He grabs it from me, and the glass lamp base on the table crashes to the floor. 'Look what you've done now,' I shout. 'Emma loves this.' I bend down to pick up the shattered pieces of glass. 'Just go, please.' I can smell stale alcohol on his breath. He bends down and I think he is going to help me pick up the glass. Instead he tries to kiss me. 'Get off!' I pull away. 'Please go.'

'I'm not going till we sort this out,' he says relentlessly. 'I want to make it up to you.'

'You're going now. Go,' I repeat.

There's a knock on the door. Quickly I stand up and put the broken pieces of lamp on the table. 'Katie, are you all right?' I hear Mark calling. I open the door.

'Look who it is,' Sam sneers. 'Your knight in shining fucking armour!'

Mark pushes past him. 'I was worried.' He touches my shoulder. 'Are you all right?'

'Fine. He won't leave.'

Mark turns to Sam. 'I think you should go.'

'I don't give a fuck what you think.'

I actually feel embarrassed that I went out with this person. Mark opens the front door and stands there holding it.

Sam grabs his jacket and walks towards him. 'All right, I'll go,' he mutters. Mark and I briefly exchange relieved looks, but then, just as Sam is about to leave, he turns around and with one lethal blow punches Mark in the face. He staggers backwards and his glasses fall to the ground.

'Sam, stop it!' I scream as he is about to have a second go at Mark. I plunge forward and grab his arm. Sam pulls away from me and proceeds to step on Mark's glasses. 'It's like a lion fighting a flea,' he says, grinding them into the ground, satisfaction written all over his smug face. 'No fucking contest.'

'Sam?' I hear Mark saying in a quiet flea-like voice.

Sam turns his head. 'Did that hurt?' He puts on his baby-like voice again.

'Not as much as this.' Mark belts him in the stomach.

Sam holds himself steady and starts to laugh scornfully. 'You can do better than that, can't you?'

'That is enough!' I shout at them both, stepping between them. 'Go home,' I plead with Sam. 'And Mark, just leave it, OK?'

I watch Sam stagger down the steps. He looks so miserable and alone. I never wanted it to end this way. 'Sam!' I call out.

He doesn't even turn around now. 'Shut up, Katie, I've had about enough of you anyway. I'll leave you and lover-boy to it.'

★ ★ ★

Mark lies with his head on my lap and I rest the packet of frozen peas against his chin. 'Next time we see Sam, we can pelt these little bullets at him,' I say, remembering Mark's pelting frozen peas line.

'If this were a film, I would have pushed Sam against the door and punched him back twice as hard,' Mark says dejectedly.

'How's the hand?'

'Painful. I feel like a loser.'

'You did hit him, though. Well done.'

'Yeah, right. If you hadn't stepped between us he would have mashed me to a pulp.'

I adjust the position of the peas. 'I don't know what I would have done if you hadn't come. How does it feel now?'

'Not good. Carry on.'

'It's funny, but I was terrified of losing Sam. When Bells came to stay, I didn't tell him about her until she'd arrived. He had no idea what she'd be like. I was so nervous he'd do a runner, that he wouldn't want to know me.'

Mark sits up and turns to me. 'I remember you telling me this when we first met. That's stupid, Katie.' His tone is uncomfortable.

'I know. There's no excuse.' I can't stand the idea of him thinking badly of me. 'Bells wasn't a part of my life at all then, not until she came to stay. I only saw her as this person with the potential to put Sam off. I know it sounds cruel, but that's how I felt. I've had a lot of growing up to do. You know, he thought we could just go back to the way things were,' I utter incredulously. 'He didn't even call me to see how Mum was, someone I've lived with. I would have called him, whatever had happened between us.'

'What did you ever see in that man?' Mark asks impatiently.

'There is a good side to him, I promise. I know he was behaving like an idiot tonight, but he's got no-one, Mark. No support from his family, he never talks about them. He has no real friends to confide in, only lads like Maguire. I didn't enjoy seeing him so unhappy. He does have a good side,' I repeat again. 'At least he doesn't pretend to be anything he isn't. I could learn from him there. I mean, who was I trying to be? Perfect Katie with her perfect life?'

Mark's tone softens. 'You shouldn't have to pretend to be anything. He shouldn't have made you feel like that.'

'It's easy to blame Sam, but it wasn't all his fault. My own insecurities were just as much to blame.'

Mark nods. 'You wouldn't put yourself through all that again, though, would you, with the next man you meet?'

'No way,' I say. 'I've learned my lesson.'

'Men aren't worth it,' he adds with his familiar wry smile.

'Thanks for coming round tonight. No-one's done anything like that for me before, Mark. You're a real mate. I owe you.'

'Well, you could get me some new glasses?'

We look at Mark's glasses, smashed to smithereens; the black frames now a wonky S-shape.

We start to laugh. 'It's the least I can do,' I agree.

36

It's a Thursday, late afternoon, and Mark has asked me over for supper. I left the shop early this afternoon as Eve and the new assistant, Jackie, were able to manage without me. Jackie is bright and enthusiastic about her work. She also designs and makes knitwear. I am going to sample some in the shop.

I sit on the stool behind the breakfast counter in Mark's kitchen. There's a pile of paperwork in front of me, his red pen scrawled across the sheets. Essays on *The Mayor of Casterbridge* with that dreaded underlined word at the end of the assignment: 'Discuss'. I start to swivel round on my stool and play with the gadget which adjusts the height. 'Weh-hey!' I say, sinking closer to the floor. 'I like these, where d'you get them from?'

'Conran.' He opens the fridge. 'No bloody milk. What do you feel like eating tonight?'

'Why don't we go out?' I suggest. Mark and I have never 'gone out' apart from that one evening when we watched the school play. Normally he cooks me supper but I'm getting a little bored of spaghetti Bolognese.

'Go out! Do you think our friendship has reached that stage?' he asks, laughing.

'I think we're ready. Did I tell you, I've seen a flat I love?'

'You're moving?' he asks, and then wonders why he is surprised. 'I forget you're living with Emma and Jonnie sometimes.'

Emma and Jonnie haven't met Mark yet. 'You have mentionitis . . . ' Emma said to me the other day while we were shopping for her wedding dress, Emma towering above the skinny shop assistant.

'Mention what?' I threw her a funny look.

'Mentionitis. You talk about him all the time. Are you scared of introducing him properly to us? Now, what do you reckon?' she asked me, unable to hide the desperation in her tone. She shuffled awkwardly from one foot to the other.

I made a disapproving sound.

'You have to imagine what it would look like in the correct size,' the shop assistant reproved me, her fake blond ponytail swishing down her back. The dress did not do up properly. It was being held together by elastic bands which were looped around the little buttons at the back. All the dresses in the shop seemed to be made for midgets.

'I'd like to meet him,' Emma told me as I helped her out of the dress.

This might sound ridiculous, as if I am in a school playground, but I don't want to share Mark yet.

'Katie?' I hear him say now. 'You do that a lot, you know.'

'Sorry? What?'

'Retreat into your own world, develop this kind of glazed expression. What are you thinking about?'

'Um, I was thinking about Emma and Jonnie. I wish they'd move out and let me take over their house. So inconsiderate of them staying put, isn't it?'

Even Mum detected a change in me when I last called. 'You're in such a good mood. Has it got something to do with Mark?'

'No, he's just a friend.'

'Blah blah blah,' she said, followed by a sniff of boredom. 'Love comes along when you least expect it. You have to take a chance, Katie. If you like this man, tell him. If you don't, well, move on. You have to go out at every opportunity, never turn an invitation down, because you never know who you might meet. When I first met your father . . . '

As Mum rattled on, I realized how annoying she can still be.

'Where's the new flat?' Mark asks me.

'Ravenscourt Park.'

'Renting or buying?'

'Buying. I'm finally taking the plunge. I'm looking forward to living on my own.'

He leans against the counter. He's wearing the new pair of glasses that we bought together, almost exactly the same model as the broken ones, with black rims. I also persuaded him to buy a pale blue round-necked jumper without holes in the elbow. 'Has the wife dragged you out shopping?' said the man in Marks & Spencer, rolling his eyes when I told Mark to try on yet another style.

'Calling Katie? Where is Katie?' Mark prods me again. 'Sounds perfect. When are you moving?'

'Just before Christmas.'

'Shit, that's less than a month away.'

'I know. Emma and Jonnie are throwing me a Christmas-stroke-leaving party in two weeks, Bells is coming down to stay and you'd better be around too, I'd like you to come.'

'I'll try and fit it in,' he says, and I throw his red marker pen at him.

'And Jess, is she around?'

'I'll ask her.'

'Why don't you live together?'

'What, besides the fact that she lives in Edinburgh? Anyway, I hate the idea. You live together and then you just merge into a married blob. Really boring. We both lead quite independent lives and I like it that way.'

'How's her ankle?' I don't really care how it is but I know I ought to acknowledge she is around.

'It's fine. Right,' he says, 'tea? Or maybe you need something stronger?'

'Tea would be great.'

'You put the kettle on, I'll get the milk and the marshmallow biscuits.' He picks up his house keys off the counter and walks out of the room.

Mark's mobile starts to vibrate against the table. 'Can you get that for me?' he calls. I can hear him putting on his coat. The front door shuts.

I pick up the phone tentatively. I don't like taking calls for other people. 'Hello, Mark's phone,' I say in my best secretarial voice.

'Who's that?' a voice says abruptly. Is this Jess?

'It's just Katie.'

'Just Katie, this is Sasha Fox. Is Mark there?'

'Not right this minute.' She is terrifying.

'It's his agent, can you get him to call me back,' she says, more as a demand than a question, and hangs up.

I put the phone down and start to walk around Mark's flat. I wonder if she has news on the book? She must have. I feel nervous for Mark. I decide to put some music on. I have a quick look through his CD collection and decide to put on some Coldplay, but when I open the box it's not in there. It's Kylie. I can picture Sam's outraged expression. I put Kylie on instead and am about to walk back into the kitchen when I decide to take a quick detour into Mark's bedroom. Along the corridor, past the bathroom, and then three steps down and I'm there.

It's a large airy room with a big double bed and a smooth carved oak headboard. It doesn't smell stale or of boy's socks, I am pleased to note. Mark has shutters instead of curtains and there's a newspaper lying across the white duvet. He's reading *Life of Pi* and next to the book on his bedside table is a silver-framed photograph. Jess is sitting on a boat wearing denim shorts and a spotted bikini, and Mark stands next to her proudly holding a barracuda. She's annoyingly pretty. Why can't she have a gap in her front teeth or unfortunate facial hair? I feel like Glenn Close in *Fatal Attraction*. What's wrong with me? I press my fingers to my temples. Perhaps I am coming down with something? I don't think I have been quite myself lately.

I hear a door shut and run back up the stairs, tripping on the last step. I decide to go into the bathroom, slam the door shut and flush the chain. Then I open the door casually and walk back to the kitchen.

'Who was it?' Mark asks, clutching the bottle of milk.

'Your agent.'

'Really? Ms Sucha Fox?' He grins nervously then sits down on the stool next to me and starts to fidget with his hands, twisting them together until I hear the joints crack.

'Stop it,' I say, wincing. 'That gives you arthritis.'

'Sorry.' He takes a deep breath. 'What did she say?'

'You've got to call her back. Call her now, she must have news on your book.'

'Did she sound in a good mood? Could you tell?' he presses me.

'She was a bit abrupt,' I confess. 'Go on,' I say, pushing the phone towards him. 'Ring her.'

'What if it's bad news? Rejections from every publisher she has approached, saying I'm a useless crap writer?' He sits forward and puts his head in his hands. 'Katie, I've worked so hard on this book. I've had scripts rejected before, I don't know why I carry on, it's awful. It makes you feel like a fool, a failure, less than an insect. If it's a no, I'll be miserable.' He stands up, paces the room and then sits down again. 'I'm feeling a bit nervous actually.'

'I can tell,' I say, longing to hug him for his insecurity. Instead I pat his leg. 'Come on, stop being a drama queen.'

'I can't help it.'

'Look, your agent must believe in you. I think she would have e-mailed you if it was bad news,' I suggest.

'Good point. Although she didn't before.'

'Do you want me to go?' Please say no. I am dying to hear what Ms Sucha Fox has to say.

'No, stay,' he urges, taking the phone. 'Forget the tea, can you get me a proper drink?' He stands up and starts to pace around the room. He walks into the sitting room and I follow him. He opens his desk drawer.

'Mark, slow down. What are you looking for?'

He waves a pack of cigarettes at me. 'For emergencies.' He turns Kylie off. 'OK, wish me luck,' he says, punching in the number.

⋆　⋆　⋆

I am making vodka and tonics in his kitchen. I have butterflies in my stomach. I'm thinking of ways to console Mark. 'It's their loss,' or, 'Did you know J. K. Rowling had masses of rejections, and look at her now!' No, that's a lame thing to say. 'Did you know Virginia Woolf, Beatrix Potter, Honoré de Balzac and many other famous writers all had books self-published at some stage in their career? It's the latest trend. That could be an option.' I read that in a weekend magazine. Mark stands in front of me looking as if he's just been given a parking ticket. He slams the mobile onto the table. I wait for him to say something. When he says nothing I tell him I am sorry and promptly hand him a neat vodka.

'Sorry for what?' He takes a large gulp of vodka. 'Penguin are going to publish it next year. You're right, I can't be bothered to cook supper. We are going out to fucking celebrate!'

'I can't believe it,' I shriek, moving forward to hug him.

He picks me up off the ground, and twirls me around. 'I am going to be published, Katie, can you believe it? Thank you, God! Thank you, GOD!'

'Hurray!' I shout, wrapping my arms around him and laughing at the same time. He puts me down and then opens the fridge. 'We need a drink. No champagne, bugger.'

'I'll go and get some, my treat.'

'Deal. I can't believe it,' he repeats

incredulously, circling the kitchen as if he is drunk. 'Ms Fox better not get run over by a bus or the publishers burn down or go bust or . . .'

'CALM down.' I smile at him. 'Right, I'll be back in a sec.' I find myself skipping along the road like an excited toddler.

'You look like a cat who's stolen the cream, and eaten it too,' the man at the off-licence says.

'My friend's just got a book deal.' I pause. 'Penguin, you know,' I add for effect.

'Wow,' he acknowledges, taking my money. 'Tell him, many congratulations.'

Aren't people nice? I love life, I think to myself. Why do people say the British are chippy, that they don't like people fulfilling their dreams? There's not a chip in sight today.

★ ★ ★

When I return, I hear Mark talking in the kitchen. I stand there quietly and listen before joining him. 'We can celebrate when you get back . . . you don't have to do that. OK, we'll see. How was the journey? How are your parents? I know! I can't believe it either. What am I doing tonight? Well, I think I'll have a few celebratory drinks.' I notice he doesn't say who with. 'Yes, I will have one on you, J.' He's listening to her and now he laughs. There's another long pause. His voice turns softer. 'I know, I wish you were here too,' he finishes.

Of course she is the first person he wants to ring with the news. This has to be one of the biggest, proudest moments in his life and he ought to be with her, not me. Why do I feel like second best? It only takes one phone call from Jess and — bam! Back to being Katie the good friend, someone to have a laugh with. I can't stand feeling like this.

'Love you too,' I hear him say.

That's it, enough dreaming, Katie. Don't feel disappointed. Mark and you have a great friendship, get on well, but that's as far as it goes. End of story, as Sam would say.

I need to go into the kitchen, have one drink and then go home. I need to accept this for what it is. I don't want to be second best; I won't let myself feel like this. I clutch the bottle of champagne and brace myself as I walk back into the kitchen.

★　★　★

'Why do you have to go now?' Mark asks after we have had one glass of champagne together. 'I want to celebrate. Come on, have another.' He starts to refill my glass. 'Let's go out dancing.'

I push my glass aside. 'Sorry, Mark, I think I might be coming down with something,' I say vaguely. 'Emma had this twenty-four-hour sick bug. It hit her out of the blue.'

Mark whacks himself hard. 'It's come on, just like that?'

I frown at him.

'Katie, you can't be ill. You were fine half an hour ago. Is something wrong?'

'I think I need to lie down.' I can hear myself whining and it's pathetic but I don't want to stay. I can't stay.

Mark feels my forehead. 'You *are* quite warm.' He lifts my chin and holds my face up to his. 'But this is my night, I don't want you to go.'

'I'm sorry.' I put my hand over his and gently remove it. I kiss him on the cheek. 'Well done, Mark. I'm so proud of you, author *extraordinaire*.' I pick up my bag.

He follows me to the door and then I feel him clutching at my hand. 'Why are you really going?'

'What?' I splutter, unable to turn round and face him.

'I'm trying to figure out if I've done something wrong, said something, in the space of ten minutes? I don't want you to go.'

'You've done nothing wrong, honestly. 'Bye, Mark.' I kiss him on the cheek one more time.

37

Sometimes I panic at night. Am I going to work in my shop for the rest of my life? Not that it's a bad life. I am lucky to have my own business, but should I be striving for more? What if Mum has a relapse or something happens to Dad? Or to Bells? What if I end up an old maid? We all assume we are going to meet someone, but what if we don't? What if I end up a bitter old lady who sits on a brown sofa stroking my spoilt cat which I feed fresh prawns? Or I start pushing around small yappy dogs in a pram because I never had children and went completely potty? That could be me in years to come. It's that 'What am I doing, where am I going?' question which quietly nags me during the day but screams at me at night. When I wake up, I calm down. Mum is all right. Dad is happy. Bells is fine. I have a job. I have good friends. I know I am going in the right direction. I have a lot to be thankful for.

We always want what we can't have, don't we? When I was about six I used to pray over and over again for blue eyes like Dad's. 'Your eyes are the colour of the sea,' I used to tell him as a child. I would rush home to see if the mirror showed the faintest change of colour in mine. They stayed green. The colour of a murky pond, I thought. I could not understand why God didn't answer my prayers.

When Bells was born I prayed that she would get better so that I could have Mum back to myself.

I stopped going to church when I was a self-conscious fifteen-year-old, but I still pray. Just don't tell anyone.

★ ★ ★

Mark stands at the front door, trailing his bike behind him. I haven't seen him for a fortnight. He left a message on my mobile but I didn't ring back or go round to his flat. However, I had to make contact when Bells arrived so I asked him if he wanted to go to the cinema with us tonight. Bells is staying for the weekend and will be around for Jonnie and Emma's Christmas party tomorrow evening. She wouldn't forgive me if she didn't see Mark.

His hands are covered in grime and his left cheek is smudged with oil too. His hair is even more all over the place.

'Did you fall, are you OK?' I ask. What's he

doing here? It's only two o'clock.

'Nearly. The chain came off.' He grimaces. 'Clunk, in the middle of the street.'

'Hello, Mark.' Bells rushes up to him and claps him on the back.

'Hi, Bells! How are you?'

'You have car like Sam?' she asks.

'No,' he admits, almost in apology.

'Why?'

'Because I don't. Anyway, how are you?'

They hold hands and her little device vibrates. 'I should have known,' he laughs. Bells is rocking forward and clapping her hands together.

'Come in,' I tell him. He chains his bicycle to the gate and follows us indoors. His mobile rings and he quickly takes the call.

'That was Jess, she can come tomorrow,' he tells me, putting his phone back in his rucksack.

'Great!' I reply.

Damn, bugger and shit.

'It'll be good to meet her properly,' I continue in this horrible cheery tone which I don't recognize as my own.

'That your girlfriend?' Bells asks.

Mark nods.

'You gonna get married?'

He looks at me and I titter cheerfully. 'Bells, don't be so nosy.' I can't get rid of this merry persona — ironic when I feel anything but. We go into the kitchen. All my washing is hanging on the drier next to the washing machine. Mark is standing in front of a line of my knickers and bras. There's one particularly attractive pair of grey pants with a hole in just the wrong place. I wish I could touch a button and they'd all disappear.

I put the kettle on. Bells hands round some fig rolls. 'Shut eyes,' she says as she holds something towards Mark. He looks at me, then back at Bells. I'm still smiling like a clown. 'Go on, don't worry, it's not a toad,' I laugh. 'Well, I don't know actually. I suppose it could be.'

'OK,' Mark whimpers. 'But I want a fig roll. I love fig rolls. The children do this at school sometimes. Made me sit on a whoopee cushion once when we had Joanna Lumley in to speak about acting. Deeply humiliating.' He squeezes his eyes shut.

Bells plants a square of mouldy cheese into his hand. It has fur all over it. From the way her shoulders are heaving up and down I can see she finds this hilarious, especially when Mark throws it back at her, shouting, 'It's alive, it's alive! Are you always like this, Bells?'

I tell him about Bells planting sanitary towels around Mum's dinner table, the story which Sam found so repulsive but Mark and Bells find extraordinarily funny. Bells is deeply proud of this tale.

'Mark, Bells and I have to go out in a minute, we're going to Sainsbury's and . . . '

'Sainsbugs,' Bells says, and proceeds to roar with laughter again.

'I promised Emma I'd get a Christmas tree and some food for tomorrow.'

'I'll help.'

'You look a mess, you can't go out looking like that.' Why am I sounding like his mother now? I can't bear being so conscious of everything I say and do around him.

'So what? You always say you shouldn't care what people think.'

'Um,' I shrug my shoulder, 'yes, you're right.'

'Give me ten minutes?'

'OK. Ten minutes.'

★　★　★

The supermarket is packed with shoppers and 'Jingle Bells' is playing in the background.

'Mark, what are you doing for Christmas?'

'Mum and Dad are in New Zealand this year with my brother the sheep farmer.'

'You're not going?'

'I can't.'

'Why not?'

'It's too expensive to fly out for a week. Anyway, they're coming home for the new year. I need to save a bit of money for next year,' he adds.

I nod. 'What's happening next year?' Mark looks pre-occupied and doesn't immediately reply. 'You're not going to be on your own at Christmas, are you?' I say.

'No. I'm seeing Jess and a few friends.'

'Where does Jess live?' I realize I already know the answer. Why is there this sudden need to fill the space between us with words?

'Edinburgh.'

'Oh, yes, of course. Edinburgh, that's a long way away.' Why is every word I say so flat and obvious?

'Excellent,' he mutters out of nowhere, looking distracted. 'Where's Bells?' We both glance around, and walk up the aisle until we see her at the delicatessen counter talking to the man behind the trays of olives and cold meats. He is wearing a hat with a silver Christmas star pasted onto the front. I can hear her asking him how old he is.

'Any more news on the book?' I sound like an interviewer. I realize it doesn't matter because Mark is not even listening to me. He's watching Bells put on the man's silver-starred hat. 'Mark?' I prod him. 'You're a world away. What are you thinking about?'

'Sorry.' He turns to me. 'I've got something on my mind.'

'Anything I can help with?'

'No,' he says too harshly, as if I am the last person who can help him, followed by a calmer, 'It's school, something's come up that I need to think about.'

'What?'

He's about to tell me but then appears to have second thoughts. 'Mark, you're worrying me, why are you looking at me like that?'

'I need to work it out for myself first,' he says. Bells crashes into our trolley. 'Race you to the . . . ' He looks at me for inspiration.

'We need mini-sausages and Parmesan cheese.'

'Race you to the sausages!' Mark says as he tears off with Bells.

★   ★   ★

Mark, Bells and I are queuing for popcorn. Bells buys a barrel of Coca-Cola. We're about to see Hugh Grant's latest film. 'You want Coke?' she asks Mark and me.

'Not another one?' he gasps. 'Bells, you'll have Coke coming out of your ears. I must

413

buy some Coke shares, the industry does well out of you.'

'Not funny, Mark.'

If I drank that much I would spend more time on the loo than watching the film, I tell her as we walk to screen number five.

We sit down next to a young couple. I am in the middle. Bells is laughing at the Cornetto advert. I turn to put my hand into the popcorn. Mark leans towards me and takes a handful. Our hands meet and stay there. I am aware of every move he makes, each touch.

I hear noisy shuffling of feet. The couple sitting next to Bells are moving seats. 'Sorry, excuse me,' they are whispering as they step over people's feet. The woman's stiletto boot stabs into my little toe and I hold in the pain. I am not going to let it ruin the evening. Don't say anything, Katie, I tell myself. I want to shout ARSEHOLES and struggle to restrain myself. The only reassuring thing is that I don't think Bells has noticed, has she?

'Excuse me?' I hear Mark saying as he stands up. The auditorium has darkened as the film crackles onto the screen. It's deathly quiet except for the sound of crisp and sweet packets being opened and ice-cream wrappers being peeled off. The couple turn around. 'I'm sorry to stop you in your tracks but is there something wrong with your seats?' I can feel everyone listening. 'Because if there is, maybe you should report it?'

They look at one another sheepishly. 'I think we should be in the row behind,' the man weakly gives as an excuse.

'You should be ashamed of yourselves,' Mark says quietly, but firmly, and sits down again. The film begins.

He takes off his glasses, wipes them clean on the sleeve of his jumper and then puts them on again. He looks tired, something is worrying him. I wish he would tell me. I look at him as he watches the film intently. He must be aware that I am looking at him because he turns to me. 'What? What is it?'

'Thank you.' I touch his hand and we link our fingers.

'What for?'

'For telling them off,' I whisper.

'Shh,' we hear from the row behind.

We both turn back to the screen, withdrawing our hands quickly.

I love Mark for speaking out. The only thing is that Bells is now painfully quiet. I hand her the popcorn but she doesn't take any. I think she understands far more than I give her credit for.

I think she always has.

38

Bells sits on my bed as she watches me get dressed. I am wearing a pale blue jumper tied at one side with a ribbon, jeans and pointed shoes with a small heel.

I brush my hair in front of the mirror and see Bells in the reflection. She's rummaging through my makeup bag, picking out lipsticks, powder and generally making a mess. 'What's this?' she asks, holding up an eyelash curler. 'You and Mark gonna get married?' she then asks randomly.

'Me marry Mark? I don't know,' I laugh as I tie my hair back and then let it loose again. I place a large sparkling black beaded flower to the side of my head. I can't decide whether to wear my hair up or down. 'It's an eyelash curler, by the way,' I add.

'Why?'

She's now trying to put on some of my nail varnish. I bought a new shimmering silver polish which Bells watched me apply earlier. 'Er, I don't know. He hasn't asked me,' I reply simply. 'We're not even dating.' I'm watching her carefully, to make sure she doesn't spill the polish all over Emma's white bedspread.

'Not same as you, am I?'

She has never asked me this question directly, although I know she has asked Mum. I don't know what to say. Oh, please, someone tell me what is the right thing to say? I can't lie and pretend she is, just to please her. Bells will see right through that anyway. Then again, she could still meet someone, couldn't she? I turn round and see a great circle of silver, the size of a ten-pence piece, on the white linen. 'Bells, look what you've done!' I rush over to examine the stain.

She throws the bottle across the room and it hits the wall, polish oozing out and onto the carpet.

'Bells, stop it! What's wrong? Why are you so angry?' I quickly retrieve the bottle and put the top back on tightly.

'Can't do like Katie,' she shouts, and starts punching one hand with the other, silver smudging across her palms. 'Not same,' she says firmly. 'Not normal, am I?'

I sit down next to her. 'What's brought all of this on?' I ask gently.

'Not normal,' she emphasizes again, cross that I do not understand what she is saying. 'People stare, not nice.'

'Bells, you're normal to me, to Dad, Mum, to all the people who love you.'

Bells doesn't look convinced. She's heard that one before. 'Not like Katie.'

'Why do you want to be like me? I'm not half the person you are.'

'You beautiful.'

'That's not what makes a person,' I say adamantly. 'Don't you ever think that.'

'Not beautiful like Katie,' she repeats.

'Well, I'm not a good cook like you. I can make chips and steak, and that's about it. And a boiled egg. I'm like Dad.'

She still looks upset.

'Look at the way you ran the house when Mum was so ill. I don't think you realize how much you can do, Bells.'

She stops hitting her hands together and laughs weakly. 'Am good cook, aren't I?'

'You are. This stuff doesn't matter, it really doesn't,' I say, holding the nail polish in front of her. 'It's all pretty superficial. You are you, don't ever change. Wave, smile, say hello to people like you always do.' I am thinking of the time when Bells was in my shop and I was ordering her not to say hello to customers. 'Or if they're being just plain rude, you stare back, don't let them get away with it. You can rise above all that, Bells. That's why people love and admire you. Look at Mark, or Eddie at the deli, or Robert and Ted, Mr Vickers, or the *entire* football team for that matter. My

God, I've never seen such a fan club.'

A small smile lights Bells's face.

'I feel like we are really getting to know each other now,' I stumble on, 'and I love being with you. I don't know about you, but I think that we are all looked after by an angel and I think you are looked after by an extra-special one.'

'What's her name?'

'She doesn't have a name like you and me. She's 'Bells's angel'. You see, she's given your name.'

Bells thinks about this. 'Mum have angel?'

'She definitely has one.'

'That's why she better. Mark have one?'

'I'm sure he does.'

'You pretty,' she says again, looking at my clothes. Bells is wearing a patchwork skirt, with a black evening top from the shop, and around her wrist is a black leather bracelet with silver studs. She's also wearing her three small stud earrings in the left ear. 'Won't ever look like you, will I?'

'I haven't got your beautiful coloured hair.'

'Mum's hair,' she says.

'Yes, Mum's. You're very lucky. Do you still want to put some of this nail varnish on?' I ask, holding up the pot.

She gives me her hand and I carefully apply the silver over her short bitten nails. 'Look,

I've made a mess too.' I smile, carefully wiping away the excess nail varnish with a tissue. 'You are you, Bells, Katie is Katie, Mark is Mark. If we were all the same, life would be pretty dull, don't you think?'

'Yes, Katie, that's right. Thank you, Katie.'

★ ★ ★

'Can I get you another drink?' I ask Eve who has brought Hector along too. He is looking plumper than usual and is wearing a royal blue tank top.

'Katie, what a great party!' She's already tipsy.

'What a lovely home,' Hector adds, looking around the room.

Emma, Bells and I decorated the Christmas tree with great big silver and gold balls, silver, red and gold ribbon, and chocolate Santas wrapped in silver and gold foil. Emma put fairy lights in the kitchen and bunches of holly in the windows with fake robins nestled in the leaves. We made canapés all day. Sausages, cheese puffs, mini-mince pies. If I have to wrap one more shrivelled prune in bacon I shall go mad.

'Eve, I wanted to thank you so much for keeping the shop going these last few months. I couldn't have done it without you.' I am giving her a large bonus this year.

'It is no matter. I was happy to. You know, Mr Vickers helped me too. He likes to count the day's takings.' She smiles widely. '*Mon Dieu!*' she exclaims, hitting my arm. 'I tell you, Mr Vickers, he is amazing! He sorts out my love life. He tell me to go for Hector, that looks are not the most important thing in the world.'

Ouch! Poor Hector, but to my surprise he finds this rather funny.

'Excuse me, I am here,' is all he says.

Then they both start to laugh together, Hector gently nudging her against the hip, and it is the most touching thing I've seen.

'Oh my God! How did you get that bruise the size of a tennis ball?' I ask Eve. It's on her left arm, near the elbow.

Hector chuckles. 'I might not be number one in the looks department but there are other departments I'm rather good at,' he says as he walks away from us proudly. Eve looks at me mischievously as she twists a strand of her long honey-coloured hair. 'Hector and I, we have sex last night,' she whispers. 'Against the bath sink, on the kitchen table, on the . . . oh, what is the word?'

'The bed?'

'*Non!* Katie, you are so boring, so dull. We

make love everywhere. By the fire, on the . . . '

'That's enough!' I laugh, putting my hands over my ears. 'Stop it. Actually, I'm wildly jealous,' I add. 'You seem very happy.'

'I am. Touching wood.' She leans across to touch the mantelpiece. 'You must be sad to leave your friends, no?'

'I don't want to live with newly-weds.' I smile. 'We were doing the table seating plan today and that was bad enough.' I tell Eve how we sat for hours writing down the guests' names on small coloured Post-it notes, and then tried to arrange them around imaginary tables. At one point Jonnie shouted and swore at Emma, telling her he didn't want any of her 'fucking doctor friends'. Emma and I were speechless. Jonnie rarely loses his temper. Emma then fired back, telling him it was unfair for anyone to have to sit next to his parents. I was with her on that one, but thought I'd better not utter a word unless I saw my name next to Hamster Hermione's.

The doorbell rings again and I can hear Mark's voice. 'You must be Mark,' I hear Emma say. 'Well done about the book! I've heard so much about you.'

Oh, Emma, don't say things like that.

'I can't believe we haven't met before,' she blunders on. 'Hello,' she says to Jess.

Jess is wearing a sea-blue coloured satin top over jeans. She barely has any make-up on but her skin is flawless. Then I catch sight of Mark, and before I know it I've bolted upstairs and run into my bedroom, swinging the door shut. I don't think he saw me. My heart is beating so fast that I expect to see it jump out onto the floor. I realize I have never felt this way about anyone before. I don't know what to say or how to act in front of him any more. I don't recognize myself. Keep calm, Katie, I tell myself, only to feel my face getting redder and hotter. 'What is meant to be is meant to be,' I mutter. 'You don't really believe any of that rubbish, do you? God, stop talking to yourself.'

I splatter on some green-coloured cream which promises to reduce the redness of my skin. I spray myself with perfume which smells like lemon zest. I adjust my hair, pinning it up, then letting it down, then pinning it up with a pretty sequined flower. 'Take a deep breath and count to five.' Finally I return to the party.

* * *

Bells stands at the CD player with Mark. The Beatles start to sing. She holds a can of ginger beer towards him, her silver nails sparkling.

423

Mark looks as if he has tumbled out of the washing machine. His hair is ruffled and he's wearing dark jeans with a loose white shirt and surprisingly trendy trainers. He puts the can down and takes Bells's hand. They start to dance. 'Can't dance very well,' she is saying.

'Doesn't matter,' Mark shouts above the music.

'Mark and I learning ballroom dance,' she adds, and laughs as he twists her around. 'Again!' she demands.

'You can't take your eyes off him, can you?' Emma says, sneaking up on me.

'Don't be silly, I was watching Bells dance.'

'He looks at you too, you know.'

'Really? Does he?'

'A lot, but you don't care, do you?'

'No, no.'

'Rubbish, Katie. This is me, Emma, your best friend. I know you inside out and back to front. You like him, I mean, *really like him*, don't you?'

'I can't do anything about it, though,' I sigh, still watching him. 'I've had quite a few boyfriends, but I've never had one who became a really good friend first. Like you and Jonnie. You are so lucky to be out of the rat race.'

'I had my first boyfriend when I was seven.

He was the child of a friend of my parents and he used to come and stay.'

'I remember this story. You used to steal his bicycle so he would chase you around the garden and lie on top of you.'

'It was such an amazing sensation, although I couldn't work out why.' She starts laughing.

Mark looks in my direction and smiles before turning back to Bells. 'It stinks, doesn't it? And there's nothing I can do.'

'What do you mean? Come on, you can do something.'

'He has a girlfriend.'

'OK, but why don't you tell him? Give yourself a chance, at least. What have you got to lose?'

I watch him with Bells. 'Everything,' I reply simply.

★ ★ ★

'Katie?' Mark says quietly, taking my hand and leading me out of the room. We stand alone, facing one another.

'Yes?' The music dies out.

'There's something I want to tell you.'

'Tell me,' I whisper.

'I don't know where to start.' He looks at me, absorbing every feature of my face. His finger gently outlines the curve of my cheek.

'What is it?'

He takes his hand away but I long for him to touch me again.

'It's all over between Jess and me. I think it has been for a long time. I have wanted to say this since we first met but I haven't had the courage. I had to say something tonight; I can't keep it a secret any longer. I am hopelessly . . . ' He stops. Please don't stop.

'Yes?'

'I am hopelessly . . . '

'Where are you moving, Katie? Katie?'

'I'm sorry,' I say, shaking my head free of fantasy. Jess is standing in front of me. 'I've found a place in Ravenscourt Park,' I tell her.

'Talking of moving, isn't it wonderful news about Mark?'

'Sorry?'

'Mark? He's been offered a transfer to Edinburgh.'

'He's moving away?' I know Jess is watching me. I feel as if I am on stage, thrust into the limelight and I have forgotten my lines. 'No, I didn't know.'

Jess looks genuinely surprised. 'Well, he only just found out. I'm sure he was going to tell you.' There is definitely a hint of pleasure in her voice that I didn't know. She stands back from me. 'I'm surprised he hasn't told you. I thought you saw him last night? I can't understand why he didn't mention it.'

'When's he going?' Emma intervenes, allowing me to try and compose myself.

'January. This new school has great drama facilities and he'd be involved in the Edinburgh Festival. It's too good an opportunity to miss. I think it will be good for our relationship too,' she continues in this soft calm voice, but still watching me carefully. 'It's hard being separated, I think Mark and I need to spend more time together.' The way she looks at me makes me feel uneasy.

'I heard my name being mentioned,' Mark says, returning. 'I don't know where Bells has gone. We need some more music.'

'Jess was telling me about your move to Edinburgh,' I tell him. 'Congratulations.'

Mark's smile rapidly disappears. 'Jess, it was my news to tell.'

'Sorry, I didn't realize it was a big secret,' she says, her eyes widening.

He shakes his head irritably. 'Katie, I've got to go.'

'What, now?' I blurt out.

'Jess, are you ready?'

She frowns. 'Right, I'll get my coat.'

I don't want him to go. I can't bear it. Mark walks ahead of me. 'I was going to tell you, I've only just made the decision,' he tries to explain.

'I wish you had,' I say quietly.

'Katie, I'm sorry.'

I am sure he wants to say something more. 'Happy Christmas,' he finally mutters, leaning forward to kiss me on the cheek. I can hear Jess's footsteps behind me.

And then he's gone.

39

Bells and I are catching the train home together for Christmas. The day after the party I moved into my new flat with the help of Jonnie. It was strange leaving. I felt like I was facing my first day at boarding school as we unpacked the boxes.

My mobile starts to ring and Mark's name appears in the screen.

'Are you still in London?'

'No, Bells and I are on the train.'

'The choo-choo,' Bells announces.

'Katie, I am sorry.'

'Look, it doesn't matter.'

'No, it does. You're a good friend . . . '

There's that word I hate. Friend.

'Well done,' I speak over him. 'A book deal and now Edinburgh. What a year! What's the name of the school?'

'Katie, I really need to talk to you.'

'That Mark?' Bells asks. 'Hello, Mark.'

'Hi, Bells,' he says in a quick flustered tone. 'Katie, it's about the other night . . . '

Bells takes the phone from me. 'Happy birthday, Mark.'

'It's not my birthday, Bells, not yet, but

thanks anyway. Can I have Katie back?'

'When are you leaving?' For an insane second I allow myself to imagine he is going to tell me he isn't going.

'In two weeks.' There is a pause. The line starts to crackle as the train goes through a tunnel. Mark is saying something but I can't hear.

'Mark, I'll see you in the New Year. And it's great news. I'll miss you, though.' I swallow hard.

'Hello, Mark,' Bells repeats. 'Happy birthday.'

He doesn't say anything back to her this time. 'You're coming to my birthday party, Katie, aren't you?'

The line crackles again.

'I can't hear you,' I say. The line goes dead.

I put the mobile in my bag and wait for him to call back. I want him to call back, but he doesn't.

★   ★   ★

Christmas is good fun and I stay on for New Year. I have never seen the New Year in with my parents and Bells, well, not since I was about twelve, so this one feels important.

On New Year's Eve, Aunt Agnes joins us, bringing home-made crackers. Agnes is ten years older than my dad. She is dressed in a fur coat and scarlet beret with scarlet lipstick to match, and is wearing a solid silver heart pendant which looks as if it came from an expensive Bond Street jeweller. We discover Aunt Agnes has met someone, through setting up a fundraising scheme in the community to raise money for a children's hospice. His name is Peter. Since Uncle Roger died two years ago she has lost at least two stone in weight. 'Aunt Agnes, you look amazing,' I tell her. 'How do you do it?'

'Thank you, darling,' she says, eyelashes fluttering over her almond-shaped eyes. 'The secret is I don't make home-made chips and Black Forest gâteau any more.'

We put on our paper hats, tell silly jokes, and light indoor fireworks. Bells has a snake. It looks like a brown pill, but once lit turns into a black mamba. Mine is a cowboy smoking a cigarette which, when I light it, puffs out smoke. At the stroke of midnight we all drink to Mum's health. Her cheeks look flushed from the alcohol and she is getting emotional. Her hair is very short and soft, like fluff. She still covers it with her patterned silk scarves. Bells asks if she can look at the scar again; and Mum guides her hand across the back of her head. Bells touches it gently.

Mum, Dad, Bells and I are watching *Who Wants To Be A Millionaire?*, the special New Year Celebrity Edition, and Simon Cowell is taking part. It's my last night at home before I head back to London.

'I can't believe this cretin is phoning a friend. It's D, you fool!' Dad says when the phone rings.

'Maybe he's phoning you, Dad,' I suggest.

'Darling, can you get that?' Mum asks, her eyes glued to the screen.

Seconds later he comes back into the room. 'It's Mark.' Dad hands me the phone and settles back in his seat.

I shove it back in his direction. 'I'm not here,' I mouth at him. NOT HERE, I scribble on a piece of paper and wave it in front of him.

'Mark, can she call you back?' Dad puts the phone down. 'I don't like lying, Katie. Make sure you call him.' His attention returns to the television.

'Why don't you want to talk to Mark?' Mum asks. 'I thought he was a good friend.'

'Um, yes, he is,' I say, watching Simon Cowell deliberate.

'Katie?' Mum presses. 'Has something happened?'

432

'Mark's moving away from London,' I tell her.

'Unless your old father is missing anything, why is that so bad?' Dad doesn't look away from the television.

'He's going to Edinburgh.'

'Hmm,' Dad acknowledges. 'You'll miss him. He's a very nice young man. What's he going to do in Edinburgh then?'

Parents never get it, I think to myself.

'Oh, darling, do shut up,' Mum says. 'You're getting the wrong end of the stick, as usual.' She turns to me. 'Look, I'm not blind. Something is going on here, more than just Mark moving on,' she says. 'Why won't you talk to him?'

'I don't feel like it, I just want to watch this.'

Mum sighs impatiently. 'Come on, Katie.'

'OK,' I give in, 'I do like him, but what's the point if he's going away?'

'Much worse things can happen. It's not the end of the world, is it? It doesn't mean you won't see him again,' she reasons.

'I know, it's just I've got so used to him being around, I'll really miss him. I kind of feel like he's my soul-mate, if you know what I mean?'

'I know exactly what you mean.' She looks sideways at Dad, who sits in the large armchair wearing his leather slippers,

433

squinting at the television.

We both smile. 'He was attractive when he was younger,' Mum whispers to me.

'He's asking the audience now, can you believe it?' Dad says, outraged. 'They won't know,' he tuts.

'This must sound so . . . ' I can't think of a word to use after everything Mum has been through, ' . . . silly to you,' I finally say.

'No, darling. What's silly is if you don't tell him. When are you seeing him next?'

'His party, tomorrow night. It's in Battersea. His parents are going and everything.'

'And you're going too, aren't you?'

I look unsure.

'You love him?' Bells suddenly asks. She's lying on her front on the floor, leaning on her elbows, watching the television. I hadn't been aware she was even listening because she had been so quiet.

'No,' I stammer, caught off-guard by her directness.

'Stupid Katie.'

'I am not,' I bite back, thinking I have not been called stupid since I was little.

'Stupid, isn't she, Mum?'

'Stop calling me stupid,' I gasp. Then I remember how I told Bells over and over again how stupid she was when she cut out the labels.

'Do you love Mark?' Mum asks.

'What? You love Mark?' Dad chips in now.

I bury my head in my hands.

'Oh, darling, do keep up. I think you're right, Bells,' Mum says. 'She's stupid if she doesn't tell him.'

They all look at me expectantly now.

'How do I tell him? He's going away. He has a girlfriend. I don't know how happy he is with Jess, though.'

Mum shrugs her shoulders. 'What have you got to lose?'

'My pride?' I suggest.

'Well, it is a risk, but you've got to ask yourself this question. Is Mark worth the risk?'

I think about this for a second. 'Yes, one hundred per cent,' I concede. 'I've never met anyone like him.'

'Right, well, in that case, you have a very large vodka, you go to the party, you walk over to him and be brave. You tell him exactly how you feel.'

'That's right,' Dad says now. 'Men need a bit of encouragement too, you know.'

'Maybe it wasn't meant to be,' I say in a final bid to spare myself from humiliation.

'That's the easy way out, only cowards say that,' Mum says with a sniff.

Mum and I stand at the top of the stairs. We are about to go to bed. 'Buy yourself a pretty dress for the party,' she says, touching my face. 'Don't wear black. Red is your colour. Wear red,' she insists. 'It goes with your dark hair. And wear your hair up.'

'Anything else?' I smile.

'No, that's it.'

We kiss on the cheek.

'Thank you,' I say, putting my arms around her. 'I love you.' It is the first time I have said that to her since I was a child.

'I love you too.' It is the first time she has told me since I was a child too. I feel a glow of warmth in her arms, something I realize has been lacking for years.

★ ★ ★

'Is it for a special occasion?' the shop assistant asks me. I have rushed out to do some last-minute shopping before I go back to London.

'My friend's birthday.' I twirl around in the dark red dress again. It's full-length with cross straps at the back, kind of Fifties-style, and I am thinking I could wear my black cardigan edged with lace over the top.

'Well, you'll knock 'em dead,' she tells me. 'That dress is *made* for you.'

I look in the mirror again to make sure she's not lying. I don't have time to look anywhere else. No, she's right. 'I'm going to get it.' I smile. It is Mark's thirty-fifth after all, I justify the decision to myself.

★   ★   ★

'If you knew the exact address it would help,' the cab driver says defensively. Of course he is right but I am too flustered to apologize. I just want to get to the party now. Not only have I forgotten the invitation, but also I was late arriving back in London because my train was delayed. It took me nearly three hours to get back to my flat. My flat. That sounds good.

Back to Mark. I can almost see the invitation with the address on it. Mark is having the party at a place I've never been to and I cannot remember the name of the venue. The invitation's sitting on my bed. Bugger, bugger, bugger.

'We're going round in circles,' I fret, looking at my watch again. It's now nine-thirty. I'm nearly two hours late. I pick up my mobile and call Mark. It's his voicemail again. 'Mark, I'm on my way, I'll be with you very soon.' I hang up abruptly. 'Wait! I think we missed the turning. Turn around.'

'I can't turn around here,' the cabbie snorts, windscreen wipers going up a gear. The rain is pelting down now.

'Do a U-turn.' He keeps on driving. 'I will tip you,' I call out loudly.

He shakes his head as he wheel-spins and drives in the other direction.

'Well done.' I vaguely remember Mark telling me the venue was close to Battersea Bridge and the power station. We have gone way too far past the bridge.

The cab driver almost tips me out of his car and into a large puddle when we finally arrive. 'Get the address next time,' he growls, but smiles when I hand him an extra £5.

* * *

I step into a large room filled with people but can hear only one person talking. It's speech time already. This place is like an indoor conservatory, with green spidery plants, a fountain, and I am standing in front of a statue of a lion. There are small candles lighting the misty room, giving it a warm glow.

A tall thin man with glasses stands next to

438

Mark who is wearing a faded blue shirt with a darker jacket. I beckon a waitress with a tray of drinks towards me and smile gratefully, taking a glass of champagne.

'I promised my son not to go on too long and embarrass him tonight, but what I do want to say is how proud we are of him.'

Everyone 'Aaahs'. Mark turns a little red and fidgets with his cuffs.

'I am not going to stand here and tell you how wonderful he is, nothing is more irritating than a proud parent. Don't want to sound like those circular letters you receive at Christmas, relaying one triumph after another.' Everyone laughs. 'Mark broke the news over Christmas that he is being posted to Edinburgh for a year. We are very happy as he will be closer to us, and I would like to wish him all the best for the year ahead.'

Everyone cheers except me. Everything I have felt during the past week starts to creep back, the realization that he is actually leaving. People start to mingle again and I am determined to make my way over to Mark now otherwise I will never do it. I clutch the present in my hand.

'Katie!' I hear him call. Mark is pushing his way through the crowd towards me. He knocks one lady's handbag and quickly turns back to say sorry. Now he is standing in front of me. 'How come you're so late?'

'Happy birthday.' I gently brush his arm.

A pretty girl in a crushed velvet dress approaches Mark and they talk briefly, giving me time to breathe properly and compose myself. Finally he's free to talk to me. 'Why have you been ignoring my calls?'

Why do you think, Mark? Surely it's not that hard to work out?

'Here's your present.' I hand him the small parcel, wrapped in blue with a ribbon.

He appears completely uninterested in it. 'Why are you late? Why bother to come at all?'

'Mark, I'm here now.'

'Well, it's rude to turn up nearly two hours late.'

I don't tell him I forgot the invitation because I was too preoccupied buying my outfit, which he hasn't seemed to notice at all. 'Mark, my train was delayed. I'm really sorry.'

'I was worried something had happened, or you weren't coming. You could have called me to say you were going to be late.'

'I did, a few times. You didn't pick up.'

He frowns heavily before turning around. 'Mum, this is Katie.'

'Katie, how lovely you could make it,' his mother says. She has tinted copper highlights and is wearing a deep blue silk top which matches her eyes. She has a warm smile that is so familiar with that dimple. 'Mark was wondering where you were, Katie. He was worried.'

He walks away.

I force myself to talk to his mother when all I want to do is follow him and apologize. I have hurt him. I should have returned his calls over Christmas. He deserves much more. He's done so much for me and I cannot even turn up to his party on time and congratulate him properly. I am a lousy friend.

'It's wonderful news about Mark going to Edinburgh, isn't it?' his mother says.

'Wonderful,' I repeat distractedly.

'Edinburgh is such a vibrant city . . . ' she goes on.

I realize I am doing the very thing Mark and I curse people for doing at drinks parties. I am looking over her shoulder to see where he is.

The tray of drinks is handed round again, and I swiftly take another glass.

Mark's mother continues to talk to me, but all the time I am desperately hoping he will come back. I can see he is getting pulled in every direction. Then I see Jess, dressed in a dark trouser suit with a bright pink lace camisole beneath. He talks to her briefly before another girl interrupts. They all start talking together. Someone is clearly telling a story because everyone in the group is now laughing. I can't slip into their group to try and talk to Mark again. I'd be out of place. All I want to do is go home. At the same time, I can hear Mum's voice over and over again.

★　★　★

'Why don't we share a taxi?' one of the other guests suggests. I had just asked reception to call a cab for me. 'I'm going in your direction so it makes sense.'

'Fine.' I turn round and see a tall man with smooth blond hair. 'If you're sure?'

'Of course. It should only be another ten minutes or so.'

'I might wait outside,' I say, 'I need a bit of fresh air.' It's raining quite heavily but I don't care. Other guests are starting to leave, walking out of the front doors, opening up their umbrellas and dodging puddles.

The man with blond hair joins me and offers his jacket. 'I'm Tom, by the way, and I think this is ours,' he says with relief as a silver car pulls into the drive. I lean back into the comfortable padded seat. I am a coward. I didn't say anything to Mark. I close my eyes, trying to block out the evening. Ten minutes later our cab driver beeps the horn so furiously I have to open my eyes to see what's going on.

'He didn't indicate, the fool,' Tom explains when I ask what happened. 'So, how do you know Mark then?'

'We were kind of neighbours,' I reply flatly. That's the simplest explanation. 'You?' I feel I have to ask.

'We work together. We're going to miss him when he leaves.'

'Yes, me too.'

'He deserves it, he works hard. I hope he gets some time to let his hair down, though. Edinburgh's such a great place. He needs to really enjoy himself, meet someone and have a good time.'

I sit up. 'He has a girlfriend, though. Jess.'

'No.' Tom shakes his head. 'He's a dark horse when it comes to his personal life, but I know he's split from her. She's a gorgeous girl. Don't know how he does it, that Mark,' he chuckles to himself.

My heart beat starts to quicken. 'Why did they split up?'

'I think they both realized they were good friends but nothing more. It's difficult when you've known someone for years and then you try and be more than mates. It's a weird change. I did it and it was disastrous! We were much better off as just friends. There was no chemistry between us, it was the strangest thing. You would think you'd have the best chemistry with someone you love and know so well, but I felt like a stale piece of bread when I was with her. Guess it doesn't work like that.'

'Tom, I've got to go back to the party,' I tell him.

He turns to me in surprise. 'Why?'

'There's no time to explain. Please, please,' I beg.

'Only when you tell me why.'

'Just because.' I hold my hands together as if in prayer.

'The party was about finished anyway.'

'Can you turn round? I *have* to go back,' I tell our driver.

The driver continues to speed along the road. 'Stop the car then, I'll walk!'

'I'll turn round when it's safe to do so,' he says primly.

'Stop the car, NOW!' I insist.

'Please could you turn around?' Tom asks politely. 'We will tip you extra,' he adds.

We spin round, the tyres squealing, and start heading back to the party. This seems to be my night for U-turns and extra tips.

'Thank you, Tom.' I plant a kiss on his cheek.

'I should share cabs with girls more often.' He smiles. 'I have jet lag, you know, I want to go home.'

'I'm really sorry, I need to say something to Mark.'

He looks at me curiously. 'And it can't wait till morning? Well, I hope it's important after all this.'

★   ★   ★

I run up the spiral stairs again, my clothes dripping water on the steps and my hair wet against my face. I can't hear much noise, the party is definitely over. The caterers are washing up glasses and packing them back into brown boxes. Candles are being blown out, trays of food carried back to the kitchen. The only noise I can hear comes from the water fountain with cupids on either side. 'Did you leave something behind?' one of the waiters asks.

'No, where's Mark?' I ask breathlessly. 'The man who was giving the party?'

'I think he's gone.'

NO! He can't have gone. Please tell me he hasn't gone. I sit down by the fountain and catch my breath. I can't believe it.

I hear footsteps approaching me.

'What are you doing here?' He doesn't wait for me to answer. 'Did you leave something behind?' There is an edge to his voice.

I am so relieved to hear Mark's voice, even if he is still in a bad mood. 'No, I did not leave anything behind,' I say firmly. The atmosphere is so tense that the caterers start to talk again and pretend to be absorbed in washing up the glasses and plates.

Mark walks over to the other side of the room and carries on packing his presents into boxes. He's not looking at me. 'Why didn't you tell me you had split up from Jess?' I ask him.

'Well, why do you think I was trying to make contact?'

I acknowledge this. 'I'm sorry, but . . . '

He interrupts me. 'You've been acting so strangely since I told you about Edinburgh. You won't let me talk to you about it.'

'Well, I don't want you to go, that's why!' I burst out.

'I think I've worked that one out. So this is your way of telling me? By acting immature, not returning my calls. I know you were at home when I called at New Year.'

'All right,' I say, 'I was. I was watching Simon Cowell on *Millionaire*.'

Mark almost smiles. 'But tonight? Turning up late and . . . '

'Will you stop and listen to me? Leave your bloody presents alone.'

Finally he looks up. 'Bells is right. You *are* a traffic warden.'

'I don't want you to go. Why would I? I'm happy for you, but Edinburgh . . . It might as well be Timbuktu. I hate the idea of not being near you. I got it all wrong,' I admit, 'I thought you were still with her, and now I've discovered you're not, and I can't tell you how happy that makes me because . . . ' I stop. Have I said too much?

'Carry on,' he says.

'I've realized how much you mean to me. I think I may even be . . . '

'What?' he gently encourages.

I can't believe he is making me say it. 'I think I love you.'

There is a long silence and I know everyone in the room is listening. 'I don't think I love you,' Mark says.

'What?' I say quietly.

'I don't think I love you,' he repeats, but then he moves forward and kisses me. I must be on a movie set, this does not feel real. I have to pinch myself when we pull ourselves apart.

'Guess what?' Mark smiles. 'I don't think I love you because I know I do.'

And then the caterers start to clap.

'Turnham Green, please,' we tell the cab driver.

'You idiot.' I push Mark's arm. 'Why didn't you tell me you'd split from Jess? You could have written or told me when I was going home on the train.'

Mark puts a hand through his hair. 'I know, but I had Bells in the background wishing me a happy birthday and then you wouldn't listen. Besides, I hadn't told Jess yet and I wanted to see you.'

'So I went through all of that agony for nothing. I was the one who had to say 'I love you' first.'

'I'm sorry, Katie, I should have finished with Jess a long time ago. We were trying too hard to make it work when in reality we were never more than friends. I knew how I felt about you after we went to the play together. I just didn't know how to break it off with her. I've known her for over twenty years but that's no reason to stay with someone.'

'Is she all right? When did you tell her?' I ask. I can't imagine Mark leaving me.

'Just after Christmas. She's fine, I think. Deep down I know she realizes we've done the right thing. I mean, she came tonight which says something, doesn't it?'

'Yes, definitely. You're old friends and that means a lot. Have you opened my present?'

'It's here.' He starts to unwrap the blue paper and I watch every line and expression on his face.

'I can't believe you found this.'

It's an original copy of *Uncle Lubin's Adventures*. I tracked one down on the internet.

'So, Edinburgh. Do you think long-distance relationships work?'

'This one will,' he says, clutching the book. 'You'll come and stay as much as you can?'

'What if you like it so much you want to stay for good?'

'We can cross that bridge when we come to it.'

'If I do come and stay there's one condition,' I tell him seriously.

'What?' He takes my hand.

'There's a spare room made up for Bells.'

Mark sinks back into the seat. 'As it happens I've looked into that. I've already bought posters of the Beatles and David Beckham.'

'And Stevie Wonder?'

'He will be pinned to the wall too.'

'Well, how can I refuse when you put it like that?'

'Good. So when can I expect you?'
'When are you leaving?'
'Next weekend.'
'How about the week after that then?'

THE END

We do hope that you have enjoyed reading this large print book.

Did you know that all of our titles are available for purchase?

We publish a wide range of high quality large print books including:
Romances, Mysteries, Classics
General Fiction
Non Fiction and Westerns

Special interest titles available in large print are:
The Little Oxford Dictionary
Music Book
Song Book
Hymn Book
Service Book

Also available from us courtesy of Oxford University Press:
Young Readers' Dictionary
(large print edition)
Young Readers' Thesaurus
(large print edition)

For further information or a free brochure, please contact us at:
Ulverscroft Large Print Books Ltd.,
The Green, Bradgate Road, Anstey,
Leicester, LE7 7FU, England.
Tel: **(00 44) 0116 236 4325**
Fax: **(00 44) 0116 234 0205**

ALL THIS WILL BE YOURS

Phil Hogan

Stuart Dutting is happily anticipating his semi-retirement from the family carpet business. He's looking forward to spending more time with his wife Diane, and to his daughter Rachel taking over the old firm. But all is not a bed of roses. Oscar, Diane's son from a previous marriage, receives a bequest from the father he never knew. This raises spectres from Diane's past, and the whole family feel the certainties of small-town life move beneath their feet. So the Duttings do what families do at times of crisis. They stop talking to each other.

THE MAN WHO WON

Guy Bellamy

Writer Andy Devlin's debts spiral out of control and he's forced to sell his home to pay them off. Andy finds himself unable to afford a new place to live. By a quirk of fate, calamity strikes his two closest friends and, for the first time, the three friends are split up. Brad has a dramatic change of fortune and sets about buying a luxurious home in the country for a neighbourly reunion. But his act of generosity will create more problems than it solves . . .

THE WIFE

Meg Wolitzer

Joe and Joan Castleman are en route to Helsinki. Joe is thinking about the prestigious literary prize he will receive and Joan is plotting how to leave him. For too long Joan has played the role of supportive wife, turning a blind eye to his misdemeanours, subjugating her own talents and quietly being the keystone of his success ... This is an acerbic and astonishing take on a marriage and the truth that behind the compromises, dedication and promise inherent in marriage there so often lies a secret ...